D0965459

DANIEL M. BENSEN

JUNCTION

This is a FLAME TREE PRESS book

FLAME TREE PRESS
6 Melbray Mews, London, SW6 3NS, UK
flametreepress.com

Distribution and warehouse:
Baker & Taylor Publisher Services (BTPS)
30 Amberwood Parkway, Ashland, OH 44805
btpubservices.com

Thanks to the Flame Tree Press team, including:
Taylor Bentley, Frances Bodiam, Federica Ciaravella, Don D'Auria, Chris Herbert, Matteo Middlemiss, Josie Mitchell, Mike Spender, Cat Taylor, Maria Tissot, Nick Wells, Gillian Whitaker.

The cover is created by Flame Tree Studio with
thanks to Nik Keevil and Shutterstock.com.
The font families used are Avenir and Bembo.

Flame Tree Press is an imprint of Flame Tree Publishing Ltd
flametreepublishing.com

A copy of the CIP data for this book is available from the British Library and the Library of Congress.

HB ISBN: 978-1-78758-096-1
PB ISBN: 978-1-78758-094-7
ebook ISBN: 978-1-78758-097-8

Printed in the US at Bookmasters, Ashland, Ohio

DANIEL M. BENSEN

JUNCTION

FLAME TREE PRESS
London & New York

CHAPTER ONE

On Camera

Daisuke Matsumori faked a smile and held out a dead mouse. The little corpse dangled by its tail, its eyes closed, its toes clenched, observed by the cassowary.

"Ah, he sees it," Daisuke stage-whispered at the camera. "See how he's focusing on it. Look at those forward-pointing eyes. Like a little tyrannosaurus, isn't he? All right. Here he comes."

The cassowary charged. Its beak gaped. The horny casque on its head cut the air like a shark's dorsal fin. Hairlike black feathers streamed behind pumping legs. The claws on its inner toes flashed, each the length of Daisuke's middle finger, ready to disembowel him if he made a wrong move.

Daisuke kept smiling. He even managed to keep his eyes from shutting as the flightless bird dashed past him, snatching the mouse from his hands. The cassowary ran until it got to the other end of the enclosure, then stretched its neck and choked its snack down with a toss of its wrinkly blue head. Its orange wattles jiggled and suddenly the cassowary was ridiculous again. Someone without Daisuke's experience would see only a fluffy puppet, prancing to entertain children.

Which was why Daisuke wasn't surprised when he heard his director say, "Cut! No, it's still not right. Not enough danger."

Daisuke allowed his smile to drop. "It could have killed me."

"Maybe, but it didn't *look* like it," said Yoshida from behind the camera. "We need to film you fighting something with more *horror.* A snake, a shark, a crocodile, or something."

"We've done crocodiles," said Daisuke.

"So we'll do crocodiles again. That's what the Iron Man of Survival does! You throw yourself at dangerous beasts. You eat bugs. You gush about how splendid nature is." Yoshida made chopping gestures with his hands. "So tell the animal handlers to take us to their biggest reptile. And let's lose your shirt, okay? Smear some mud on your chest."

Daisuke suppressed a sigh and turned to the handler standing in the cassowary cage with his animal-control pole held ready. "Thank you," Daisuke said in English. "That was very good. Now I must wrestle a crocodile. Okay?"

"Okay!" said the handler, obviously thrilled to be part of a Japanese wilderness survivor show.

Was I ever that happy to be doing this work? Daisuke tried and failed to summon up some pre-divorce enthusiasm. *At least this guy's salary won't all go to a bunch of lawyers. Even the cassowary gets a mouse out of the deal.*

"Stop frowning!" said Yoshida. "While the camera is running, that expression on your face is hard to look at."

Yes, I am close to burning out. Thank you for your concern.

But Yoshida was right, damn him. Searching for control, Daisuke rubbed the groove on the finger where he'd once worn his wedding ring. The ring was no longer there, but the skin where it had been still bore a subtle groove. He could feel it, even if he could no longer feel Eriko's cool fingertips on his lips or hear her voice before he left for a shoot. "Switch on that smile," she'd told him, and he had. Daisuke had flashed his teeth like magnesium flares and ridden the dazzling expression to his spot as the star of the most popular nature show on Japanese television.

The cassowary growled at him, a basso rasp evocative of wild boars and hungry dinosaurs. Careful not to turn his back on the murderous bird, Daisuke let himself out of the cage.

Yoshida scratched the back of his bald head. "It's just one more series, right? A month in the jungle and then *vacation*! What are you going to do with all that free time?"

Brooding, mostly. But what Daisuke said was, "Let's find those crocodiles."

"And take off your shirt," said Yoshida. "I was serious about that."

Of course he was. *Well, at least I'll be cooler when I'm shirtless and smeared with mud.*

The Port Moresby Nature Park was insulated from the noisy chaos of the rest of the capital of Papua New Guinea, but it was still too hot, and far too humid. The air still felt like it would be more efficient to breathe through gills. *Why couldn't NHK have put my farewell performance in Kamchatka?* Daisuke yearned for rustling larch forests and crystalline streams, but his most highly rated series of survivor shows had taken place in a jungle. Therefore, according to the merciless logic of funding, so would this last expedition.

On their way to the crocodile pool, Daisuke, Yoshida, and the cameraman passed under the malevolent gaze of the giant praying mantis statue at the center of the park. They were supposed to be establishing the scene before Daisuke was whisked away into the leech-filled marshes of the New Guinea lowlands. There, he would spend the next few weeks grinning into the camera as the elements punished his body, before going back to eating microwaved rice in his empty apartment while despair shriveled his soul.

Suffering is the core of my career, thought Daisuke. *What an asshole I must have been in my previous life to deserve this.*

The satellite phone on Yoshida's belt rang.

"Hello?" The director's sweaty forehead folded with sudden confusion. "Who may I—? Ah, yes, sir! Of course, sir." He thrust the phone at Daisuke. "It's Mr. Takeda."

"Yes?" Daisuke took the phone and pressed his producer's chilly growl to his ear.

"You can speak English, right?"

"To some extent," Daisuke said, sharing a wary look with Yoshida. "Ah, you might not have been aware of this, sir, but we are in the middle of a shoot—"

"It's over!" barked the producer. "Pack up. Prepare for departure."

"Departure, sir?"

"Huh?" Yoshida snatched his phone back with nothing more than a perfunctory nod and a "Thanks, Matsumori."

He wouldn't have done that last year. When his job was my favor to him and not his to me, my director would have let me hold that phone for as long as I damn well pleased.

Stop, Daisuke ordered himself. There might still be a camera trained on him. This might all be some bizarre stunt by NHK to insert drama into Daisuke's final performance.

That meant he couldn't let the bitterness he felt show on his face. Daisuke was as much a trapped performer as that flightless bird in its cage, forced to turn somersaults for food.

Daisuke rubbed his empty ring finger, pretending he could forget that he was standing under the glare of his future audience. Now, what could he do with his hands? How about wipe off some of the sweat piling up over his eyebrows? Yes, that would look natural.

The phone conversation had gone on too long. If there was still a camera on him, there was no way they were going to use this footage. And even if they were, the audience would certainly expect some curiosity on the part of the Iron Man of Survival. "What's going on?" Daisuke asked his director. "What's happening? What's wrong?"

His director waved him away. "Sir, I'm afraid that that is impossible," he said into the phone. "The money is already— *Canceled*?"

Daisuke allowed his face to show surprise, but none of the relief or fear he felt. He didn't have to drag himself through the New Guinea swamps. He could just drag himself back to Tokyo. *Think of all the extra rice I'll be able to microwave.*

Yoshida wiped his own brow, his face red. "So, are you saying we should just go home?"

The director pulled the phone away from his ear as if it had bitten him. That allowed Daisuke to hear that his producer was *giggling* like a schoolgirl.

"I'm not saying anything about going *home*," the producer said.

Daisuke grabbed the phone back from Yoshida. "What does that mean? Are we supposed to shoot in another location?" He reached for patience and the appropriate honorific language. "I'm sorry, sir, but I must have told you that this shoot was going to be the last. And I'm not in good health, either. In addition, in Tokyo there's, um, an important meeting—"

"Your wife's pack of lawyers can wait, little Matsumori," chortled his boss. "But the helicopter isn't waiting."

Surely a little anger would be expected of him at this point. "What damn helicopter?"

The phone crackled. It was hard to tell, but Daisuke thought he heard a door slam back in the NHK office. Voices rose in the background and the producer's syntax flipped from brusque command to obsequious servitude. "Yes. That is right, sir. I will do so, sir. I will tell them immediately."

Yoshida hissed through his teeth. Daisuke knew what he was thinking: *Who could possibly be high-ranking enough to make the tyrant of NHK programming excrete oil like that?*

"You will prepare to fly immediately," said the producer, back in authority mode. "If you don't, you will be fired and maybe dead and condemned forever as traitors to Japan and the whole human race!"

"Sir, what are you saying?" Yoshida pleaded into the phone, losing his honorifics as his desperation mounted. "Who're you saying is flying to where for *what*?"

But Daisuke could already hear the chop of rotors. On the off chance those hidden cameras were still rolling, he struck a pose, chin up, finger pointing. From beyond the bug-eyed fiberglass head of the praying mantis, a helicopter appeared in the sky.

Back in its cage, the cassowary growled.

★ ★ ★

"This is Daisuke Matsumori, the Iron Man of Survival," he found himself saying three hours later. "As you can see, I'm in a helicopter, not a Land Rover. I am not going to my scheduled destination on the Karawari River, but to Indonesian Papua, where…well, I'm sure my esteemed viewers saw this footage before I did."

The Indonesian journalists that were this helicopter's other passengers had shown Daisuke the images: a series of photographs taken by a cell phone camera, time-stamped yesterday. Daisuke would have seen them on the news in his hotel room if he hadn't been at the zoo since before dawn.

The first photo was of a hole in the ground. Soil and rock sloped at a strange angle down to a blue and white distortion – something that was obviously not a glitch in a digital camera, because a human arm stuck out of it. In the next photo, the arm's owner was climbing out of the hole, the distortion behind him like a chromed bubble reflecting a sky clearer than the current weather in New Guinea, and with a different kind of sunlight.

Daisuke cleared his throat and spoke again into the mic on his headset and to the camera in front of him. "There is a wormhole in New Guinea," he said. "On the other side, there is a planet very similar to ours, although not exactly the same."

Whoever edited this footage for distribution might choose this pause as an opportunity to insert the next pictures Daisuke had seen: a snow-dusted mountainside that matched no landscape on Earth, lots of pictures of animals, plants, worms, more worms…. The photographer was apparently a biologist. An Australian woman who'd come here to study birds and found herself in the center of a geopolitical maelstrom. Daisuke hoped he'd get a chance to interview her, but that job would probably go to Nurul.

"There is life on the other side," said Daisuke. "Amazing life. Those animals are not giant caterpillars or scaly sea cucumbers." He chuckled, and if the sound was forced, nobody would be able to tell through the helicopter noise. "They are alien life, products of an evolutionary process entirely separate from ours."

And if those 'aliens' turned out to have been cooked up in some animator's computer, Daisuke would look like an absolute fool. Were his producers setting him up to fail? Was this some oblique punishment for his marital problems? An excuse to fire him?

Daisuke glanced out of the window of the helicopter and dismissed the possibility. Not that his bosses wouldn't be so vindictive, but he doubted they could rope the Indonesian military into their schemes. Those were Indonesian attack helicopters flanking the civilian model that carried Daisuke. Whatever this wormhole really was, important people were taking it seriously.

"I have been chosen…." prompted Nurul.

Daisuke blinked and refocused his eyes. His new director was seated next to him, impeccably dressed and made-up as if to announce the weather. Even flying a thousand meters above impenetrable alpine wilderness, Nurul Astarina looked as unruffled as if standing in front of a blue screen. Daisuke admired her professionalism.

"That's your line," she said into her own microphone. "'I have been chosen for the honor….'"

Daisuke waved his hand in front of his nose. "I am sorry, Ms. Astarina."

"Nurul, please." She smiled. "I *did* say."

Daisuke had traveled the world long enough to stop being embarrassed about calling coworkers by their first names. "I'm sorry, Nurul," he said, "I was just…."

Just what? Shocked? Overwhelmed? Burned out? Ambivalent about whether he really wanted to travel to another dimension and be eaten by alien worms?

"Ten minutes to wheels down," the pilot said into Daisuke's awkward failure to complete the sentence.

"Don't worry," said Nurul. Like the pilot and Daisuke himself, she was speaking English. "It *is* an awkward situation."

That was putting it mildly. Nurul had been reticent about the goings-on in the Indonesian government, but Daisuke could guess that a lot of people in Jakarta were still furious that big-brother USA had landed its soldiers on their territory. The rational thing for Indonesia to do would be to roll over and play nice, but politics wasn't always rational.

Lines were being drawn, ultimatums made, sabers rattled, and someone in the UN had seen this smoking powder keg and said to themselves, *Why, this looks like a job for a Japanese television personality!*

"I apologize," said Daisuke. "Of course, I am very happy to have this opportunity to—" he felt ridiculous saying it "—explore an alien planet.

But I am very surprised there isn't an American person they wanted to lead the expedition? Or Australian?"

"I don't think there is time for that," said Nurul. "I was told they needed people who they could get through the wormhole today."

And that was another thing that bothered Daisuke. The international response had crashed down on the Papuan Highlands with ridiculous speed. Mere hours after that Australian biologist had sent her alien photos to everyone in her address book, the sky had started raining American and Australian paratroopers. The Indonesian jeeps had arrived only a little later, and now it seemed there were two armies growing up around the wormhole, each making threat-displays at the other. Nobody had shot anybody yet. At least, not in any official capacity.

"This is all very fast, isn't it?" Daisuke said. "Why don't we wait until tomorrow? Do they think the, ah, wormhole will go away?"

Nurul stared back at him, eyes wide. "I don't know."

"Of course," said Daisuke, not at all reassured. Was he here as somebody's patsy? A scapegoat in case things went wrong? Or just someone more personable than the typical soldier? A propagandist?

And if the photographs were genuine, that made Daisuke's position even more precarious. Three years ago, he would have taken the opportunity to explore a new world with lavish thanks and quite a bit of private ego, secretly certain he deserved it. Now, though, Daisuke could feel suspicious unease. Was he really just the first appropriate person they could find? Why did they need to work so fast? Why couldn't the American, Indonesian, Papuan, and Australian governments hammer out territorial claims quietly, then open a joint tour company and start charging admission?

Not that he had any choice in the matter. Daisuke was unequipped to imagine what a real encounter with extraterrestrial life would mean for him personally, but he knew how his public persona ought to react. Would the Iron Man of Survival turn up his nose at an offer to accompany Charles Darwin? Mamiya Rinzō? Lewis and Clark? It was impossible for him to refuse.

Look at it this way, Daisuke. Maybe an alien will eat you, and you won't have to go back to that empty apartment.

"We can always do this on the ground." Whatever her own private worries might be, Nurul gave Daisuke a smile indistinguishable from truth. "I'm sure they'll keep us waiting."

Daisuke laughed politely, but said, "No, no. Let's do at least one more take. I'm ready."

His director turned to her husband and said something in rapid Indonesian. Rahman Astarina had so far exchanged no words with Daisuke other than "Ya", "Okay", and "I what's your pilem", which Daisuke had eventually understood as "I watch your films." His wife's English, however, was better than Daisuke's.

"Whenever you're ready," said Nurul while Rahman gave a thumbs-up. She gave her husband a smile, and Daisuke tried to ignore the sullen swell of envy at a functioning married couple. *What did they do to deserve their happiness?*

Daisuke rubbed his ring finger and smiled. "I have been chosen for a great honor, and I promise that I will do my best to fulfill the responsibility that has fallen into my hands." He bowed to the camera, his audience. "To uphold the ideal of peaceful scientific exploration for the good of all humanity." He looked out the window, past the attack helicopter, to the jungle below. "Now, my friends, into the unknown."

★ ★ ★

They settled onto the ragged soil of what until yesterday had been a native village. The natives were gone, replaced by soldiers in green and blue hats who chopped trees, built walls, and, now, aimed their guns at Daisuke.

Daisuke swallowed and tried not to focus too much on the weapons as he followed his pilot and the Astarinas across the impromptu landing pad. They passed through a cordon made of stacked logs and barbed wire, and emerged into a circular enclosure surrounded by more logs. Raw-edged stumps stuck up from the mud, all supporting crates of equipment and stacks of binders. Soldiers yelled into walkie-talkies or at each other. Most ominous of all was the circle of uniformed men, guns out, facing inward as if prepared to face an invasion from the hole at their feet.

Which is exactly what they are doing, Daisuke realized with a chill. If that thing in the middle of the soldiers' formation wasn't a wormhole, it was something equally unknown and dangerous.

Orange light shone from the hole and slid off the muzzles of the weapons pointed into its center. Daisuke was reminded of chimpanzees he had once seen fishing for termites, poking grass stems into holes in the ground and waiting for something to bite.

"Matsumori-*san*, this is Syahiral Hariyadi," said Nurul. "Colonel in the Indonesian National Armed Forces."

Daisuke looked around to see a short, powerfully built man in a green uniform and black beret. The colonel looked up at Daisuke, his wide, smooth-skinned face just a little large for his body.

"Oh yes, 'the Iron Man of Survival'," said Hariyadi, his accent round and dense as a cannonball. "They told me you'd be here, and that I was expected to join you in your ridiculous propaganda piece. Well, the UN may have time to shepherd minor celebrities around, but I have a duty to ensure the future prosperity of my country." He jerked his chin at the Astarinas and said something in clipped Indonesian, then nodded at Daisuke. "You may stay here and wait for someone to put you somewhere."

For a dizzy moment, Daisuke nearly agreed with him. But by the time he had translated "You're absolutely right, sir, I don't belong here," into English, his career-progression instincts had caught up with him. Daisuke had built a career on saying the right thing at the right time. That, and throwing himself into danger. He did both now.

"I agree, Colonel, I *was* brought here very suddenly," he said. "I still don't understand the hurry, but the Americans seemed very insistent." Daisuke saw now why they'd chosen him, a Japanese man, for this job. An American or Australian wouldn't have been able to talk like this to an Indonesian soldier without antagonizing him.

Hariyadi curled his lip, angry, but not at Daisuke. "Of course the Americans are insistent. *They* know any delay will strengthen the position of the Republic of Indonesia and our rightful claim on the resources within our borders."

That sounded serious, but nobody would expect the Iron Man of Survival to debate politics. "I see, sir," said Daisuke. "I don't know about politics, but I am very eager to see what is on the other side of the wormhole."

Hariyadi's lip remained curled. Daisuke's eagerness, false or true, didn't seem to gain him much traction with the colonel.

In a flash of inspiration, Daisuke realized who the next person to speak in this scene should be, and looked at the Australian pilot who'd flown them here.

"Sir," said the pilot as if on cue, "we have orders from Colonel Pearson."

"Who does not outrank me," said Hariyadi.

The gun-toting men around them tensed, and Daisuke couldn't help but wish someone was filming this.

"I am eager to explore," he repeated. "Not only out of a love for the unknown, but as a means of showing what wonders the human race is capable of. You will play an important part in that story, Colonel, if you are to come with me."

Hariyadi only grunted, but it was the grunt of a man imagining his name in the history books.

Daisuke looked at the pilot again, and again the soldier received the subconscious signal that he should speak. "Do you have a communication from the United States government or the UN that countermands my orders, sir?"

Hariyadi glanced up at the sky, then down at the wormhole. "No," he said. "If I do receive such orders, I will place these civilians under protective custody. Understood?"

"Affirmative," said the pilot.

"Yes," said Daisuke.

Hariyadi turned an ironic expression on Daisuke. "Let us not waste time. Matsumori-*san*, may I invite you into the newest territory of the Republic of Indonesia?"

"Film," whispered Nurul. "Film!"

Daisuke glanced from the camera to Hariyadi to the funnel-shaped hole in the earth. The circle of blue at the bottom seemed to stretch away, pulling Daisuke with it as his left thumb found the groove in his ring finger.

Switch on that smile, he told himself, and jumped through the wormhole.

CHAPTER TWO

The Far Side

Imagine a mirrored ball at the bottom of a pit. That was how Daisuke might have described the wormhole to viewers, but that wasn't accurate. A mirror would have shown nothing but the dark rocks and earth around it. The wormhole, however, was blue, white, and green. The colors were an incomprehensible smear at its edges, but at the center, they twisted into an image of sky and trees. Mountains in the background like none on Earth.

Not a ball, but a three-dimensional hole, thought Daisuke as he bumped and slid down the shallow slope of the pit in the soil of the New Guinea Highlands. And that still didn't capture the feel of the thing.

The wormhole *pulled*. Even while falling toward it, Daisuke felt as if he was stuck on the floor of an upward-accelerating elevator. He was descending faster than mere Earth gravity should account for, and as the wormhole swelled in Daisuke's vision, the image of trees and mountains gained depth. A wave of cold, like diving into a calm lake, and Daisuke passed through, plunging feet-first into another world.

Blue sky above him. Green trees around him. And people. More soldiers. Details he couldn't see because he was still sliding down an incline. The inner surface of the pit on Earth had become the outer slope of a hill…somewhere else.

Daisuke tried to get his feet under him, but the gravity kept increasing the farther he got from the wormhole, and his knees creaked as he tried to force his downward momentum into a different direction. In the end, the best he could do was to slide down the hill on his ass, legs tucked in front of him, boots flat against the grassy ground. Then at least he could spring to his feet quickly once he slid to a stop.

He was in a military fortification just like the one on the other side of the wormhole in Indonesian Papua back on Earth. Nothing other than interplanetary travel could explain the way the sun was so large and orange, or the way Daisuke was so heavy. His feet interacted with the ground wrong, as if he had just stepped onto land after a long sea voyage. Even the air felt different

– thicker, laced with scents that Daisuke would never be able to describe to the audience at home.

Which was unfortunate, because despite its alien smells and sensations, the other side of the wormhole *looked* very much like Earth. Beyond the bustle of muddy soldiers, silver-tan grass rippled across the flanks of the hills. The sky was a clear, pale blue, hung with hawks. Birdsong punctuated the sounds of machinery and men's voices. Pretty, but the land around the wormhole was boringly un-alien in every way that would show up on camera.

Cameras. Daisuke looked around for his audience and remembered his role.

"I'm here!" he said. Then, since the soldiers waiting to welcome him likely didn't speak Japanese, he said, "Hello!" in English.

Nobody answered him. Nobody was even watching him. The people gathered here, those who didn't have other jobs to do, were staring up at the crown of the hill, where the wormhole to Earth glimmered like a black pearl.

Even as he watched, the wormhole disgorged the rest of the party. Nurul managed to stumble down the hill with some grace, while her husband simply let himself roll, shielding his camera with his body. Hariyadi looked like he wanted to find the man responsible for the gravity and have him flogged. The three Indonesians slid to a stop near Daisuke and stood shakily in the new gravity, adjusting their clothes and squinting in the ginger-colored light.

"Good afternoon, Colonel Hariyadi."

The speaker was a man in an American uniform. Chin up, hands on hips, chest protruding just past his belly, he looked like a bald and aging superhero. "Welcome to Far Side Base."

"Such a stupid name," said the stumpy, grimy woman standing next to the soldier. "You might as well call this place XKCD." Her accent was Australian. Some sort of technical contractor? Not military or government, or she wouldn't have spoken out of turn. Certainly not media, or else she would be better groomed.

Hariyadi ignored the civilian woman and spoke to the man and fellow soldier. "It is I who should be welcoming you, Pearson. The fact that you positioned yourself here while I was overseeing the construction of Near Side Base is legally irrelevant."

The American – Pearson – maintained a stony expression while his companion rolled her eyes. "Are these other people supposed to be the journalists?" he asked.

Hariyadi introduced the Astarinas and Daisuke, who examined the civilian woman with growing understanding. Those rumpled khaki clothes, that greasy hair. The accent, the sunburn, the squint, her inclusion in this welcoming party. Daisuke realized who she must be. He smiled, extending his hand toward her.

"You're the biologist who discovered the wormhole."

She frowned at Daisuke, crinkling the freckled bridge of her nose. "The Nun discovered the wormhole. I'm just the one they told about it."

The who? This wasn't the time for digressions. "It's a pleasure to meet you," Daisuke persisted. "I'm Daisuke Matsumori. I'm sure you, ah, haven't seen my television program?" He laughed self-deprecatingly.

"No. But I am sorry I missed it."

Daisuke didn't miss the way her eyes flashed down his body. He suppressed the desire to run a hand through his hair.

The American thrust himself into the fraught silence. "I'm Colonel Gregory Pearson, commander of the American and UN troops of Far Side Base. This" – he nodded to the biologist – "is Anne Houlihan of the University of Sydney. It is thanks to her" – *traitorous and foolish leaking of valuable strategic intelligence*, his scowl communicated – "that we are all here."

Ms. Houlihan was the same height as Hariyadi, but rather wider. She looked like she hadn't changed her clothes, much less bathed, in a week, but if she felt intimidated to be surrounded by all these posturing soldiers, she wasn't showing it. Daisuke, a connoisseur of wilderness survival equipment, appreciated her shirt and pants as the perfect outfit for exploring new planets. Her boots, especially, looked like she'd recently used them to kick a crocodile to death. Her eyes were the color of raw honey, and her dimpled smile was bigger, toothier, and more genuine than any expression he'd seen in a long time. Her hand, when she shook his, was very warm.

"This is all very impressive," Daisuke said.

Anne looked as if she'd bitten into a leech. "This display of imperialism, you mean? You should have seen the shrine complex that was here before these dipshits tore it down."

Daisuke hid his shock. If there were a camera running, it might have made sense for Anne to steal the scene and win some support from her civilian audience. Otherwise, why antagonize her military hosts?

In any case, she should be interesting to work with. Daisuke had had expert guests on his shows before, and they usually turned stony and unresponsive – afraid of doing something foolish on camera. A few of them eventually managed to relax and be themselves, but nobody had come roaring out of the starting gate like this before.

"We are securing the wormhole," said Pearson, which might have been a response to Anne's insult, or he might have just moved on to the next line of his planned patter.

Whichever, Daisuke took the cue, twisting to look back up the hill. The wormhole at its tip was rimmed with the blue and green of this extraterrestrial mountainside, but its center was dark brown, showing the soil around its counterpart back on Earth.

"'The High Earth Hole', the Papuan natives call it," said Pearson. "Its other side in Papua is 'the Deep Sky Hole.'"

"Natives?" said Nurul. "Those would be the Nun people?"

"That's right—" Pearson looked as if he might go on talking, but Anne interrupted him.

"The Nun say they've been terraforming this place since the beginning of the world." Her side-eyed glare shuttled between Pearson and Hariyadi. "And then we showed up and started squabbling over it."

"I am not in the business of squabbling, Ms. Houlihan," said Hariyadi. "I am here to ensure the Americans do not take what is not theirs."

"No fear of *that*, Colonel." Pearson bared his teeth in an expression he probably imagined was a smile. "We, and I mean specifically we six people" – he swept them all with his stare – "are to spearhead a peaceful and multinational exploration effort, beginning tomorrow."

Hariyadi snorted and Anne scoffed. "Oh, yes, we'll just have the planet explored by dinner, won't we?"

Pearson played his trick again, answering the biologist's question while seeming to ignore her. "We will make a start tomorrow with aerial reconnaissance. The first ever flight of an aircraft on this planet." He nodded to Daisuke and the Astarinas. "We rely on you to represent our peaceful exploration efforts to the world."

Nurul only nodded photogenically, but Rahman looked as nervous as a seal hunter watching an orca swimming under the sea ice toward him.

Daisuke attempted to clarify the situation, or at least as much of it as Pearson was willing to reveal. "So, Colonel," he asked, "we have no idea what we will see out there, beyond the mountains?"

Pearson jerked his chin up. "That's correct."

"Hasn't there been…." *Damn, what was the English word?* "Haven't there been people who could see these lands before us? Or at least drones?"

"Exactly," said Hariyadi. "We should not even be here, off of Earth, where we know so little."

Pearson spread his hands. "Say the word, Hariyadi, and we'll *both* withdraw *all* of our men back to Earth."

"I get it," said Anne. "The fate of two worlds rests on the shoulders of two galahs in a dick-measuring contest."

Daisuke was unfamiliar with that particular idiom, but it probably meant that the US had spooked Indonesia into rushing its fortification of the wormhole, which had scared the Americans in turn and so forth, the two countries pushing people through to this unknown planet with insane speed. And the vicious cycle was still spinning.

"So then," said Nurul, hands crossed over her lap like a nursery school teacher, "our governments all need more information. The sooner we begin filming, the sooner we can tell voters on Earth what they need to know in order to decide these matters for themselves. Shall we film a bit more now?"

Hariyadi and Pearson looked at the journalist with identical weary expressions. Pearson looked like he was about to say something, but was distracted by an American soldier, who came jogging up to his superior.

"Sir," the soldier said, brandishing a walkie-talkie. "We got another exo-injury, sir."

"Shit," said Anne, as if the soldier had addressed her. "It's someone on the burn teams, isn't it? Why do you even need a big flat field of charcoal north of town?"

"It's, uh, it's venom." The lieutenant's head swung back and forth between Pearson and the scientist. "New kind of treeworm. Little things like maggots. Swarmed up a guy's leg when he got too close to their tree. Symptoms that followed were—"

"Swelling, probably?" said Anne. "Flushing? Hives? Generalized feeling of doom?"

"Doom?" repeated Hariyadi.

Pearson rounded on her. "Ms. Houlihan, please—"

"That's an allergic reaction," she said. "Incompatible biochemistry."

"Sir...." The lieutenant faced Pearson, but eyed the biologist as if she might charge at any moment. "We thought it was poison."

Pearson sighed and turned to Anne. "Is it poison, Houlihan?"

She shook her head. "Oh, no. Anaphylaxis will still kill the hell out of him, though. Got to jab him." She mimed punching her own thigh. "With an EpiPen."

Pearson rubbed a knuckle between his eyes. "Tell them what she said," he ordered. "Don't forget to requisition more EpiPens."

"Antihistamines, too," said Anne. "Uh, ask a real medical doctor first, though, all right?"

"Sir!" The lieutenant turned away, speaking into the walkie-talkie, relaying...Anne's orders?

Well, who else was qualified to give them? Daisuke didn't suppose the American or Australian armies employed many speculative biologists, and other civilians with the proper background would take time to track down and transport to the New Guinea Highlands. Daisuke supposed he was similarly underqualified. *So both Anne and I are bats in the village without birds.*

All they had to do was to survive long enough to be replaced by someone competent. Daisuke sidled up to Anne and bent to whisper into her ear. "On our exploration party tomorrow, what do you think we can do to avoid being poisoned ourselves?"

She turned wide eyes on him. "I have no fucking clue, mate."

"Feelings of impending doom, indeed," muttered Pearson.

★ ★ ★

Smoke swirled up from a dozen firepits, carrying the smell of roasting pork and steaming grass. Army-supplied bowls and Nun tree-bark trenchers of porridge circulated around the guests of the natives' 'welcoming party.'

Daisuke scooped his porridge up with gusto. It had been a long day.

"Delicious," he told the flickering eye of Rahman's camera. "It is so kind of the Nun people to make this feast for us."

"This is the second night in a row they've done it," said Anne. "I'm not sure they realize we plan to stay here forever." The biologist was sitting next to him, which was either a compliment to him or an insult to Pearson, who was across the firepit. Daisuke enjoyed her proximity and her conversation, which was refreshingly blunt.

"So communication is very bad?" he asked.

"Uh...." She was looking at the camera again.

At first, Daisuke had thought the biologist was pretending to be camera-shy. How could he explain her performance at the wormhole that morning if Anne wasn't a performer? But it seemed now that all of Anne's cutting remarks had just been her honest opinions.

Trying to help Anne get over her stage fright, Daisuke asked, "Do you have anyone who can interpret for the Nun?"

But Pearson, seated on the log beside Daisuke, snatched the conversational initiative before Anne could recover it. "There are only a few natives who speak Indonesian, and none who speak English or anything else."

Anne frowned. "Although they speak plenty of other Papuan languages."

"Which isn't very helpful to us, is it?" said Pearson.

"Our translators should arrive shortly," said Hariyadi. The Indonesian colonel looked very uncomfortable on his log, bowl of porridge in hand and a camera pointed at his face. He kept darting glances at the cameraman's bottle of beer.

"It will be very good to hear what these people have to say," Daisuke said to Anne, trying to make her forget the camera. "You know, I have been fascinated by New Guinea ever since my first visit here."

"You mean 'there'," said Anne.

"Ah yes. Of course, we're not in New Guinea anymore," Daisuke said, "but this place resembles it very much. The plants and the animals…." He looked off into the middle distance. "Also, the feeling of moving between worlds."

It was too much. Anne looked back at the camera and froze like a frog caught in the glare of a snake. "Um," she said, and took a swig of her own beer.

Daisuke gave up and followed her example. The beer was good: bintang smuggled in by Indonesian soldiers and a good complement to the porridge and pork. *The feast must be hard on the Muslim soldiers*, thought Daisuke, although neither Hariyadi nor the Astarinas seemed to care.

Nurul cleared her throat. "Speaking of which." She turned to Pearson, and Daisuke's trained eye caught the twitch of the journalist's hand as she realized she had no microphone to point into the soldier's face. "Can you tell us more about this village on the far side of the Indonesian wormhole? Where are we, exactly?"

Pearson cleared his throat. "This village is called Imsame. It's on the western bank of the Mekimsam River."

Hariyadi cleared his throat. "I believe she was referring to our astronomical position."

"Oh." Pearson grimaced. "We don't know. The stars are…unfamiliar."

Anne chuckled at that for some reason, but Pearson ignored her.

"Tomorrow," he said, "we'll fly out of the habitable zone around the Earth Wormhole…"

Daisuke noticed he didn't call it 'the Indonesian Wormhole.'

"…and get our first aerial reconnaissance of what the native Nun people call 'the Uninitiated Forest of Treeworms.' The Treeworm Bush. The toxic, alien ecosystem."

Nurul nodded at Daisuke, and he understood he was expected to contribute.

"Ah...." he said, and waited for Rahman to center the camera on his face before frowning seriously. "When you say 'toxic'...well, we heard of the man who was bitten by a worm and suffered an allergic reaction? Is that what you mean?"

"Obviously," muttered Anne.

Pearson shot her a smug smile. "To answer that question, I refer to our resident biologist, Anne Houlihan, discoverer of the wormhole."

Rahman turned the camera in her direction, and Anne leaned back, hands up in front of her as if the cameraman had aimed a gun at her.

"Well, um. Shit. Amino acids. We don't even know if they *have* them... no." Anne stared at her beer. "You know how you get red and pussy when there's a splinter in your finger? Pus? Shit. *Shit,* I swore again. Don't film me. I'm no good at all this..." – she made circles with the bottle of beer in her hand – "...looking like...a person. On film. Talk to someone else."

Nurul made a noise that Daisuke, well accustomed to the ways of directors, recognized as the sigh of a professional resigning herself to filming a bunch of idiots.

Daisuke, however, felt just a bit optimistic. It was refreshing to work with people who said what they meant. *And acting alongside Anne, Pearson, and Hariyadi, I can't help but look good.*

He tried to guess what Anne had been trying to say. "Ms. Houlihan, why is the land around this terraformed valley uninhabitable?"

"Um. Well. Uh." Anne's eyes slid to his. Locked there. "North. Look, Mr. Matsumori, you have to know that that's just a...a convention. We just call it 'north' because we call the direction the sun rises 'east.' Magnetic compasses don't even...wait. Shit." She closed her eyes and opened them. "Can we start again?"

"Of course," said Nurul. "Whenever you're ready."

"Ugh," said Anne. "Shit."

Pearson sighed, but Daisuke kept his face open. "Don't worry," he whispered to her. "I will help you." He angled his body on the log they shared so that he was between the camera and Anne, caught her eyes again and said, "That's very interesting, Ms. Houlihan. So we know very little about this planet, even the basic directions?"

"Correct?" Anne said it with the rising intonation of a question, but she nodded at the same time.

"Um." Daisuke tried again. "Is there anything we *do* know?"

"Yes?" said Anne. "Oh. Okay? So, this here is a rocky planet? Very Earthlike, although the gravity is higher and the stars are different. Oh, the *stars*!" The question-intonation vanished as Anne became more confident in what she was saying. "The stars are very different indeed." She snorted, as if at a joke. "But you'll see about that. Anyway, we've got mountains, we've got air and liquid water. We're going to fly over it all tomorrow in a plane that's been, I guess" – she glanced at Pearson – "disassembled and put through the wormhole piece by piece?"

Pearson cleared his throat and Daisuke tried to get them back on topic.

"Outside the valley, there is alien life," he said. "But in this valley, there are grass and trees. They are very much like on Earth. So what's going on?"

"Don't ask me, I only got here yesterday," said Anne, and looked surprised when they all laughed.

"That was a very good joke," Nurul hinted.

"Right," said Anne. "A joke."

Daisuke smiled at her. "Sorry, I should have said, why are the, ah, 'treeworms' toxic?"

Anne shrugged. "Well, incompatible biochemistry, obviously."

Daisuke had seen that one coming, and had a translation ready. "In other words, humans and other Earthly life are allergic to the treeworms?"

"At the very fucking least!" She threw her arms out and Daisuke rocked back. "This whole planet must have a totally different vocabulary of amino acids. If they even *use* amino acids. God, I wish I could do some proper science here." Anne shook her head, sending blonde curls flying. "I haven't a clue what's going on at the molecular level or how this fits in with the bigger picture of the ecology. I mean, it's a whole bloody big planet out there!"

Pearson cleared his throat again and Rahman centered the camera on him.

"Good job," whispered Daisuke as Anne wiped the sweat off her face.

"*Thank* you, Ms. Houlihan. Now," Pearson addressed the camera, jaw working as if the general wished he had a pipe stem to chew on, "I must stress that we have things well enough under control now to do the sort of research necessary to determine how great a danger this planet presents."

Anne made an unattractive noise and Daisuke tried to gain control of the scene before she ruined all his work. "I don't know anything about politics or military things. Maybe you can explain to me: why is the wormhole so dangerous? If no one can live outside the valley, then all we have here is a small tribe of natives."

"And surely, if the natives can handle it, so can we," said Nurul.

Pearson glared at the Indonesian journalist. Daisuke was put in mind of an owl pinpointing a distant mouse. "Excuse me if I gave the impression that our mission here was to protect the Earth from aliens. The truth is the opposite. There are many players on the international theater vying for power here, for use of this new planet's resources. It is my mission, and Colonel Hariyadi's" – he gave a gracious nod to his counterpart – "to ensure that the various interests here are balanced peacefully."

"So you say," said Hariyadi, raising his palms. "Balance."

Daisuke would have been happy to let the scene close there, but Pearson had to have the last word. "Transparency is also very important to the American government, of course, and we see it as our responsibility to our descendants to keep a record of these historic events." He cleared his throat. "To that end, we will have you all fitted with one of these."

He tugged at a lanyard around his neck and pulled out a palm-sized black device, a bit smaller than a smartphone. "This is a body camera. It will record video and audio of whatever you're facing. Battery life of over a week. Please keep it on and unobstructed at all times."

Anne muttered something like, "Oh, of all the—"

"Cameras for everyone?" Daisuke said, thinking about what being on camera all the time would do to his and Anne's every single interaction. It was going to be an exhausting and awkward couple of days, with him poking and prodding her toward the basic semblance of humanity. "Is this…really necessary?"

"Yes," said Hariyadi. "The stakes here are higher than you seem to realize."

"What?" said Anne, glaring at Pearson. "You want us to collect your intelligence for you?"

"He wants us to put a sweet civilian face on the military struggle here," said Nurul.

"We want you to establish our innocence," Hariyadi corrected.

Daisuke kept his face blank while wondering what on Earth 'establish our innocence' was supposed to mean.

"What the hell does that mean?" said Anne.

Pearson looked out toward the natives, celebrating around their firepits. "It would be a shame if I, or my esteemed colleague Hariyadi, were torn apart by aliens and everyone assumed it was foul play." He scowled. "And by 'a shame' I mean 'World War Three.'"

Daisuke knew that tone. Pearson was about to launch into a speech, probably about how America was nobly trying to stop Indonesia from indulging in an illegal land grab.

That wasn't a speech Daisuke's audience, or Daisuke himself, needed to hear again, so he looked for something distracting.

"Isn't that our host?" he asked, pointing.

The Nun chief, a proud display of masculinity in feathered headdress, sash, and meter-long codpiece, left off haranguing the chefs and the central firepit and bounded over to theirs.

Nurul directed Rahman to swing his camera toward the spectacle, and Pearson deflated, looking sour.

"Please translate for me," Daisuke whispered to Anne, and bowed to the man. "Thank you for extending this opportunity to all mankind."

Anne said something in halting Indonesian and their host answered rather more fluently.

"This is Tyaney, the man who originally found me and showed me the Deep Sky Hole," said Anne. "He says he is happy for all the foreigners we have brought to buy things from his people. He's, uh, happy to offer us second helpings of our meal as well."

"For what price?" asked Pearson. Anne shot him a poisonous look and Tyaney spoke again.

"He says," Nurul said, when it became clear that Anne hadn't been paying attention. "He says that his…newest wife?…has brought us more food."

"Oh. Hello, Sing," Anne said. "*Selamat malam.*"

Sing did not respond. The chieftain's shaven-headed wife was covered in a sort of raincoat made of fur-lined straw. Her face was round and rather heavy-featured, dominated by a mouth too small for her teeth. With deep-set eyes and a long, slightly hooked nose, Sing might have been anything from fifteen to a malnourished twenty-five.

Tyaney yelled something at her, and the little woman ducked her head, presenting more folded-bark dishes. The foreigners took what was offered with varying degrees of politeness.

"So that's Tyaney," said Anne. "He's the one who found me and brought me to the wormhole in the first place. His father was alive to see first contact with the outside world, but Tyaney's been all the way to Jayapura. He's decided to act like I'm his best friend in the…both worlds…and he's our best source of information. I just wish he wasn't…."

"An asshole?" Pearson asked.

"No," said Anne. "He's just brought the attention of the whole world down on his little village. A village the army has completely evacuated now. How do you think he feels about that? How do the rest of the Nun feel about him? The shit he's dealing with is more complex than anything Pearson or Hariyadi have on their plates."

Tyaney screamed something at Sing.

"So?" said Rahman. "He is asshole."

"All natives treat their wives like that," said Nurul, giving her own husband a tender look.

Anne's jaw muscles visibly clenched. "No, they don't."

Tyaney yelled something at them, or maybe at his wife again. Anne said something to him, which made him laugh, and Anne scowled.

"What did you tell him?" Daisuke wondered if he ought to tell Anne not to antagonize Tyaney. That some of the native guides on his various shoots had been unpleasant people, but he'd needed to work with them, and had refrained from commenting on their customs.

"Ms. Houlihan told him she would bring him and his wife with her on the plane tomorrow," said Hariyadi, "and he just said, 'My wife? Don't be ridiculous.'" The Indonesian colonel smiled. "I hope you have learned your lesson, Ms. Houlihan. You do not understand the natives as well as you think you do, and you have no authority to invite them on military expeditions."

"Houlihan discussed it with me, Hariyadi," said Pearson. "I gave her the go-ahead."

"And who will give up their seat to allow your biologist to bring her pet Nun on board?" Hariyadi leaned forward on his log, stabbing a finger toward his American counterpart. "You are making unilateral decisions that strain both our missions. That is unacceptable."

Anne took a swig from her bottle and cawed in sarcastic laughter. "Human politics. I never thought it could get any stupider, but here we are." She raised her free hand and wiggled its fingers over her forehead. "It's like ants stealing from a picnic being racist to each other."

Daisuke decided those fingertips were supposed to represent antennae. He was starting to feel the beer.

"Well, who do you think set up this picnic?" Anne leaned back into the shadows and took another drink. "Whose food do you think we're stealing? You dipshits invade the Nun's home because they don't have tanks and attack helicopters. But when you meet beings that can make permanent wormholes leading to *your* home? What happens then?"

The fire popped in its pit. Somewhere, beyond the feasting soldiers, insects buzzed.

"You mean you believe that aliens made the wormhole?" Daisuke asked.

"We are aware of that possibility," said Pearson. "Another reason our mission of exploration is so important."

Anne gave a scornful grunt. "What exploration do we need? Just look the fuck up, mate."

Daisuke squinted, trying to parse that phrasal verb.

"Look up." Anne patted Daisuke on the shoulder, and the skin under the spot where she touched hummed with pleasant warmth. Her face was very close to his, and her eyes were luminous in the firelight. "Look at the stars."

Daisuke looked up, past the smoke into the cold night sky, pricked by unfamiliar stars, girdled with—

He sucked in a shocked breath and Anne laughed.

"What are you…?" Nurul looked up and gasped, and Colonel Hariyadi cursed in Indonesian.

Daisuke felt a rare, true smile break across his face. Over their heads, lines of lights marched across the sky, twinkling white, yellow, red, and blue. The lights curved off to the east and west, following the path of the sun to the southern horizon, as ordered as pearls on a necklace.

"They might just be stars," said Pearson.

"Those aren't stars, you tosser," Anne said. "Those points of light orbit this planet. We're looking at a ring system."

"Like on Saturn and Neptune?" Daisuke clarified.

Anne made an impatient sound. "No, it isn't like Saturn. *That* one's made of ice and rock, but *this*" – she poked her beer bottle upward – "this ring is made of fucking wormholes."

"*Yeli im*," said Tyaney into their astonished silence. The Nun chieftain had come to stand behind Hariyadi, his penis-sheath pointing toward the fire, his face aimed at the sky.

"What did he say?" asked Daisuke.

"*Yeli* is a deity like the Rainbow Serpent," said Anne. "*Im* means 'sky'."

"The men call it 'the Nightbow'," said Pearson. "Showing it to newcomers is somewhat of a hazing ritual."

"The Nightbow," Daisuke said. "What is it? Who made it?"

"Yeah," said Anne. "Wouldn't it be great to try and find that out?"

★ ★ ★

The rotting treeworm lay in the center of a circle of dead grass like a fish in an extremely unappetizing breakfast box.

The morning sun bathed the south-western slopes of the mountains in light that was just a little too yellow. And the scent Daisuke had smelled up by the wormhole wasn't just a hint on the wind anymore. The alien reek was all around him, not exactly chemical, not exactly fetid, just...*strange*. Foreign. Bad.

"Is it safe to touch with my boot?" he asked.

Once Anne had assured him it was, Daisuke proceeded to prod the alien corpse with his toe. It flopped over, the size and shape of a child's fist, the eye-stalks and frills on each end of its tube-shaped body as ragged as old leather. Below it was mucus and dead grass. No maggots or other carrion eaters, as if the worm had bled poison. In a way, it had.

"Tell me what you smell," Anne instructed. She was squatting in the grass, looking up at him with her blonde hair and honey-colored eyes.

Daisuke tried to think more about the chemicals assaulting his nose and less about the freckles on the bridge of hers. "I smell yogurt," he said. "Grass. Strong alcohol."

"Correct," said Anne. "At first I thought the alcohol might be just a by-product of its metabolism, like with yeast? Now I think treeworm biology actually uses the stuff as a solvent." She chuckled. "Which means they must have some pretty wild structural compounds."

Daisuke was beginning to see how he would be able to get Anne to relax on camera. Like most technical specialists, she got so few chances to talk about her interests with normal people that she needed barely any encouragement to lecture. Now he just needed to preserve this energy while they were filming. Perhaps the little cameras they had around their necks would get her used to the big one Rahman used.

Anne shoved herself to her feet, puffing a little in the gravity. "And that's not all. Look over here!"

Daisuke watched her, feeling a smile tugging at the corner of his mouth. How long had it been since he had taken it upon himself to explore a new environment? Back in his show's first season, when he'd just been a voice speaking from behind the camera? Then it had turned out that viewers liked watching Daisuke fling himself at dangerous organisms. At the time, he'd thought he did too. Not that any of the video the wallet-sized bodycams captured would be usable. Daisuke didn't even try to angle the inadequate little lens at Anne or the objects of her study. He just...wanted her to tell him more. There was nothing he would rather do on this chilly, high-gravity, odd-smelling morning.

Pearson had called Imsame a village, but it wasn't really. The place was only currently full of people because the Nun had been displaced from their permanent home on Earth. On their walk here, Anne had explained what Tyaney had told her: the Nun weren't supposed to *live* in Imsame, but worship here. And in this case, 'worship' meant 'build dams'.

Nun dams were man-high, crescent-shaped walls across the river, linked together to create a series of pools shaped like the scales of a fish. Holes could be opened in these walls to let in water, then closed to allow the settling-out of detritus from the treeworm forest upstream. The Nun carefully collected sewage and agricultural waste from the Terran ecosystem, which they dumped into the pools, killing any alien organisms that might be living in them. A stinking pool became a pond, then a marsh, then finally a grassy space on which the Nun could plant windbreak trees, sheltering and feeding pigs and game birds. After enough time, the soil was ready for crops, and the human-friendly ecology thus ground slowly upstream, a green and leafy glacier.

Daisuke walked over to where Anne squatted over another dark lump. This second treeworm had decomposed into a little mound covered in lurid green growth, which extended maybe a centimeter onto the soil around it. Another centimeter out and the ground was brown and dead, then a more normal green, dotted with tiny Earthly plants and the tracks of insects and birds.

"Ah." Daisuke groped for vocabulary he hadn't used since college. "That is succession."

"In both directions," said Anne. "See the alien algae growing on the contaminated soil? We're looking at the border in a very small war."

Daisuke smiled. "Is our side winning?"

"Oh yes," said Anne. "Thanks to the Nun. Here's a trick I learned from them."

She spit on the ground. Daisuke, thinking of Amazonian chicha-making parties, watched as the spongy alien growth under Anne's saliva changed from the color of absinthe to the color of old ivory. Creatures the size of grains of rice tumbled, writhed, and inched away from the spot where Anne's saliva had landed.

"There's a lot of talk at Far Side Base about protecting the Earth from alien plagues," Anne said, "but it just isn't an issue. The organisms here…their cell walls are dissolved by amylase. *We're* invading *them*."

Daisuke remembered the soldier from yesterday who had been stricken with an exotic allergic reaction. Before he could remember the necessary vocabulary to bring up the subject, though, Anne shifted sideways in order to harass some other plant life.

"See this horsetail?" She poked it. "The one like a little Christmas tree? See those weird brown bristles sticking out under the green shoots? I think they're for shading the ground. Preventing water from evaporating, controlling solute concentrations. And smell this." She plucked a nodule off a fat green succulent and passed it to Daisuke.

It resembled the ice plants Daisuke had seen growing along the beaches of the Garden Route in South Africa. When he squeezed the little green lump, a drop of clear liquid emerged from a hole at one end. He sniffed. "More alcohol."

Anne raised an eyebrow at him. "And why might that be?"

Daisuke blinked, rusty wheels turning in his head. Alcohol could be used to poison alien life…except no, the aliens made alcohol too. "Some kind of mimicry?" he said, then immediately shook his head. "No. The treeworms keep alcohol inside like blood. And when they die," he said, light dawning, "the blood dries, leaving their poisons behind. This plant drops alcohol on the ground to wash those chemicals away."

"That's my guess too. The plants are flushing ethanol-soluble compounds away from their roots. Or methanol, because who knows? If we turn out to be right, I'll name this species after you." Anne smiled up at him. "Good show, Daisuke." She pronounced it 'Dye-Sue-Key.'

Ha. This was getting more like college all the time. "Thank you," said Daisuke. "But the pronunciation is 'Dice-Kay', not 'Dye-Sue-Key'." It was an explanation he'd given so many times it came almost automatically, along with the college-era pickup line. "*Daisuki* actually means 'I love you'."

Anne's face went bright red. It was a fascinating phenomenon to watch, like dropping an octopus into boiling water. "Shit!" she said. "Sorry!"

Daisuke waved a hand back and forth in front of his nose. "I don't mind. Really, I shouldn't say anything about it. If you say 'I love you' on film, it will be very good for our ratings." Although probably bad for his divorce proceedings.

"And we're always on film, aren't we?" Anne stood, flicking her bodycam. "Fuck, I hate dealing with people." She glanced back at him. "Except you."

She was asking for help, and Daisuke felt a sharp jab of annoyance at this woman for having problems he needed to deal with. Wasn't it enough that *his* life was falling apart? He shook his head and brushed his left thumb along the ridged base of his ring finger. *No wonder she left you, you asshole.*

Daisuke's boots were already halfway sunken into the polluted mud. Shit, how much time had he wasted out here with just the stupid little body cameras recording this?

Anne pushed a sweat-dark blonde curl off her forehead. "What?"

"I'm sorry. We are in a difficult situation." Daisuke turned, looking out past the dams to where the river curved around a broad, flat plain. Last week, Anne had told him, that plain had been a treeworm forest. Now, it was a flat, charred field: an impromptu runway for the airplane.

"You want to catch up with the others?" said Anne. "I suppose if we're late to the plane, Pearson and Hariyadi will yell at us." She sighed and started walking, Daisuke following behind.

Anne spoke as if to the settling pools, loud enough that Daisuke could hear her. "And I know I'm going to have to do some more yelling to get Hariyadi to let Tyaney on the plane, and yelling at Tyaney to let on his wife. And they're all going to have these fucking cameras.... Do you think you can help me? Give me some acting tips?"

Daisuke frowned down at the walls along which they walked. On either side of him, milky green water bubbled and stank. He did not want to speak at the moment. He wanted to climb into the treeworm forest and watch the poisonous life flee from his spit.

"Tips," he forced himself to say. "It will get easier to ignore the camera after practice. For now, I only say 'don't worry'. I know what I'm doing. When we're on, I will ask you questions and give you distractions from the camera. Just respond to me."

Daisuke watched the work crews on the hills, burning back the treeworm forest. He wasn't a real biologist. He might have been, but he'd gone the route of fame and fortune instead of solitude and study. It had seemed like a good idea at the time, except now here he was with less than no fortune, squeezing out the last drops of his fame like alcohol from a mutant cactus.

"You think that'll be enough?" Anne said obliviously. "Believe me, mate, I'd love to just talk to you, but there's also the problem that everyone behind that camera hates me."

"You mean Colonel Pearson's men?"

"They've classified everything they could, Daisuke." This time she pronounced his name correctly. "They would have classified the whole planet's existence except I sent those photos I took to everyone I knew. I have no idea how much of the real story is getting out. Or what people back on Earth think of me."

"Many people on Earth call you a hero."

"And the ones who don't? The soldiers sure as hell think I'm a traitor, and *they're* the ones with guns! Last night, and the night before that, I woke up dreaming of standing in front of a firing squad. Can you give me any tips about *that,* Mr. Cheekbones-and-stubble?"

Daisuke nearly missed his footing and fell into a settling pool. Anne was flirting with him. And, once he'd regained his footing, he realized how scared she must be.

"Well?" demanded Anne. She'd turned to look at him.

Daisuke tried to look away from her chest and the camera that hung there. He rubbed the stubble she'd mentioned, considering how best to translate the extremely idiomatic phrase on his mind. "Um. Fuck them."

She raised a pale eyebrow. "Pardon?"

"It doesn't matter what they think of you," Daisuke elaborated. "You talked about simulating humanity on camera. Well, everyone simulates humanity all the time. Everyone is an actor. Everyone is faking. Playing a part."

"You mean you think I should manipulate people?"

"Manipulate is a very negative word, but...." The next sentence was tricky. Daisuke spent a moment composing it while they walked. "What else should you do with the people who don't think you are a hero for discovering this world? They deserve to be manipulated."

Daisuke wished someone had given him that advice back at the start of his career. Then he might have stayed a real person with real emotions, and not devolved into a puppet animated by a hollow, glowing box. A 'TV personality'.

"Entertain them," he told the biologist, feeling like Kōji Yakusho, an actor whose style Daisuke had always striven to emulate. He managed not to say "Shall we dance?" replacing that incomprehensible movie reference with, "Just follow my lead."

"Okay." Anne turned back toward the airplane and strode ahead, leaving Daisuke to muddle along in her trail until they reached the airfield.

The Mekimsam River looped away from the eastern wall of the valley and its bank went from a half-meter-wide shelf between cliff and riverbed to a wide, flat field. People were on that field, burning back vegetation and erecting equipment. Daisuke recognized a short conning tower, and, like a fish baking on a bed of charcoal, the gleaming white lozenge of their plane.

"If you're wondering why it isn't a helicopter we're flying in..." Anne said, "...a helicopter could land anywhere. A plane can only land here, where Pearson's or Hariyadi's people can shoot it down if they want to."

She was speaking too loudly. A passing soldier hefted his flamethrower and glared at her, and Pearson, standing next to the plane with Hariyadi and the Astarinas, put his hands on his hips and yelled back.

"Thank you for finally showing up! I'm glad you appreciate keeping this unknown hostile valuable environment under control."

"And good luck with that, Colonel!"

Daisuke's head came up at the new voice. It had come from the plane, from whose hatch now swung a man with a suntan almost as painful to look at as his Hawaiian-print shirt.

"Hello, my friends!" said the man, contacting the ground with a high-gravity *thump*. "Welcome to the plane ride to nowhere!"

The man – presumably their pilot – was no taller than Daisuke, but about twice as big around. Daisuke was reminded of a compressed, sunburned version of Wakanohō Toshinori, the dope-head Russian sumo wrestler. That may have just been the man's accent, though.

"Ladies first." The Russian swept off an imaginary hat in a bow, and took Anne's hand to kiss. "A pleasure to meet you, my dear Ms. Houlihan." He turned to Daisuke and executed another bow, one he probably believed was Japanese. In any case, it did not include hand kissing. "*Konichiwa*, Matsumori-*san*."

He straightened. "Culturally appropriate greetings having been accomplished, allow me to introduce myself. I am Mikhail Sergeyevich Alekseyev. You can say 'Misha'. Easy even for Japanese, right?" He winked at Daisuke, who hoped one of their cameras was getting this display. This was annoying as hell, which meant the average viewer would eat it right up.

"We ready to go?" Pearson asked Misha.

Misha grinned, showing a set of teeth perfect enough to grace the jaw of an American. "Soon, soon," he said. "When my little plane is done guzzling his breakfast. You can already climb in. The black man and his woman are already aboard."

"The black man and his what?" said Hariyadi while Pearson rubbed his temples.

Tyaney's head popped out of the hatch, followed by his too-young wife.

The Nun man was formally dressed in a simple grass smock and western-style raincoat. He'd tied his hair into a poof at the back of his skull, and if he was wearing a penis-sheath, it must be a fairly modest one.

"*Ibu* Anne!" Tyaney called to them, followed by a stream of angry Indonesian.

"You tried to take him off the plane?" Anne's brows lowered and her jaw firmed. Daisuke widened his stance in preparation to stand against her next burst of righteous wrath.

Colonel Hariyadi turned to Pearson and contributed to the confusion. "I was under the impression that you and I were to accompany this mission."

"Of course we're accompanying it," said Pearson. "We have to be on that plane!"

"Not according to the Papuan," Hariyadi said. "Or maybe I should say 'not according to Ms. Houlihan', who invited him."

Anne wheeled on the Indonesian captain. "Yes, and we discussed this last night. You saw me invite him."

Hariyadi jerked his chin up. "And I rescinded that invitation."

"I agree," said Pearson. "We talked about this, Ms. Houlihan. There's no space on the plane. The colonel and myself, our aides, you and Matsumori and the Astarinas—"

"And I!" said Misha. "Unless the tiny black woman can fly my tiny airplane." He laughed.

Pearson ignored him. "That's nine people. We don't have space for one extra person, let alone two. No." He turned to Anne. "Tell him he can go on the next flight."

Anne braced herself as if to attack the two trained soldiers. Daisuke wanted to get this over with, but he wasn't inclined to side with the military. Plus, he'd promised Anne he would help.

I've faced down more violent primates than this, anyway. Once I imagine these men are male macaques, the next step becomes clear.

Daisuke stepped to the side, not quite between her and the snorting soldiers. He centered his stance, bracing his arms on his hips and raising his chin into a position of calm dominance. The focus of the scene shifted onto him as easily as swinging a spotlight.

"The natives will look very good on camera," he said. "Much better than extra soldiers."

Pearson rolled his eyes. "I don't care how it looks."

"Yes, you do, or we wouldn't be here, would we?" said Anne. "With these bloody cameras dangling off our necks. And anyway, it's their bloody planet! The Nun discovered and started transforming this place while our ancestors were still figuring out basic agriculture."

"We do plan to use this footage, don't we?" Daisuke asked.

But Anne had pushed Pearson too far. The soldier didn't even look at Daisuke as he said, "Damn it, Houlihan, can't you ever just do what you're told?"

Anne's lower jaw slid forward. Daisuke was reminded of the leopard that had nearly eaten him. "If Tyaney and his wife aren't going, I'm not going."

"Fine." Pearson flung up his hands. "Hariyadi and I will give up our aides—"

"I shall not!" Hariyadi took a step forward, shoulders stretching in an effort to make himself look bigger. The move might have been wise against a real leopard, but not a pissed-off biologist. "What if we simply left you on the ground, Ms. Houlihan? Or perhaps in prison?"

Daisuke found himself suddenly between them. Odd. Was that his instinct to help Anne, stop arguments among his crew, or put himself in the center of attention? And where was Rahman and his damn camera? Daisuke glanced around. Yes, Rahman had quietly lifted the machine to his shoulder. Now, he grinned and gave Daisuke the thumbs-up.

"All right, now...." Daisuke said, putting his palms up. "There is no need to fight." He could almost hear the voiceover: *Tensions were high from the very first day, but I did my best to calm rumbling bellies.* What would that be in English? 'Tame savage hearts'?

"Stay out of this, Matsumori," Pearson growled.

Daisuke ignored that. "I agree with Anne," he said. "There is nothing your aides can do on camera, colonels, and the natives might provide useful—"

"Be quiet." Hariyadi stabbed a finger at Anne. "And *you*, tell your native guides to exit the aircraft."

They were pressing in on Daisuke from both sides, rumbling. He was trying to figure out how to make his exit look good on camera, when Anne snarled, "You know I'm trained to castrate primates, right?"

Pearson took a step back. A second later, Daisuke and Hariyadi finished translating that sentence and followed his example.

"What did you say to me?" Hariyadi hissed, face darkening.

"There's lots of ways to do it, too," Anne said.

Hariyadi's mouth opened, shut, opened again. But before he could make any sort of coherent response, Pearson laughed.

"Maybe my aide and I should stay on the ground and let you fly off with Houlihan." He tipped the biologist a wink. "He might not come back in one piece, but oh, the footage!"

"Ya!" said Rahman.

"Da!" said Misha.

Hariyadi looked around him, as if remembering where he was. He let out his breath and straightened, tugging his uniform down over his chest. "Colonel Pearson, our orders were clear."

Pearson shrugged. "My superiors didn't tell me anything about how many sergeants to take on the first reconnaissance flight. If we both leave our aides here, the natives can come with us. Eh?" He smiled paternalistically up at Tyaney, who turned his head aside and spat.

Frowning, Hariyadi glanced from Pearson to his own aide.

"I don't care," said Misha. "I fly Americans, Papuans, Martians, whatever. As long as weight is not exceeded."

Hariyadi nodded to himself, gripping his bodycam. He no longer looked angry. He looked determined. "Very well," he said and glared up at Tyaney. "He had better be worth the aggravation."

Tyaney's lips stretched and he said something in Indonesian.

Nurul translated, looking amused. "He says, 'Since the shattering of the Yeli Worm, the world has looked to us to enforce the borders between countries. Now you will not turn us away.'"

"Right," said Pearson, rolling his eyes. "Good. If we see any treeworms in the plane, you can spear them."

To his evident annoyance, Nurul translated that too, as well as its response. "The country of the *dung yo* is only our closest neighbor," Tyaney said. "There are many others. On this trip, I expect to spear something *really* interesting."

CHAPTER THREE

Junction

Daisuke lowered himself into the seat across the narrow aisle from Anne, who was shivering in her seat as if with cold. No, he realized, the biologist was shaking with fury.

"Anne," he said, leaning toward her. "Are you all right?"

"God!" she whispered. "Pearson! I very nearly attacked a trained soldier with a good twenty kilos and probably twenty years of combat experience over me. What was I *thinking*?"

Because of course that delightful threat hadn't been playacting, as Daisuke would assume coming from anyone else. Anne had really meant all those things about castration. Why on Earth should that be so attractive?

"Hey," said Daisuke.

"What?" Anne knuckled her eyes.

"You were right. The Nun deserve something from us." Daisuke smiled at her, projecting warmth. "I think—"

"Ding!" shouted Misha. "Thank you for flying Air Misha, Austronesia's best choice for smuggling, drug running, and sexual tourism since I deserted the army."

Daisuke jerked up and away from Anne, staring at the back of Misha's head. The massive Russian was directly in front of them, squeezed into his pilot's seat like a bear in a bathtub. "Now, I am kidnapped by some other armies," he continued in a voice that boomed down the fuselage of the plane, "so now *everything* is by book! This is a non-smoking flight. Yes, even marijuana. If you've got any smokes, bring them up here to me right now. I'll trade you some of the whiskey I got up here." He held up a two-liter Coke bottle full of yellowish liquid and sloshed it, steering the plane one-handed.

"Where exactly did you find this fellow?" Hariyadi asked from the seat behind Daisuke.

"In a Malaysian prison," came Pearson's voice from behind Anne. Daisuke wondered at the odd choice. Surely there were people in one army or another qualified to fly this kind of plane. Or was that the problem? One army or the other? Perhaps, like Daisuke himself, Misha was a compromise, the representative of a country with little stake in this planet.

"Thanks," said Anne. "It's good to hear I'm not totally crazy." She was leaning across her seat's armrest toward Daisuke. He tried not to look down the collar of her shirt.

It would be unutterably sleazy of him to seduce the first unattached woman he stumbled across post-separation. *Not even post-divorce, come to think of it.* If Anne wanted a relationship with Daisuke, she was a very poor judge of character. Probably she couldn't see below his polished exterior persona. What would she do if she found out that there was nothing under that exterior but a howling vacuum?

She was looking at him. With the ease of long habit, Daisuke directed the conversation away from anything substantive. "What do you think he meant, your native friend?"

"You mean Tyaney? I don't know," she said. "Hariyadi translated him correctly, though. 'Many other countries.' He might mean other habitats. These mountains will be full of little microclimates."

The rotor throbbed and acceleration pushed her back in her seat. People and charred ground blurred past her window. More normal sensations. Daisuke could be flying off to any shoot in Siberia or Canada. Then the plane slid into the air and the ground scrolling below him was no longer black, but absinthe-green.

The wormwood forest grew dense and lush along the banks of the river, a wilderness of parasols and tangled cords that might be vines or snakes or something else entirely. Things moved in the shadow of the plane.

"Oh hey," said Misha. "Alien monsters. You guys see them too, right?"

"'Countries' might mean many things," said Daisuke. "Do you think we will meet other…ah, groups of natives aside from the Nun?"

Anne shifted her attention from the window to him. "We're traveling due west, and Tyaney was very clear about there being no other people over those mountains. How could there be? The land is poisonous."

"Tyaney said 'country', but he meant the sort of 'country' in 'big sky country'," said Daisuke. "It means an area. A region."

Anne nodded. Her breathing was back under control, he saw. He was helping distract her. "It would make sense for the Nun to have different names for different habitats. High mountains. Marshes. Deserts. Even oceans."

The plane banked and the view from Anne's window tilted up to show the deep and chilly sky. Dark specks floated out there in the air. Or maybe those were just motes in Daisuke's eyes.

When the plane leveled out and the ground came back into view, it had faded from native candy-green to a washed-out chartreuse, wrinkled and veined like the skin of a very old lime.

"I am thinking," Daisuke said. "Those places the Nun can't travel to. They can't leave the Deep Sky Country and survive. Which means there is no way Tyaney and his wife can be our guides. This" – he nodded out his window – "will be just as new to them as to us."

Anne's mouth twisted. "So that dipstick just wanted a joyride after all. After I stuck my neck out for him." Her hands clenched around her seat belt. "I'm the idiot for letting Tyaney manipulate me. Jesus Christ, but I hate people."

A cough from behind Daisuke. That had been Pearson.

Daisuke glanced at Anne's reddening face, and decided to switch the conversation to another track. "Should we ask him what he wants? Tyaney, I mean."

★ ★ ★

"Tyaney! Do you think you can get free rides in planes from me?"

That was exactly what Tyaney thought. He had needed to show his people that he was still in control of the situation in Imsame. But now here he was, surrounded by the Them, and he had to be careful. The chief of the Nun composed his face into an expression of hurt confusion and said, "No, *Ibu* Anne. I gave you my wife to use as a guide. She knows the countries around here. Ask her anything. I'll translate."

That seemed to rob Anne of her initiative. The red woman blinked, looking confused and guilty. "Um," she said. "Well. What do you mean? How can Sing know about this poisonous forest? People can't live there."

"No," said Tyaney, quashing his impatience. Ever since the Them had invaded, it had been nothing but nonsensical questions and annoying orders. "No one lives farther away from the High Earth Hole than my newest wife, Sing."

The Indonesians had turned around in their seats and trained their camera on him. Good. Tyaney stared bravely into it. "Sing's people are savages," he said, using the offensive racial epithet used by the Indonesians to refer to his own people, "but they know all about the different countries."

The red colonel, Pearson, demanded something in his language.

"How far has Sing traveled?" Anne asked, after a hot exchange with the man.

Tyaney nodded and grinned. "I kidnapped her from the mouth of the Death Wind Pass, the one south of Imsame, where the Death Wind River joins the Mekimsam. She has seen the Death Wind Country, the—" He paused, looking for the word in Indonesian. "Toy…maker Country? Yes. The Signal Fire Country, the Ripe Blood Country. The Treeworm Country you already know."

"What are you telling the Them?" asked Sing, sitting uncomfortably in the seat across from him.

"They want to kill you," Tyaney told her with satisfaction. "They know you're a witch. A toymaker-user. I'm convincing them you're better use to them alive. Don't forget that I have control over the Them as they have control over this flying machine."

Sing said nothing. If only Tyaney could know he'd impressed her. That she thought he could command powers as great as her own. Then maybe he could relax and stop being so afraid of the woman he'd taken to be his wife.

"Ask them if their machines can destroy the Death Wind Country," she said.

"My newest wife asks: can we fly to the Death Wind Country and burn it as we did the wormwoods?" He shuddered. Such a thought would never have occurred to him. But who knew what the Them could do? They were almost as frightening as Sing.

★ ★ ★

Daisuke waited patiently for Tyaney and Anne's incomprehensible exchange to end.

Others were less patient. "What the hell was all that about?" demanded Pearson.

"That," shouted Misha from his pilot's seat, "was request from Grass Skirt Princess to firebomb the next valley over. You know, she may have a point. Look out your windows."

Daisuke looked. They were crossing the spine of the mountains west of the Deep Sky Country, where the green vegetation gave way, not to snowy or rocky peaks, but something brown, rippling like floating hair.

"*Apa itu?*" asked Rahman, with the intonation of 'what's that?'

"*Soko Mekaletya,*" Tyaney said. "*Di sana Soko Heng Tokwey.*"

"They're the names of places," said Anne. "'The Country of the Something', and that's the Country of the…Sun Ground? The Ground Sun?"

West of the hair, the mountain slope was a brilliant, canola-field yellow, which cut off abruptly at the lower elevations. Something gleamed there in the cup of the valley, gray and steely. It was mist, and as Daisuke watched, it parted, swirling around the black back of a flying animal the size of an orca.

"Fascinating," Anne whispered.

Pearson jerked around in his seat. "What *is* this? Is that thing dangerous?"

Pearson's demand was probably addressed to the universe in general, but Tyaney answered as if he understood, "*Soko Bou Deibuna.*" Followed by something in Indonesian.

"The Death Wind Country," Anne translated. "I don't understand. Something I'm missing...."

The shadow of their plane had crossed the Death Wind Country and was now rippling up the valley's western slope. Animals the size of goats bounded across a landscape of giant grapes, or piles of spaghetti, or spilled intestines.

"*Soko Ining Eng*," narrated Tyaney.

"The Country of Ripe Blood?" Anne asked herself. "Oh," said Anne. "Oh, I see. Fucking *wormholes*."

A mound topped by a shimmering blue sphere flashed by. Then another fringe of waving brown tassels, like a mane across the ridge of mountains, and the land changed again.

"What wormhole? Explain," Pearson demanded.

Anne rolled her eyes. It was the expression of a specialist being forced to repeat themselves to an ignorant public. Fortunately, this was exactly Daisuke's job.

"I think she means the Earth wormhole isn't the only one," he said. "We just saw another."

"And another," Anne said, "And *another* off to the south, and they're all the same distance away from each other." She talked faster, more quietly, grinning to herself. "This is a *grid* of wormholes, each at the center of its own alien ecosystem."

"This planet is a jigsaw puzzle. A crazy quilt."

"Or," said Daisuke, "it is a railway junction."

Nurul was babbling excitedly in Indonesian. Anne spoke too, whether translating or just voicing her own opinion, Daisuke didn't know.

"This isn't just one other planet, it's...it's a network of dozens. Hundreds! If each of those wormholes leads into a different habitable world...."

"It's a defensive nightmare," said Pearson. "Hundreds of corridors for God-knows-what to come down. Or go up."

"Stop being paranoid," Anne said. "The only thing that's changed is we know this planet is even more precious than we thought. Hundreds of alien ecosystems rubbing up against each other. Coevolving. Do you know what that *means*?"

"It means we must—" Hariyadi's order was interrupted by a sharp curse from Misha. The plane bucked and something up by the nose went *bang!* The pervasive sound and vibration of the engine vanished.

Everyone looked forward. Past the pilot, the nose of the plane was smoking. The rotors spun gently in the wind of their passage through the air.

"Turn us around," barked Hariyadi.

Misha only grunted and the plane bobbed sickeningly in the air.

"We must return and report what we have seen," Hariyadi said, voice tight.

"Plane not responding," shouted Misha. "Engine broken. We crash."

"Then radio back to base," ordered Hariyadi. "Now, while we still have line of sight. It is imperative—"

"Play with radio and we all crash and die," Misha said. "I land plane now."

Hariyadi, face gray, turned to scream at Pearson. "You! You did this! I'll see you dead before I—"

"Crashing," said Misha. "Still crashing." The plane dropped a meter as if falling off a stair. Daisuke could feel his body tugging upward against his seat belt, his hair and viscera making the same effort to stay at the plane's previous elevation, clawing at the sky as they fell.

I knew we were going to crash, came Daisuke's own voice in his mind, narrating the tragic event as it unfolded. *We had made the most important discovery of human history, and we would never be able to tell anyone.*

Misha pushed on the yoke and the plane lurched. Daisuke was now looking down at the back of Misha's chair. His guts felt like streamers trailing behind him. They were diving.

The landing gear clunked into position under the floor.

The landscape rushing past out the windows now looked more like bad computer graphics than real life. It was a rolling purple plain, littered with geometric objects like corkscrews, obelisks, pleated sheets, spiny spheres. A squadron of man-sized donuts rolled into the shadow of a giant crystal rooster comb as the plane hurtled past.

Wind screamed over the fuselage of the plane, vibrations rippling from the metal through Daisuke's skin and bones.

They rocked. The nose tipped up. The wind died. A soft pressure urged

Daisuke forward. The gentle hand of de-acceleration telling him everything would be all right if he just curled up....

"Hold on," said Misha.

The plane kissed the ground with barely a tremble. The Newtonian pressure eased. They were down as smoothly as if they'd landed on a freshly paved runway.

Daisuke hadn't been aware he'd closed his eyes. When he opened them, the alien obelisks were still rushing past the window. Just as fast as they had been when the plane was in flight. The vibration had begun again, this time from below.

"Keep holding something!" Misha shouted.

Anne's shoulder touched Daisuke's chair. She was leaning to the left. Or rather the whole plane was slewing to the right.

Misha cursed again. In the window beyond Daisuke's head, one of the obelisks was getting bigger.

Something glittered. Flashed. Crystalline crashing like a broken mirror, and the caress of Sir Isaac became an open-handed slap. Daisuke jerked forward against his seat belt.

The plane's nose swung around, the force of the spin tugging Daisuke's head forward. Another crash. The shriek of metal from under their feet, and the plane tipped as if banking. Sparks filled the window. The wing on Daisuke's side tore off with a noise so loud it wasn't even noise anymore, but a pair of hands scooping apart the hemispheres of his brain.

Anne loomed over him. Daisuke rotated into position below her, between her and the shattered window and the rushing purple ground.

Anne fell.

CHAPTER FOUR

Food, Water, and Shelter

Daisuke awoke in the arms of a beautiful woman. Or at least with her knees pressing painfully against his hips and her elbows wedged against his ribs.

There was something warm and wet on his neck. Daisuke's throat tightened. "Anne?" he whispered.

A hard, round weight moved against his shoulder, and Daisuke's face was enveloped in a cloud of curly blonde hair. It smelled like sweat and detergent, and not at all like blood.

Anne slurped the drool back into her mouth and said, "Gwuh?"

Daisuke allowed himself to breathe out. He could feel the bruise spreading from where the seat belt cut into his torso. "Anne," he said, "are you okay?"

"Whuh?" She shook her head, scrubbing Daisuke with the mop of her hair. "What happened?"

"You fell on me," Daisuke said. "You fell on me when the plane...."

He slowly turned his head and looked down through his badly scratched window. It was possible to make out multicolored objects on the other side, squiggling around like fish in an aquarium.

"Out! Out, everybody!" Daisuke and Anne jolted as one at the sound of Colonel Pearson's voice. "Don't panic, but this *is* a downed aircraft and it *is* full of fuel. So get a move on!"

Anne floundered against him like one of the fish-things on the other side of Daisuke's window. Her arms unfolded and braced against the edge of his seat. Her weight left Daisuke, who felt suddenly cold and exposed.

Daisuke's hands scrabbled at the buckle of his seat belt. The plastic strap slid across the bruise on his chest with breathtaking agony, but none of his limbs seemed to be broken.

"Is everyone all right?" he called. "Please answer with your name. I'm Daisuke. I'm all right."

He counted eight affirmative grunts from the others before Pearson pulled Anne off him and into the aisle. She scrambled down the corridor ceiling formed by the sides of the chairs, and Daisuke followed as if navigating a mangrove forest. And would he have to worry about crocodiles here too?

Daisuke clambered up the plane's fuselage, slowly so as not to tip the machine over, and looked down.

Sulfurous steam rose from shallow, purplish mud, all rimmed about by jagged translucent shards of…ice? Mobile objects – Daisuke was forced to classify them as animals – slid and squirmed through that mud and across those shards. From here, the animals were formless blobs of shifting color, but none was larger than a cat. No crocodiles. At least, none that Daisuke could see.

"It looks safe," he called into the hatch, and slid off the plane. His boots thudded dully on what must not be ice, but textured glass. A few moments later Anne and Pearson joined him on the ground.

"You might have stayed inside," complained Hariyadi's voice from within the fuselage, "and helped with the enormous Russian."

"It's the delicious Indonesian cuisine," Misha said, breaching the hatch like a walrus. "You must blame your people, my friend."

Hariyadi made no reply as he came down after Misha. Rahman boosted Nurul out, then slid to the ground himself, clutching his camera.

Tyaney extracted himself, yelling in Indonesian. Probably something along the lines of "Where the hell are we? How are we going to get home?"

Hariyadi snapped something at the Nun man, and Tyaney snapped back. Misha said, "Where's Sing?"

Tyaney made a puffing noise with his lips, a clear intercultural signal for 'I don't give a damn.'

Daisuke turned around and pointed to where Sing was climbing out of the hatch. "There."

"I get her," Misha said, and lumbered toward the plane, growling about "careless husband" and "respect for wife".

He caught Sing as she slid out of the hatch, then the whole party put some distance between themselves and the plane.

"All right," said Pearson, after they had milled around in shock for several minutes and experienced no explosion. "Is everyone all right?"

Daisuke focused his attention on his own body. He felt bruises, yes, but no blood, no concussion, no broken bones or dislocated joints. He was just chilly. The same seemed true of everyone else. They would all be sore in the morning, but there were no injuries that required care.

Which was good, because the nearest hospital was who knew how many light-years away. Daisuke rubbed his arms and looked at the sun, now past the midline of the southern horizon. "We will need shelter," he said. "Before dark."

Anne nodded. "Good thinking. Um." She looked at Misha. "Do we have any wilderness survival stuff?"

"Da," said the pilot. "Survival." He was staring at his downed plane, jaw working under his fleshy cheek. The shadow of the wing in the light cast a slash of darkness across his face. *At that moment,* narrated Daisuke to himself, *our pilot looked like an ancient god. A trickster, full of both laughter and murder.*

"There are warm clothes and food and an emergency radio in the plane," Pearson was saying. He stood with feet planted firmly on the glassy ground, as if claiming it for himself, or as if afraid of slipping. "All the standard survival equipment. I saw it loaded myself."

"A lot of good it will do us if my plane explodes," grumbled Misha.

Sing said something. Of all of them, the native woman looked the least like she'd just dropped from the sky. Her grass cloak was no more ruffled than usual. Her shaved head gleamed as if oiled as she held her hat in one hand and pointed at the plane with the other. She spoke again, and Tyaney translated. This started an argument between him, Hariyadi, Nurul, Rahman, and Anne.

Daisuke found himself sharing a look with Pearson. *There in the wilderness,* he thought, *civilization soon began to wear away to reveal the tribalism beneath. With a common language, the American soldier became my brother. Without one, the Indonesians started to look like enemies.*

"They are arguing," Misha said. "Something about being a hero. Who's going to go into my plane and get the equipment and risk getting blown up. The black man says he will do it. You know what that means."

Daisuke wasn't sure what it meant. In any case, the only person against the idea seemed to be Anne, who was powerless to stop Tyaney from sprinting across the glass and climbing up and into the plane.

An olive-green duffel bag sailed out the hatch and crashed to the ground.

"Shit," said Pearson. "He's going to break everything. Come on, Alekseyev, help me catch stuff."

Daisuke wasn't invited, but followed anyway, putting himself into position to take the bags and hard-shell boxes caught by Misha and Pearson, and hand them off to Hariyadi and Rahman. The women found themselves at the end of the line, depositing the supplies as far from the plane as possible.

Eventually, Tyaney started throwing down ripped-up seat cushions and Hariyadi yelled at him to stop. The rest of the group pushed their pile of goodies farther away, although worrying about the plane seemed increasingly silly.

"It's not exploding." Nurul sounded almost disappointed.

"Good," growled Hariyadi. "We can examine it. Find out exactly what happened."

"What happened?" repeated Misha. "We crashed!"

"But why did we crash?" said Nurul. "Was it accident? Pilot error? Sabotage?" She was smiling pleasantly up at the Russian, but her eyes flicked to her husband, and her palm turned up in a subtle lifting gesture.

No stranger to the Tribe of Journalists, Daisuke was entirely unsurprised to see Rahman swing his camera up. He could almost hear his voiceover: *Once we were all sure of our immediate safety, tensions began to mount.*

"Pilot error?" Misha said. "Only pilot error is error of being here!" He flung his arms toward the plane. "With plane cut up, sent to space-hole, put back together. With crazy plans of crazy soldiers."

Pearson squinted at him. "Cool it with the crazy Russian act, Alekseyev."

"Oh, is my English suboptimal for you?" Misha swept an elaborately sarcastic bow in the soldier's direction. "Excuse me, please. I am stressed with crazy biologist and natives and journalist who think to play detective when we are lost on great glass nothing with no wood to burn or food to eat." He looked up. "And sun is setting."

"But what happened to the plane?" Nurul insisted.

"I say I don't know. Engine stops working, superlative pilot lands without killing even one stupid passenger," said Misha. "What, you want me to do forensic analysis on big pile of wreckage?"

That pile of wreckage now stood like a statue on a gently rippling, glassy plane. Hexagonal tiles stretched to the mountains on the northern horizon, dotted here and there with clusters of objects that looked less like trees and bushes and more like pieces on a surreal chessboard.

During the crash, the plane had slid, hit one of these things, slewed in a circle, hit another, and tipped sideways. A trail of metallic debris arced from the plane, describing the physics of its abruptly halted inertia. Much of that scrap was caught in a furrow of shattered glass that ended in two piles of gooey crystalline wreckage.

"Yes," said Hariyadi. "We must find the cause of this calamity. Because if it *was* sabotage –"

Pearson spoke over him. "This can wait until—"

Hariyadi kept talking. "– the saboteur might be one of us."

"Enough!" Anne said. "What a *stupid* thing that was to say. Why did you even say that?"

Hariyadi made a visible effort to pull himself together, reassembling his cracked mask, the liar. "Excuse me?"

"What makes you think the saboteur would be here with us now?" Anne asked. "It would be pretty bloody stupid to strand *yourself* in the middle of nowhere."

Daisuke opened his mouth to defend Anne, but, weirdly, Pearson beat him to it. "Exactly. What we need is to trust each other. Let's not play the blame game."

"Be that as it may," said Hariyadi, "we must still determine—"

Anne thrust a finger at him. "Did *you* sabotage the plane?"

Hariyadi grimaced at Anne's pointer finger as if it was made of rotten meat. "Of course not! Why would—"

"Do you plan to murder any of us?"

"Not presently, Ms. Houlihan," said Hariyadi.

Anne spun, pointing at Pearson. "How about you, Colonel? Planning to murder any of us?"

Pearson folded his arms. "I am not. It is my mission to keep us all safe."

So the American soldier had finally decided to play along with Anne. Good. They all needed to pull together in order to survive.

"How about you, Misha? Daisuke?" She pointed at each in turn. "Sing? Tyaney? Nurul? Rahman? No murderers here? Okay. So we've eliminated malice as a potential cause for death out here. That just leaves stupidity. And out here in an alien wilderness where we know literally nothing, it would be very, very stupid to stop trusting each other, okay?"

Her honey-colored eyes burned. Steam literally rose from her purple-splashed boots, planted powerfully in the shattered glass. Anne looked like she might ascend to next power-level at any moment. Even more impressive, Daisuke knew Anne was such a terrible actress, this harangue had to all be genuine and off-the-cuff.

"She is right," Daisuke said. "We must survive together."

Hariyadi nodded sharply. "Yes. Besides, we'll have time to go over the engine while we wait for rescue."

"Wait for how long?" asked Daisuke.

"We filed a flight plan, and we didn't deviate from it even as we crashed," Pearson said. "The crash site will be easily visible from the air.

It should only be a matter of getting another plane moved through the wormhole and reassembled."

"Except the last time your people rushed a plane through the wormhole, it crashed." Hariyadi slashed his bladed hand toward the wreck. "Even assuming anyone can land safely on this glass and we don't have to wait for a helicopter. We will be here for an unacceptably long time."

"Why don't we walk back to Imsame?" asked Nurul. "That shouldn't take more than four days."

"We travel fifteen kilometers of deadly wilderness with alien beasts thirsty for blood?" Misha laughed. "Crazy!"

"I am trained for survival in hostile environments," said Hariyadi. "And we have expert guides. Sing is a native, Ms. Houlihan a biologist, and Mr. Matsumori an explorer."

Pearson cut the air with his hand. "Sing has never been to this part of this planet, everything Ms. Houlihan says is conjecture, and Mr. Matsumori only plays an explorer on TV. Our chances of survival if we try to walk home are minuscule."

"And if we stay here?" Hariyadi asked. "We have no food or water."

"Actually, we have ten days' worth of food," said Misha. "Military rations in storage compartments in place of booze and drugs."

Anne let out a breath. "That's very good. We can't assume we'll be able to live off the land."

"So," said Pearson. "We have plenty of food we can eat while we wait to be picked up."

Hariyadi drew breath to argue, but Anne beat him to it. "By the dipshits who already got us stranded out here? No way. What we have plenty of food for is a hike back to the Deep Sky Country. We should be fine if we leave immediately."

Misha shook his head. "No packs to carry food."

"Help is coming," Pearson insisted. "We just have to stay by the plane so they can find us."

"And if by day nine nobody has shown up yet?" said Anne.

"By day nine we are all dead of hypothermia," Misha said.

A muscle jumped in Pearson's jaw. "You two think you're being funny? You are not helping. We have to stay here because otherwise our rescuers will have no idea where we are, not to mention the insanity of hiking through alien wilderness we know nothing about."

Anne responded, "What about the insanity of staying put in the alien wilderness?"

This scene needed direction, and Nurul was busy talking with Hariyadi, attended by the anxious Rahman and Tyaney.

"The colonel is right," Daisuke told the arguing people. "Now we have no choice but to find warmth. And water. We can worry about everything else tomorrow."

"All right," said Misha. "So where is water? Where is wood for fuel?" His boot thunked on the ground. "Out here on the glasslands?"

"Hm," Anne said. "There should be water, at least."

"'Should be'?" repeated Pearson. "In other words, you don't know?" He rubbed his chin, looking off toward the eastern horizon. "Damn, but I wish we'd brought a specialist on this jaunt."

Anne stomped her foot. "Oh, that is bullshit. There *aren't* any specialists. We're on an undiscovered planet and *I'm* the only person here who knows enough to even begin to theorize about how to keep us alive."

"Good," said Pearson. "So theorize, Ms. Houlihan, while you go through our supplies with Ms. Astarina. Figure out what sort of food and water we have."

"Why don't *you* play housewife?" Anne said, but the colonel had already spun to address Misha.

"Alekseyev! You're on first watch. You and Hariyadi. Circle our camp and keep an eye out for danger."

"You are giving many orders." In contrast to Pearson in his rolled-up sleeves and unbuttoned jacket, Hariyadi seemed to have become neater since the crash, if that were possible. His collar creaked under his chin as he nodded at Nurul. "I will go to the aircraft so I can inspect its radio."

"You'll have time for that tomorrow," said Pearson. "Right now, night's falling and we need you watching our perimeter. Unless you want to give your gun to Alekseyev?"

Hariyadi's eyes narrowed and Daisuke held his breath. But neither soldier whipped out his weapon and tried to shoot the other. Instead, Pearson jerked his head up in an approximation of a nod. "Very well. We shall inspect the aircraft tomorrow first thing."*Co-operation,* thought Daisuke. *We may just get out of this situation without killing each other.*

But it would look bad if Daisuke did nothing while his comrades worked. "What should I do, sir?" he asked.

"Oh, right." Pearson turned to him. "You and Rahman and Tyaney. Got to keep the boys busy."

The cameraman's head popped up at the mention of his name. "Ya?" Tyaney said nothing, but he turned to regard them with his deep-set, unreadable eyes.

Pearson smiled. "Any of you boys ever dug a latrine?"

★ ★ ★

"What 'latrine' mean?" asked Rahman, handing a collapsible shovel to Daisuke.

"Outdoor toilet," Daisuke said, wondering if either of their language skills would be up for this. "In my career, I have dug many."

The site they'd selected was south-west and downwind of the camp, close enough to afford protection, far enough away not to stink the place up.

"Are you ready to dig?" asked Daisuke.

"Ya!" Rahman said, and brandished his collapsible shovel. Daisuke made a mental note to keep his shovel after this job was over. Only two people in their party had guns, and Daisuke might need a weapon of his own.

Tyaney walked up to them and drawled something in Indonesian that made Rahman frown. "He says he has to…use bathroom."

"Tell him to help dig," said Daisuke.

Tyaney scowled at the shovel Rahman offered him, but took it.

It was not easy to keep up my own spirits, Daisuke would narrate this footage if he was ever so unlucky as to see it aired. *However, the spirit of the party was of more importance.*

"So let's dig fast!" Daisuke braced his feet, held his shovel over his head, gave out a cry to gather his energy and plunged the steel blade down with all his strength.

The shovel crashed through the tile's roof, sliced through its gooey interior, and penetrated maybe a centimeter into a surface as hard as limestone.

Tyaney slapped his knee, doubled over with laughter.

Daisuke pointed his shovel at the native. "Your turn."

The bottom or floor of the tile was as full of holes as a slice of lotus root. The holes, as they slowly and painfully chipped deeper into the ground, turned out to be the insides of tubes or pipes or roots. These burrowed into a substrate that was not soil so much as chalky sand. Rahman discovered this when he wedged the tip of his shovel into a crack in the tile and levered it up, releasing a white puff of dust.

The three men held their breath and stepped back until the dust had dissipated. Then it was a relatively easy job to grab the shards of floor and rip them up. Multicolored worms fled through the chalk-sand from the light.

"Aha," said Daisuke. "Rainbow worms! *Dung Yeli*, eh Tyaney?"

Tyaney said something Rahman translated as, "You dig more, maybe you find your god too."

"I think we will find hell," said Daisuke, holding his nose.

The cracked pipes released a warm milky liquid that stank of sulfur. It seemed, though, that the main pathways in this strange natural sewer system had already rerouted away from the tile they'd removed. The chalk-sand they shoveled out of the hole was dry.

"All right," Daisuke said. "I think it's deep enough." The hole had become a shaft, walled with the stalactite-like root-pipes of the surrounding, healthy tiles.

"Easy!" said Rahman.

Daisuke nodded. "Let's dig a second hole for the women." He cast about, his eye coming to rest on a pale yellow-tan tile that stood out against the purple of its neighbors. "How about that one?" he said, pointing. "It looks dead, maybe we can lever it up easily?"

"Lever?" said Rahman.

"I'll show you." Daisuke placed the edge of his shovel at the crack between the yellow tile and one of its neighbors.

"I understand," Rahman said. "Lever like 'lever lock hiking pole monopod' for camera." He stood next to Daisuke and wedged the tip of his shovel in. The yellow glass gave slightly.

Yelling from the camp. "No, I don't know what it is, just don't bloody touch it!"

Daisuke looked up to see Anne stomping away from Pearson. "I thought soldiers were supposed to take orders. If I have to explain where I get my theories from everyone will be dead before I finish sentence one. What are *you* three doing?" She came to a stop in front of them, arms folded. "What stupid busywork does Pearson have you doing, I should say."

"A latrine is necessary." Daisuke let go of his shovel. "Think about it this way. We will be the first humans to mix our waste with the local ecosystem."

"You chose one of the yellow tiles."

"Yes," said Daisuke. "I think it is dead. Maybe easy to dig up?"

"Hm," Anne said.

"So I should dig hole?" asked Rahman.

Anne held up a hand. "Wait. What's adding our waste to the soil here actually going to do? Kill all the soil microbes certainly. Hm." She frowned, thinking. "I wish there was a way we could keep our poop sealed in plastic or something."

"Absolutely not." That was Nurul, walking toward them with a wrinkled brown packet in one hand. "We have more important things to think about than sewage. Like food." She held up the packet. Unfolded, this proved to be a conglomeration of taped-together vacuum-packed packets, each covered in dense text. "Most of it is American army rations like this."

Daisuke's heart sank. He had hoped for canned food, which could be placed over a steaming hole in the ground and warmed without contaminating it. "What kind of rations?"

"'Cold Weather Meal,'" Nurul read off the largest packet, the one with a plastic spoon attached to it. "It appears to be many sachets of different kinds of powder."

"Which we will have to mix with water," said Anne, "and heat. And we don't have either."

"Should I dig hole?" Rahman asked again.

"Yes," said Nurul.

"Wait. Why do we need two holes to crap in?" Anne asked.

Nurul smiled the smile of a journalist trying to stop herself from rolling her eyes. "I would appreciate some privacy from the men. Can we perhaps put curtains around it too?"

Anne snorted. "With big pink flowers on them? This is not high on our hierarchy of needs."

"Maybe we can chop down some of those crystal trees." Nurul pointed to an obelisk growing in the distance. "And...sort of...arrange them around the hole? Anne?"

But Anne wasn't listening. Her eyes had gone unfocused, drifted to the ground. "Flowers," she said. "Red against green."

Nurul turned her attention to Daisuke. "Well? What do you think?"

"I think that won't work," said Daisuke. "But that small screw-tree might make a good weapon. Like a...." He mimed the throwing gesture, having forgotten the word in English.

"A spear," Nurul said. "Good idea. But we are back to the issue of privacy."

"Blanket?" said Rahman. "On head?"

The only blankets they had were the silvery thermal kind. Daisuke imagined the mirror-reflective, vaguely humanoid figure squatting on the field of glass, with the wing of the crashed plane rising up in the background. *We'll look like the art on a progressive rock album.*

"Good. That's settled," Nurul said. "So we do have some bottled water, as well as something called a flameless ration heater. But don't you think it would be best to save them, Anne?"

"What?" said Anne, who had been staring at the ground. "All right. I can probably find a way to get water and heat out of these tiles. Give me a second to think." Her voice dropped to a mumble. Something about yellow flowers on a purple field.

"And food?" Nurul asked. "Can we get *that* from the ground?"

Anne looked up sharply. She seemed to have taken Nurul's question as sarcastic, rather than desperate. "What the hell is that supposed to mean?"

Nurul held up her hands. "I think you misinterpreted—"

Anne stomped and the tile under Rahman thunked hollowly, like a glass drum. "What, do you expect me to conjure a feast from the purple goo? I keep telling you people, *I don't know!* I'm a biologist, not a bloody supermarket."

Nurul's mouth drew up. "I know that, Anne, but there is no one else who might know how to keep us alive out here."

"And putting it all on me," Anne ground between her gritted teeth. "Just like bloody Colonel Pearson. But I'm trying to think and I don't *know* how to get food and I'm just as bloody scared as you lot, all right? So leave me alone."

Hell, but Anne was bad at human interaction. "We're all doing our best," Daisuke tried to temporize, but Anne seemed to have offended Nurul already. The journalist snapped something in Indonesian at her husband. Daisuke assumed it was, 'When are you going to be done?'

Rahman mumbled something and bore down with his shovel.

Daisuke held his hands out. "It's all right. I will dig the hole. You can go talk to your wife." It was what he would want if there were someone here he could turn to for comfort. Or if there was someone anywhere, on any planet.

"Thank you," said Nurul, walking forward to take Rahman's hand. "I am sorry I was angry, Anne. It's only—"

Anne's eyes went wide. "Wait. Yellow tile! It must be under pressure!"

"Would you stop interrupting me?" Nurul said.

"Stop!" Anne leaped toward Rahman as he strained to lever up the bulging yellow tile.

Which exploded in a plume of steam.

★ ★ ★

Anne's legs and front flashed cold, then hot. How much damage had that steam done? That hot acid? The sort of thing that disfigured a person forever.... Anne clenched her fists. She couldn't think about that now, not with the yellow mist filling the air. Yellow would show up against purple, the glasslands equivalent of a flower. Flowers meant reproductive cells. Reproductive cells meant... something that would kill her a lot faster than some third-degree burns.

"Hold your breath!" Anne shouted. "Get out of the cloud." And then, before she clamped her hand over her mouth and nose and squeezed her eyes shut, "Help!"

She pulled herself across the tiles, thinking at every moment of how it would feel if another one shattered. Her foot throbbed. Her hands stung. *Help.*

Footsteps thumped across the glass. Daisuke, from the sound of it. He wasted no time asking what had happened or if she and Nurul and Rahman were okay. He just grabbed.

"Matsumori!" Pearson shouted. "Get the water. We have to wash that acid off her."

Acid wasn't the problem. Pollen was. Or whatever it was the tiles used for pollen. Where would water be? With their bags?

"Colonel, stop!" Daisuke shouted.

Why? What was Pearson doing? Anne swallowed past a lump in her throat. Swallowed again, and realized her lips and hands had begun to itch.

Shit. Anaphylaxis. Her body had detected something in the yellow spores it didn't like. Some misshaped protein that worked perfectly fine inside a glassland organism's body, but would bring Terran metabolism to a screeching halt. She remembered the treeworms' response to human spit. *Sucks to be on the receiving end.*

Daisuke set her down. "Allergies. Is there an EpiPen?"

"Alekseyev!" Pearson bellowed. "Where's the damn anaphylaxis kit?"

A frantic rustling as he searched through their supplies, then a gurgle and snap of plastic and clean water splashed over Anne's face. Daisuke's hands scrubbed down her belly and legs, where the yellow cloud had touched. But she couldn't breathe anymore. Her windpipe had closed. Her swollen eyelids let her see nothing but red darkness.

Thumping on the glass, as of someone heavy running. "Yes, sir?" It was Misha's voice, quite close. "Oh, holy shit!"

Holy shit indeed, Anne thought. *If they don't have an EpiPen in there, Misha is going to have to cut open my throat. That's how I'm going to die, when a Russian ex-con drug-smuggler tries to perform a tracheotomy on me.*

"It's right there," said Misha, "Yes." And someone punched her thigh. A jab like she'd been attacked with a staple gun. Cold lightning flooded up her torso. Adrenaline sped her heart, dilated her blood vessels, tore loose the invisible fist that had closed around Anne's throat.

Anne gasped in a breath of sulfurous air. Coughed. Spat and gave herself a more thorough flushing with the remainder of the two-liter bottle Daisuke gave her. She also gave Daisuke a good flushing too.

He coughed. "Water," he said. "Nurul and Rahman will need it too."

Yes, thought Anne. She still couldn't speak, but the swelling was already much better.

By that time she could stagger, trembling and bleary-eyed, to where Misha and Daisuke were kneeling over Nurul. The journalist shuddered in the grip of adrenaline, then started her own coughing, wheezing recovery. Both of them were soaking wet, and Misha and Pearson were wet up to the shoulders. Bumbleflies whirred and clinked, drinking the spore-juice, settling in a glittering carpet over the ground around the steaming hole where that yellow tile had been.

The commotion had attracted Hariyadi, who relayed Anne's orders in Indonesian, adding in other good ideas such as "drag the bags away," and "get the burn ointment."

Anne's foot started throbbing, right on cue. Her shoes and pants had protected most of the parts of her closest to the exploding tile, but some of the hot, acidic spray had gotten up one leg, and it stung like blue blazes. Nurul had gotten some spray on her hands too, and had to be seen to. Both needed another dousing with water to flush off the acid before it ate through their clothes.

By the time the adrenaline, artificially administered and naturally occurring, had worn off, the purple fog was gone, nobody had died of allergic reaction, and their clothing and luggage had been cleaned and (mostly) saved. But they only had four liters of water left.

CHAPTER FIVE

The Stars

Daisuke and Anne left the others back at camp while they scouted for sources of water, food, and firewood. Anne was more optimistic than Daisuke that they would actually find any.

"None of you pay enough attention to aliens," she said, sliding her way back across the glass toward the plane. "Didn't you notice the swimmers under the glass? The smell in the air? The plumes of vapor?"

"Well, we didn't think we were going to be exploded. But I understand you." Daisuke did his best to slide too. The glass wasn't as slippery as ice, but walking took extra concentration.

They stopped in the furrow left by their landing. The jagged metal that had once been the plane's wing had plowed up the glass tiles here, exposing bubbling, steaming, sulfurous-smelling purple slime. It did not look like a promising place to find something that would keep them alive, but Anne stopped and squatted. Daisuke followed suit.

"This stuff on the ground isn't exactly glass." Anne pressed her finger into the surface, which gave slightly. Little trapezoid plates separated, a spiderweb of fault lines radiating from the center of the plate. "There are *pieces* of glass, or some kind of silicate, yes, but they're suspended in a tough membrane. Maybe silicone?"

She scratched at the ground. Purple scum flaked off under her nails, exposing a darker, duller burgundy color that seemed to be a property of whatever was under the glassy shell.

"Some kind of algae on the upper surface," Anne muttered. "And something that eats the algae...." Her finger followed a track of clean glass that wound across the tiles. "Aha!"

Daisuke leaned his body toward hers, trying to point his bodycam at the blue blob Anne had found. "Hello there, you pretty little bugger," she said, standing, and nudged the blob with the toe of her boot.

"Is it wise to touch it like that?" asked Daisuke. "On Earth, bright colors signal poison."

"No shit," Anne said. "But you're assuming that this thing's poisons will work on me, while *I'm* assuming that it doesn't have any way of delivering venom through half a centimeter of steel-coated leather. Don't worry, Daisuke, I've kicked a lot of things with these boots and nothing's bitten my toes yet."

The blob shivered and twinkled, a tiny burning ghost. Blink, and its body shifted from blue to a hallucinatory shadowless orange. It had no legs that Daisuke could see, but it slid toward Anne like a rock sliding across a frozen pond.

"It looks like bad CGI," said Daisuke. Leaning closer, he saw the iridescent effect was the result of spines standing out from the skin of the animal. A bitter sulfurous smell hit his nose. On the tile below it, silicone caulk between the glass plates began to steam.

"Don't piss off the shmoos, Daisuke," said Anne. "They secrete sulfuric acid when stressed."

"The whats?"

"Shmoo," said Anne. "It's the technical term for a K-strategy sea urchin larva."

Daisuke retreated from the little animal. "K-strategy means?"

"Investing a lot of resources in one larva. Some sea urchins just churn out planktonic larvae, most of which die, but other produce just a few big shmoos, which are sort of blobs that grow spines. Like this." She held a hand out to the creature on the tile before her.

Its threat-display done, the shmoo bunched up into a little orange ball. Much faster than a slug, it zipped over Anne's shoe to a place where a piece of airplane had torn away the roof of a tile, exposing two centimeters of steaming purple slime.

That plume of steam buzzed with bumblebee-sized creatures like airborne crystal snails. Other animals had gathered around the damaged tile like gazelles at a miniature oasis: flattened oblongs, fuzzy coins, spiral worms, scintillating rainbow-colored marbles that rolled by themselves. Daisuke aimed his bodycam at a thimble-sized sea urchin as it walked on stiff stilt legs into the goo. Those legs flushed purple, like straws sucking up fruit juice.

"Hm," said Anne, then, apparently to herself, "I'll need to take a better look tomorrow, but I *think* what we're looking at is a system to protect life against a hostile environment."

"Hostile environment?" Daisuke asked, looking around nervously.

"I mean the air. Land," Anne said. "When animals on Earth climbed out of the sea, they took the sea with them, as blood contained in a sack inside their bodies. On whatever planet these tiles came from, life covered itself in siliceous tests…."

Daisuke tried to halt the descent into jargon. "You mean these glass shells."

"Spot on," said Anne. "They dissolve the necessary chemicals in…well, it would have to be heated water. Which they could pump…." She trailed off.

That wasn't going to play well. "Like the sewer system under a street?" Daisuke tried to summarize.

Anne rocked her head from side to side, pursing her lips. "More like an aquarium."

"Ah!" The analogy came to Daisuke. "The goldfish you scoop at a festival!"

"You what goldfish at a festival?"

"Scoop!" Daisuke grasped an imaginary paper scooper and bowl, making the familiar motions. "You know, you have to work fast before the paper breaks in the water. Don't you scoop goldfish in Australia?"

"No, Daisuke," Anne said. "We do not scoop goldfish in Australia."

"Anyway, the fish will die in the air, but you might put them in a glass bowl."

Anne was less impressed with Daisuke's imagery than he was. "Glass bowls aren't linked together via underground geothermal pipes."

"By geothermal, you mean they use energy from the interior of the Earth, I mean, the interior of this planet—"

"You called it Junction?" said Anne.

Had he? Daisuke didn't remember. It was easier to say than 'crazy quilt', anyway.

"Yes. Energy from the interior of *Junction* heats the water." Daisuke had begun the summation out of habit. Dumbing down the scientist's explanation so it would make sense to his viewers. But then he actually started listening to himself, passing his hand through the steam rising from the damaged tile.

I had been thinking of the glassland biome as if it was a puzzle that cannot be comprehended. Daisuke imagined his narration over this scene. *But now I saw it for what it was: an ecosystem. A system to support life.*

When Daisuke placed his hand against the ground, the ridged, glassy surface was warm.

"We will not freeze," said Daisuke. "We only have to lie on the ground."

"Well, yes," Anne said, squinting at him. "I thought that was obvious."

So they didn't need wood for a fire. They could make their own sauna just by cutting a hole in the ground. But as for food….

Daisuke lowered his face toward the swarming creatures and took a sniff. "Like fermented fish," he narrated for his audience, "but with sulfur instead of salt. If we have to eat this, I think even people who love *funazushi* will have a difficult time appreciating this flavor."

"Eat it?" said Anne as if in horror. "No! It's probably totally incompatible with our biochemistry. We're lucky we're not going into anaphylaxis just from smelling the air here."

"So," Daisuke said, "no food, no wood, and no water out here?"

She made a wry face. "No food or wood, certainly. But there is water under there." She tapped the tough glassy surface again. Things beneath it darted and swam.

"Can we drink it?" asked Daisuke, but an idea was already forming in his mind. "I have been in plenty of situations where I needed to purify water. You can mix hand sanitizer or alcohol or even bleach with water to kill germs. At least, Terran germs."

"Correct," said Anne. "And what about chemical pollutants? We can smell the sulfur, but what's in there that we *can't* smell? To be sure we're getting out all the impurities, we'd have to boil the stuff and collect its steam."

"I am glad to see we are thinking of the same thing." Daisuke picked up a palm-sized tile lying loose on the ground. After a once-over with his hand-sanitizer and a corner of his shirt, he had its surface clean enough to hold over the nearest hole the plane had plowed in the glasslands.

Daisuke held the glass plate high over the wafting steam. In the chilly air of dusk, water condensed almost immediately on the under-surface of the glass. Little droplets merged as Daisuke tilted the glass, ran together like rivers running down a mountain to water, or veins spreading the heart's nourishment to a man's hand. He lifted the glass high, and water bulged on the lower lip of the glass plate, shone red in the light of the setting sun, and fell onto Daisuke's outstretched tongue.

Anne watched his experiment, her brows together. "I wish there was some other way to test this. Don't swallow immediately. Any weird tastes?"

Daisuke held the water in his mouth. There was still some sour sulfur there, but no stinging or numbness. Daisuke swallowed, and smiled. "Yum," he said.

★ ★ ★

"Yuck," said Tyaney.

Daisuke agreed. Hardly chilly or shaky at all now, he forced himself to eat another mouthful of something that said *Turkey Tetrazzini* on the package, but tasted like poultry-flavored vomit.

"Is this what the American military has to eat?" Hariyadi asked.

"No rice?" Nurul asked her silvery food-pack.

"I like," said Rahman. "Good like wife cooking."

Nurul shoved him.

"We don't usually rehydrate the stuff with sulfuric acid," said Pearson.

"Very diluted acid." Daisuke spoke around a spoonful of sulfurous sweet and sour pork. "This is no worse than what's already in your stomach."

"That's hydrochloric, though," Anne contributed.

"So you mean this food is pre-digested," said Misha. "Efficient!"

Daisuke couldn't even muster a polite chuckle. It had been a long day.

The wind was cold, but the warm air rising from the ground kept their surroundings a pleasant twenty degrees Celsius. Still, he wished they had a fire. Instead, they sat on folded blankets around the shattered remains of the tile that provided them with the steam to warm and hydrate their dinner. The shadow of the plane reached over them, seeming to clutch at the sky.

The sun sank toward the south-west, its light scattering through the atmosphere, shifting the color of the sky through orange, green, and purple, fading to star-pricked black to the north. Things like glass bumblebees zipped through the dusk air, avoiding larger, rod-shaped creatures like headless dragonflies. Or would a better comparison be 'elongated, winged squid'?

"Maybe we eat animals?" asked Rahman, who hadn't touched his dinner. He asked something hopeful-sounding of Tyaney, who barked a question at Sing. Both Nun had already finished their rations, although whether from hunger or a desire to be over with a bad experience quickly, Daisuke didn't know.

"No." Nurul translated Tyaney's report from his wife. "We can't eat the animals."

"Maybe animals eat us," said Misha. "When I was on patrol, I saw something moving fast, like motorcycle. No shape. Many colors."

"That could have been a shmoo," Anne said. "A little spiny blob the size of your thumb?"

"No, size of cat," said Misha. "Big cat. With eyes."

Nurul made a sound like "Eww," and huddled closer against Rahman's side.

"And I saw things eating the glass on the ground by the plane," said Pearson. "Little balls like hard candies. Might be venomous."

"Toxic," Anne sighed. "Allergenic."

Pearson grimaced. "My point is that we're going to need to keep an eye out for little things as well as big ones."

"And what did you see, Hariyadi?" asked Daisuke. It was important to get people talking, sharing, building trust. Reminding them that they were all out here together, terrified, maybe, but not alone.

"Something like...." The Indonesian soldier paused, thinking of the word. "A sea urchin?"

"A sea urchin, yes," Daisuke said. "Anne and I saw one too, but small." He held his fingers a few centimeters apart.

"No," said Hariyadi. He held his hand a meter and a half off the ground.

"Perhaps we should sleep in the plane?" Nurul looked fearfully out at the rippled glass beyond the circle of their flashlights.

"No," said Pearson. "Too unstable."

"Plane is sideways," Misha pointed out. "How to sleep against sides of seats?"

Daisuke thought of the chalklike substrate under the tiles, and of the quicksand he'd encountered in South Africa. "I am also worried about unstability."

"Instability," Anne corrected. "But yes. After today's...accident with the sporulation tile, let's stay cautious?"

Accident? Daisuke would call it a 'disaster'. And now that the initial terror had worn off, he was thinking more and more about how stupid the whole thing would look on the video recorded by their bodycams. Of course, people who had been there would know how chaotic and impossible things could get out in the field, but their audience back home wouldn't understand. Daisuke would look like an idiot for choosing the one dangerous tile in the whole field to dig up, and Anne would at best appear to be hopelessly disconnected from the real world. After all the mental work she'd done to figure out the reproductive cycle of these alien plants, she couldn't have given more useful advice on the matter than "Yellow tile!"?

"I just don't want to sleep in the open where anything might find us," Nurul said.

"We shall continue our watch," said Hariyadi.

"So we will live long enough to die of thirst," said Misha. "May I choose devouring by monster instead?"

"We can get enough water from the steam traps," Anne said. "But we have to be *really* careful about allergies."

"Yeah," said Misha. "No more EpiPens."

"No more coffee," Rahman said. "*Ya Allah,* no more *cigarettes*!" He was smoking his last, the tip the only fire in a country of glass and hot water.

This was why Daisuke didn't voice any of his concerns. Everyone else was more worried about the basics of survival. But the disaster with the exploding tile had been caused by lack of communication. Lack of teamwork. Bad feelings.

Being on camera did something to people. It made them put on masks. I am not myself, I am *playing* myself, the grizzled old soldier, the irreverent pilot, the Iron Man of Survival. Everyone acted in front of a camera, with the possible exception of Anne, and Daisuke hoped that he could use their cameras to remind these people that they were supposed to be acting like *survivors.*

He looked up at the Nightbow, thinking about how to set the scene.

Daisuke got to his feet. Eyes on the sky, he held a hand out to Anne. "Anne. Stand up with me."

"What are you doing?" But she gave him her hand.

"Rahman, please turn on your camera," said Daisuke. "I think it is time for some wonder."

With a sigh, Rahman scooted away from his wife's side and stood, unslinging his camera.

"What the hell is it *now*?" Pearson said.

But the camera was already rolling. Rahman never went anywhere without it.

"Look at this!" Daisuke declaimed. "Gaze at a magnificent *wonder* of the alien *world*!"

The camera panned up to take in the southern horizon, which was spanned by the arc of twinkling lights – red, yellow, blue, and white.

The speech came easily. "On Earth, we have the River of Heaven, what in English is called the Milky Way. But in this place, we have the Moat of Heaven! The Milky Ring!"

"Like I said before, they aren't rings." But Anne made the 'hm' noise that meant she was thinking. "Huh. They must be wormholes."

I got her. "Really? Wormholes?" Daisuke spread his arms, thinking of his silhouette on the covers of books and boxed DVDs. "A ring of wormholes circling this planet! Shining with the light of other worlds!"

"Is that possible?" Pearson asked.

Misha turned his face up. "What is up there?"

"Same as what's down here," said Anne. "Look." She pointed.

"Pan down," said Nurul quietly.

Ha. Daisuke had her too.

It was full night now, dark enough that it was easy to see the lights shining out beyond the glasslands. There and there and there, all in a line.

"Those wormholes on the ground were probably just tourist destinations," said Anne. "Rocky planets not too much smaller or larger than Earth, all with oxygen-nitrogen atmospheres, liquid water, and life. The wormholes in orbit were probably more like the industrial districts. Or trade."

"The heart," Daisuke said, "of an interstellar empire."

Anne snorted, but nobody else did.

"God, this place just keeps getting weirder," said Pearson.

"Are you saying you believe Junction is a zoo, Ms. Houlihan?" Hariyadi asked, joining the scene. Now how would Daisuke get Tyaney and Sing to participate?

"Who could have built such a grand project?" Daisuke asked the camera. "Can we ask our local experts?"

"You mean Tyaney?" said Anne. She said something to the Nun man, who had been quietly licking clean the inside of his food pouch.

He said something, at which Hariyadi scoffed. "Pft. Superstitions and fairytales."

Nurul cleared her throat. "He says the lights of the Nightbow are not doors. That's not how it is at all. He says, 'Do you want to hear the story of how the Nightbow came to be?'"

"Absolutely," said Daisuke.

Tyaney shone the flashlight on his own face.

"Ah!" Misha said. "Campfire story with no fire! But at least my ass is warm."

Tyaney spoke, and Nurul translated. "'Quiet everyone. Once, there was a man who climbed the *Yeli*. The *Yeli* was a worm. It was a tree. It was a rainbow. In the night sky it was *Yeli im*, the Sky Worm, what you call the Nightbow. It held apart the sky and the earth. The man climbed the tree because he stole a woman from another man."

"I know this one!" cried Misha.

"This story is very interesting," Daisuke said, hoping the pilot would take the hint and shut up.

"The man whose wife was stolen grew angry," Tyaney said. "He commanded his brothers and sons and cousins to help him chop down the *Yeli* so that the young man and the young woman would fall back to the earth.

"The axes hurt the *Yeli*. Like a worm cut in two, it slithered in two directions. One part, down into the deep earth, the other up into the high sky.

"The young man and the young woman thought they were safe in the sky, but because the *Yeli* was really only one, it had made only one hole: in the earth was the Deep Sky Hole, in the sky, the High Earth Hole.

"The old husband of the woman rushed through the hole and found the young man and chopped off his head. The blood from the wound leaked into the ground of the Deep Sky Country and poisoned it so no good crop could grow there. But the young bride wept and her tears cleansed the land, so some crops could grow, but only where her tears had fallen. Then she ran into the cold jungle beneath the Nightbow and gave birth to the adulterer's child. That is the origin of the people born under the Nightbow, on poisoned ground. People like Sing."

Rahman swung the camera to point at Sing, who bowed her head.

Even that worked. Tyaney was either casting Sing as a villain, or himself. *Later, I will worry about whether either of those possibilities is true.*

"Excellent," he said, clapping. "A great story." Now to use it to weld his crew together. "Anne, what is your analysis?"

"Huh?" she said, "I'm not an anthropologist."

Just co-operate with me, damn you. Attractive as her authenticity was, Daisuke wished his co-star would be a little less impossible. Any other talking head would have been happy to babble out some half-baked theory about the myth they'd just heard, and that was all Daisuke needed.

"No need to be archaeologist to see Tyaney doesn't respect his wife the way a husband should," said Misha.

"You have a theory about where the wormhole comes from," Daisuke told her patiently.

"Oh. Well. Right. A zoo," Anne said. "Maybe. With some sort of containment around each wormhole to keep the biomes separate. But when the containment failed, the biomes spilled out, spreading until they came up against an incompatible biome from some other wormhole."

Good. Now they all knew Anne's role in the group. Nurul took the cue with admirable professionalism.

"Thank you, Anne," she said. "We count on you for your understanding of this place."

Anne's shoulders tensed up. Her head snapped around. "Hey, I'm doing the best I can."

"I know," said Nurul.

Damnit, Anne. "She wasn't being sarcastic," Daisuke said.

Anne blinked at him. "Really? Oh. Shit. Shit!" She pounded the glass with her fist. "You know what? I'm going to go." She stood up. "Go away for a minute. Scout the perimeter."

This wasn't at all what Daisuke had wanted. "Uh," he said. "Wait." But she was already stomping away.

Daisuke looked at the rest of his crew. They were looking at him.

"Well?" said Misha. "Go after her."

Daisuke did.

Walking away from the others and their flashlights was like diving into a subterranean river. The Nightbow was not as bright as Earth's moon would have been, and a fog was rising from the warm, moist ground, obscuring the stars and wormholes above.

Creatures buzzed or hooted or tinkled like crystal bells, invisible in the fog. Strange cold drafts coiled and whispered through the rising columns of steam. Stars and wormholes peeked through the fog, creating a velvety gloom thicker than mere darkness, as menacing and intimate as sharing a sauna with a psychopath.

"Let's go back to the others," he told Anne when he caught up with her.

"I'm not scared of the dark," she snapped. "Although I am disappointed at the lack of bioluminescence," she said, as if to herself.

"It's all right," said Daisuke. "Nobody is angry at you because you misinterpreted—"

"Of *course* they're angry at me," Anne said. "I nearly got Nurul and Rahman killed. I wasted all of our water. And I keep being just a *flaming* bitch about everything on top of it."

Daisuke had not expected that, but he should have. Anne must be feeling guilty. He glanced at the bodycam hanging off her chest and thought of how to respond. Right. "It's my fault," he said. "I chose the yellow tile. Without you, Nurul and Rahman would be dead."

Anne didn't seem to be listening. She walked slowly into the cold wind from the north-west, staring at the steaming ground in front of her. "And before that, Nurul wasn't badgering me about the food. I just thought she was, but all she wanted was some comfort. Some, just, some empty promises. 'Everything's going to be okay. Don't worry.' Same with Pearson. And I'm just *bad* at that, all right?"

Daisuke couldn't think of anything to say in response to Anne except *"True"* so he kept his mouth shut and followed her.

"You work with people," said Anne. "Everyone on this crazy trip works with people in one way or another, except me. I work as far away as possible from as many people as possible."

"So you're bad with people," Daisuke said. "That doesn't make you a bad person." Eh. That hadn't sounded as trite in his head. Hopefully his viewers wouldn't judge him so harshly.

"I'm an asshole is what I am," said Anne, who seemed to have completely forgotten about their future audience. "I automatically assume the worst of everyone. And I blow up way too easily. You know when I was in uni I actually kept track of which of the rows I started had a legitimate cause? I stopped after my roommate found the graph and we had a row about it."

Daisuke fell back on his original plan: give everyone a job. "We don't need you for your people skills. We need you to understand this place and protect us."

Anne stopped walking. Her chin jerked up and down. "I know. And I'm scared I can't do it."

"You can," said Daisuke.

"That's easy for you to say." Anne flapped a hand at him. "You're Mr. Survivor-man. You've been lost in the wilderness a hundred times."

"Never wilderness as dangerous as this."

Things whizzed through the beam of his flashlight, as large as cats, sliding across the ground like giant pale hockey pucks. He had no idea what they were, or what they would do if they attacked.

"Are those dangerous?" he asked.

"Probably not," said Anne. "Small nocturnal predators like squid or bats. What would be the terrestrial equivalent? Shrews?" And, as if she hadn't just demonstrated her indispensibility, "Anyway, you can actually, you know, *talk* to people. Make them do what you want. I see how you keep defusing arguments." She sniffed. "Despite my efforts to the bloody contrary."

If I was good at people, I wouldn't have a dent on my finger where a ring used to be. But Daisuke wasn't about to say that.

"That's what you're doing now, isn't it?" Anne looked up at him. "You're trying to manipulate me into being a productive member of the team. No." She closed her eyes and flapped her hands in front of her face. "I don't mean manipulate, that sounds bad, but...I don't know. Just. It'll be hard." She opened her eyes and looked into his. "I trust you."

"You shouldn't," said Daisuke, and nearly bit his tongue off. His eyes went to her bodycam. *Shit. I shouldn't have said that. Anne handed me the perfect ending for this scene, and I flubbed it.*

She frowned. "What do you mean?"

"I mean…." Daisuke scrambled for some platitude to put her off, but nothing came to him. A warm breeze wound up his leg. Why couldn't he stop looking at Anne's bodycam? *Don't look into the lens, you fool.* "I…I mean. I am not so good with people." He rubbed the place where his ring had once been. "I have a wife. We are in the middle of a divorce."

"Uh," she said. "Oh. What does that have to do with anything? She's not even on this planet."

Anne was, though.

"My wife cheated on me," said Daisuke. And there it was. He'd said it. He'd broken his promise and talked about his divorce on the public record. And it had been easy. Like leaning against what you thought was a solid wall to find it was only painted paper. Like taking a bite of a stinking durian and finding out how good it actually tasted.

"She didn't bother to hide it," he said into Anne's silence. "I was angry about that at the time. The way she let me find her with her boyfriend. It would hurt my reputation and my career. But it never got out." *Until now.* But it felt too good to tell the story. "Now I wonder if she wasn't trying to do me a favor. Give me an excuse, you know. Otherwise we might still be together, our hearts dying."

"Oh. Wow. I'm sorry, Daisuke."

He looked down at her face. Wormholes and stars swam, reflected, in her eyes. She hadn't mispronounced his name this time, but Daisuke still heard 'I love you'.

Daisuke cleared his throat. "Call me 'Dice'," he said. "And I shouldn't have told you all that."

"I'm glad you did, though," said Anne, entirely failing to back off. "So you're definitely available then?"

Perhaps this was a good time for more truth. "Not really. The divorce isn't finalized." And somewhere in the night, a gun went off.

So, a bit too much truth, there. Anne didn't say anything as she led the way back to the campsite. That wind from the north-west was even stronger now, and all they had to do was turn around and walk with it, as fast as possible without stepping on any yellow tiles.

Flashlight beams flicked through the fog like the legs of a giant panicking insect, centered on a spot of glass between Anne and Daisuke and the 'fireplace' where they'd eaten their wretched dinner.

The crew was gathered around a lump of pale flesh the size of a large cat. Hariyadi seemed shaken and Pearson grim, while Nurul was excitedly whispering at Rahman's camera. The journalist was all but rubbing her hands together, which meant something juicy had happened. Tyaney and Sing looked like spectators at a chess match. Misha just looked grumpy.

"I was asleep," he said. "You wake me up next time, it better be a bear. Or at least something with claws and teeth." He examined the corpse. "Or legs. Or a mouth. Or a head."

Rahman squatted, focusing his camera on the creature, and despite everything, Daisuke felt the narration welling up inside him. "Come with me," he whispered to Anne. "Follow my lead."

"That," he said, striding from of the darkness, "is a shmoo. A larger version of the creature Anne and I saw earlier. Amazing, isn't it?"

"Your viewers might not agree," said Pearson. "This thing looks like ten kilos of snot in a plastic bag."

"Less fearsome creatures than this have killed people," said Daisuke, and looked at Anne.

For a wonder, she took the cue. "Just ask anyone stung by a box jelly. Assuming that person hadn't yet gone into cardiovascular collapse." Anne knelt by the corpse, carefully avoiding the pool of steaming liquid around it. "What happened here?"

"It was I," said Hariyadi. "I was on patrol and my flashlight beam shone off something. There were eyes in the dark, like a cat's."

"The eyes of a shmoo," Daisuke clarified.

"We have got to change that name," Nurul muttered.

"It attacked my boot." Hariyadi lifted his foot, showing a splash of discoloration across the toe.

"Acid burns," said Anne. "Hm. So these things excrete acid when stressed, as well. Or…I'm thinking of that smaller shmoo eating its way through the silicone calking of its tile…. Is what we're seeing here a feeding strategy? Or both?"

"Misha, we have found your teeth and claws," Daisuke said.

"Oh," said Misha. "Goody."

"Hey." Anne looked up at Hariyadi. "That was a really dumb thing to do. You see a glowing-eyed creature snarling at you from the shadows and you *kick* it? You don't even have real boots." She stomped her steel-toed monsters for emphasis.

"I did not kick it," Hariyadi said stuffily. "I stood still. It…" he coughed, "…ran at my shoe. Or to be precise, it *moved*. Without legs. I kicked it away, giving me enough time to draw my weapon and shoot the beast."

"Nice to know bullets work on these things," said Pearson.

"But...but...." Anne seemed to be struggling with the urge to get angry. If so, she lost. "That was *really* stupid. You had no idea what shooting that thing would do. It might have exploded like a balloon full of acid. The bullet might not even have penetrated. Or it might have gone all the way through and ricocheted off the tile under it and hit you. The bullet might have set off another exploding tile."

"We should be careful," said Daisuke. "Anne is right. We don't know what's out here."

"What's out here is one less shmoo, anyway," Misha said. "How did it run with no legs, I am wondering."

"Yes, Anne," said Daisuke. "How does it run?"

"You want me to dissect this thing now?" Anne said.

"Yeah," Pearson said. "You said we don't know what's out here. It's time to change that."

Daisuke nodded encouragingly at Anne. Rahman, behind his camera, gave her a thumbs-up.

Anne blinked and rubbed her face. Smoothed down her hair. "All right," she said. "It's time for an alien autopsy. Everyone come shine your torch on the shmoo. And Daisuke, turn it over with your boot, all right?"

Under the light of their flashlights, the creature was a bruised gray, like mashed banana. The bullet hole was visible as a puckered scar, from which oozed steaming whitish liquid.

"The bullet was stopped inside the shmoo's body," Anne said. "But it didn't hit a bone. This thing doesn't seem to have any. And this steaming discharge. Nothing alive could be that hot. Not *while* it was alive. But when it was pierced by the bullet... the way its body flopped when Daisuke moved it.... Press into its side again, Dice."

She winked at him and Daisuke's heart flopped over.

"Look at that," said Anne, prodding the shmoo. "Look how it sloshes around. Several layers with blood and viscera between. Not a tube-within-a-tube like us but...bags-within-bags."

Daisuke summarized for the camera: "So this creature is like several water balloons, one inside the other." He looked down at his steaming boot. "All filled with acid?"

"Can't be," said Anne. "There's only acid in this outermost layer, the one under the skin. The reservoir of sulfuric acid is sandwiched between what must be some very tough barriers."

"So how does this thing hunt?" asked Daisuke.

"Probably with these." Anne pointed at a transparent, centimeter-long spine, one of hundreds that dotted the creature's tough skin like the quills of a porcupine. "Let me.... Dice, you got a pair of pliers on you?"

As it happened, Daisuke did. He plucked his multi-tool from his utility belt and passed it to Anne. Her warm fingers brushed across his.

"Don't want to touch this thing with bare skin," she muttered, clamping the pliers to the tip of the spine and pulling. The spine slid a good five centimeters from the shmoo's body before it stuck.

"Hm," said Anne. "These spines go all the way to the core of the animal. I bet they're for sucking up the juice of the prey animal. The shmoo doesn't even have to inject digestive enzymes like a spider. All it has to do is pierce the inner layer that protects a glasslands animal from its own acid."

"As I did, when I shot it?" Hariyadi asked.

"But the bullet didn't go all the way through," said Anne. "It pierced the outer layer, the inner one, the gooey center of the animal, but got lodged here." She prodded a black lump in the rapidly deflating mess. "Against the other side of the inner layer on its way out."

"Damn, that thing must be tough on the inside," Pearson said.

"It would have to be, to defend against exactly the sort of attack it uses on its prey." Anne scooted around the shmoo. "Where are those eyes? I can't seem to find them."

"It seems a fragile existence," said Hariyadi. "A walking chemical reaction."

"You've just described yourself," Anne said. "Ever see someone with a gut wound? Same problem."

Daisuke heard a sharp intake of breath and realized that maybe Hariyadi *had* seen a gut wound digest a man from the inside out. Perhaps the dear colonel had *caused* one.

"Ah," said Anne, "*there* the eyes are. Interesting."

"Interesting?" Daisuke prompted.

"I can feel the lenses inside," Anne said, prodding the sagging body with the plier nose of the multi-tool. "They're embedded in the tough inner membrane. But how does the organism see out through its outer skin?" She brushed the tool around the glass spines at one end of the oblong body, smoothing them into a swirling circle like the petals of a chrysanthemum. "Shine your light here. At this angle."

The chrysanthemum petals blazed suddenly with blue light. As Anne poked them, the light flicked to green, then red.

"Aha," she said. "These spines aren't just transparent. They can conduct light all the way through to the core of the animal. It can even tune its visual system by slight adjustments to the angles of these...what...optical spines?"

"Like...." Daisuke's brow furrowed as he worked on a way to dumb that down. "Uh...a periscope? Eye glasses?"

"Like a weird alien eyeball made of millions of tiny prisms floating in acid," said Anne. "That's what it's like." She pushed off her knees and looked up at Hariyadi. "These things are going to be a problem."

"If we stay here," Nurul said.

"We're staying here," said Pearson, and turned to Anne before the journalist could respond. "Houlihan, how do we solve the problem?"

"Well, it's not like we can dig a moat to keep these things out." Anne rapped the glass ground with her knuckles and Nurul flinched. "And I don't know how much luck you'd have if you tried to kick it, or even step on it. A bullet works, but only two of us have guns."

"So," said Hariyadi. "As I said before, we must retire to the plane. I don't believe these shmoos can climb into planes, can they?"

Anne nodded. "The plane would be more secure—"

"If it wasn't in danger of blowing up," Pearson said.

"Oh!" Hariyadi shook his head in disgust. "Surely the plane is safe by now. It is not even burning. Alekseyev, will it explode?"

Misha gave an aggressive sort of Russian shrug. "I know that how? I must examine my plane, his engine. Not until tomorrow."

"First thing tomorrow morning," said Hariyadi.

"In the meantime," Daisuke said, "I know how to make some weapons."

"Yeah?" Pearson said. "Out of what?"

"Bamboo. Tree branches. Rocks...." Daisuke shook his head. "None of those around here. We might use shovels?"

"You know," said Pearson, "I like that idea, Matsumori. Astarina, you know where the collapsible shovels are? Issue one to whoever's got next watch. Houlihan, Tyaney, and I'll come too. Three people, two shovels, one gun. We'll keep us safe the rest of the night."

Hariyadi grimaced. "And what of the next day?"

"Well," said Pearson, "we'll just have to shoot that alien when we get to it."

CHAPTER SIX

Staying and Going

The morning light slashed across the glasslands and into Daisuke's eyes like a sickle on a chain. He licked at his mossy teeth while Misha grunted and cursed at the nose of the plane. Finally, the engine cowling of the Cessna fell to the ground, ringing against the glass.

"Fuck, Alekseyev!" said Pearson. "Do you want to set off another explosion?"

Misha just kicked the cowling away across the shattered ground. Like the rest of them, huddled together in the lee of the sideways airplane, the pilot was probably sore from a night spent on the heated glass, queasy from a partially pre-digested breakfast, and less than eager to march out here and perform an autopsy on the plane.

"Is this really necessary?" Anne asked.

"Well?" said Hariyadi.

"Eh!" Misha grunted, shoulder-deep in the mechanical bowels of the plane. "What butcher reassembled my plane like this? Sloppy! No wonder my steering was so much like slug."

"Alekseyev," Pearson barked. "Why did we crash?"

"Oh yes." The pilot extracted himself from his plane and wiped his hands on his pants. "Good news. We can camp in cold plane, hold big glass spikes, fight alien motorcycle slugs, no problem."

"Huh?" said Rahman.

"Plane will not explode," Misha said. "Inert. Whole thing. Electrical system is baked."

Pearson sighed. "You mean fried?"

"Yes. Fried. What was I thinking of?"

"How did it happen?" Hariyadi demanded.

Misha threw up his hands. "How, how, everyone is asking how. How did plane crash? I tell you. Electrical system fried. How is fried electrical system? Probably there is too much electricity in one place or not enough in another.

You want better explanation, you should have brought electrician. Or maybe stayed home."

"Electrical system?" said Hariyadi. "What about the radio?"

"Fried," Misha said. "Also eaten up."

"What?" said Hariyadi, Nurul, and Anne at the same time.

"These animals," Misha reached into the engine and pulled out a glass ball the size of a snail, candy-colored with complicated grooves around its surface, "they eat electronics. Etch them like acid. Silicon, right, Anne?"

"Silicone," said Anne, reaching out. "Let me see that."

Misha handed it to her. "Why bother with examinations? We are really stuck here. We have no choice but waiting."

"What about other radios?" Hariyadi insisted. "Walkie-talkies. Is anyone here carrying one?"

"I have one, of course," said Pearson. "But we don't have line-of-sight with base and Junction doesn't have satellites to bounce signals off. But the fact that we didn't return yesterday means they'll know something is wrong. They'll be looking for us."

"So you say."

Pearson smiled unconvincingly. "Colonel Hariyadi, I thought you were a man of faith."

"If you mean am I religious," said Hariyadi, "yes. I am registered as Muslim, and I wonder how I would have gone had I the misfortune to be born in your country, Colonel Pearson. Americans make much of their pluralistic society, but in fact—"

"In fact, we don't get sidetracked easily," said Pearson. "We will stay here."

"Why must I?" Hariyadi spread his palms. "I can take half the supplies and set out for the base with Nurul and Rahman, and the natives." He scanned their faces. "And anyone else who wishes to accompany us."

Pearson had stopped smiling. "You know I can't let you do that."

"Ah." Hariyadi squared his shoulders. "And here we come to it. Precisely how do you intend to stop me?"

Daisuke's back teeth were pressing together painfully. His hands drifted toward his belt. Feeling for his knife. *If Hariyadi were a wild boar, he would be lowering his head, pawing the ground, his bristles ruffed. Preparing to charge. If he were a boar, my knife might do me some good.*

"Take your hand away from your gun, Hariyadi."

"You first, Pearson."

Daisuke remembered a duel between two rival male baboons he'd seen in

South Africa. *We are all primates out here, stranded so far from the savanna that gave us birth. The only way we can possibly survive is by remembering that we are more than animals.*

"Colonel Pearson," he said. "Colonel Hariyadi. Remember we depend on one another to survive. Now is not the time for mistrust."

"Quiet, kid," said Pearson.

Daisuke was careful not to get angry. "What do you think will happen if you shoot?" he asked.

"You can't threaten me," said Pearson.

Hariyadi turned his head, never losing eye contact with Pearson, and said something to Rahman. The cameraman shook his head, eyes wide and frightened.

"Of course Rahman's not going to 'take Daisuke down,'" said Anne, who had apparently understood Hariyadi's order. "What the bloody hell is going on here?"

"What does it look like?" Misha said. "They are trying to figure out whether they should shoot each other."

Anne flung up her arms. "Well, maybe we should fucking let them."

"Be quiet, Anne," growled Pearson. "You have no idea what's going on."

"No!" Anne walked toward him, either having forgotten the man had a gun or else horrifically brave. Daisuke wished he could tell her so. "*You* have no idea. You think you're the colonel of a bunch of soldiers in enemy territory, and you're not. You're a mad old codger with a gun, squaring off against another mad old codger with another gun as if you're in a Wild West saloon. None of us are your soldiers, and we don't take your orders." She grabbed his right arm. "Now stop this."

Anne was large and solidly built, but Pearson was larger and heavier and better trained. Daisuke knew the only reason the soldier did not smash the biologist to the ground was because he couldn't afford to take his eyes off Hariyadi.

Pearson's voice trembled from between gritted teeth. "Ms. Houlihan, let go of me."

"Daisuke," said Anne. "Go restrain Hariyadi. Misha, come help me with Pearson."

"No way." Misha backed away as Nurul stepped forward.

"Anne, stop," she said. "You'll get shot."

"Nobody's getting shot," said Anne. "*Daisuke.*"

Maybe Anne was right. Maybe they could really pull off this...mutiny?

Daisuke walked toward Hariyadi. Slowly, with his palms out so as not to spook the dangerous and skittish beast. "Sir," he said, "I think Anne is right. If you will please take your hand away from your weapon...."

"Enough of this!" Pearson twisted his arm out of Anne's grasp, shoving her away from him. Breaking eye contact with Hariyadi.

The Indonesian's lips stretched, his shoulders squared, his fingers clenched around his pistol.

Anne shrieked. Rahman cried out and dived at Daisuke, but too late to stop Daisuke from hitting Hariyadi.

Daisuke hugged Hariyadi with arms and legs, throwing his weight to the side. He should have overbalanced the smaller man and brought them both to the ground. Instead, Daisuke found Hariyadi's arms around *him*. Now he was flying through the air as before, but upside down. The glass ground slapped all the air out of his lungs.

Daisuke had once spent a very lucrative two weeks in the Philippines learning how to wrestle crocodiles. He remembered now how much fun that had been, and how trained soldiers were not crocodiles.

Hariyadi stood above him. His gun was out. Daisuke's mouth was open, but no words could come out. His lungs spasmed in his chest. A broken vessel in his eye bled red across his vision. A gunshot reduced his world to whining, throbbing darkness, and it was almost a relief.

Something wet splashed on his face. Something warm. Salty tasting. Sulfurous. And...itchy?

"You *fucker*," Anne screamed. "Who has a canteen of water? Pour it on him before—"

"I know, damn it."

Water gurgled, but not onto Daisuke's face. He had to wait, face heating and swelling, until finally cool water trickled down his hair, as welcome as rain in a desert. Daisuke's eyes stung and itched as if he'd taken a face full of powdered mustard, but he knew that if he touched them, things would only get worse. All he could do was lie there, water running down his face, weeping the allergens away.

"I could have shot *you* instead of the ground," Pearson was saying. "I could have. Don't forget it."

Hariyadi made a furious choking sound.

"Is he going to live?"

"How should I fucking know?" came Anne's voice.

"I think so," Misha said. "Hariyadi got smaller dose than Nurul, and she is still living."

Daisuke blinked the tears out of his eyes. His face still itched horribly, but he could see Misha kneeling over Hariyadi's prone form, Anne red-faced and Nurul livid. Pearson standing over them all. The American soldier had shot a tile between Daisuke and Hariyadi, splashing both of them with alien goo as debilitating as pepper spray.

"You fucking psychopath!" said Anne. "You could have killed him." She jabbed a hand at Daisuke. "You could have killed both of them."

"But I didn't. I'm not the bad guy here." Pearson looked out over the glasslands. "You'd better remember that the next time an alien attacks."

★ ★ ★

"Would you please speak English?" Colonel Greg Pearson told his charges.

The Astarinas, who had been gossiping in Indonesian, fell silent. Houlihan, though, dug her heels in.

"This is insane. What you're doing is insane."

Pearson looked off into the distance so he wouldn't have to look at her face. Tiled purple folds of land stretched to the western horizon. Sing, the native girl, walked ahead of them, scouting for danger.

Once Pearson had gotten control of his anger, he asked, "What's insane? Looking for weapons? For other supplies we might use?"

"There won't *be* any supplies," Anne said, blunt as a mallet. "We got water, sort of, and heat, and that's all this ecosystem is going to give us. That and a case of anaphylactic shock. Or something else. Something we don't even know about yet."

Pearson didn't ask her what she thought they should do, but she told him anyway. "Hariyadi is *right,* Pearson. We have to get out of here. Hike back to Imsame. If we leave today, we can get there—"

Too soon, Pearson knew. And even if he didn't, he had his orders. "No," he said.

Anne stopped walking. "What? Just 'no'? Fuck you."

Pearson lowered his head. Prayed to God for strength, not to mention forgiveness. Small shmoos and candy-bugs rolled between his boots. Other creatures swarmed under the glass. When he turned, he could look at the scientist without wanting to shoot her.

"Or maybe, Ms. Houlihan, you don't know everything about this situation," he said. "Maybe, if you had all the facts, it'd be *your* actions that'd seem insane."

Anne folded her arms, squinting in the sun. Nurul and Rahman were looking at him too. "And what facts would I need to make sense of dragging along a cameraman to film your gloating?"

"I am not gloating," he told them. "I am separating Hariyadi from his countrymen while he has a chance to cool down and consider the situation. I am trying to prevent him or any of the rest of us from coming to harm." Or anyone back on Earth, although these civilians couldn't know that. If only they would let Pearson protect them!

"Also," he said, "I actually need you to scout for *actual* danger," – Pearson swept his arm across the rumpled horizon – "so the next thing that nearly kills someone—"

"—isn't an accident?" interrupted Anne. "You want me to scour this pristine world for new weapons for you, Colonel?"

Nurul whispered something to Rahman, who aimed his camera at Pearson. They were plotting something, weren't they? God above, were they trying to force him to shoot them?

"We need to know it all," Pearson said, ignoring the camera as best he could. "Weapons, food, dangerous predators…."

"…shmoos of unusual size…." said Anne.

"We need to gather as much intelligence as possible about this place," Pearson said as reasonably as he could. "We'll be staying here for quite some time."

"Yes," said Nurul, walking toward them. "So. *Do* you see anything dangerous around here?"

"I wish I wasn't the only person you could ask that question to," Anne said. "Sing is a better wilderness survivor than I am, I'm sure."

The native girl looked back at them, expression and motivations impossible to read. They weren't in land she knew.

It had been a good idea to let Houlihan bring Sing and her aggravating husband on this trip. Not that it would have been difficult to neutralize Hariyadi's lieutenant, but every advantage Pearson could gain, any dirty trick he could play, would be worth it if he could prevent the coming war. Even if no rescue came and he died out here, even if everyone in this party died, it would be worth it if he could just keep Hariyadi away from his people back in Imsame.

"Since we were stranded here yesterday, our lives have already been at risk twice," said Nurul, apparently to the camera her husband was swinging around. "Once, when the ground exploded under us. Another, when we were attacked by a strange and savage creature."

"And once again when we were menaced by killer apes," Houlihan muttered at him.

Pearson gritted his teeth. It was like the woman was missing part of her brain. Even a dog was smart enough to roll over once you established dominance, but the biologist just kept pushing, even when she was clearly in the wrong. Who had nearly killed half their party and wasted their entire water supply by failing to do her damn job.

The thought made Pearson look down at the ground, suddenly nervous it might blow up under him.

"Don't worry," said Anne. "No yellow tiles here."

"Assuming yellow tiles are the only thing dangerous out there," Pearson said.

"We can't assume any such thing. Which is why we can't stay here."

Maybe that was her problem. Scientists were like lawyers and politicians and other people who thought that words mattered. That if you just *talked* about something long enough, you'd accomplish something.

Well, Pearson had tried that. He'd tried words and explanations and that lunatic Hariyadi had nearly shot him. They *were* going to stay here because Pearson was under orders to kill anyone who tried to leave. He couldn't tell the civilians that, of course, because then they'd try to figure out where the orders came from, and why. Which would blow this operation's deniability all to hell and probably get Houlihan and the rest locked up in some federal prison. But Pearson couldn't tell them *that*, either. So, just don't engage. Don't talk. *Act.*

"You know what I'd like?" Pearson stopped walking. "I'd like a spear." He pointed to one of those weird twisted glassy structures they called 'screw-trees'. "Maybe if we chop down one of those?" Scrupulously, he added, "Would that be safe, Ms. Houlihan?"

She looked at him levelly. "I don't know."

Pearson ground his teeth. "So find out."

One thing he could say about her, the woman was no coward. She stomped right up to the potentially deadly screw-tree and knelt close to its base. "Okay," she said in lecture mode. "This thing is a helix, a flat double sheet of glass that grows in a spiral. It's slightly wider at the bottom, but not by much. Separated into wedge-shaped segments. Each one has its own internal reservoir of purple goo. Some structures on the edge of the screw…little yellow fruits? Flowers? Hmm. Oh! And look at this little beauty, like a Life Saver, rolling around. And here's a bumblesnail we haven't seen before…."

All right, that was enough technical chatter. "Is it likely to explode if I cut it down?" Pearson asked.

"No," said Houlihan with admirable certainty. "But I don't think you can carve the tip into a point. It's all hollow glass."

Damn. "Any other way we can use it for a weapon?"

Anne shrugged unhelpfully, but Sing, who had climbed to the top of the nearest ridge, had begun to point and yell.

Pearson's head whipped around. His hand went to his holstered sidearm. "What's that?"

"Urchins!" shouted Nurul, as Rahman squatted and focused his camera between two outcroppings of forest-reef. There were two creatures there, like glass medicine balls suspended on six-foot spines. Spines that would make excellent weapons.

Mottled purple viscera squelched around the inside of the glass balls, crawling up the inside of the central balls like giant amoebas. Overbalanced, the balls tipped forward, and the urchins rolled closer to the humans.

"They must be high browsers," Houlihan said. "I wonder...." and she trailed off into irrelevant speculation. Pearson didn't much care about what the urchins ate, as long as it wasn't people. All he cared about was the spines these things carried, which would make excellent spears. He drew his gun.

"Don't shoot it, dipshit!" Houlihan cried. "We have no idea what will happen."

He was getting real tired of that word. But Pearson controlled his temper and lowered his gun. "Do you think it will explode, Houlihan?" Better keep the questions simple.

"Probably not," she said, "but still."

"You have a better way of killing it?"

"Why don't we just watch and learn a little before we start killing?"

Sing squawked something in her language. She was looking at the ridge behind the urchins. Had she seen something? Was that look on her face fear? It was hard to tell, she was so damn stoic. Pearson kept his gun out.

The urchins made another laborious, rolling 'step' toward the humans.

"Do you think they're attacking?" asked Nurul. "Are they dangerous?"

"I doubt it," Houlihan said. "It looks like it has a top speed of maybe three centimeters per second."

Sing yelled, and this time there was no mistaking her fear.

"What?" said Houlihan, looking around, but Pearson had already seen it.

From behind the ridge emerged a purple-green, lozenge-shaped object about six feet long. Glassy spines glittered on its surface, those down the center axis flowing from aft to fore with the smoothness of a conveyor belt.

As Pearson watched, it stopped, bunched its sacklike body and turned its forward end toward him. Rosettes of prismatic spines opened like two eyes, shimmering glossy black.

A giant shmoo.

Pearson already had his gun centered between those weird, flowerlike eyes. "Don't worry. I won't let it get too close."

Houlihan drew breath like she was about to protest, but the shmoo had even less patience for her than Pearson. It blurred forward in a shocking burst of speed and smashed into one of the urchins. The plant-eater threw itself, not away, but toward its attacker, maybe trying to pierce the shmoo's body with its spines. Glass screeched off glass, and a shattered spine as long as Pearson's leg went spinning across the tiles.

"No need!" Nurul picked up the spine, provoking nothing from the shmoo but a subtle change in color and a sucking noise.

Sing was yelling something, which nobody present could understand. Did she know something about these aliens? Did she see some other danger? Where the hell was that useless slob Tyaney the one time he might be useful translating?

Now the shmoo was on top of the urchin, pushing its head into the hole left by the urchin's spine, its body shimmering and flashing the artificial blue of an ice slushie.

"Whoa," said Houlihan. "Some kind of optical effect there. Prismatic spines?"

"It's smoking," Nurul observed, her voice quiet and awed. She was right. Foul-smelling steam bubbled up around the face of the feeding predator and the tips of the urchin's still-intact spines.

"More sulfuric acid," Houlihan said. "The shmoo is pumping the acid up into the body of the urchin. Dissolving all those clever silicone valves. And incidentally digesting all the flesh inside."

The feeding predator was oddly beautiful. And it wasn't just the rainbow colors that shimmered along its body. There was a purity to its purpose there. Eat or starve. Live or die. Do what you must. None of the compromises you have to make as a human, as a soldier, as a good man.

The urchin's guts had gone from purple to bubbling black. Witch's brew in a cauldron. Another spine broke off and fell to the glassy ground with a clang.

The shmoo shifted from blue to yellow and looked up. Those sunflower eyes scanned across the dropped spine, then the journalists, then Pearson.

"Ah!" said Nurul. "The spears you wanted, Colonel. Shall I get them?" She reached out toward the dead urchin and the living predator.

"No. Stay back, Astarina." Pearson strode toward them, pistol ready to defend the stupid civilians. Why couldn't just one of these people have the self-preservation instincts God gave a fruit fly?

"We can wait until that thing is done eating," he said.

"Not if the shmoo's digestive juices break the spine apart," answered Nurul. "Then it will no longer work as a spear." She grabbed the spine and pulled it toward her, knocking it against one of the other spines as she did so. The urchin twisted under the feeding shmoo, smoke pouring from cracks in its armor.

"What are you bloody doing, trying to bring that whole thing down on top of you?" yelled Anne. "Come away before that thing sees you, you dickheads."

"She's right," Pearson said, although he suspected he was one of the 'dickheads'. He was nearly between the journalists and the predator now. "I'll shoot that thing if it attacks, but there's no need for that. Let's all just—"

Nurul dropped the spine, which clattered loudly on the glass.

The shmoo flared yellow. Spines along its back and belly blurred as it reversed and swerved around the corpse of the urchin. Eye-rosettes expanded and contracted, focusing on Nurul.

Goddamn suicidal goddamned civilians! Anne the biologist would probably stand back and let nature take its course, but Pearson was a moral person and he had a mission to protect these suicidal idiots. He braced his legs, raising his arms, sighting on the shmoo. Once he saved her life, he was going to rip that stupid journalist a new one.

The shmoo's body bunched like a cat about to pounce. There was no doubt it was going to attack Nurul if Pearson didn't stop it. Wishing he had his earplugs in, Pearson squeezed off a single well-placed shot.

The shmoo did not die. It *rippled* like he'd thrown a rock in a pond, and not a large rock, either. It reversed farther, shimmering yellow and red. Clear fluid dripped from a hole in its side, smoking where it touched the glassy ground.

Pearson swore. "I didn't kill it."

"Obviously not," said Anne. "Listen. Move away from that thing."

Pearson raised his foot. Took a step back.

The shmoo swerved around. Eye-rosettes expanded and contracted, focusing on him. It bunched its body.

Pearson shot it twice more. It was like shooting a bag of wet cement. A bag of cement being fired at him out of a cannon.

Nurul screamed and the shmoo smashed into Pearson.

* * *

Daisuke was on his feet before the echoes of the gunshot had receded into the glass hills. His show's theme song pumping in his head, Daisuke was running before he had even heard Nurul scream.

His boots rubbed and slid over the glass tiles, turning every slight uphill grade into a skating slog, nightmarishly slow. They'd have to cut this footage, turn the music slower with a minor key. Not that anyone was filming him right now, or they could get completed footage to a film studio for editing. Maybe there would be no editing. Maybe he and his party would all die out here, torn apart by whatever was making Nurul and now, horribly, Pearson scream. Maybe Daisuke's next deeds, whether foolish or heroic, would go entirely unrecorded and unremembered.

Anne's party hadn't gone far, but Daisuke's thighs burned as if he'd run a mile by the time he crested the final hill and saw them.

Anne, Sing, and Nurul: there by the spiny corpse of a glass urchin the size of a cow. Nurul was still screaming, pointing at the place where Pearson lay, covered by what looked at this distance like a yellow beanbag chair. Then the yellow darkened to burnt umber, swirling with hypnotic white and blue. The predator shmoo reared up over Pearson's prone body like a monstrous slug and turned chrysanthemum eyes on Daisuke.

Pearson made a sound that was not a scream. It was a death groan, the sound the human animal makes when it has given up hope of survival. If Daisuke had ever heard a fellow human being cry out like that, he would have ended his career with something as stupid and dangerous as what he was doing right now.

Going downhill should be like skiing, right?

Or maybe sledding. Daisuke sat on the glass and pushed himself down the hill feet first.

"What the bloody fuck are you doing, Daisuke?" Anne's voice joined Nurul's. "Go for his gun! No! You can't use the gun on it. Bastard's bulletproof."

Of the three women, Sing was the most helpful. While Nurul wrung her hands and Anne yelled contradictory instructions at him, the Nun woman twisted one of the spines off the urchin's corpse and threw it to him.

The spine was roughly the size of an elephant's tusk. The transparent cone wasn't weighted like a spear, so it spun in the air and bonged against the ground some ways away from Daisuke. But he could still stand, scoop the weapon up, and use it against the bulletproof monster that was digesting Pearson.

Remember, gentle viewers, I am a professional. I have encountered big cats, venomous snakes of various kinds, and great white sharks in their natural environment.

His encounter with the leopard had been made under the full knowledge of the gun held by the park ranger standing off camera. He'd handled venomous snakes, but only with vials of antivenom at hand. Swum with sharks, but only from inside a cage. His 'wilderness adventures' had always been safe, scripted things, as full of real danger as a plastic replica of puffer fish sashimi.

Now living glass slid under his hands, pounded beneath his boots, rose up in a hallucinatory sack of color before him. Spines extended from the body of Daisuke's enemy, beaded with fluid. A hellish smell rose with Pearson's groans.

Gathering his spirit, Daisuke gripped the spine in both hands, and plunged it down.

The spine pierced the outer layer of the shmoo's body with a slushy pop. Sank. Stuck on a membrane as tough as a plastic tarpaulin. Slid off.

Daisuke spun away before his momentum could smash him into the shmoo's body, which was now gushing acid.

Clear fluid dribbled out of the new wound and its outer membrane sagged, but even as Daisuke watched, a foamy scab formed over the hole he'd made between the creature's eye-lenses. These remained fixed on Daisuke as the animal rolled off Pearson. It did not crawl, for it had no legs. Nor did it slither like a snake, nor slide like a slug. The drive belt of spines along its prime meridian spun and the dire shmoo followed Daisuke as smoothly as a rolling motorcycle.

Daisuke ground his boots against the glass, bleeding off his momentum. Shouting, he raised his hands over his head to present a bigger silhouette. A cautious leopard would have backed down and slunk away, but the shmoo did not seem intimidated. The creature flattened, fattened, mounded up its rear end, while the eyed front grew narrow and pointed as a shark's snout.

Daisuke had time to think, *It's changing its gear ratios.* Before the drive belt spun up to speed and, with a sound like ice water in a vacuum cleaner, the shmoo charged.

The thing could accelerate horrifyingly fast, but Daisuke's human legs gave him the advantage of agility. He could jump out of the way and spin, while the shmoo was forced to swerve to face him again. Daisuke thrust with his spear, but rotten-smelling slime splashed onto his hands. Skin burning, he fumbled. The tip of the spear slid off the shmoo's side, and he didn't even break its outer skin. The shmoo hunched up and spun its drive belt.

So, gentle viewers, in fighting this creature, I was less lion-tamer than toreador. A good thing I fought the bulls in Andalusia. But oh it would have been nice if I had a cattle prod handy.

The spiny skin on the monster's back blurred with motion and it sped toward him as if on a track, leaking digestive juices and throbbing with bands of vibrant color.

It was easy to imagine how this strategy might confuse an unarmed prey animal. *I, however, had my crystal staff.* Daisuke braced himself in a modified long frontal stance, right knee bent, right foot forward toward the charging predator. His left leg swept back behind him, knee straight, left foot turned perpendicular to the force of the attack. He lowered his lance. Raised its butt so the tip slanted upward.

The shmoo struck it.

Daisuke's weight was thrown from his forward foot onto his back. The butt of the spine cracked against the ground, slid, but he pressed that rear boot down, giving himself the leverage to force the spine forward, past that tough inner membrane, into the shmoo's body.

For a moment, the rear half of the shmoo was lifted into the air by Daisuke's weight on the other end of the lever of his spear. Daisuke stared into a pair of eyes like obsidian flowers. Inside the baggy body of the predator, something tore.

Foaming brown fluid squirted down the length of the spear. The shmoo jerked, tried to reverse. Couldn't. Its body shimmered with orange and yellow, which faded to white, which became a dark and foggy gray.

The eye-lenses disassembled. The spines sagged. Blood and acid bubbled through Daisuke's spear, now sticking out the front of a motorcycle-sized lump of shapeless flesh.

The shmoo was dead and Daisuke was alive.

"I…I did it," Daisuke mumbled in Japanese, and staggered backward into Anne's arms.

"*Yatta,* indeed," she repeated at him. "You bloody nong."

"Wow!" That was Rahman's voice. "Great footage."

Daisuke twisted against Anne's warm support to see the cameraman giving him a thumbs-up. Misha was there too, smiling along with Nurul, Tyaney, and Sing.

The only person not smiling was Colonel Hariyadi. "Excellent work, Mr. Matsumori," he said, striding toward the gun on the ground. "Now to see if your American ally is still alive."

Pearson was sprawled across the bloody glass, groaning. "I'm alive," he said. "You bastard. Can't kill me."

"Of course I won't kill you, Colonel Pearson." Hariyadi pocketed Pearson's pistol. "I am not, as you say, the 'bad guy'. I am only the guy in charge." He spun on a heel. "Ms. Houlihan, Mr. Alekseyev. See to Colonel Pearson. Make sure he is ready to move. The rest of you, break camp. We leave within the hour."

CHAPTER SEVEN

Breaking Camp

"Is Pearson all right?" asked Nurul. "Is he dead?"

"No," said Daisuke, "but his legs—"

"Oh, *alhamdulillah*!" Nurul collapsed as if her lower spine had been severed, knees thudding against the glass. Rahman cried out and bent to hold her, while she wept with relief. "He's not dead. It didn't kill him."

Daisuke knelt by the couple. "What happened?"

Nurul pulled her face away from Rahman's chest. "What? Oh. Well, we saw the urchins. Anne was talking about them...the shmoo attacked."

"It attacked Pearson?"

"No." That was Rahman. "It attack urchin."

"We went closer to film it," said Nurul. She looked up at Rahman. "Oh why was I so stupid? I didn't think it was dangerous," Nurul answered herself. "It was busy eating. And we needed that spine."

"But you dropped the bloody thing on the ground, and the noise attracted the predator's attention," Anne said. "Pearson shot it, but all that did was divert its attention."

"Pearson was trying to protect you," Daisuke summarized. "He made it angry and it attacked him."

"Yes," said Nurul. "I had no idea he would do that. I didn't even think he was paying attention to me and Rahman. He was too busy arguing with Anne."

"Arguing with Anne?"

Nurul squinted at him. "Why are you asking all these questions, anyway?"

Because I am suspicious. First the odd, rushed, slapdash nature of this whole expedition, as if someone were grabbing civilians at random and stuffing them into a plane with Pearson and Hariyadi. The unexplained crash and Pearson's irrational insistence that they stay put. Then his mauling, and now they were marching back to base as if that had been the plan all along. Daisuke had experienced more unlikely chains of coincidences, yes, but that was out in nature. Human beings were more organized. Humans schemed. They were capable of evil.

"Well," he said, thoughts a ball of mating vipers. "Of course I am a television person, just like you. I am concerned about how this will all look on camera."

Nurul smiled a journalist's smile. "Why, you will look like a hero, Dai."

Her bodycam stared up from her chest. Daisuke's and Rahman's were also working, collecting audio. Daisuke must appear to be as he always was: a simple, nature-loving survivor-man. He must not let his suspicions show. "Thank you," he said, and extracted himself from the scene.

Hariyadi, Anne, and Misha were still squatting next to the unconscious Pearson. Unsurprisingly, they were still arguing.

"We can't move him," said Anne.

"You are thinking for spinal trauma and concussion," Misha said, rummaging through his first aid kit. "This is acid burn."

Pearson shivered, muscles on his skinned legs twitching. There was plenty of blood on those legs, and on his chest too, but almost none on the ground. The tiles under Pearson, perhaps in defensive reaction to the acidic discharge from the shmoo, had pulled themselves tight, opening gaps like the walls of a honeycomb. The contraction of the tiles made them slightly higher at the center than the edges, and the blood ran down their sides, drained away into the chalky sand below.

"Shit," Anne said, "shit shit shit. Daisuke, bullets didn't pack enough force to puncture the membrane between the acid layer and that thing's internal organs. If your spear hadn't either—"

"It will be all right," said Daisuke.

Pearson groaned, not like a man waking up, but like a dying animal, as if every exhalation tore something out of him.

Plastic rustled and clunked. "Ah," said Misha. "Morphine."

"But I meant we shouldn't drag him across country to the base," Anne said.

"Well, I agree. I didn't want to move before, and now we have crippled soldier to drag." Misha peeled the plastic wrapper off a disposable syringe.

With disturbing ease, Misha found a vein and injected Pearson with rather a lot of brownish liquid. The groaning became a slow wheeze like air being let out of a bicycle tire.

"And yet go we must," said Hariyadi. "You know better than I, Ms. Houlihan, how we cannot stay in this place. Lack of food and water, poisonous plants, and now dangerous carnivores? If you care about Pearson's survival at all, you must agree with me."

"Yes," Anne said, looking at the gun the Indonesian colonel had already strapped back on his hip, "we must."

Hariyadi's hand went to the weapon. "You can't think I would shoot you."

Misha snorted. "No. As you said, you in charge now, Colonel." He closed his first aid kit and shrugged. "If you say 'go', we must go."

Hariyadi nodded gravely. "Thank you, Mr. Alekseyev."

"No." Pearson's eyes were closed, but his breath hissed through his mouth. "Can't go. Damn you, Alekseyev, we're staying."

Misha frowned, his mouth a deep and almost comical crescent in the center of a field of black stubble. "Needs more morphine."

Anne took the old man's hand. "Don't talk." Her voice cracked. Was she angry she had misjudged the soldier? Worried that Pearson might die thinking she hated him? What was she thinking? Daisuke suddenly wasn't sure he could know.

She took one of the soldier's leathery hands. "Hey," she said. "It'll be all right."

The hand clamped around hers. "Whose are you?"

'Whose'? Was the man delirious?

"It's me," said Anne. "Anne Houlihan."

"No, goddamn it." Pearson grunted and opened his eyes. "Whose are you?"

He had probably meant to glare at her, but shock and pain and drugs turned his gaze as soft as tofu. "You're not one of ours."

Daisuke frowned. Pearson didn't *look* delirious. Only in terrible pain.

Anne looked as confused as Daisuke felt. "What is he talking about?"

"Nothing." Pearson's eyes drifted shut, opened. "Shit. I hate being like this. Vulnerable. No!" He tried to fend off another syringe from Misha, his free hand flapping like a crippled fruit bat.

Anne's sigh clouded the air in front of her face. It was getting colder.

"Daisuke," said Misha. "I am thinking maybe we make stretcher. You know, drag him back to camp?"

"A stretcher?" Daisuke asked. "I could lash a frame together out of logs." That was an audience favorite. "But where can I find logs?"

Anne looked up from Pearson. "What about the urchin spines?"

"An excellent idea," said Hariyadi. "But it will have to drag him farther than back to camp."

"Yes, yes," Misha said. "I know."

"Good. I shall meet you there in no more than half an hour." Hariyadi turned and left, shouting crisp orders to Rahman and Nurul in Indonesian.

"Just stay with me a minute," Pearson mumbled. "Protect you. Stay."

"I will," said Anne. She couldn't have arranged this accident. Could she have? She did hate Pearson. She had been arguing with him right before…no. She must be innocent, Daisuke assured himself as he collected urchin spines.

A tiny cold needle pricked the back of Daisuke's neck. He looked up, and caught another snowflake on his face. The clouds above them were dark and low. Cold air pressed down on them like a cloud of poisonous gas.

On Earth, the snow would have been a major problem. Daisuke's exhausted, panicked brain was halfway through calculating how he could make a shelter and save them from freezing to death when he noticed that the snow wasn't piling up. It melted when it hit the warm ground, forming puddles that drained into the honeycomb cracks that had opened between the tiles. Swirls of steam rose around Pearson and the dead urchin like smoke from a funeral pyre.

Each urchin spine was about two meters long and surprisingly flexible, tapering from fifteen centimeters at the base to two at the tip. Within a rubbery silicone sleeve, rings of glass gave the spine its strength. He could lean his whole weight on the tip – and he had put more pressure on it than that when he'd skewered the shmoo – but he could also flex the spine like a green sapling. It should work as well as wood for the stretcher.

Daisuke jogged back to camp and found a length of nylon cord he could use to bind together five of the urchin's spines. After another jog and a few minutes of tying and stretching, the result was less a stretcher than a sledge – two spines pointing forward to act as runners and the other three forming the cross braces.

Pearson did not protest or even open his eyes while Daisuke and Misha tied the wounded soldier to the sledge. His breathing was very shallow.

"I'm worried about the amount of morphine in him," said Anne.

"Addiction is not biggest problem," Misha answered. "Bigger problem is when morphine runs out. Or if someone else gets hurt."

"No one else will get hurt." Daisuke pulled a knot tight under Pearson's armpit. "Misha will be our doctor. Anne will find things like the urchin spines. I will make things with them. We help each other."

Anne swallowed and smiled, blinking rapidly. "Thanks, Daisuke."

Daisuke banished his foolish suspicions. "Sure." The clouds were darker now. "We should get back to camp." He grabbed a loop of the cord and fitted it above his eyes like a headband. With a grunt, he took a step over the glass. The sledge squealed behind him.

The sledge design came from Greenland, where the ground was snow and ice. Warm glass was a less co-operative substrate, and Daisuke was sweating by the time they reached camp. He tried not to think about pulling this thing all the way to the mountains to the east. And then up them. And down them again. *Just think about what a great montage the footage of the journey will make.*

"Finally," said Hariyadi, who was overseeing Nurul and Rahman as they packed the supplies. "Mr. Matsumori, this luggage is for you to load on your sledge. Ms. Houlihan, this is your pack. You will walk in front with me. We need you to scout for danger."

Tyaney and Sing watched the preparations to leave, neither offering to help nor asking questions. Sing had been with Pearson when he was attacked as well, hadn't she? Tyaney had told them Sing knew nothing of this environment, but could Daisuke take the man at his word? Tyaney might be lying, Sing might be lying.

But why would the Nun want to harm Pearson? Why would they want anything? They were so distant. So alien. *I will have to speak with them,* Daisuke resolved as he crawled over the sledge, making the camp's baggage fast to it. *Use Nurul or Anne as an interpreter.*

"Mr. Alekseyev!" Hariyadi yelled. "For the last time, make yourself ready."

Misha was sitting on top of his backpack. "I say we should spend night here. We can be safe in plane. And we don't know our way."

"I know the way," said Hariyadi. "It's due east."

"Our compasses are not working, Colonel. And if sky is cloudy we cannot see the sun." Misha looked upward and held out his palm, catching snowflakes. "Maybe Sing knows a way to navigate?"

"Hm. Well, we can just use the screw-trees," said Anne.

Misha looked at her.

"Because the thread of the screw is always angled so more surface area faces south?"

Misha squinted.

"Because Junction has no axial tilt? Therefore the sun is always directly over the equator? Therefore the light is always coming from the south?"

Misha blinked. "Oh."

"We are lucky to have access to your expertise," Hariyadi said. "Now get up."

Misha lumbered to his feet. "Colonel say 'go'. I go."

So did the rest of them.

The sledge did not work as well as it might have. On flat ground and when the spaces between hills were empty, Daisuke could make fairly good progress. Too often, though, the hollows were home to spindly screw-trees. The 'plants' grew into each other and fused into impenetrable land reefs that had to be avoided, with two men heaving on the sledge while another pushed it sideways up the hill. The higher-than-Earth gravity did not help either.

Once, the whole grunting mass of Daisuke, Pearson, and the sledge lost its traction and crashed into the reef they were trying to avoid, prompting the angry response of a swarm of bumblesnails. The coiled-shelled creatures darted back and forth through the air, buzzing their glassy wings and questing with their spines for something they could inject with venom. But by the time Daisuke opened his eyes, the swarm had dispersed. Nobody collapsed of either toxic or anaphylactic shock.

It continued to snow as they trudged dutifully eastward. Water ran down the hills, but did not pool between them. The cracks between the tiles opened to drain away the liquid, and without the support of their neighbors, the tiles became increasingly unstable. Daisuke found himself wobbling, as if he walked on rocks set into quicksand. Which meant—

The sledge rocked and tipped sideways. Pearson groaned. Daisuke cursed.

He turned in his traces to see that one side of the sledge had turned up a tile and fallen into the sandy, watery hole left behind. It took him, Rahman, and Misha pulling in tandem to haul the raft out of its hole and up the shallow incline of the nearest hill. Cursing and straining, they left a trail of uprooted tiles behind them. Pearson screamed with every bump.

The 'vegetation' at the crest of the hill was very different from what grew in the wetter hollows. Shorter, denser, more heavily sculpted by the wind. Misha sagged against this hill-reef. "We camp here?" he asked, and at Hariyadi's nod said, "I will help Pearson."

"Oh, this snow is *dreadful*!" said Nurul. "It's so cold and wet. And we can't even build a fire. Thank goodness we're leaving this awful place."

"Well, we can get warm if we break a tile," Anne said. "Although I do wonder what will happen if we can't get dry. Trench foot?"

Daisuke did not want to think about that picturesque English term.

"Yes," said Hariyadi. "We can erect a tent over him and tie it to these trees. Daisuke, Tyaney, that's you." He repeated that in Indonesian, then for some reason switched back to English to say, "Rahman, help Ms. Houlihan erect a steam trap. Nurul and I shall prepare the food."

Everyone fell to their assigned tasks. All except Sing, who hadn't received any instructions. She simply sat where she'd been standing, arms wrapped around herself, legs folded against the warm, wet tiles.

"Poor woman," said Rahman, following Daisuke's gaze. "She can't talk. Husband maybe think she is pig or dog. These natives, huh? I tie tarp this tree? This one?"

"You just don't understand how Nun marriage works," Anne said, then switched to Indonesian.

Rahman raised his eyebrows at her and asked a question in the same language.

Whatever he said, Anne evidently could think of no response. All she did was shake her head and mutter something about 'bulletproof racism'.

"Sing knows how to survive out here," said Daisuke. "We do not." And, as an idea occurred, "We can ask her about what sort of challenges to expect in the next biome." It would be a good excuse to draw Sing into their crew.

"How she understand question? How we understand answer?" Rahman asked. "Tyaney translate? I don't trust him one bit."

"We can try," said Anne. "Now, we need to break this branch." She grasped a corkscrew of glass spiraling out of the mass of the reef under the tarp. "Can you do it with your shovel?"

Glass shattered and steam billowed out of the tree, rising with the mist already coming off the ground to condense against the tarp.

"Go get a bucket to collect the water," Daisuke said, wondering how it could be that nobody had thought to talk to Sing before. "I will get Sing. And Tyaney to translate for her."

They didn't want Sing and Tyaney to feel threatened, so they'd kept the size of the crew small for this scene. Hariyadi was content to review the footage later. Misha had, with some convincing, gone off and amused himself elsewhere. Nurul had argued that she would be a better translator than Anne, whose Indonesian was rather worse than Tyaney's, but Tyaney didn't like Nurul. He liked Anne, and Anne liked Daisuke. Daisuke just wanted to make sure nobody got murdered during this important conversation.

Now they sat in a circle around the steam trap: Daisuke, Rahman, Anne, Tyaney, and Sing.

"Rolling," whispered Rahman.

Daisuke nodded to Anne. "Go ahead. Just focus on Sing and Tyaney."

Anne, who had been looking anxiously at the camera, swallowed, and fidgeted against the warm glass. She asked a question in halting Indonesian.

Tyaney turned and snapped something at Sing. Daisuke didn't speak the Nun language and knew nothing of their customs, but it was very hard not to interpret the man as vilely cruel to his wife.

It was also hard to tell what Sing thought of her husband, or indeed any of the people here. Her round face was expressionless, her eyes slitted. She looked like a woman in half hibernation, waiting for the world to become worth participating in.

Tyaney repeated his question, then interrupted Sing when she began to answer. Sing responded, then stood with the economy of movement of a person who has lived most of her life outdoors. Tyaney flinched back as if afraid his wife might kick him, then yelled something that sounded angry.

Sing didn't appear to notice. She stood over them, face hidden by the tarp stretched over the steam trap. Water dripped from the underside of the tarp as Sing pressed on the top with a finger.

When Daisuke stood, he saw that the steam trap had cooled and collected a thin crust of snow. Sing was drawing in the snow with her finger. Her whole hand. She clawed four furrows into the snow. She spoke, Tyaney mumbled something, and Anne translated.

"These are the valleys that go in the same direction as the wind."

Sing shifted position and drew her finger down the first valley.

"To the east, the Deep Sky Country, home of the Nun."

Sing pointed to the rightmost groove.

"This is here. The Warm Ice Country, which we know of, but which no person has ever visited before now."

Anne's brow creased as she translated. "How could you know about this place if no person has ever visited it?" She repeated her question in Indonesian. Both she and Rahman gasped at the answer.

"What?" asked Daisuke.

"He...." Anne blinked. "He says, 'The animals that Sing knows visit it sometimes.'"

Daisuke thought of the woodland creatures in *Snow White*. "Know? What animals does Sing know?"

"I asked him that," said Anne. "Tyaney is describing them...." She listened to Tyaney, who was still talking. "I don't understand. Rahman, did he say *calamari*?"

"Ya," said Rahman. "Calamari."

"Like squid?" Daisuke asked.

"He says no, not like squid. Like calamari." Anne shrugged in mystification. "Now he's talking about a fancy seafood restaurant he ate at in Jayapura?"

Daisuke suspected there was a translation problem somewhere along this long and unreliable line. "Ask him if these talking animals are helpful."

"No," said Tyaney. "Very dangerous." He was glaring at Sing as if daring his wife to disagree. *Not that we would know if she did.* Still, Daisuke had the strong impression that the Nun man was lying.

"So we're going this way?" Daisuke asked, indicating their eastward path to what must be the first of two mountain ranges. "Do Sing's people know anything about these mountains?"

There was some discussion there, from which emerged that two mountains stood between the crew and their destination. Anne guessed that they were inhabited by two branches of some third biome, an alien ecosystem different from both the glasslands and the wormwood forest.

"'She knows the place well and we will be in no danger,'" translated Anne, "but that's just Tyaney bragging, I think. Plus he says, 'Don't worry, I'll keep her under control.' Whatever that means."

They would have to keep an eye on the Nun woman, was what that meant. Her own husband didn't trust her. But Daisuke was already thinking suspiciously about everyone else, so why not add one more to the list?

"Will we be able to eat the animals in the mountains?" he asked. "Drink the water?

Tyaney chuckled.

"Sing says there is no food to be had in the mountains, but after we cross to the other side, we will be in the…." Anne paused. "Uh. Ripe Blood Country?"

Tyaney pointed at the valley between the two mountain ranges, in the middle of the map.

"The Ripe Blood Country. And there we can replenish our supplies of meat and water and…."

Anne stopped translating while Tyaney hissed a question at Sing, who answered with a short negative.

"Just meat and water. You cannot eat Ripe Blood plants."

Anne asked another question, pointing at the next mountain range, the last before the Deep Sky Country and safety.

"After the Ripe Blood Country, we only have to cross the Death Wind Pass and we will be home."

That didn't sound promising.

Sing drew her finger through the gap between the inner and outer mountain ranges and said something Tyaney and Anne translated as: "The

Death Wind River runs here, between the Ripe Blood Country and the Ground Sun Country. The river runs through the Death Wind Pass."

"If there's a river, I can build us a raft," said Daisuke.

"No," came the answer. "No rafts on the Death Wind River. It is impossible."

Tyaney made an addendum. "If we stay high enough up, though, we should be fine."

"What does that mean?"

"I already asked him," Anne said. "He says, 'Where the Death Wind can't get us.'"

That sounded ominous. "So this Death Wind," said Daisuke. "Is *that* another tribe of natives? Or calamari aliens?"

"No," Anne translated for Tyaney. "No people until we get to Sing's village, and there we must be very careful, because they are savage and dangerous witches."

"What?" said Daisuke, but Tyaney was still talking.

"Then we will be only a day's walk from Imsame and the High Earth Hole."

Tyaney nodded as if at a job well done and turned away. After a moment, so did Sing.

Daisuke couldn't help but notice that Tyaney had glossed over the exact nature of the 'Death Wind'. And now he was turning as if to leave.

"Wait," Daisuke said. "Ask him what exactly is the Death Wind?"

Anne did, and Tyaney rounded on her, waving his hands as he shouted in Indonesian. He stomped on the map Sing had made, smearing it into illegibility.

Rahman snapped something that sounded insulting, but Anne held up a hand. She said something, which Tyaney interrupted, spitting what must be deadly invective as he grabbed Sing's arm. Still cursing, the native dragged his wife away.

"I assume the conversation is over?" asked Daisuke.

"Of all the bloody fucking dipshits!" Anne stomped as well, though not, Daisuke noticed, before checking the color of the tile under her foot. "That sneaky little...." She snapped her jaw closed and massaged her temples. "Sorry. I must have made some mistake. Insulted him somehow."

"What did Tyaney say?" Daisuke asked.

"Asshole," said Rahman.

Anne shook her head. "He thinks we're trying to cut him out of the deal. That if he tells us too many details about the way back to Imsame, we won't have any reason to keep him alive." She looked at Rahman. "*Benar?*"

Rahman nodded. "He say we have map, we don't need Tyaney, we kill him. Crazy!"

Daisuke thought of Pearson. "Yes," he said. "Crazy."

★ ★ ★

Daisuke's suspicious mood only deepened when they rejoined the others and heard Pearson's agonized ravings.

"Get that goddamn camera out of my face. I'm going to—Jesus Christ Lord *Almighty* but my legs hurt." Pearson stopped swatting at Rahman and grasped his upper thighs, gritting his teeth.

"Is there anything you can do for him?" asked Hariyadi.

"No," Misha said. "I have washed the wounds and wrapped them in gauze. That is all that can be done for acid burns."

"Maybe put…" Pearson sucked air through his teeth, "…baking soda on them or something."

"That would be a bad idea," Misha said. "Besides, we have no baking supplies. Or water."

"We have the water from Anne's steam trap." Daisuke held up a plastic envelope that claimed to contain 'BBQ pork'.

"Now sir, you must have another bite of your…" Misha squinted at the bag sloshing in his hand, "…hamburger with bun."

Pearson narrowed his eyes. "I'll tell you what, Alekseyev. I'll eat that whole bag of reconstituted pig vomit if you tell me I'm going to be able to walk again."

Misha looked at Anne, who stiffened, horror written in every line of her face and body. But if the biologist was no doctor, she was no coward, either. She told the soldier what he needed to know.

"Your legs were injected with sulfuric acid, probably about as concentrated as the hydrochloric acid in your stomach," she said. "There was no…uh… mechanical processing," she made clawing and chewing motions with her hands, indicating a shmoo softening up its prey, "and I'm happy to see there's no sign of allergic reaction…"

"…because all allergens have been digested, maybe," said Misha.

"…so," Anne said. "I think you'll live."

"I'll live." Pearson glared at Hariyadi. "In enemy custody."

Daisuke quietly ate his dinner and watched.

Nurul made an angry humming noise, but Hariyadi only raised an eyebrow.

"Even if I were your enemy, Colonel Pearson, I think you would have greater problems to worry about."

"Yes," said Pearson. "Such as being a cripple on an overland hike through uncharted territory on an alien planet populated by monsters, through the snow, and *uphill.*"

"Exactly," Misha said. "Now finish your dinner or no injection for you."

"Oh yes. How could I forget the incipient morphine addiction to add to my list?" Pearson squeezed his lower arm and held out his wrist to Misha. "Give me my fix, doc."

Anne looked away.

Daisuke could guess why. It wouldn't be the sight of the needle going into his vein, but the look on Pearson's face. The loosening. The weakness.

"Ah." The soldier sighed and flopped onto his back. "Not that I give a damn anymore, but Hariyadi, you are going to kill us all."

"I do not plan to kill anyone, Colonel Pearson."

"That may be so, but it's going to happen," said Pearson. "Just turn around and go back to the plane, would you?"

Nurul murmured something and Hariyadi frowned. "What do you know, Colonel Pearson?"

"I know," Pearson said, "a war is coming. That's what you're marching us into."

"Damn this stuff is strong," said Misha. "Almost makes me jealous."

"What war?" Hariyadi asked. "There will be no war. The politicians in Jakarta and Washington may shout all they like, but out here, it is military men who make decisions. Men like you, Colonel, and me."

Pearson laughed. Everyone flinched back from the sound.

"Oh," said the old man. "Oh fuck that hurts so good. Hariyadi, you are a crazy fucking maniac."

Hariyadi grimaced. "He is out of his mind on drugs, the poor man. I—"

"Yeah," Pearson said. "And I'm a stupid old fool. Or at least my country is making me act like one. Let me talk, dammit!"

"Sir," Misha said again, "it would be unhealthy for me to give you more morphine."

"So don't do it, comrade." Pearson put his hands behind his head. "Just lie back and listen."

"I don't think—"

"That's an order," snapped the soldier. "You got your fairytale from

George of the Jungle over there" – he jerked his thumb at Tyaney, who was squatting next to Sing, back turned on the people speaking incomprehensible English – "so now it's time to hear the white man's story of Junction.

"Once upon a time, once upon a time, someone punched a big hole in South Pacific geopolitics." Pearson chuckled woozily. "A wormhole. It warped space and time and also money and politics, which are more important. Give me a drink."

Daisuke handed him their water bottle, filled from the steam trap.

"Ugh," said Pearson. "It's still warm. Papua New Guinea fell apart, torn to pieces by just the *hint* that Australia, the US, and China might end up on different sides of this conflict. Australia and the US smashed a pro-Chinese coup by the Papuan military, and sent those soldiers to the Highlands to get killed by Indonesians.

"Because even if the Indonesians couldn't get to the wormhole first, they'd be damned if they were going to let the Americans and Australians have it all to ourselves. Whoops! Did we dump defoliant on the rainforest around the wormhole *again*? And napalm too this time! Well, the people who made those mistakes will be punished, you have our word on it! And the people who shot at you? Terrorists, of course!"

"That is not at all what happened," Hariyadi said. "There *were* terrorists around the wormhole. Papuan separatists and religious fanatics. The Indonesian army was given orders to pacify the region. Orders that came from our government, which means," he sneered, "it came from yours."

"Heh," said Pearson. "Don't I know it. Your army is nothing more than a bunch of mercenaries hired by the highest bidder. Except for a few... troublesome...patriots like you." His voice had grown warm and muzzy. "Anyway, Australia was also torn between a government that knows its best interests aligned with the USA, and increasing anti-American sentiment in the populace. There was a lot of talk about avoiding a 'second Gallipoli'. There was a hard deadline on the current American/Australian/New Guinean alliance: the next Australian election."

"Next year?" said Anne.

"Time flies when you're having a civil insurrection," Pearson said. "Now, China. China was much more cautious and pragmatic. Their fleet of warships south of the Philippines just sort of showed up there to ensure nobody did anything regrettable.

"So the USA" – he placed his hands on his heart – "was feeling the heat.

They managed to get their people on the ground at the wormhole site, but how to justify their presence? Internationally, it's all nods and smiles about exploring the opportunities of the wormhole in coalition with all of humanity. Why, yes, China and Russia and Europe, you're invited too. Internally, though, the only way to keep goodwill flowing from the American public was by whipping up a state of frenzy. Indonesia is a clear and present danger to the security of the wormhole. And did someone say 'terrorists'? The New Guinean armed forces were trained by China! And even the Australians are going to turn against us! If anyone is going to do anything 'regrettable', you bet your ass it's going to be us. Fuck, my legs hurt."

They were all silent for a moment.

"What exactly," said Hariyadi, "was that load of paranoid fantasy supposed to signify?"

Pearson didn't appear to hear him. "There are two kinds of countries in this world. Stupid countries and crazy countries. Indonesia's going to do something crazy, which will prompt the US to do something stupid. Turn back to the airplane, Hariyadi. Let us hide there while the world burns on the other side of those mountains."

"Meaning that we should sit here and be safe while the world burns?" Nurul asked. "That's not a very brave philosophy, Colonel."

"That's not what I said," snarled Pearson. Then, more quietly. "I'm no coward."

Hariyadi stood. "This is all purest nonsense. Do you have any facts to back up your wild accusations?"

But Pearson had closed his eyes. His breathing had become shallow and fast. Sweat stood out on his forehead.

"Enough," Misha said. "He is not a well man."

"I am aware of that." Hariyadi rubbed a hand over his face. "All right. We shall set up a rotation for night duties. Guarding and monitoring Colonel Pearson…."

Daisuke volunteered to drag Pearson into his private tent and take the first shift with the wounded man. He had halfway hoped for a chance to talk to him privately, but the soldier remained in his sweating, pale, drugged unconsciousness. Daisuke managed to stay awake until his watch ended, at which point he switched with Nurul and crawled into the men's tent. The warm, wet air rising from the ground condensed into rivers that ran down the outside of his blanket and the inside of the tent. *It's like a chilly sauna,* he would tell his audience. *A chilly sauna on a broken bathroom floor.* The ground under him was hard and not at all level.

Eventually, Daisuke fell asleep. He dreamed he was back on the plane and they were crashing. The plane sank through the air as slowly as if through quicksand, scrawling above it a trail of black smoke, like a message written in grass-style calligraphy. *Do not trust them.*

Tyaṇey shrieked.

Daisuke jolted awake and crawled over Misha and Hariyadi to the tent flap.

It was day and the sky was clear and cloudless. There was no snow on the ground. Nothing that suggested any snow had ever fallen here.

Tyaney screamed again. Daisuke didn't understand the words he used, but he knew shocked profanity when he heard it.

"What is it now?" said Hariyadi, blundering out behind Daisuke.

Tyaney pointed back the way they had come.

Daisuke looked west. They had covered depressingly little distance, and the plane was still visible. Although they had apparently climbed farther uphill than he had thought. Either that or the plane was....

"Christ on a bicycle!" Anne shouted from the flap of the women's tent. "The bloody plane is sinking!"

The plane was at the center of a vast sinkhole. Shallow, but growing deeper as the waterlogged sand under it gave way. The water steamed in the bright morning air, air that teemed with clouds of swarming life.

Daisuke thought of the contracted tiles and how they had slipped and ripped out of the ground under the sledge. About the much heavier plane. About the fact that there were no boulders or other heavy objects lying anywhere on the glasslands.

"Goodness," said Daisuke, watching the ground claim their plane. "Look at the diameter of that sinkhole. If we had stayed there...."

"We didn't," Hariyadi said. "We shall take it as a sign."

"Well," said Misha, emerging from Pearson's tent, "here is another sign. He is dead."

CHAPTER EIGHT

Gushing

"Colonel Pearson is dead?" Hariyadi nearly shoved Daisuke off the hill as he whirled to face Misha. "How did this happen?"

Misha only shrugged his sagging shoulders. "I don't know how he died. No marks on body. Simply, he is not breathing." He looked at Daisuke. "You gonna help me?"

"Help?" Daisuke echoed.

"Help move body. Help bury body."

Daisuke blinked. Well, of course they had to bury Pearson. They couldn't very well drag the corpse with them over the mountains. A corpse. One of their number had died.

"No," said Hariyadi. "We can't bury him. We don't have time."

Anne rounded on the soldier. "Would you like us to leave *your* corpse out here when *you* die?"

Hariyadi raised an eyebrow. "When I die?"

"When all of us die, she means," Misha said.

Anne just looked bleakly at the ground.

And that's when I knew I had to intervene. Daisuke found himself stepping forward and clearing his throat, checking to see where Rahman and his camera might be.

"We will bury Colonel Pearson's body," he said. "Misha? Get the shovels."

"Okay," said Anne, while the Russian sloped off to the sledge, "but then what?"

"We will all dig together," Daisuke said. "Just as all together we will help each other to survive. We will not give up."

"Okay?" Anne said. "But I meant 'what about decomposition?' The bacteria in his gut will go some way toward breaking his body down, but they won't thrive in quicksand. Local bacteria and scavengers can't digest him. His nutrients will be wasted. Just totally inaccessible."

Daisuke prevented himself from asking "so what?" If anything, the ninety kilos of biomaterial donated by Pearson would help terraform this place. But the habit of long training took over and what Daisuke ended up saying was, "Perhaps his body will form the basis of an Earthlike ecosystem. Future explorers might find here an apple tree growing in the oasis made by Pearson's sacrifice."

Anne just sniffed. Was she fighting back tears? Why? She'd never liked Pearson. She'd barely been able to exchange a civil word with him. Daisuke might be excused for shedding a manly tear for the fall of a gruff old mentor, but what sort of relationship drama had Anne established? Romantic antagonism?

Daisuke realized with a twist of self-loathing that he was thinking like a TV personality. What had Eriko called him? An eggshell with nothing inside? *This is a funeral, and I can't even summon up the humanity to be* sad*?*

Apparently not, but if Daisuke couldn't be a real human being, he could sure as hell *act* like it. He rubbed his ring finger and composed his expression into heavy grief. "Let's get the body."

Pearson's body itself showed no signs of struggle. The corpse lay on its back under a silvery thermal blanket, its arms limp at its sides, its skin waxy and bejeweled with dew. Its mouth and eyes were closed. The man looked more peaceful than he ever had when alive. Daisuke muttered a prayer to Amida Buddha as he squatted at the corpse's head and slid his arms under its armpits.

"So what happened?" asked Hariyadi as Misha and Daisuke waddled past with their grisly cargo. "Allergy? Shock? Poison?" His eyes scanned Daisuke's face, Misha's, Anne's, narrow with suspicion.

"Well, we can rule out poison," Anne said. "The shmoo injected him with *something*, but I doubt bioactive molecules from aliens would have anything like the intended effect on humans."

"Allergies?" Hariyadi pressed.

Anne made a considering noise. "I wouldn't be surprised if it wasn't even the shmoo that killed him, just his own immune response to the alien germs that took up residence in the wounds ex post facto."

"What's going on?" Nurul mumbled, climbing out of the women's tent. She shivered under her thermal blanket, glaring blearily at the rest of the party as if looking for the person who had turned down the thermostat. Then her eyes fell on Daisuke and Misha. Pearson's body. She stiffened, her face setting like cement.

"Pearson is dead," said Anne.

"Oh!" Nurul's blanket fell to the ground as she put her hands to her mouth, revealing clothes stained, and in some cases eaten right through, by glasslands effluvia. Her forehead furrowed with shock and distress. "That's— How terrible! Was it his wounds that killed him?"

Anne sighed. "I suppose it must have been. Shock. Delayed shock. It's not like we can do an autopsy on him out here. Or a decent burial." She ran her hands through her hair, while Nurul ducked into the men's tent, where Rahman was still asleep. Tyaney lurched out of the tent a few seconds later as if shoved, his expression foul. The Nun man turned back toward the tent, opening his mouth, but backed away from the sound of muffled weeping.

"Okay," said Misha. "We bury him. If we don't die of exhaustion carrying body down hill. Come, Daisuke."

It turned out that moving Pearson's body was the most difficult part of the burial process. With only a little pressure from the edge of a shovel, the tiles that made up the ground of the glasslands popped out of their sockets. The chalky sand below was entirely dry and easy to shift.

Small creatures like hard candies made of glass tinkled out over the ground as the humans emptied out a grave. What would such creatures make of Pearson's body? Would it poison them? Would they die of an immune reaction? Daisuke grimaced at the thought. He'd experienced the early stages of anaphylaxis himself.

Daisuke remembered burning pain, swelling of the eyes, nose, and throat. Anne clawing at her own skin, her rictus grin of pain and terror.

Pearson's body, however, was as peaceful as a Buddha.

Too peaceful. Daisuke forced himself to keep digging, kept his expression neutral. Pearson couldn't have died the way Anne said he had. It was still possible that Junction was simply a very dangerous place – more dangerous than the worst bush Daisuke had ever trekked through.

Or maybe, gentle audience, it is not Junction that is dangerous, but the human soul.

CHAPTER NINE

Postmortem

The body of Gregory Pearson, Colonel, United States Air Force, became a flattened mound of sand between two glassy ridges. Hexagonal tiles turned on their sides formed a fence around the grave, the fishlike organisms within wriggling as they died from exposure to Terran biochemistry. The body might last forever, mummified under the crossed root-pipes the expedition had left on top of the grave.

Or Pearson's body might already have vanished into a sinkhole like the one that had swallowed the plane. A ferocious predator might have chanced upon the grave and dug it up. The person who was responsible for the death might be walking alongside Daisuke right now. The chilly, damp air smelled of sulfur.

And yet the glasslands were beautiful. The sun, still low in the south-east, sprayed off the reef-topped crests of the hills. Glassy animals swarmed in the air, splitting the light with their prismatic shells, populating the misty air with rainbows.

Glass squealed under the runners of the sledge as Daisuke pulled their baggage. It was hard work, full of backtracking and rerouting around ridges that all seemed to run in the wrong direction, but Daisuke was no stranger to hard physical labor. Plus, this way he could keep all of his suspects in view.

Hariyadi marched at the head of their little expedition, Pearson's gun in his hand. They were marching toward Imsame even now. The wounded Pearson hadn't been able to stop them from leaving camp. *He would have slowed us down, though.*

Tyaney and Sing walked next to the colonel, the woman hand in hand with her husband, occasionally exchanging a few words. The Nun guides had barely reacted when they learned about Pearson's death. Was that just because Daisuke didn't understand their special signs of grief? Or did they really not give a damn about the life or death of a Westerner? And Pearson had put Sing in danger, antagonizing the wildlife like that.

Pearson had put Nurul in danger too, and as loyal Indonesians, they might not like the way the American had tried to take control after the crash. That is, the destruction of Misha's precious airplane. And the Russian had been the one to discover Pearson's body. He was also the one who had administered Pearson's morphine. Pearson, who had died so peacefully.

And Anne. The one who so clearly hated Pearson and everything he stood for. The one who had argued with him before his death. Who had been with him when the shmoo attacked, and who knew more about this environment than anyone. Murder by applied ecology?

Anne might be a murderer. *Any* of Daisuke's companions might be a murderer.

Stuck in his frightening thoughts, Daisuke failed to give enough berth to a reeflike outcropping of screw-trees. One of the runners of the sledge caught on a finger-high nodule and Daisuke was nearly yanked off his feet as the sledge turned into an immovable fixture of the landscape.

Anne and Misha were the closest, and so first to turn around in response to Daisuke's swearing and calls for help. It took all three of them to lift the sledge off the obstruction and push it clear.

"What are you doing?" Hariyadi called. "You are too far behind."

Daisuke wiped his brow. Tiny creatures like the beads of a necklace zipped through the air, tasting his sweat and dropping away. He looked out at the glasslands, rising in hills like ripples in a pond to lap at the stony feet of the mountains.

"Oh man," said Misha. "That is going to be a bitch to climb with this sledge."

"You know," Anne said, "I've been thinking."

Daisuke looked at her. "Thinking?" He panted.

"I'm thinking about how we might be able to improve on your sledge design." The smile Anne turned on him made her red, sweaty face look very good. An apple he was sure would be deliciously sweet. If only he could be sure it wasn't poisoned.

"How would you like some wheels?" asked Anne.

★ ★ ★

The herd of wheelers grazed on a glassy meadow between two lines of foothills. The creatures, each the size of a monster truck's tire, were the mottled purple of glasslands camouflage, rolling their ring-shaped bodies slowly across the tiles.

"I saw these things from the plane," Daisuke said. "Do you think that they can become the wheels for our sledge?"

Anne frowned. "We know that. I explained it to you an hour ago."

"He's speaking for the camera," Nurul whispered to her.

Anne looked around at Rahman and the camera, her frown deepening. "Just let's be a bit more careful this time, right? I mean, you gave the eulogy for the last guy who tried to approach a wild animal."

"The shmoo was a predator. Those are grazers." Nurul pointed to the ground, where sagging, blackened tiles showed where wheelers had been feeding. "The trails we followed—"

"I know that! And rhinoceroses are also grazers. And horses, kangaroos, even sheep can kill people."

Daisuke cleared his throat. "Do you think these wheel animals are dangerous?"

"Well, look at them!" She thrust out her hands at the nearest wheeler. It was five or six meters away, a thick glass hoop with spines around the rim. "I have no idea how they move themselves, but if they're eating the tiles, that means they have a way of getting through the glassy test and into the soup inside. I'm thinking a powerful radula assisted by acid at high concentration."

After taking a moment to remember that test and radula meant 'shell' and 'tongue', Daisuke nodded and summarized. "So you believe these things drill into the glassland ground and suck up nutrients like—"

"Shut up, Daisuke!" Anne stomped. "This isn't a bloody TV show."

Daisuke jerked. Looked up. For a second, he stared into the lens of the camera.

"Hey," said Rahman.

Daisuke quickly refocused his eyes. Looking into the camera? When was the last time he'd made that amateur mistake?

"I know," he said. "I know this isn't a TV show. But this is what I know. And Nurul and Rahman. It's why we're here." *Or so we are supposed to assume.*

"Like how you keep analyzing every creature we see," said Nurul. "Or how Hariyadi keeps yelling and giving orders. We all have our roles."

"Yes, well, my role is to tell you when you're about to do something stupid and dangerous." Anne sighed. "But we need a way to carry our supplies."

"It can't hurt to try," Nurul said.

"Can't hurt *you,* you mean." Anne gestured at the camera. "You're going to be behind the camera, not in front of it."

"We will stand in front of the camera together," said Daisuke.

Nurul waited the appropriate beat before slashing her hand through the air. "And cut!"

When they'd repositioned everyone and gotten the "Ya" from Rahman, Anne, and Daisuke had put one of the wheelers between themselves and the camera. Daisuke held his urchin spine in his right hand and a collapsible shovel in his left.

"So, Anne," he said, "what do we have here? I'd say this is the strangest organism we've discovered so far, how about you?"

Anne sighed and rolled her eyes. "Just stab the bloody thing, Dice. Stab it right through its bloody axle."

Daisuke had spent a long time memorizing random English vocabulary. "That's no axle," he said, hoisting his urchin spine. "*This* is an axle."

Her glare cracked. "What are you doing?" she giggled. "Is that Crocodile Dundee you're trying to do?"

Daisuke just smiled, trying to remember who Crocodile Dundee was.

"Just poke the alien, you dipstick. I'll tell the camera how this creature works."

"You have theories?" asked Daisuke.

"Of course I have theories. Rolling as a means of locomotion isn't unknown even on Earth. There is a spider that spreads its legs out and turns its body into a wheel. There's a beetle larva that rolls up and does the same. What we're seeing here is similar. I just don't understand how this thing propels itself...."

"Let's find out." Daisuke smacked the wheeler with his spear.

Anne grabbed his arm and pulled him back. "Jesus Christ, Daisuke! I was kidding about the poking."

The wheeler rolled as if pushed, but toward Daisuke, rather than away. It pivoted and from its flat rim a spike pistoned out, spraying steaming fluid.

Rahman and Nurul jerked back. Daisuke and Anne had already stepped out of the way.

"So we know how it defends itself," Daisuke said, once he was sure his voice would remain level. "Do you think that spike also moves the animal?"

"Hmm," said Anne. "Maybe in emergencies. But look at how it rolls and pivots. There must be something heavy moving around inside it. Changing its balance."

"Changing its balance?" Daisuke prodded.

"Stop wasting time!" Hariyadi yelled at them from beside their travois.

Anne flapped her hands at him, then formed the fingers into a ring. "Imagine a worm swallowed a rock and then its own tail. Now the worm is a hoop standing on its rim with a heavy rock inside. It swallows the rock further down its gut, which causes it to overbalance and roll."

"I see," said Daisuke, thinking of his career. "Like a clown forever cursed to do somersaults."

Anne squinted at him. "Huh?"

"All right." Daisuke squared his shoulders. "Let's see if we can make a wheel." He raised his spear, then, thinking, switched the shovel into his right hand. With the spear in his left, he reached out and prodded the wheeler, which shot out its defensive spike. Daisuke rushed in close and brought the shovel down on the spike where it met the rim of the wheeler. He leaped backward, away from the digestive juices that flooded out of the shattered hole he had made.

Daisuke glanced at Anne, wondering if his destruction of the native wildlife would bother her. Anne only stared at him for a second before frowning and holding her hands up. "What? You killed it. Congratulations."

The wheeler rolled away from him, smoking fluid sluicing down its side. Its internal organs bubbled and spasmed, and defensive spikes extended, retracted, extended again. A hole in the inner rim of the wheel vomited black tarry material. The animal rolled to a stop.

"Let's get a move on." Anne walked to the wheeler, grabbed its rim, and held out a hand. "Give me that spine." Daisuke handed it to her, and she thrust it through the center of the wheeler. There were bits of glass there, hollow and brittle as old light bulbs.

"Aha," said Anne. "As the wheeler grows, it flees away from its center, increasing its diameter faster than its body's girth in an attempt to gain torque. That leaves an empty space around the hub. An...that's not an axle? The urchin spine is the axle? So what's the hole? There's got to be some technical name for the hole in the middle of a wheel."

"I don't know." Daisuke shoved on the spine, now threaded through the middle of the dead animal. Trailing acidic slime, it rolled.

"Well," said Anne. "At least we invented the wheel."

★ ★ ★

The tiles rolled by under Daisuke's feet. Every time he looked up, the mountains were closer, rising from the sparkling plains like the head of a black dog from a diamond-studded collar.

"I think I can see the next biome," said Anne. "Do you see where the glass sort of peters out? Then there's bare rock, and above that…." She squinted. "Something dark."

"What are you talking about?" Hariyadi shouted, even though he wasn't more than a few paces from them. In fact, Daisuke realized, the Indonesian soldier hadn't allowed them to get more than a few paces away since that morning. *What is he afraid we might do?*

"Can we get to the mountains before sunset?" asked Hariyadi, who hadn't bothered to wait for an answer to his first question.

"I think we might," Daisuke said. "Maybe if—"

Anne smacked him across the chest with the back of her arm. "Careful!" She pointed with her free hand at the yellow tile in front of Hariyadi.

The others turned at Anne's shout. Rahman called out a question in Indonesian and Misha said, "Almost step on landmine again, Colonel?"

"I saw it. I knew it was there." Hariyadi took a dignified step to the side. "These things are becoming quite a nuisance."

"They do seem more common," said Daisuke as he skirted the dangerous spot. "Maybe we are in a less stable part of the glasslands."

Anne swatted at a bumblesnail as it tumbled through the air past her head. "Oh, no. Isn't it obvious? After the snow melted into water, the glasslands are, um, blooming."

"And singing," Misha said. "Or is that sound in my head?"

"No," said Daisuke, "I hear it too." It had begun as a subliminal rumble, a fluttering in the chest that Daisuke had only felt before in Africa, when elephants were nearby. Now, though, he could tell the subsonics came from the ground.

Anne cocked her head, eyes narrow. "And the pitch is rising."

As if it had been waiting for her to notice it, the sound shifted to the sound of boulders grinding together.

Hariyadi surveyed their surroundings. "There's steam coming out of the cracks around that yellow tile. What does that signify?"

"You know what?" said Anne. "I think we should all head up a hill. Uh. Right now."

Daisuke knew better than to ask for clarification. As he turned in his traces and hauled his cart back toward the safety of a hill-reef, the whistling rose in pitch from earthquake to church organ. The ground vibrated under Daisuke's boots. He pulled harder on the cart. "Help!" he called.

A few moments later the cart lurched behind him and Misha grunted. "I push! I push! What is noise?"

"A signal." Anne appeared in Daisuke's peripheral vision, her expression worried, but not panicked. "Look at those swarming bumblesnails. Or, no, Daisuke, don't look. Focus on your climbing. I think that whistling is calling them here."

Daisuke didn't have to look. Tiny bead-gnats swarmed him. Animals crawled on the glass at his feet, legless stick insects dragging filmy bags like parachutes, trying to catch the wind and get up into the air.

"It's like of the scent of a cherry tree in bloom, calling the bees," said Anne. "A musical perfume."

"Yo-is*sho*!" Daisuke groaned, hauling the sledge up the hill a half-meter at a time. It wasn't until he got to the top that he could appreciate Anne's flower analogy. Yellow spots speckled the purple glasslands like a color-shifted prairie in bloom. The air over those 'flowers' was thick with flying creatures from the size of bees to hawks, darting, whirling, attacking, and escaping from each other as the pitch of the whistling grew higher and louder.

"It's like an old-fashioned teakettle," Anne said, looking out over the swarming glasslands. "And it's about to boil over."

That was a good comparison. Daisuke looked around for Rahman and found the cameraman already at work, showing Daisuke a thumbs-up from behind his equipment.

Daisuke gave the camera a big smile. "We should be safe up here," he said for the folks at home. "Safe from the…steam-spawning of the glasslands." And then as the howl rose in the air, "Perhaps we should set up some kind of protection."

"I had wanted to get out of this cursed place before nightfall." Hariyadi puffed up the hill behind them, looking annoyed. "Protection from what? Are we in fact safe on this hill, Ms. Houlihan?"

Anne rubbed her mouth. "We might want to erect tarps to protect us from the, um, splashing."

Hariyadi yelled orders at Rahman, Nurul, and Tyaney. Anne answered their plaintive-sounding questions in Indonesian and said in English, "I'm sure it will all blow, um, blow over before sunset."

She was right. The sun had just barely touched the horizon when the glasslands exploded.

The howl became a whistle, which rose to the shriek of an air-raid siren. The sound reached its crest, and every yellow tile became a spume of boiling fluid. Drops spattered on the tent they'd erected.

"It reminds me of watching whales breach off Hawaii," said Daisuke. Then the smell hit them.

"Whales from hell," Misha said.

Rahman clamped his hand over his mouth, but he kept filming.

Anne pulled one of the edges of her jacket over her mouth. "Probably shouldn't breathe this stuff in!" she yelled through the fabric.

So they were silent for the next few minutes, until the sharp, sulfurous stench died away. Then another tense period, waiting for the yellow goo to stop raining on their tent. Daisuke made sure his back was to the camera before shutting his eyes and monitoring himself for signs of incipient allergy.

Time passed and nobody fell to the ground in a seizure. They let out sighs of relief, but shallow ones.

"Now," said Anne, eventually, "we need to start thinking about animal life."

Daisuke opened his eyes. Beyond the tarp, the glasslands looked as if they'd been spray-painted. Yellow slime covered the ground, and it writhed with life.

Wheelers and urchins trundled between things like shaggy carpets and animated rolling pins. Shmoos ambushed and battled their prey while overhead, baton-shaped hunters darted through clouds of bumblesnails. High above the glasslands, the last red rays of the setting sun shone on parasail-shaped scavengers, circling in the warm updraft from the mass steam-sporing.

Nurul murmured something to Rahman and then said in English, "Daisuke, can you take a step to the side?"

She wanted to get a wider angle. Daisuke turned and put his hands on his hips, framing the scene with his torso. "Ah," he said, "what a glorious spectacle of nature. The miracle of reproduction!"

"Ah," said Misha, "geysers of plant semen. What's that word, Daisuke? *Bukkake*?"

Daisuke made a disgusted face.

Rahman giggled and, thank goodness, put the camera down.

Nurul squinted at her husband. "How do you know about *bukkake*?"

"Well, how do *you*?" asked Misha, and burst into laughter at her blush. "Ah, when a married couple finds they share a fetish—"

"Shut up, Misha," Anne said. "I'm thinking about sulfur-reducing bacteria."

"Oh, were you?" said Misha. "I was thinking about—"

"On *Earth*," Anne said heavily, "they live in hot springs and hydrothermal vents or deep underground where they can get at elemental sulfur. Here, it seems like there's a lot of sulfur just freely available in the environment. More than there should be." She cocked an eyebrow at Daisuke, as if offering him a puzzle. "Like there's more oxygen than there should be on Earth."

Daisuke got it. "You mean glassland plants produce sulfur the same way Earth plants produce oxygen?"

Anne shrugged. "It's what I'm guessing. Clearly there's enough oxygen in the air to keep us alive." Anne breathed in demonstration. "Maybe enough blows in from other places. Maybe plants here *also* produce oxygen." She nodded to herself. "Yes, it *would* be odd for the aliens who designed this place to link up a planet with a poisonous atmosphere."

She was developing a real presence on camera: solid and loud. Daisuke found he liked watching the biologist as she lectured. Found it hard to stop, actually.

"But what if organisms like that evolved a way to mine the sulfur they needed out of the ground?" Anne asked.

Of course, she got no answer, but she went on anyway. "Perhaps," she said, "by using strong acid to dissolve boreholes into the rock? Heat becomes a problem, but silicate valves are grown in the bores, shunting water from one place to another, cooling the tunnel system and transporting dissolved minerals."

Daisuke was trying to put together a metaphor to encapsulate all that when Hariyadi said, "How can we ever build cities in a hell like this?"

"Why should we need to?" asked Anne.

"To stop acid from glasslands eating through crust of planet," Misha said.

"I was thinking more of establishing a claim to the land," said Hariyadi.

Anne shook her head, setting her halo of curls swinging in fascinating little arcs. Daisuke would love to find out what those curls felt like around his fingers. "We don't need to save Junction from the glasslands. This ecosystem has its own system of checks and balances."

"Maybe on home planet." Misha pointed west, toward where they assumed the glasslands' own wormhole sat. "Here, on Junction, we have only part of ecosystem. Spill-over from ancient alien zoological gardens. Maybe it eats hole in planet, makes super-volcano."

"Nonsense," Anne said. "If that could happen, it would have happened some time in the past however many million years and we'd see evidence of it on Earth. Volcanic ash spewing out of a hole in the New Guinea Highlands."

Hariyadi made a skeptical sound. "How could you possibly know that that Indonesian wormhole is so old?"

Daisuke frowned. What the hell was he doing thinking about caressing Anne's scalp when super-volcanoes or alien slime could kill them all at any moment? *Or if not natural forces, then human agency.*

"What?" said Anne. "It's obvious? The plants growing at the edge of the

Earth biome aren't like anything that actually lives on Earth. There are fish in the Nun settling pools that *eat* plant matter from the treeworm biome! You think that kind of adaptation happens over a long weekend? And, uh…." She looked introspective. "I haven't talked about this before, but I'm pretty sure I saw teeth on one of the birds the Nun roasted for us. So, the Deep Sky Hole has been there for a long, long time. Like, Cretaceous-long."

"And for how many million years since aliens put wormholes here?" Misha pointed up toward the darkening sky and the unnatural arc of the Nightbow. "Connections to how many other stars? Hundreds? Thousands? In all that time, one of those stars will become red giant, no? Or become nova. Why do we not see wormhole belching stellar plasma all over place?"

"Because we'd be dead if we were close enough to a nova to see it," said Anne.

Daisuke looked into her eyes. Saw the stars reflected there. "So," he said, "why are we not dead?"

"Because we are careful," snapped Hariyadi. "Enough idle speculation. Ladies, we need dinner. Daisuke, you should have made a steam trap already."

"Ladies?" Anne said. "*Ladies?* How about *you* make dinner, Hariyadi? Since even though I may be a woman, I actually have an important job to do, what with observing our environment and making deductions that keep us alive. While you…."

"Please help me with the steam trap, Anne," Daisuke begged.

"I keep you safe," said Hariyadi. "I make sure the whole party is coordinated and organized. It's the difference between life and death."

"Yes, yes it is. Yes, you do." Daisuke looked around for a camera, but Rahman was just staring at him, probably not getting five words in the conversation out of ten. Well, they were all wearing bodycams. Daisuke oriented himself to Hariyadi's and performed.

"We all do what we must to survive," he declaimed. "That is what we should learn from Pearson's death. There is no room in our group for fighting. No room for suspicion." He lifted his right fist to chin level. "We protect each other so we can survive."

Hariyadi raised an eyebrow. "Should I applaud?" He let out an angry breath. "Go make us a steam trap, Mr. Matsumori, and take Ms. Houlihan with you."

He glared at Anne, as if daring her to disagree. Nurul and Rahman whispered at each other. Misha looked extremely entertained. Sing and Tyaney were sitting silently, ignoring both each other and the rest of the party.

"Please come," Daisuke whispered, and walked out from under the tarp.

Anne followed him a moment later. "Oh hell," she said. "*People.*" She spat the word like a curse.

Daisuke smiled. As lost as he was behind the persona of the Iron Man of Survival, a person with no mask at all was like a drink of cool water in the desert. He walked across the slippery glass, selecting a tile to smash and some words of comfort to say. "You do not need to be a people person. Just a survival person."

"Is that supposed to be sarcastic?" Anne demanded. "Pearson died trying to protect Nurul and me." She looked away. "Protect us from something I should have seen coming a mile off. Dig into that tile. No, that one."

Anne pointed and Daisuke plunged the shovel into the tile. The plume of steam that came out was smaller than usual. Perhaps the glasslands needed time to recover from its sporulation.

"I am wondering whether the thing that made Pearson allergic might get us too?" he said, once they had the steam trap erected.

Anne frowned, considering. "Well, he *might* have died from anaphylaxis. Or maybe it was poison or shock or, or anything. Fast-acting silicosis from all the glass-coated pollen?" She waved her hand in front of her face as if to dispel poisonous smoke. "I don't even have a magnifying glass. I have no idea what's in this air and it could be almost anything. You keep making assumptions like we're on Earth, Dice, and we're not."

She was right. Pearson's death could have been caused by anything. Their own deaths could be caused by anything. Not a comforting thought.

"So," Daisuke said, trying not to feel the tickling of spores in his nasal cavities, "it's a very good thing we're leaving this environment quickly."

"I suppose," said Anne. "Good thing we don't have a crippled soldier to slow us down."

Whatever relief Daisuke might have felt was gone now. Anne had just outlined her motive for getting rid of a deadly drain on their resources. Hell, Daisuke was halfway convinced *he* should have killed Pearson.

He looked at Anne, her hips drawn as if with broad strokes of a big, round-tipped brush. Himself, lusting after her, suspicious of her, making dinner, trying to keep his tenuous grip on his role to play. Wishing he could have sex with Anne even when it was entirely possible she'd murdered Pearson. Sex and power. Scheming and sneaking. Dominance games. Death. *We are eight monkeys, still trying to do what monkeys do, even though we are so very far from jungle.*

"You're awfully quiet," said Anne.

"It has been a long day." He glanced at her bodycam. *And I don't want to interrogate you.*

"Hey," Anne said. "You just looked at my bodycam." She put her hand over the device. "Are you afraid of saying something that might get recorded? Or doing something? Because I can take this thing off."

Daisuke stared at Anne.

"That sounded like a come-on, didn't it?" she said. "Uh.... Well, maybe it is?" She hefted the bodycam in one hand. "How about it?"

Their eyes met and his heart jumped as if he'd touched his tongue to a battery. A sour taste filled his mouth. The same taste he got right before he forced himself to jump onto a crocodile's back or fling himself up an escarpment. The thrill of danger.

"Shit. I said the wrong thing, didn't I?" Anne gave a short, sharp sigh. "Look, Dice, I don't enjoy feeling like I'm back in high school. I'm not good at this, okay? So would you stop trying to send me subtle signals and tell me whether I should keep pushing or whether I'm embarrassing myself?"

"I'm the one who should be embarrassed," said Daisuke, "and I'm the one who should apologize. I...." He forced himself to say something the Iron Man of Survival would never say. "I don't know what to do."

She folded her arms. "Oh, I get it. You aren't interested."

"No no!" Daisuke fumbled for the right words. "You are very interesting. I mean, I am...interested. I am just...." He looked down at his own bodycam. "I am just confused. When there is no camera, I don't know what to do."

"You...want to record us pashing?" Anne asked. "That's pretty weird, Dice. I'm not judging, but I'm not into that."

"No. No." Daisuke held his hands up toward her, feeling as if he was propitiating an idol. "I don't want cameras for...that reason." They'd called it 'making out' in America. Presumably 'pashing' was the Australian equivalent. "It's only...." *Can I even express this thought in my own language?* "I know what I should do in front of cameras," Daisuke attempted. "Like you know what to do with an alien ecosystem. Right?"

She rocked her head from side to side. "You mean you're a professional TV guy the same way I'm a professional biologist. Okay. But I'm talking about what happens when we..." she tugged distractingly at her shirt, "...hang up our work clothes."

"Nothing," said Daisuke. "There is nothing else in me."

"What do you mean, nothing?" She examined him as if he were a new species of nematode. "Dice, you're gonna have to unpack that for me."

Her expression was open and concerned. Honest. As opposed to Daisuke, the fake hero, the pseudo-biologist, mimic-detective, the TV personality.

Self-disgust gushed up from the glass-coated bedrock of Daisuke's personality. He was off script. The Iron Man of Survival wouldn't talk like this.

And yet, who knew when they would stop surviving? Pearson had managed to unburden himself before his death, but would Daisuke be so lucky?

He cleared his throat, forced himself to speak. "My wife was right."

"Uh," Anne said. "…oh?"

"My wife said…." Daisuke tried to assemble a coherent translation. "'You have a pretty face, but you're hollow. Like an egg with nothing inside. I could crush you with one hand.'"

Anne blinked. "Your wife said she would crush you?"

"She wrote it in an email."

Anne snorted. "The bitch."

"No," said Daisuke. "She was right. I never showed her my…insides?" She squinted at him and Daisuke reviewed his phraseology. "I mean what I have inside. Only showed her outside." He brushed his hand across his chest. "The shell."

Anne squatted next to him, close enough he could feel her body heat. "Well." She looked down his torso. "What have you got in there?"

Daisuke's laugh came without warning. A bark that echoed off the glass ridges around them. A herd of wheelers left off their grazing on the reproductive slurry coating the valley below and rolled off in search of quieter pastures.

"You," said Daisuke. "You are…you have no shell at all. An egg with no shell."

She squinted. "So like frog spawn? I can live with that."

"Most women would be insulted by the comparison."

Anne's grin turned self-deprecating. "Most women would have worked their wiles on you a lot smoother, probably."

Daisuke flicked through his mental English grammar book. Yes, this sentence should work: "Maybe it's better to be bad at people than to be bad at being a person."

"Well," Anne said. "That just means we're complementary." She placed a hand on her collar. "Insides without outsides…." She put the other hand on his chest, where it warmed him. "And outsides without insides." She raised an eyebrow at him. "So can I fill you up?"

Daisuke laughed again, leaned to the side, and kissed Anne.

Overhead, the Nightbow shone with the light of other stars.

CHAPTER TEN

Marital Relations

They didn't have sex. That would have to wait until Anne could finagle a private tent. Or failing that, a patch of ground that wasn't coated in allergenic yellow slime.

But Daisuke was definitely on Anne's 'to do' list. That was the thought Anne had gone to sleep with and the thought she'd woken up with. Just grabbing Daisuke's face and rubbing it all over her. Letting those strong, long-fingered hands explore a different kind of wilderness.

"So," said a voice from her elbow, "are congratulations in order?"

Anne looked around to see Nurul, now looking less like an airline hostess than one of the broke college students who sleep in the airport. Although Anne shouldn't be critical. She probably looked less human than the things growing on the mountainside around them.

"I don't know what you're talking about," Anne said, failing to suppress her smile.

Nurul smiled in return. "I've known you two were going to end up together since we met in Imsame. And the way you looked at each other this morning while we broke camp, even Hariyadi figured it out." She nodded back down the slope. "That's why he's marching so far back, the coward."

Anne didn't see the logic. "He's scared of Daisuke and me having sex?"

"More like, he's scared of talking about it," said Nurul. "He is a man of a certain age, after all."

Anne and Nurul had indeed outdistanced the rest of the party by a fair bit. The slopes of the mountain had proven surprisingly amenable to wheeled vehicles, but it still took Daisuke, Rahman, and Misha working together to keep their heavily laden cart moving up the zig-zag game trail.

They'd only been climbing for a couple of hours, but already the air was cooler and thinner, if less sulfurous. The morning sun shone up the length of the mountain range, casting deep shadows across their folds and gullies, throwing glittering highlights off of hill-reefs and, still visible in the distance, the wing of their airplane. The fuselage of the plane had vanished into an irregular lavender carpet that Anne supposed was some kind of weedy secondary growth. And under that scab, were the glasslands digesting the metal and plastic in the plane or just growing over it? If she came back in a year, would that wing still be there, waving hello as it now seemed now to wave goodbye?

If she came back in a year, what would be growing over Pearson's grave?

Anne shivered, angry at herself for ruining her own good mood, and guilty she'd been in a good mood in the first place. She should be grim. She should be mourning, literally, not chasing after rugged Japanese celebrities.

The only thing that made Anne feel better was that Daisuke had clearly felt the same way. He'd asked her to talk to people about Pearson's death, probably because he wanted to get some good footage of grieving.

Anne actually agreed with him. *They should* try to keep him alive in their memories. Because God knew Anne hadn't given the man much credit while he was alive. She'd been content to deal with him as a stereotype, but she'd been like a layperson walking across the desert and saying, "It's just sand," totally ignorant of the struggles going on under the surface. The ceaseless work that it took for organisms there to just go on surviving under the lethal sun.

Pearson hadn't been some meathead caricature. He'd been a whole person, full of complicated self-contradictions, as rich and diverse and productive as anyone. And now he was gone, his body turned into a battleground of two different types of microorganism. Wasted. Fuck, was she crying?

"What's wrong?" asked Nurul.

"God, I'm sorry." Anne sniffed, poking at her eyes, churning with embarrassment and sadness and horniness and curiosity and who knows what. "I'm sorry. I'm a mess."

"It's all right." Nurul looked at her, face scrunched up as if she was wrestling with an internal decision.

"He was a very difficult man," she said, finally. "A hard man. Still I am… horrified he's dead."

Horrified, yes. Because Pearson was a worthy individual who should not have died, or because Anne was afraid the same might happen to her? Or maybe just horrified at her own selfishness.

Nurul shook her head, maybe clearing away her own grim thoughts. "Do we have enough food and water to get over the mountain?"

"If getting over the mountain only takes us a day," said Anne, "maybe."

"But that should be enough, right? Didn't Sing say that there is a sort of oasis ahead, where we can eat the animals and drink the water?"

"Yes, and I would like to believe her," Anne said, "but even if she's right, there's still this biome between us and the oasis." She sniffed. "From the smell of it, I'd prefer not to drink the water here."

The rocks around them were almost entirely bare of life except for odd little glassy bubbles and a sort of brown slime. Every now and then the wind would swirl down the mountain, bringing with it a smell that made Anne think of sewers and rotting corpses. Or maybe that was just her imagination.

Anne looked downslope, wondering how she might indicate that she'd rather let Daisuke catch up to her, then just sort of kiss him for a while. "You don't want to wait for the others to catch up with us?"

"We wouldn't be very good scouts if we stayed with the convoy. Besides" – Nurul swept her hand up the slope – "Hariyadi wants to push forward until we get to the tree line."

"The reverse tree line, I'd call it." Rather than the normal succession of trees to grass to bare rock, this mountainside went from glass reefs to bare rock to rotting sludge, then something rustling and brown.

"All right," she said as they started up toward the tangled mountain jungle. "But you don't need to keep to my pace. Feel free to take a rest and let your husband catch you up."

Nurul did not get the hint. "Actually I thought since our primary TV personality is currently employed as an ox alongside my husband, I should take the opportunity to enjoy one of your famous alien talks."

Of course Anne would really rather talk more about Daisuke. But there was a fair chance that Nurul would remind Anne that once they made it back to civilization, Daisuke would drop Anne like a homely potato. So. Stick to biology.

"Sure," she said. "I'll try not to get us attacked by poisonous spores or vicious beasts this time." Anne immediately regretted the joke. Her teeth ground together and she suppressed the urge to stomp, furious with herself. Jesus, a man had died!

Nurul favored her with a smile, teeth a perfect white crescent. "Thank you."

The sun rose high and the glasslands died out from under them. The lowland tiles became fishbowl-sized globes, then shrank to the size of grapes, then vanished, leaving the ground bare except for pencil-thin root-pipes and purple algae. Farther up, the pipes were broken, then absent. A shiny, chocolate-colored patina appeared on the sunward side of rocks, and then….

The Seattle Public Library

Capitol Hill Branch

Visit us on the Web: www.spl.org

Checked Out Items 2/24/2020 16:30

XXXXXXXXX4117

em Title	Due Date
010095880141	3/16/2020
unction	

# of Items: 1

enewals: 206-386-4190

eleCirc: 206-386-9015 / 24 hours a day

nline: myaccount.spl.org

ay your fines/fees online at pay.spl.org

"Is that hair?" Nurul asked. "An animal?"

"Maybe," said Anne. "Or an old wig. Or the remains of a man buried up to his scalp in the talus."

Nurul squinted at her. "You're not serious, are you?"

"It's some kind of plant."

"Well, why don't you go examine it and tell me about it?" Nurul flicked her bodycam. "Daisuke's not the only one who knows how to help people look good on camera."

Anne realized their previous conversation about pashing was now recorded on military hardware. Hopefully they'd never declassify this stuff, and only some poor intelligence analyst would have to know Anne's shame.

Biology. Let's focus on biology.

Trying not to be self-conscious, Anne brushed the clump of brown filaments with her foot. They flopped limply aside. "More like thin noodles than hair," she said. And, still thinking of Daisuke. "Soba-weed." God, did her voice sound weird? Was she standing the right way? And what *smelled* so bad?

Her nose twitched at the smell of sewage. So did Nurul's.

"Ugh! I wouldn't want to eat noodles that smelled like that," the journalist said. "Are we going to spend another three days hiking through this stuff?"

Anne tried to stop staring at the camera lens and just answer the question. No wonder Daisuke was half-crazy. "Um. Not according to Sing's map. She said this biome only runs down the spine of the mountain range." And, as the thought occurred to her, "Why that would be? Is there a wormhole at the top of the mountain? Why doesn't this biome extend all the way down to the foothills?"

Nurul made an encouraging noise through the hand she had placed over her mouth and nose.

Anne toed an odorous brunette tussock as she tried to visualize the map Sing had drawn. "Sing says this biome dominates the upper slopes of the next mountains over too. But again, not in the valley in the middle. *That's* home to three separate biomes. So…the ultraviolet light up here or the low pressure or low temperature or something else gives this stuff an edge?"

That seemed to be the case. The vegetation grew larger and more varied as they climbed, and fortunately less rank. Or maybe that was just Anne's nose getting used to the rotting garbage smell of this mountaintop biome. She breathed deeply, then breathed again. The air was definitely rarefied up here, who knew how high above sea level. Who knew if Junction even had seas.

They made good progress. Anne had been afraid the weird ripply forest would prove to be impenetrable, but the game trail continued right between them. Hip-high soba-weed swished gently between stands of bamboo-like tubes. Except the brown cylindrical stalks didn't move like bamboo. They were too flexible, too fluid. Looking up at the undulating plants, now four meters tall, Anne was reminded of a kelp forest, which meant....

"You look like you're thinking something interesting."

Anne turned to look at Nurul. "Sorry, I was just remembering going scuba-diving in the Giant Kelp Marine Forests off Tasmania. There are these tall undulating stalks of seaweed."

"Yes." Nurul gave a little clap. "Good delivery. Good image. Now, why didn't you just say that when the thought struck you?"

Anne frowned. "You mean just say everything I think out loud?"

"Not *everything*, maybe, but everything interesting," said Nurul. "You're an expert on biology, so people will want to hear whatever you have to say about it."

"That's never been my experience," Anne said. "Most of the time people react like what I'm saying is either boring or gross or insulting."

Nurul steepled her hands in front of her chest. "Anne, I promise I will tell you when you are boring or insulting. Trust me."

Anne couldn't help but smile. "Okay."

"Good." Nurul tilted her hands so the tips of her fingers pointed at Anne. "Why do these plants remind you of seaweed?"

"That's not important," said Anne. Oh, that had been rude, hadn't it? She looked at Nurul who mouthed, *Keep talking.*

Anne took a breath. "My point is that these plants shouldn't be able to stand up under their own weight. Look." She reached out to the nearest stalk, preparing to feel its texture. But then she remembered she was on an alien planet, in a brand-new biosphere, and it would be a phenomenally stupid idea to go around squeezing the wildlife.

"What's wrong?" Nurul's voice was just a bit higher than professionalism would dictate.

She's remembering the last time we went walking together.

"Don't worry," Anne said. "Just let me find a stick or something? I'll whack one of these, um, kelp-trees with it."

They both cast around for a suitable prodding tool, peering into the undulating foliage that lined the trail.

"I can't see anything," said Nurul, "and if you think we shouldn't touch the plants...." She reached tentatively toward the soba-weed. "Keep your hand away and trust my boots," Anne said.

"Your boots?" asked Nurul, but Anne was already standing on one foot, stretching the other into the undergrowth. Brown hairlike strands parted harmlessly over her foot as she swept it back and forth.

Something tiny, hard, and zebra-striped bounced off her tough boot. Nurul shrieked, but Anne only hopped backward, keeping an eye on the creature, which had fallen onto the path. About the size of the tip of her pinky, the animal writhed on the dirt, pushing out with a muscular organ like the foot of a clam or a human tongue. Except that instead of a simple bag of fluid-filled muscle, this organ was a hollow tube, which could turn inside out and slip over the round little animal like a sock. The creature was now half as long as Anne's pinky and twice as fat, rolling around in a circle as it brought to bear a sharp little spine.

Anne ducked aside just as that sock-foot flipped itself inside out, launching the animal into the air. "Huh," she said as it sailed through the space where her head had just been. "This biome's equivalent of a flea? A parasite that jumps on a single foot like a tongue. A...linguipod."

"Is it dangerous?" Nurul asked. She had pulled her elbows in close to her body, as if cold.

"Hm? Maybe." Anne considered. "See that color pattern? That striking black and white? Might be a sign of poison. That little thorn on the front could certainly deliver a dose of venom."

It probably wouldn't do anything to humans, of course, unless they happened to be allergic to it. But still. "Stay away from the soba-weed," said Anne. "And step out of that linguipod's flight path."

Nurul squeaked and jumped at the same time as the little creature. Its leap arced across the path and toward the weeds on the other side. Before it could land, the linguipod was snatched from the air by what looked like a twisted-up towel.

"Ooh! Would you look at that?" Anne rushed past Nurul, to where the soba-weed was still rustling. She gave the undergrowth a prod, then a kick, and a hollow log toppled out of the soba-weed.

The log was about the length and thickness of her forearm, with thick branches along its fibrous sides. One end was capped by a pale growth. Some kind of mushroom?

"Aha," said Anne. "A log. Just the sort of thing we need." She leaned toward it and the log moved. "Or...maybe not?"

The folds of pale flesh that Anne had mistaken for a mushroom pulsed. Turned inside out. Became a tube. A trunk. An everted proboscis, peppered with eyespots and lined with teeth.

Anne slowly straightened and backed away. The proboscis stretched after her. The stiff woody limbs rattled against each other and the creature's tubular body scuttled around to bring Anne into reach. That wasn't a log at all, but a woody shell.

"What about that?" said Nurul. "Is *that* thing dangerous?"

Anne sidestepped a jab from the proboscis, slid forward, put her toe under the creature's edge, and flipped it onto its back. "Not anymore," she said, and watched as its proboscis curved around, trying to lever the animal back onto its feet. It had six legs, Anne saw, arranged not in pairs, but in staggered rows down its sides. And there was also something strange about how they moved.

"Look at this," she said, belatedly remembering the bodycams. "Each leg is connected to the, um, trunk, just like the branch of a tree. No joints. The branch extends out and down until it terminates in a sort of cap. The cap moves, but not by muscle-power. See these strands of thread that extend from the cap to the trunk? This animal is…what? *Operating* its limbs, like a puppeteer."

They watched the log-worm as it rocked back and forth, trying to right itself.

"Still, though," said Anne, "I wouldn't touch it. I wouldn't touch anything here until we get a better picture of how this biome works." She sighed. "Hopefully Sing will be able to tell us something useful about this place. Otherwise we'll just have to—"

"Kick things and hope?" Nurul shrugged. "It's not as if we're live. We can always edit this footage to look like you always found whatever you were looking for on the first try."

Anne wasn't listening. She frowned up at the impossible, bendy trees. "Not to mention the fact that I still don't know what these damn trees are made of. Hell. It's as if the animals evolved lignin as their structural chemical and the trees evolved, what…fucking algin?"

"What's algin?"

Anne blinked, annoyed. "It's the stuff they extract from kelp to make your ice cream thicker and I don't know what I'm talking about, do I? I don't want to say something stupid like 'plants here use algin as a structural component'."

Nurul made soothing gestures. "Remember, we can always edit to make you sound cleverer. Now, what was that about ice cream?"

Anne sighed. "My point is I have no idea whether what's in these plants is actually algin. In fact, now that I think of it, I'm sure it isn't, because algin only forms a gum when in the presence of water, and we're not floating in water. See, that's why I don't want to open my mouth before I finish thinking. I wasn't making any grand scientific observations, I was just distracted by how similar this stuff is to kelp."

"So talk about that," Nurul suggested. "How is it like kelp?"

"Isn't that obvious?" said Anne. "This stuff has the same kind of holdfast cementing the stalk to rocks and boulders. No root system. Which is also crazy on land. And…." She pointed up. "The same fronds high above. And *that* doesn't make sense either."

She didn't wait for Nurul to ask the inevitable 'why not?' but went right on. "See how they flap? They're like flags or streamers, which is great if you want to summon the king. But it's rubbish for photosynthesizing. Kelp fronds flap like that because they need to stir the water around so they get access to oxygen, and because the surface of the water holds them up, so access to sunlight isn't an issue. The situation's reversed up here, so why? And the way they bulge out at the top like…oh, blow me."

Nurul jumped. "What's wrong?"

"This is why I didn't want to muse out loud," said Anne. "Everyone at home will think 'why didn't that moron immediately figure out that these things are being held up by buoyancy?' Just like kelp, except instead of air they're filled with something lighter than air."

She looked triumphantly at Nurul, whose eyes were glazed with incomprehension.

"In other words," Anne said, 'these trees are balloons. Filled with hydrogen, probably. Which" – she snapped her fingers – "they crack out from water or methane or something with the help of ultraviolet radiation, which they can only harvest at high elevation, where the air is thin!" She pumped her fist. "Yes!"

Nurul applauded. "Oh, I understood most of that."

"Thank you!" Anne took a bow.

"Okay," Nurul said, "now let's turn around, get the camera, and film this whole conversation over again."

★ ★ ★

When Anne and Nurul returned for the second time to the convoy, it had barely moved.

"You have to stop," Anne told the gasping Daisuke and Hariyadi as they strained at the towrope. "You're going to rupture something." The air was much thinner here, worse than Anne would have thought possible for a mountain this short. Her heart was pounding with the effort of just standing here, and so was her head. She could only imagine how bad off the men were.

Daisuke strained, face red, eyes squeezed shut. "Keep," he groaned, "pulling. Even when vision goes gray, pull. The peak of the mountain is there, and you will come to it."

Misha just cursed in Russian from behind the cart, where he and Rahman were pushing.

Nurul went to go pat her sweating husband on the head and tell him how manly he was. Anne took a more pragmatic approach with Daisuke.

"Listen, Dice," she said, " you have to stop now before you collapse because I don't want to carry you."

"Have to," he wheezed. "Over mountain. No food here. No fires."

"Well, of course we can't light fires," said Anne. "The whole damn forest is full of hydrogen. But look. We have food, and we can get water here. Or at least, that's what Sing told me last time."

"So," Hariyadi groaned, "ask her."

Sing was walking behind the cart hand in hand with Tyaney. Or rather wrist in hand. Anne didn't want to map Western standards onto Nun culture, but it did look very much like Sing's husband was dragging her up this mountain. He was squinting into the shadows off the trail, but as Anne approached his eyes darted to hers and his lips parted.

"Ah, *Ibu* Anne, how nice of you to join me. Are you going to look after my wife for me while I go piss?"

"No." Anne shook her head and it pulsed with pain. "I wanted to ask Sing about something."

"You can ask her after I piss. Here. Take her hand. Hold on tight."

"Wait," Anne said. "No. Why do we need to watch her?"

"Just make sure she doesn't do anything."

"Why would she do anything?"

Tyaney rolled his eyes. "Because she's a witch and we are in her country! She wasn't born on Earth like us, remember? She's corrupted. Just help me, all right?" With a grunt, he slapped Sing's wrist into Anne's grip and jogged back down the track.

"Damn it," said Anne. She let go of Sing and said, "I'm sorry. Uh…okay?"

The woman just looked at her, expression stony. Anne wondered if the woman was immune to altitude sickness, or just good at hiding it.

"We will need to do something about Tyaney," Misha said. Apparently pushing the cart did not take all of his attention.

Anne sighed. "I don't know...I don't speak Nun. Maybe we're misinterpreting signals, but—"

"But Tyaney is abusing her," Misha said.

"Tyaney is dog," said Rahman, who had apparently been listening too. "He is...*egois*?"

"*Da*," said Misha. "*Egoistichnyy*. Egoistic. Selfish."

"Everything he's done has been for the sake of his tribe," Anne protested.

Misha smiled as he heaved at their cart. "Tribalistic, then. Is not much."

Anne rolled her eyes. "Look, we have zero context for Nun culture."

"So we get context," said Misha. "Talk to Sing. Teach her English."

"Why not learn her language?" Anne said. "Why not teach her Indonesian? Or Russian for that matter?"

"Because English is easy," Misha said. "Like baby talk."

"*Din-lulum!*" said Sing. "*Metek aleb-ti-a. Din-lulum!*"

"Yes, exactly."

"Shut up," Anne said. "That wasn't baby talk. That was her own bloody language." Anne followed the woman's pointing finger. Kelp-tree stalks grew closer together than trees in a Terran forest, and their tassled balloon crowns blocked most sunlight from the forest floor. Visibility dropped off sharply, except where a narrow, rutted path branched off from their main street. Anne could look down the side path and make out a humped shape in the darkness. Something moved on top of that shape. Something...spun?

"What that?" asked Rahman.

Anne took a step toward whatever that was, but Sing's hand closed on her wrist.

"*Deibuna*," the small woman said. "*Metek aleb-ti-a*."

"This is impossible," Misha said. "Everything Sing says must to be translated through Tyaney. We *need* the primitive asshole."

Anne wanted to check out the spinning thing in the forest, but first she'd have to deal with Misha's casual racism. "Would you stop that?" she said. "Tyaney isn't 'primitive'. He isn't a 'savage'. He's just a person."

"Just an asshole," Misha said. "He literally says his wife is a witch!"

"Translation error."

Misha folded his arms over his chest, creating a wall of hairy muscle between himself and Anne. "Very well. What about actions, then? He sold out his tribe as soon as he figured out that they were sitting on a strategic resource."

"He figured out how to leverage the tribe's assets into a position that would defend them against invaders," said Anne.

"No, that was you who did that. Tyaney just wanted to sell to highest bidder," Misha said. "I know. I know he went to Jayapura. Bought some guns. Learned some new things about wormholes from science fantasy movie. Then went back to village full of ideas and weapons. Went through wormhole and conquered people on other side. Took daughter of chief as newest wife."

Rahman nodded. "Yes. Tyaney say."

"What sort of sensationalist garbage is that?" Anne said. "You think Sing is *a captured princess*? Where the hell does that story come from?"

Misha shrugged, then leaned into the cart for another push. "Listen what he says about her. He talks about capturing her. He says her people are evil. He looks at her like she is new Mercedes he just stole."

"Okay, enough of this," said Anne. "We're talking about Tyaney and Sing like they're another couple of aliens we're observing. They're people. We just need to talk to Sing."

"Oh," Rahman asked. "How?"

"Yeah," said Misha. "Know any words in Sing's language?"

"Just a few," Anne admitted. "'Tree'. 'Worm'. 'Water'. 'Country'. Um, 'house', I think."

"Water? We need water!" said Rahman.

Of course they did. Anne looked around. The side path with Sing's spinning thing was well behind them now. No point in doubling back, but maybe she could learn more from their native guide.

"Okay." Anne leaned down and caught Sing's eye. The woman had been looking into the soba-weed as if afraid of ambush. "Um, Sing? Water? *Mek*?"

Sing looked up. "*Mek? Yo metek aleb-ti-a sam mek.*"

"Uh," said Anne, but the Nun woman pointed at the nearest kelp-tree.

"*Yo*," she said. "*Yo sam mek.*"

"That means 'tree something water'," Anne said.

"Tree water," Sing seemed to agree.

Anne thought about that. "Well, that would make sense, wouldn't it? Look down and you don't see any soil. Just bare rocks with the holdfasts of the plants clinging to them. But they must have some way of storing the water they need, and the only place it could be is inside. Plus, it would make good ballast against the lifting power of hydrogen."

"So she says water is in the trees," said Misha. "Okay. Stop!" he yelled, and let go of the cart. Hariyadi and Daisuke groaned from the other side.

"Sing," said Misha, lumbering toward her. "You say water is in tree?" He removed from his belt an extremely scary serrated hunting knife, nearly as long as his forearm. "Like here?" He gave a kelp-tree a whack with the flat of the blade. It thunked and sloshed like a rubber wine cask.

Sing jumped at the noise, looking around as if afraid of drawing attention.

"Quiet, Misha," said Anne. "There might be predators."

"Human ones only, I think," Misha said, and smiled at Sing. He held his thumb up. "Tyaney good?" He turned his thumb down, frowning. "Or Tyaney bad?"

Sing frowned. "Tyaney."

"Just as I thought," Misha said. "We must rescue her."

"You have no idea if she understood you," said Anne. "Or if you understood her. We have no idea if there's even water in that tree."

In answer, Misha gave the tree a slash with his knife and jumped back to avoid a stream of thick black mud. It stunk like a latrine and wriggled with creatures like rings of calamari. Anne turned away before she could be sick, taking her eyes off Sing.

"Oh! We can't drink that!" said Rahman.

"Where is water, Sing?" Misha asked. Then, spinning around, "Sing?"

"What?" Anne caught a glimpse of the soba-weed swaying like a curtain, obscuring Sing's footprints. The woman herself was gone.

"She ran away." Anne was nearly bowled over by Misha, who leaped into the undulating undergrowth after Sing.

"Follow me!" he shouted, already invisible behind waving brown tendrils. "Before the trail gets cold."

Anne jumped in after him and was running before she could consider why. Was she rescuing a woman from her abusive husband or securing a vital source of intelligence? Or just acting to spite Tyaney, who'd made a fool of her again?

Anne stopped herself. She couldn't just plunge headlong into the alien bush with no more protection than a pair of boots and some rancid clothing. But if they lost Sing, all the rest of this expedition would be a headlong plunge into alien bush. They needed Sing to tell them what was safe and what was dangerous. And the trail was getting cold.

Anne passed through the curtain of soba-weed and the light dimmed. The forest was stinking, somber, and cold. It whispered and thunked with the sounds of kelp-trees sliding past each other. And there was something else. Some kind of animals making xylophone-like *klonk*ing or *pokk*ing sounds from the soba-weed. Anne imagined a log-worm striking its own shell with a biological hammer.

The kelp-trees moved in the wind, parting to let dazzling spears of sunlight pierce the coffee-colored understory gloom. Anne blinked, squinted, tried to retain some semblance of dark-adapted vision. If she faced north-east, she could put her back to the afternoon sun, which cut off her view of half the forest. Sing could be standing three meters south-west of her, and she'd be obliterated by the dazzle.

Misha had, either consciously or not, turned away from the sun and run east, parallel to the track. As she watched, he bulled through a wiglike clump of soba-weed, which rustled.

"Stop!" called Anne, "we have no idea what's—"

"Fuck!" Misha reeled back, a lobster-sized log-worm dangling from his upraised foot.

"It's okay. It's okay," Anne said, walking up to him. "This thing doesn't have any equipment hard enough to get through your boot leather. Just put your foot down and give it a chance to disengage."

"Or…." Misha growled and slashed his terrifying knife through the log-worm's proboscis. Its shelled body clunked to the ground, bleeding milky fluid.

"There," said Misha, taking a step into the bush, "now we…*fuck*!"

He held up an arm to shield his face from a rain of bullet-sized linguipods.

"And that is how she will kill you."

Tyaney was right behind her. How the hell had the bastard snuck up on her?

"What do you mean?" Anne tried to look less frightened and more pissed off. "Tyaney, what's going on between you and—"

"Sing is a witch," Tyaney said. "As I told you. She can command the creatures of this country to do her bidding." He pointed at Misha. "Already they have killed the fat man."

"I am not dead," Misha said, but winced. "Ow." He flicked his hand, sending a squadron of linguipods flying.

"Let me see that." Anne grabbed Misha's hand and peered at the bleeding pinpricks the little animals had left behind.

"No swelling, no heat," she said. "Misha, do you feel any stinging, tingling, numbness, itching, dizziness?"

"I know the symptoms of snakebite and anaphylactic shock better than you do," snapped Misha, pulling his hand back. "I'll be fine. Unlike that little wife-beating weasel." He glared at Tyaney, who sneered back and uttered an Indonesian idiom about dogs.

Anne gritted her teeth. Of all the time for alpha male dominance rituals. "Right!" she said, and clapped her hands. The noise echoed like a gunshot between the swaying stalks.

"Do you want to find Sing?" Anne demanded in Indonesian. "If so, follow me."

"You can't track a witch in her own wood," Tyaney said. "We don't know anything about this evil country."

"You don't know anything?" demanded Misha.

"No. I come from Earth, remember?"

Anne wasn't listening. She had squatted, looking at the ill-lit ground.

Fine threads, delicate and thin as the hairs on a baby's head, clutched the upper surfaces of the stones. The fuzz carpeted the ground everywhere except where she and Misha had stepped, where their boots had overturned pebbles and crushed the tiny plants.

"What are you doing? That won't work," groused Tyaney as Anne waddled down the path of disturbed vegetation, past Misha.

Sing had run through the plant life without fear of poison, so....

Anne swept her hand through the soba-weed and flinched back from a rain of linguipods. She moved, swept out her hand again. Another attack from the little parasites. And again...nothing. The soba-weed to the north-east was free of linguipods. Because the creatures had already attacked someone else? Sing, for example?

"Look," she said, "in a forest on Earth we would look for..." she switched to English, "...spiderwebs and crushed grass. Here we have disturbed baby's-hair weeds and triggered linguipods, but it's the same thing."

"What?" said both Tyaney and Misha, equally baffled.

Anne stood and pointed into the bush. "Sing went that way."

Tyaney did not look impressed. "Let Misha go first. He can spring her other traps."

Misha either didn't understand or ignored the comment. He did indeed insist on going first, though, carefully parting the weeds with his booted foot before taking each step.

"Misha," Anne said, "I should go first. I know how to read the ground."

"You think you do," grunted Misha, taking another step.

"I *think* I just bloody proved I can read the ground, Misha, so let me take the lead."

Misha waved a hand in front of his face, as if dispelling smoke. "Sorry, Anne. I am not angry at you."

"This is too slow," Tyaney said.

"Shut up," Misha replied in his terrible Indonesian. "You hurt your wife, you dog."

"Yes," said Tyaney. "*My* wife. Mine. You think you can take her from me, red man, and have her peoples' magic for yourself?"

"You animal," Misha said, at the limit of his Indonesian vocabulary. "You pig. You dog."

"You called me a dog already, you leftward-shitting, swollen-jawed, sagging-bellied, burned-skinned pile of babbling afterbirth."

"You're not helping," said Anne. "Misha, check the ground ahead of us for linguipods. Tyaney, why did Sing run away?"

"Because certain death is better than staying with her bastard husband," Misha said in English while Tyaney said, "To find her toys, probably. She told me the local ones were wild and untamed, but I don't believe her."

"Toys?" repeated Anne, thinking she'd heard wrong. "Like the things children play with?"

"Eh," Tyaney said. "In my language we call them *mekaletya*."

"*Meka letyat?*" said Misha.

Anne struggled to recall what Sing had said with so much fear in her voice. "Is that like *Metek aleb-ti-a*?"

Tyaney shrugged. "*Metek aleb-ti-a* means 'a small thing that gives a lot'. *Mekaletya* means…how would you say it in Indonesian? Maybe 'toymaker'."

"Tyaney," Anne said, hairs rising on the back of her neck, "what exactly are toymakers?"

"They're, what do you call it? 'Evil aliens'," said Tyaney. "When we raided Sing's village, the damn things killed three of my men. Clearly, Sing wants to finish the job now."

They emerged onto a rut in the ground barely large enough to qualify as a path.

"There," whispered Tyaney. "Of course she came to them. *Ibu* Anne, if you want use of Sing, we must find her now before she—"

Something clattered behind them. Misha swore under his breath and jumped back from the object he'd stepped on. "It's all right," he said in disgust. "Just another damn log-worm."

Except it wasn't. Or at least, not anymore.

"Dead," Tyaney said.

Misha kicked the empty wooden shell into the middle of the path, where it rolled to a stop, empty and skull-like.

"That way is the toymaker nest," Tyaney said, pointing south. "We must go back into the bush and circle around. It is death to stay on this path. Let the fat man go first to absorb all the parasites."

Misha had something to say about that, but Anne was no longer listening. As she watched, a second log-worm joined the shell Misha had kicked.

Except it wasn't. Instead of a wrinkled fleshy mouth, this thing's front end was capped by a purplish, hexagonal pane, very much like a glasslands tile. Instead of marionette-legs, it pushed itself forward with an octet of finger-length legs. And it – Anne squinted for a better look – it rolled.

Two thin wooden cylinders like the wheels of a steamroller squeaked as the legs pushed the animal forward. On its back, an L-shaped organ twitched back and forth like a tail…no.

Anne's mental models broke and reformed. The half-meter thing she saw twitching its way up the path was not an animal. It was a toy boat. A wooden artifact with wheels, oars, and a little periscope on top.

Tyaney said something that was probably a curse in his language. "Stay back," he said. "Do not provoke it. We are not enough to defend ourselves."

"But…but…that's…." Anne swallowed, her throat suddenly dry. "That's a wooden fucking *robot*."

She had been speaking English, but Tyaney wasn't listening anyway. "Disturb a single toymaker and the rest will never forget us or stop until they have killed us all."

As if to underline the ridiculous pronouncement, the little boat stuck out an oar and patted ineffectually at the empty log-worm shell.

When the shell only spun harmlessly, the little boat nosed closer. Its two front oars, which Anne now noticed were shaped less like paddles than salad spoons, clapped onto the shell's sides, pressed, and lifted. The oars, now arms, locked into place with an audible *klak*, suspending the log-worm shell over the ground. On its six remaining oars, the boat pushed itself through a four-point turn and trundled back down the path.

Anne and Misha stared after it, mouths open. Gradually, their shocked silence was filled by a sound from down the path as of tiny xylophones, or mating frogs, ticking wooden clocks, or an army of tiny gnomes, hammering away in the darkness of the forest.

"So," said Anne, very carefully in Indonesian, "that was a toymaker?"

"No," Tyaney said, "the makers ride inside the toys like we rode inside the airplane."

Which made what they'd just seen a sort of mining engineer? Collecting raw material from the forest? No, more like a caddis fly larva building a shell out of found materials. Facts clicked into place. "Let me guess," she said, and switched to Indonesian. "Inside the toy there is stinking black stuff and white things like rings of calamari."

Just like they'd seen living inside the kelp-trees. Except *this* species, the toymakers, didn't live inside trees, but the shells of dead log-worms. Something of Nurul's lessons must have rubbed off on her because Anne had no trouble coming up with an analogy. "As if a bird built wheels onto its nest."

"People build things with wheels too," Misha said. "What if these creatures are true tool-users. Can we talk to them?"

Anne shook her head and shrugged. "I would love to find out." She switched back into Indonesian and asked Tyaney, "The thing down the path is the toymakers' city?"

"Nest," corrected Tyaney. "Sing will be with them. If we stay off the path and make our way toward the nest, we may be able to see her. Then I will throw a rock and hit her on the head."

"What?" hissed Misha.

"If she falls without damaging any toymakers, they will ignore her and we can collect her." Tyaney finished.

"No," Anne said. "We might kill Sing."

"If Sing directs her alien hordes against us, we will surely be overwhelmed," said Tyaney.

"No," Anne said again. "No violence. We go to the nest. We find Sing. We talk to her."

"That's a stupid idea and you're a stupid, blind red woman," said Tyaney, but Misha was already lumbering into the bush. Anne had intentionally made her Indonesian simple enough for the smuggler to follow.

Tyaney snarled and threatened, but he had no way to stop them short of injuring them. And even if the Nun man thought he'd be able to overpower a pair of fit and bulky 'red people', he knew as well as Anne how vulnerable he would be here in the kelp-tree forest by himself.

"You are being stupid," he said, "and selfish. You want to take Sing from me and use her to lead you home. You can kill me then and take my share of the food."

There was more noise from the path beyond the soba-weed. Wooden oars clattered against rock.

"Of course we're not going to kill you," Anne whispered back at him.

"But you're right we need Sing. You must be..." – she groped at her meager vocabulary – "...a good husband to her."

"Arrogant red woman!" said Tyaney. "You think you know my wife better than I do? She's mine. I know her. I know where she is and what she's doing."

"No, you don't," Misha said. He had stopped at a new, smaller path. One of many Anne could see, all radiating out from a clearing just beyond the smuggler. There, built up around the holdfast of a huge old kelp-tree, was the toymaker city.

It was made of log-worm shells of varying lengths and diameters. Some had been split to form crescents that had been somehow glued together to form larger, flowerlike structures. Others had been glued side-to-side into honeycomb patterns or end-to-end to make segmented tubes.

There were other materials in use as well. Anne noted hexagonal glass plates and glass bowls the size of her head and realized who had made the path down the mountain to the glasslands and why.

The linked-cylinder architecture reminded Anne of an illustration she'd seen of proposed habitats on Mars. *That or someone hired Jim Henson to design toys for a construction-equipment-worshipping cargo cult.*

And all of it was in motion. There were vibrating guy-wires, spinning windmills, circling trains, oars, and lever-arms that paddled and pistoned, chopped and scooped and carried. There were at least a hundred variously sized land-boats, all bustling into and out of the central mound.

What there was not, was Sing.

Misha snorted in disgust. "You lied. She is not here."

"But Sing came this way." Tyaney looked at Anne, apparently baffled. "She must have. You tracked her, didn't you?"

"I tracked her to the path," Anne said. "She probably used it. Or crossed it and kept going. If these things are as dangerous as you say, Sing probably walked *away* from them."

"No," said Tyaney. "She must have come here. These evil creatures are hers to command."

"And how would he know that?" Misha asked in English. "His witch doctor tell him?"

Anne shook her head. She hated to leave sight of these fascinating wooden tool-users but.... "We have to find Sing. If she didn't go down the path, she must have gone up it."

"Don't walk on the path!" snapped Tyaney. "It's death to step on a toymaker."

And they'd never be able to avoid that. The path, which had been empty less than fifteen minutes ago, now swarmed with wheeled vehicles, most of them headed back toward Daisuke and the others.

Anne was about to suggest they go back through the woods the way they'd come when a noise like a fanfare of tiny xylophones erupted from the clearing. The central mass of the city, a rough pyramid of stacked cylinders that Anne had thought of as little skyscrapers, separated from the rest of the buildings and slid across the ground. Another fanfare, and the mass of towers jerked forward again. The whole thing, she saw now, was on wheels, rolling pins the thickness of her thigh.

Anne noticed the silken netting strung across those towers, the cords that she had thought of as guy-lines, but now realized were…reins?

She focused on the ground, and saw several large land-boats dig their oars into the ground. Xylophones tinkled, reins went taut, and the mass of towers rolled another half-meter down the path.

"Seems the toymakers are on the march," Anne said.

"Yeah," said Misha, "right toward our caravan."

CHAPTER ELEVEN

Toymakers

Daisuke lay on his back, breathing.

It was good to feel the rise and fall of his rib cage, the pulse of blood from his temples to the soles of his feet. His shoulders and thighs ached. So did his head. Sparks swam in his eyes. Nerves tingled in the tips of his fingers and the pit of his stomach. Even the heavy gravity of Junction felt pleasant now, a gentle hand pressing him against the flesh of the planet.

The chocolate-colored tubes of the forest swayed above him like the strands of the hair of a sunken giantess, swimming with strange and wonderful life. A lobsterish creature climbed jerkily up a stalk, hunted by a floating predator the size and shape of a Children's Day *koinobori* windsock. The ghostly pursuer billowed through the air toward its prey, darting out the brown dagger of its proboscis. Wood *thock*ed against wood and the lobster clunked hollowly onto the rocky ground. The killer windsock undulated downward to finish its meal.

Daisuke wondered why the forest floor wasn't littered with wooden shells. Was there something that ate them? Alien termites? Or perhaps something lived inside those shells? Alien hermit crabs? He smiled, anticipating asking that question of Anne.

And speaking of transmitting genes.... There was a whole biological circus grinding into motion now within Daisuke. A process that started with a glance, a smile, a kind word, a touch, or a kiss, and ended in the next generation. *Yes, gentle viewers, this is what it feels like to be a naturalist in love.*

He'd had girlfriends before his marriage and a few flings afterward. The difference had been startling. A semi-famous, theoretically wealthy, attractive man, Daisuke had found new sexual partners easy to acquire. The reproductive itch was easy to scratch, even if only for a few nights at a time. If only he had liked any of the women he'd slept with. Or they him, come to think of it.

Now, Daisuke certainly enjoyed *Anne*. And any doubt as to whether she reciprocated had been thoroughly squashed last night on the glasslands. He was breathing. His heart was pumping. Daisuke felt, as with all his endorphin highs, a nirvana-like state of unawareness, as if he was dissolving into the ever-spinning wheel of the gaudy living world.

That would be the part of the trek he'd edit out. Just say, "That was the most difficult day of my life," and skip ahead to the next exotic animal attack.

Whose idea had it been for Daisuke to haul this cart up a mountain, anyway? It had proved to be an excellent way to keep him too exhausted to focus on detective work. Not that he was very good at it, anyway.

Anne believed Pearson's death was an accident. Maybe he should trust her. *Trust her and kiss her and undress her....*

"Mr. Matsumori! Get up!"

Hariyadi was standing over him, voice tight with suppressed anger. Or was that fear?

"What happened?" Daisuke opened his eyes. By the shadows on the path and by the fact that he was still exhausted, he couldn't have been asleep long. "What's going on?"

"Sing ran away." That was Nurul, more obviously afraid than the soldier. "Anne and Misha ran after her, and Tyaney ran after them. We need you to track them down."

Anne! In trouble? Daisuke tried to spring to his feet, but his upward trajectory went sideways as every muscle in his back and legs seized up at once. Damn him, how could he have forgotten to stretch before lying down? All that time in Tokyo offices had made him soft.

"I'm fine!" Daisuke waved away Rahman's and Hariyadi's hands as he steadied himself against the cart and tried to rub some life back into his calf muscles. "What happened? Why did Sing run away?"

"You can ask her yourself when you find her," said Hariyadi. "You don't need me to tell you that our survival depends utterly on her on-the-ground knowledge."

"What about Anne?"

"She's also a priority," Hariyadi conceded. "We need her expertise. And Misha has the most medical training of any of us."

The colonel didn't mention Tyaney on his list of priorities, Daisuke noticed, which was a mistake. Even ignoring the questionable ethics of leaving someone to die in the wilderness just because he was a bit of a jerk, they needed Tyaney to translate for his wife. Calling Hariyadi out on his mistake would be counterproductive, though, so Daisuke simply resolved to rescue everyone. "When did they leave? Which way did they go?"

"Only a few minutes ago." Nurul had huddled in under Rahman's arm.

She asked him something in Indonesian and he pointed into the weeds on the south side of the path.

"We must go now," said Hariyadi. "Once we find them, we can reconvene at the cart."

Daisuke tended to agree. *With the party split in two, we could not afford to split up further. Aside from the aid and comfort company may bring, most predators will avoid a group of three or more humans. And thinking of which....* "Rahman," Daisuke said, "do you have a weapon?"

"No weapon," said the Indonesian. "Only camera."

My decision was easy to make. "Take my knife." Daisuke threw the small tool to the cameraman, who fumbled and dropped it.

"We don't have time for this," said Hariyadi.

"No more going into the wilderness unarmed," Daisuke said. "Now, sir, if you would give me your other gun?" He held out his hand as if expecting Hariyadi to actually agree.

"Absolutely not," Hariyadi said.

Of course, narrated Daisuke. *I wasn't one of his men. He would have gladly given the gun to Rahman, but Rahman would have been more dangerous to us than to any lurking predators. Nor would Hariyadi hand over his weapon to Nurul, a woman. Not unless the alternative was giving the weapon to me.*

"Although I suppose distributing resources would be better ...." Hariyadi sighed and unbuckled Pearson's holster from around his waist. Not meeting Nurul's eyes, he thrust the weapon in her direction.

"So the three of us are armed," said Nurul. "What about you?"

Thank you for the straight line. Looking as grim and badass as he knew how, Daisuke turned and removed an urchin spine from the cart.

"This is ridiculous," Hariyadi said. "What can you do with a spear?"

It's like we've rehearsed this. In answer, Daisuke swept the spine through the nearest clump of weeds, provoking a hailstorm of jumping, zebra-striped parasites.

"Anne calls those linguipods," said Nurul. "They might be dangerous."

"Then I will go first," Daisuke said, firmly in persona. "Now, follow me."

Now, hope that I can actually find the trail. Daisuke had certainly accompanied enough real wilderness trackers, pumped them for information, even spent time on camera following the instructions they'd given. He'd only been wrong about half the time.

As if he knew exactly what he was doing, Daisuke withdrew his flashlight from its belt-pouch and flicked it on. The beam of reddish light cut through the forest gloom, showing where the carpet of grasslike weeds had been disturbed by the passage of human feet. A blind man could have followed those tracks.

Oh thank goodness, thought Daisuke. *I would have looked pretty stupid if I'd sent us wandering in circles while Anne got eaten by carnivorous windsocks.*

The tracks led south, then turned east and paralleled the path for a ways before crossing a smaller trail. Or…no. Daisuke studied the rocky ground of the little trail, much harder to read than the hairy forest floor. "I think one person went that way." He pointed forward to the curtain-like fringe of weeds on the trail's other side. "The other three…." He shone his flashlight on the ground. Anne and the others had not crossed the trail, but turned south and paralleled it.

"Why didn't they follow Sing?" Hariyadi asked.

"Why didn't they use the path?" said Nurul.

"Because they learned something." Daisuke looked around the forest, its murky depths undulating with hidden dangers. "They saw something." *Something I should have seen before now.* "First Sing, then Anne and the others. They were…afraid of the paths." He imagined he could hear the minor bars of the song in his soundtrack titled 'Danger'. "And what else might be using them."

The four of them stood very still, watching the forest sway. Balloons rubbed and rumbled against each other. Something in the woods made a noise like the clacking of the bamboo arms of a hundred *souzu* deer-scarer fountains. The air held the burned-vanilla musk of rotting wood over the ever-present stink of sewage.

"So," Hariyadi said, "cross the trail. We must be close to Sing."

"We must be close to Anne and the others," said Daisuke. "You should all cross the trail and go after Sing. I will turn south and rescue Anne. And the others, of course."

"No," Hariyadi said. "We will not split the party again."

My thoughts exactly, but what about Anne? "Sir," Daisuke said, but Hariyadi did not allow him to finish.

"Go straight ahead, Mr. Matsumori. We need your expertise to find the native woman."

Daisuke paused, considering what Hariyadi would do if he simply turned and ran away toward Anne. *And how would it look on camera? Valiant warrior protecting his lady, or coward fleeing his duty? How much do I care about that?*

"I said, go straight ahead." Hariyadi rested his hand on his holster.

"It would be very foolish to shoot me," said Daisuke, careful not to let his anger show. He *would* rescue Anne. Screw this tiny tin-pot dictator and his guns.

He would have simply turned and walked away if Nurul hadn't pierced him with her gaze and said, "You aren't considering putting all our lives in jeopardy for the sake of your libido, are you?"

Daisuke opened his mouth. Closed it. *Thank you, Nurul.*

"And even if you save Anne," Nurul went on, "what good will it do if we lose Sing? Do you want Anne to die of starvation or dehydration or poison or animal attack without Sing's expertise to guide us?"

Daisuke let out his breath and gave a sharp nod. "All right," he said, and parted the weeds that separated them from the trail.

To the north, the trail rejoined the main path, where their cart rested, abandoned. To the south, down the path, wooden wind chimes ticked and clonked. Ahead, the weeds swarmed with linguipods.

"She didn't cross the path," said Daisuke.

"So which way did she go?" Hariyadi asked. "South or north? East or west on the main path or back into the forest? And what is that sound?"

"I don't know, sir." The path was rocky and bare of vegetation. Perhaps one of his expert consultants could have seen tracks in it, but he sure as hell couldn't.

Hariyadi cursed again. "We'll have to split up. Rahman, you run north, Matsumori, south."

"Wait," said Daisuke.

"No. You have to start now to have any hope of catching her up."

"You were right before. We shouldn't split up." Daisuke tried to arrange his thoughts. "Maybe we can predict where Sing will run, given what we know about her motivation. What were you doing before she ran away?"

"Talking," Nurul said.

"Talking? You were talking to her? How?"

"With only small words," Rahman said. "'Water', 'tree', 'death'. You know. But she *can* learn English, *insha Allah.*"

"Death?" said Daisuke. "She said 'death'?"

Nurul asked her husband something in their language. Rahman responded and Nurul put her hands to her mouth, nodding thoughtfully. Hariyadi barked an order, which caused Rahman to widen his eyes and take a step back, hands coming up between him and the soldier. Nurul spoke sharply to her husband, who shook his head, but stopped protesting.

Cut out of the conversation, Daisuke tried to think of something intelligent to do. What had scared Sing, and how would she try to escape it? Not by running down the paths. Not by running through the forest, at least no more than necessary until she found…a better way to escape.

Daisuke looked up.

Windsocks chased each other through a canopy of chocolate-colored balloons. Climbing log-worms clacked and scuttled. And there, three meters up, her legs wrapped around a kelp-tree stalk, was Sing.

The Nun woman had either found or made a knapped stone hand axe, which she had used to carve finger- and toe-holds into the kelp-tree's tough, gummy tissue. Now, slathered with stinking black goo from the plant's interior, she was sawing away at the material that bound the hydrogen-filled plant to the ground.

For a crucial moment, Daisuke simply stared at the woman. She must have heard them, must have known they were hunting for her. But she wasn't even looking down. Sing was totally focused on the task of untethering her balloon from the ground, mouth set, eyes wide as if with panic.

Now Daisuke's ears registered the fact that the bamboo-rattling sound was much louder. Closer. And from the sound of it, someone was walking, dragging something heavy up the trail toward them.

Hairs shivered up Daisuke's shoulders and neck.

But before he could say, "We have to get off of this trail," the creature emerged from around a bend.

It was the size of a compact car, huge and irregular and turreted. A mud-and-wood castle on wheels. Glassy eyes peppered its surface; arms flapped and spun and clutched in all directions. Tentacles or vines spread from its forward face and vanished into a scuttling mass of...little wooden cars?

Or little boats. Oar-like wooden limbs bristled from their sides. Some were hitched to carts. Others were capped by wooden arms carrying more knapped-stone implements. Flint knives glittered, glass-tipped scorpion tails ratcheted back. Pairs of slings counter-rotated. Bladders inflated with gas.

"Toys," whispered Daisuke.

Hariyadi stared, whining deep in his throat. Daisuke had seen it before, when one of his cameramen had been cornered by a leopard. The cameraman hadn't been armed, though.

"Shoot it!" Nurul screamed.

And Hariyadi opened fire.

The bullets struck the largest animal, or machine, or whatever it was. One of its four thick towers blew entirely apart, while two more ruptured, spraying black effluvia, strings of wooden disks inscribed like old Chinese money, and white ring-shaped worms. Toymakers.

Some of the calamari rings were caught by folding wooden arms like tiny construction robots. Many more of the toymaker organisms fell to the ground, and were lost under grinding wooden wheels.

The knocking of hundreds of wooden hammers became louder and higher pitched. A percussive alarm. A howl of toymaker rage.

★ ★ ★

"Oh, you idiots!" yelled Sing. "I don't want to have to see you die." Of course, they didn't understand her.

Weeping, Sing sawed harder at the kelp-tree stalk. The balloon above her swayed in the wind that would carry her away from this nightmare and back to her brother.

She must hurry. The Them and Tyaney might still snatch her back and re-imprison her. Deeper in the forest, Anne was gesticulating, saying something in her brash way to Misha and Tyaney. Had the Them woman seen Sing? Was she telling her companions to capture her? But the men did not look up. They ran down the path toward the place where Hariyadi, the slack-bellied fool, had shot the cargo carriage.

The toymakers were a gathering caravan, mobilized around the large cargo carriage. Their most likely destination was the lower western slopes, where they would gather glass to trade with Sing's people. And what a story that would be when she returned home. *I know where the glass comes from*, she would say, and her brother Yunubey would embrace her and everything would be all right again.

The caravan was crippled now. It no longer had the resources to travel down the mountain, so their only course of action now was to punish those who had damaged their cargo carriage. Make an example of them.

The Indonesians were shouting at each other; Hariyadi and Nurul ganging up on Rahman. None of them even spared a glance at the oncoming toymakers.

"You fools," said Sing, sawing. "Get off the path or they'll fill you full of darts."

The work was slow and awkward. The toymaker blade she had stolen was little more than a chip of stone, and Sing had to bend in half in order to bring it to bear on the stalk below her feet. The flexible brown material did not cut easily, and the effluvia that dripped out of the interior of the plant made her work slippery and uncertain.

And now, Hariyadi was pointing at her with his gun.

"Oh, you bent-backed, pus-filled sister-fucker," Sing said.

Thunder echoed again in the kelp forest and Sing jerked. Not, she realized, because her body had been pierced by one of those tiny metal arrows, but because her kelp-tree was sinking. She looked up at the balloon, now sagging, and cursed Hariyadi all the way to the ground.

Daisuke yelled something, which Hariyadi cut off with a curt order.

"No!" Daisuke said, one of the Them words Sing had come to recognize.

Hariyadi now pointed his gun at Daisuke. And all the while, the toymakers drew closer.

"You stupid, deformed Them!" shouted Sing. "Stop flailing that weapon around. The toymakers will kill us all unless we give them a sacrifice."

Daisuke seemed to understand her. He turned to Hariyadi and the toymakers closing on them. The oars of land-canoes rippled like a centipede's legs. Man-o'-wars made their stealthy way through the air between the stalks, the spring-loaded weapons hanging under the hulls swiveling to aim at the humans.

Either Daisuke didn't see the gathering enemies, or he didn't understand the danger they posed. "Sir, please," he said, "We— Ugh!"

The closest man-o'-war fired. Its plastic, stone, and glass bolt shot through the air and lodged with a sickening *thump* in the center of Daisuke's chest. He screamed.

★ ★ ★

A scream rang through the alien forest just as the bolt struck a kelp-tree right behind Misha's head.

Misha swiped out at the miniature blimp that had shot at him and knocked it spinning. "They have fucking *crossbows*?" he growled.

"That was Daisuke," Anne said. "Come *on*, I said." She bolted toward the sounds of battle, and Misha could do nothing but follow her. Sing might be there.

"Wait!" wailed Tyaney from behind them. "Don't leave me!"

Misha stopped to take his bearing and pain flashed up his shin. Hissing through his teeth, he hopped back, away from another damn toy-creature. This one waved an obsidian knife, dripping with Misha's blood.

He kicked the little bastard out of the way and called to Anne, "I thought you said the forest would be safe!" Shit. That English had been too good. But his leg stung like a motherfucker.

Anne didn't seem to notice the lapse. She was up the path ahead of him, dealing with her own attackers. "I didn't think somebody would start shooting at them— Ow! Christ, that's sharp! It's like they kicked a hornets' nest."

Which meant that Sing was in danger from more than just that kidnapping slimeball Tyaney. To rip that sweet little princess away from her family and turn her into a virtual slave? Misha swore he would kill the man if the toymakers didn't beat him to it.

"Come now!" he shouted, running past Anne.

Trees and soba-weed flashed past him. Little murderous wooden dolls. Some of them were airborne.

Speed was the key. These things moved like windup toys. Lots of strength, but not much speed and no flexibility. A single soldier in body armor could obliterate this alien threat with his hands. But Misha had no body armor. He didn't even have a baseball bat.

Misha had to make do with his crushing boots and punching fists. More obsidian-blade slashes. More blood loss. He'd suffered worse. And Sing needed him.

He broke onto the path, Anne and the disgusting native trailing behind him. He stood, took a moment to scan the scene. There was Sing, crouching next to Daisuke, who was lying flat on the ground.

Daisuke groaned and slapped at the crossbow bolt sticking out of his chest. It wobbled. Stuck, Misha saw, in the TV man's bodycam. The lucky bastard had just had the wind knocked out of him.

"Get up!" Misha yelled at him.

Hariyadi had the same idea. The other soldier stopped yelling orders at Rahman and addressed Daisuke. "Get up! We fall back! Back to the cart." He switched to Indonesian. "Get the…" *something* "…woman."

Sing, he must mean. Misha sprinted toward her, ducking to avoid a rock hurled by a miniature catapult.

"Back!" shouted Hariyadi, and another gunshot slammed against Misha's eardrums.

"Stop bloody shooting!" That was Anne's voice. "Disturb a toymaker and they'll hunt you down and kill you!"

"A bit late for that advice," Misha muttered. He reached out toward

Sing. She would know how to stop this. He would save her, and she would save them all.

* * *

Tyaney burst onto the trail, keening a Nun battle cry. "Oh, infelicitous witch born of cursed blood. All the spirits dead and unborn cry for your blood to be spilled. Cleanse it! Cleanse the hateful taint of the— Gah!"

He flinched back, but not far enough. The toymaker smashed into the side of his head, spraying bits of wood and glass. Tyaney stumbled, cold effluvia and warm blood sheeting down his face. That toymaker hadn't flown under its own power. Someone, some *person*, had thrown it at Tyaney.

Tyaney turned, snarling, ready to kill whoever had attacked him.

He saw every toymaker on the path had focused its periscope on him.

Tyaney looked down at the stinking black slime on his hands. Whoever had thrown that toymaker at him, they had marked him for death.

"No," said Tyaney.

A ballista bolt whizzed past his head. A rock smashed into his hip. He stepped backward, and a little wooden body rolled under his foot. Tyaney fell backward, down among the bustling toymakers. Obsidian blades flashed on all sides.

"Help me."

But the Them were retreating, running back to the cart. They wouldn't help him. They didn't like him. Tyaney wasn't part of their tribe, and now he'd never have the money or power to force the Them to obey.

"To the cart!" Hariyadi's voice rang through the forest. "Now, while they're distracted."

By butchering me. A sharp pain in his chest. Another in his leg. Now Tyaney knew how a tree must feel when it was felled by puny humans. Chopped into pieces.

Wooden wheels and stone knives blocked out his vision.

* * *

They ran toward the cart. Misha carried the protesting Sing and Anne tugged on Daisuke's arm as he stumbled along after, blood dripping down his front out from under his skewered, life-saving bodycam.

Behind them, the toymakers clacked with apparent glee as they chopped into Tyaney with their stone and glass hammers.

"Got to get the cart," Anne muttered as if to herself, tugging on Daisuke. "No point in escaping the toymakers if we starve."

Daisuke was in no position to judge her logic. Most of his brain was consumed with the pulsing agony from his chest. His body camera swung free, spinning around the fulcrum of the arrow that had pierced it. *At least it isn't embedded in my chest. At least I am not being butchered like Tyaney.*

Stones turned under his feet. Cold, stinking air burned in his chest like a vanilla-scented outhouse. His vision narrowed and darkened. Tyaney's screams cut off.

A restraining tug on his arm. Daisuke stopped. Blinked.

The cart was there. It lay waiting for them like an old forgotten treehouse. The site of so many childhood adventures that now, in the light of lethal adult experience, looked small and useless. A toy.

"Everyone, push," commanded Hariyadi. "If we can get past them before they're done with Tyaney, we might have a chance."

So Daisuke, bleeding and trembling though he was, took up the strap at the front of the cart and heaved. His vision blurred and washed red. *Broken blood vessel in my eyeball. Don't worry, gentle viewers, it's happened to me before. I've never lost a native guide, though, and I can't recall a time I was shot in the chest. Gentle viewers, never has your humble wilderness survivor been so close to… not surviving.*

The cart ground forward.

And never have I wanted to survive quite so much.

Daisuke felt the heat beside him. The solid presence of Anne Houlihan. She was yoked together with him like in that Buddhist aphorism.

"Ready and heave!" came Hariyadi's voice from somewhere.

The ground rolled out from under him and Daisuke flailed with his legs to stay upright. His feet found the ground. Bit in. Pushed.

Daisuke's chest was a roiling ball of agony. He blinked, but the blood did not clear from his eyes. The stalks of kelp-trees swayed and rushed past them. The cart rattled down the path, past a scuttling scrum of murderous little wooden robots, through the hostile, alien woods.

Until they hit the wall.

CHAPTER TWELVE

At the Wall

The cart rumbled under Daisuke. The kelp-trees rushed by overhead. Shapes flashed up there like ghosts or hostile aliens.

"Stop!" shouted Misha, and Anne said, "Of all the— A bloody wall?" before she lurched to a stop. Daisuke kept running for a few steps, the cart slewing behind him, before he tripped and nearly fell onto what, yes, appeared to be a wall.

It was a palisade of the woody skeletons of log-worms, cut to make sharp stakes and driven into the ground at an angle. Fortunately for Daisuke, that angle was downhill, the sharp points of the logs facing away from them. Rather than impaling him, the palisade had only stopped him.

Had Sing's people built this wall? Had their expedition made it to human habitation at last? But no. Sing didn't know this place. And the stakes protected the kelp-tree forest. This wall had been built by toymakers.

Daisuke risked a glance behind them. The forest was still and silent. No bamboo rods tap-tapped their coded messages of war. But how much noise need an armed clockwork dirigible make? The ambush could be drawing in around them even now.

"We need to cross this border," Daisuke croaked. He coughed, rubbed his chest. His shirt was sticky with blood, but the flow seemed to have stopped. It just felt like that time a kangaroo had kicked him. And the familiar weight of the bodycam around his neck had taken on a strange new imbalance. It tugged on his shirt as if something was holding it.

Daisuke examined the shaft protruding from his chest. It was made of wood. It had a divot at the end where it could fit into a firing mechanism. It even had three stubby fins to help it fly true. Daisuke only realized as he clapped his hands around the crossbow bolt what a stupid thing that was to do. But instead of debilitating him with pain, wiggling the bolt only pressed painfully against the bruise on his chest. Glass tinkled.

With trembling fingers Daisuke unbuttoned his shirt and pulled out his bodycam. The thick square of plastic came free, spinning at the end of its strap, bleeding bits of plastic and electronics around the shaft of the crossbow bolt that had impaled it.

"Dice, you okay?" Anne was out of her harness, standing sideways between two of the logs of the palisade.

Daisuke probed his breastbone. "Barely a scratch," he said in wonder.

"Good. So get a move on."

He did, slipping off the cart and pressing his painful way between the palisade logs. There was another fence beyond them at knee height, followed by a third at the level of his ankles. Definitely toymaker work.

Animal carcasses hung impaled from the stakes or lay decomposing on the ground. Some were mere piles of unidentifiable slime and scales. On others it was still possible to make out thick legs and long, curving claws. One of the corpses was the size of a brown bear.

Daisuke crossed the wall. The others were already on the other side arguing. "How will we get cart over bitch wall?" Misha complained.

"We cannot abandon our supplies," said Hariyadi. "And we must move quickly."

"Oh right. You're the one to give orders, Colonel Start-an-Interstellar-War," Anne said.

"Shooting it seemed the best thing—"

"I'll bet it always does, to you." Anne's face was red, her hands on her hips in full aggression mode. "But guns didn't work on the shmoo and they sure as hell didn't fucking work on that toymaker. Are you—"

Wait, Anne, Daisuke tried to say, but inflating his lungs began a coughing fit that totally failed to stop her from saying, "Are you trying to get us killed?"

Hariyadi drew himself up. Put his hand on the butt of his pistol. "I am not responsible for Tyaney's death. I am not responsible for Colonel Pearson's. I have done my utmost to preserve the lives of everyone on this mission—"

"No," said Anne. "That was me. I'm the one who's been keeping us alive. You've just been ordering me around as if, as if your bloody rank means anything out here. It was bad enough when you weren't actively endangering us all, but now? Oh no, mate, now I'm done with putting up with you."

Hariyadi's expression didn't change. His hand didn't move, either. "I did what seemed prudent."

"Prudent?" Anne stomped on the corpse-strewn earth. "If you hadn't blown up their convoy, the toymakers would have gone right past us and Tyaney might still be alive."

"Or that 'convoy' might have been a weapon that would have killed us all rather than only one of us," Hariyadi said. "It's all very well to point the finger of blame after indulging in hindsight, but we need a leader."

"Correct," said Anne, "but here's *my* question: why the hell should that leader be you?"

That question seemed to shock Hariyadi. He blinked, mouth working as if he'd never before considered the implications of letting someone else run the expedition.

"Of course it should be me," he said. "I have experience in leadership. I brought us to this point."

"Except for the two who died," Anne pointed out.

"More would have died had I not kept my head and given the orders that saved the rest of you." Hariyadi raised a finger before Anne could muster an objection to that. "And, had I not shot down Sing's balloon, she would have stranded us here."

Sing was squatting a little way down the slope with a blanket wrapped around her.

"Poor girl," said Misha. "She needs help."

Did she really? Had Tyaney really abused Sing, or had she been abusing *him*? Had those toymakers been an accident, a distraction, or a weapon? Had Tyaney's death been an accident or…not? No answer seemed to be forthcoming.

Daisuke felt the attention of the group swing back around. He could almost hear Anne spinning her mental engine, getting ready for what she thought was another round of rational argumentation. Had she forgotten Hariyadi's gun?

"So." The word rattled in Daisuke's chest, but Hariyadi's attention snapped onto him like a targeting laser. *Well, that's not so different from a spotlight.* "I think we should make sure the toymakers are gone, then try to move the cart to this side of the wall."

"If we can trust Sing," said Nurul.

This earned her a growl from both Anne and Misha.

Nurul grimaced. "If we can understand her, then."

There was more grumbling, but Daisuke had stopped paying attention.

At some point, they had crossed over the mountain. The ground east of them sloped into a clouded valley, then rose up again in another fold of mountain, this one colored a bright and artificial-looking yellow. At least the parts of it that weren't cloaked in shadow.

"Night is coming," Daisuke said. "We have to make camp fast."

"Right," said Misha. "Making camp. Nothing here but rocks and mud. Is too much to ask for hotel? Or at least McDonald's?"

"We can erect tents," Daisuke said.

Hariyadi grunted something, and Nurul said, "We can burn those fence posts."

Everyone agreed that was a great plan, except, apparently, Sing. Sing waited under her blanket until Daisuke had dug through their supplies, found the axe, and made his first chop against the wall. The Nun woman screeched like a demon.

Daisuke straightened slowly, his heart slamming against the inside of his bruised chest. "What?" he said. "What is the problem?"

"I can understand two words of what she says," Misha said. "'Toymakers' and 'death'. Maybe Sing thinks our vandalism of wall will cause...what is word?"

"A curse?" said Anne.

"Reprisal," Misha corrected. "If aliens knock hole in your civic infrastructure, what will you do?"

"But how do we know if the native is right?" Hariyadi asked.

"If Sing's our expert, she's our expert," said Anne. "She says don't cut down the wall, so we won't."

Daisuke thought of a cold dinner of surplus American army rations and felt like weeping. He looked down at the hatchet, shut his eyes tight. Sighed.

He turned. "What should we do, Anne?"

It was like watching a spotlight shift from Hariyadi to Anne. She was their leader now.

She didn't seem to notice. "What should we do? Obviously, we should make camp. Get the stuff off the cart. Misha, make sure Sing thinks this is a safe place to sleep. Better get the first aid kit too, for Daisuke. Anybody else have any wounds that need taking care of?"

"I will get the first aid kit," said Daisuke. While he was unspooling medical gauze and uncapping the tube of antibiotic ointment, he snuck a quick peek at their supply of morphine.

"What's the matter?" Anne said from behind him. "You hurt worse than you look, Dice?"

"No," said Daisuke. "No. I was just.... How much morphine did we use on Pearson?"

"How much did Misha use?" Anne asked. "Two syringes' worth, I think."

And indeed there were two empty spaces in the plastic roll. *So Pearson didn't die by overdose*, thought Daisuke, *but he didn't die by allergy, either. And now Tyaney is dead as well. And less subtly this time, as well. Killed in a second animal attack.*

"You want some help with those bandages?" asked Anne.

"No," Daisuke said, but she already had her arms around his chest. Her face was hot, pressed up against his cheek.

"Don't die," she whispered.

"I will try my best." He leaned down. Brushed his lips across hers.

Shouts from the cart.

Anne started. "What now?"

Misha was standing on the unpacked cart, axe in his hands, engaged in a shouting match with Hariyadi. It was hard to make out exactly what they were saying, but Daisuke didn't have to understand the conversation; he could see the problem. Behind Misha, Sing had stood, shrugging off her blanket, exposing the object she'd been holding.

It was woody and brown, about the size of a watermelon. A periscope like a bent drinking straw poked from its nose, swiveled toward him.

"*That's* why Tyaney called her a witch," whispered Anne, probably to herself. "Her people know how to tame toymakers."

Daisuke shivered, as if hearing the voice of a ghost.

Hariyadi's head swiveled toward her. "So, Ms. Houlihan, you think the toymakers are intelligent? What sort of threat do they pose?"

Anne only shrugged unhelpfully. "Well, I wouldn't say 'intelligent'. The toys are more like a termite mound. Part of the animals' extended phenotype. They don't *engineer* those land-boats, they just build them. And the land-boats built according to bad designs don't work, so their builders die and don't pass on their faulty genes. Or maybe…." She tapped her fingernails against her teeth. "Or what if the designs for the vehicles aren't coded for in genes at all – just a behavior where the toymaker worm observes an artifact like a cogwheel and then chews a piece of wood into a replica. In that case, the cogwheel is the replicator and the worm, genes and all, is just the machine it uses to reproduce itself."

The silence that followed was, depending on the source, uncaring, baffled, impatient, and infuriated.

Daisuke cleared his throat. "And what about threats?" he asked, walking toward the others and hoping the biologist would follow his lead.

"Yes!" barked Hariyadi. "What is the Nun girl going to *do* with that thing? Summon the other toymakers to chop us all to pieces? Or just help her run away again?"

"Hm. Good question," Anne said, as Hariyadi audibly ground his teeth. "Well, a toymaker could be a hunting animal like a falcon. It might carry messages. It might work as a sentry like a guard dog. They might even work as stores of information like books.... May I?"

Anne had stopped in front of Sing, and held out her hands, palms up in the fading light.

Sing said something that probably meant that that would be a very bad idea. But she glanced past Anne at Hariyadi and bit her lip. Seeming to come to a decision, Sing held out the toymaker vehicle for Anne to inspect.

"*Din-lulum*," Sing said, with the intonation of 'look'.

Daisuke looked. Or rather, peered over Anne's shoulder.

Sing's toymaker had no oars or wheels, only a set of immobile hooks along its underside, bracketing a bulbous, barbed device like a wasp's stinger.

"Oh," said Anne. "I see."

Daisuke glanced back at Hariyadi, who was grinding his teeth again. "What do you see, Anne?" he prompted.

"It must be one of the flying ones," Anne said. "A little wooden dirigible. Or a balloon, since I don't see any propellers or other way for it to—"

"*Din-lulum*," said Sing again and gave the balloon a little shake. Holding its hull firmly with her thumbs, ring, and little fingers, she tapped the wood with the nails of her pointer and ring fingers in a quick, odd little rhythm. In a high voice, Sing spoke, but not to Anne or any of the other humans present.

Daisuke's hackles rose.

The toymaker rang like a xylophone in counterpoint to the music. It shuddered in Sing's grip. The wasp stinger twitched and rotated.

Still chanting, Sing let go of the creature, which bobbed, weightless in the air. The stinger swept around, provoking hisses from Hariyadi and even Misha, but ended up only pointing toward the wall.

Sing cried out and gave a sharp double-click with her tongue against the roof of her mouth. The toymaker fired its weapon.

With a cartoonish *sproing*, the barb shot out from the 'stinger' like a harpoon from a spring-loaded gun. There was even a thread connecting the harpoon to the gun. The thread unwound from the end of the harpoon, now quivering in the palisade wall. That line went taut as the little balloon winched itself forward, winding back, until the little round body was perched, flush against the log.

"Huh," Anne said. "A spring."

This time Daisuke didn't wait for Anne to clarify her gnomic mutterings. He just asked, "What have you realized?"

"Oh, well." Then Anne noticed everyone was looking at her. "Nothing.

Just that if that's a spring in there, it probably comes from the inside of a treeworm, which lives, uh, one, two, three, four biomes away." She nodded to herself. "Plus we saw them collecting glass. I'd say the Nun have plugged themselves into a pretty extensive trade network. Impressive."

"Yes," said Daisuke, thinking about how Sing might have murdered her husband. She would have known that getting toymaker fluids on him would make him a target. Even if she had not been in a position to pick up a toymaker and hurl it at Tyaney, might Sing have simply ordered one of her wooden minions to smash itself into him? Did her mastery of the creatures extend to compelling them to suicide? And she had been with Pearson when the shmoo had attacked, hadn't she?

"We have to talk with her," he said. "We will ask her what she plans to do with that thing. How will it solve our problems?"

"How will we do that?" Hariyadi asked.

Daisuke turned to Anne, the only one of them who knew any Nun. "Can you ask her?"

"I'll try," said Anne. "Um, *mekaletya*, uh, why? *Dan mekaletya?*"

"*Dan meteklyetya ub-ak do?*" Sing squinted, shook her head. "*An dan nu meteklyeta ara diin-ny-en heib-lam.*"

"Enlightening," Hariyadi said.

"*Keb-lum. keb-lulum.*"

"That means 'listen up'," Anne said.

The toymaker clacked and clicked, shuddering with the force of whatever internal mechanism it used to make the signals. Invisible in the shadows beyond the wall, other toymakers answered.

Anne hissed through her teeth. "It's *talking* to them."

Daisuke saw Hariyadi stiffen and injected some calm. "I think it is warning them off. Like a guard dog."

Anne nodded. "Sing is on our side after all."

Hariyadi made a face while Nurul said, "At least Sing is on her own side, but we knew that already."

The toymaker made a *klack-klack* noise, a wooden mirror of Sing's tongue-click. There followed a hollow *klunk* as a hatch opened on the little balloon's roof. Inside, an animal shaped like a slice of calamari in an ink-black sauce contracted and relaxed.

"Hm," said Anne. "A doorway? An airlock?"

"A sphincter?" Misha said.

Sing turned to him and made pointing gestures toward her open mouth.

She nodded and pointed west into the kelp-trees. "*Jibna*," she said. "*Mek*."

"That's 'food', I think, and 'water'," Anne said. "She's telling us it's hungry. It's going to need toymaker biome material. Um, *Yoyo mekaletya bin?*"

Sing gave a Rahman-esque thumbs-up and Anne shrugged. "I guess she's going to go back into the forest."

Hariyadi said something complicated and probably sacrilegious in Indonesian, but evidently decided he had better things to do than keep Sing from venturing back into the forest they'd just fled. "We need food as well," he said. "Nurul, please prepare it while the rest of us disassemble the cart."

They worked together in silence as the sun slid behind the mountain they'd crossed. Ginger-colored light sprayed across the bruise-colored sky, and suddenly it was night.

But not dark. Daisuke could still see his hands clearly. His skin glowed like raw honey, the color of Anne's eyes.

She noticed it too. "Wha—?" Anne straightened from her work and looked eastward. "Light reflecting off the other side of the…no. Ha!"

Daisuke knew that noise. That was a sign of another miracle of Junction. Smiling, he looked past Anne at the other side of the valley, which shone.

It was as bright as moonlight, but as warm and alive as a candle flame. Light the rich yellow of sea urchin roe flickered and danced in intricate branching patterns across the slopes of the mountains across the valley. It was not fire, but light. Light running like water, or the electricity of firing neurons. Ki-energy made visible.

"What did Sing call it?" said Anne. "The Ground Sun Country? The Lighthouse Country?"

"It isn't…." Daisuke groped for explanations. "It can't be a city?"

"No. Humans would never string their street lights in such a crazy array," Anne said.

She was right. Illumination spangled out of a central bright spot like dew on spiderwebs or fireflies on the branches of a tree.

"Damn, I wish I could know what lives over there," she said.

"Whereas I wish we could return home alive," said Hariyadi, "and in good time. Are all the tents erected? If so, I shall take first watch, along with—"

"*Lihat!*" Rahman said, pointing excitedly down the length of the valley.

At first Daisuke didn't see much. The Lighthouse Country blazed in loops and skeins like an earthbound galaxy. Its warm light illuminated the mist that clung to the river as it ran toward the valley of the Deep Sky Country….

"What?" Daisuke said. He fumbled with his utility belt, snapped open his binoculars, focused on the lights he could see at the mouth of the river. These were not Lighthouse Country yellow, but flickering red with clearly visible columns of smoke.

"Campfires," said Daisuke.

"People," Rahman said.

Daisuke passed his binoculars to Anne, who passed them to Rahman, saying, "Nun natives? Camped on the other side of the valley?"

"Marvelous," said Rahman. "They help us! We walk to river, only thing."

'The Death Wind River,' Sing had called it, although Daisuke wasn't sure he wanted to remind the others of that.

"We shall see tomorrow," Hariyadi said. "In the meantime, we still have the business of survival to attend to."

Nurul asked the colonel a question in Indonesian, which he rebuffed with a curt growl. In English, he said, "I shall take first watch. With Rahman."

Nurul asked another question and Anne's brow wrinkled.

"What do you mean, 'enough time'?" she asked in English.

Hariyadi shook his head. "Never mind. Get some sleep. Rahman!" He said something to the cameraman, who gave the soldier a disgruntled look, no doubt tired of being ordered around. Nurul spoke, but Rahman only shook his head and slouched away down the hill. Hariyadi said something under his breath and took off in the other direction.

A less exhausted Daisuke would have pursued one or the other of the men and tried to mend fences, but Nurul and Misha were already making their way toward two of the tents. The third....

Anne was looking at him. Her eyes were nearly black in the amber illumination of the Lighthouse Country. Did he want to offer to share a tent? Would she say yes? Would that be wise? Yes, probably, and possibly not.

Daisuke cleared his throat. "I think I will stay awake for some time. I will watch the light on the mountain."

Anne looked away. "Sorry," she said. "Uh. Good night."

Well good. I've either confused her, mortally offended her, or stopped her from murdering me in private. Maybe all three? Daisuke watched light flicker over the hill, considering. Another member of their party had died. Again, the biology of this planet had killed him. And Tyaney, like Pearson, had been a difficult person to like. He had especially antagonized Anne. And aliens had butchered him.

It wouldn't be enough to convict Anne in a court of law. *Especially if the judge was in love with her...* Daisuke shook his head as another thought occurred. *Or especially if the judge was in the middle of a messy divorce and no longer trusted love...* What if his attraction to Anne, rather than biasing him in her favor, made him suspicious of her?

Small animals clicked along the rocky ground. Downslope, larger beasts hooted and whistled. A zipper unzipped.

Anne crawled out of her tent and advanced on him. "Hey," she said in a sort of shouted whisper. "Can I marvel at nature with you?"

Daisuke nodded deeply.

"I doubt that's bioluminescence." Anne faced the glowing mountainside, close enough for him to feel the heat radiating off her. "More likely that's reflected light from a wormhole. See how it's brighter in the middle? So for some reason, the vegetation there spreads the light from its home world across the mountain. I'm thinking of the way the Humongous Fungus in America shunts nutrients around an area the size of, what was it, eight square kilometers? What do you bet that all of the trees in that glowing forest are all just scions of the same rootstock?"

Daisuke watched Anne's eyes flick up to his, away, back again. She wasn't the subtle sort. She raged at her antagonists, shouted and stomped and stormed off. She didn't plot elaborate murder. Unless part of the plot was to appear prickly and antisocial in order to lower everyone's guard....

But Daisuke could go around in circles like that forever. The fact was that Anne wasn't entirely safe. She was an undescribed species caught in a beam of sunlight on the jungle floor. Possibly venomous, but beautiful and strange. Deserving of a closer look.

"It's very beautiful," said Daisuke, and put his hand around her waist. "Would you tell me more about it?"

"Hm." Anne leaned into him. "Naw. Let's kiss instead."

Daisuke put his hand to her bodycam. Not that his viewers wouldn't expect the Iron Man of Survival to kiss the girl, but that wasn't the scene he wanted to be in, right now. He wanted to be himself, expressing his true feelings for an audience of only one.

"Take that off," he whispered.

They were startled apart some time later by a clattering *thump*.

Sing had returned from the kelp-tree forest with an armload of supplies, which she had dumped in a careless pile before turning to her tame toymaker. After some more chanting, she tapped at the wooden oblong with one hand, while with the other she extended a dark object the size of an ice-cream cone.

The toymaker opened the hatch on its top and Sing fed the cone into it.

"Um." Anne cleared her throat. "Thank you. I'm very sorry about what happened to Tyaney."

Sing waved a hand, murmuring something in a tired voice. She gave Daisuke a smile and patted Anne's shoulder as she walked past her toward the tents.

Toward, in fact, Misha's tent.

"Eh?" said Daisuke.

Sing went up to the tent and gave a double tongue-click, as if she was signaling a toymaker. It worked; Misha unzipped the tent from the inside and Sing ducked in to meet him.

Daisuke turned and walked away before he heard anything more. Anne followed him, sniggering past the hand clamped over her mouth.

He tried to clear the feel of Anne pressed against him from his mind. Had the Russian conspired with the Nun to kill her abusive husband? Or perhaps he had thought he was rescuing her? Or had she murdered Tyaney as a gesture aimed at Misha? Or were the two of them just making the best of an impossible situation? He would have to talk to Misha to find out. Daisuke would have to talk to everyone....

"You want to turn in?" Anne said. "There's going to be a whole day ahead of us."

"Turn in?" She meant go to bed. Daisuke thought of Sing and Misha.

"Although, if I'm honest, I'd kind of like to take a bath first," said Anne. "I probably smell dreadful."

"No," Daisuke said, "you smell...." His brain caught up with him. "A bath?"

"Oh man, it'll feel good, Dice. A cold bath and a hot meal."

Daisuke frowned. He was missing something. "There's no clean water here," he said, "and nothing that will burn."

"Take a look downslope of us."

Daisuke did. In the light of the opposite valley, clear mountain streams shimmered amid lush folds of plant life. Bushes like piled mattresses or stacked PVC pipe, all of it as green as anything on Earth. All of it growing within ten minutes' walk of where they now stood.

For the first time since they'd crashed, the air didn't stink. It was sweet. Sharp and clean in Daisuke's lungs like the nose of a dry white wine. He hadn't realized how starved he was for the smell of photosynthesis, the sight of green plant life. It was like, after long, lonely years away at work, he had come home to his friends.

"We did it," Anne said. "We're in the oasis."

Daisuke tried to remember that they weren't actually home yet. They were barely halfway. Two members of his crew were dead, and Daisuke knew those deaths had not been accidents. But they could take a bath. They could make a fire. They were still alive, and could breathe in the sweet, green air.

"We work really well together," Anne said. "That's unusual. You know, for somebody I'm not...*just* working with. Um." She cleared her throat, looking at her boots.

"I was sort of expecting you to participate in this conversation, Dice," Anne said. "Or am I just supposed to seduce myself?" This couldn't be an act. If Daisuke was a shell with nothing inside, Anne was the yolk and white just sitting there on the mound of rice, pretending to be nothing other than what she was.

"So," she said. "What are you thinking about?"

'Eating you for breakfast' would be, perhaps, too forward. "I was thinking about how I am a shell with no egg inside, and you are an egg with no shell," he said. "Maybe that's why we suit each other."

Anne looked at him. "Naw," she said. "I think your ex-wife is wrong. You're not a hollow shell, you're just a big fucking nerd who doesn't know how to talk to human beings."

"That's...a strange thing to say."

"Ha. You mean it's the pot calling the kettle black."

Daisuke had to think for a moment before he remembered the meaning of that expression. He smiled and said, "It's better in Japanese. 'The eye-shit laughs at the nose-shit.'"

She screwed up her face. "Eye-shit?"

Daisuke rubbed the inner corner of an eye. He ignored the unmanly tear he found there and said. "You know, eye-shit. After you sleep, the stuff in your eyes. It shouldn't laugh at nose-shit, because it's all the same stuff." The word came to him. "Mucus!"

Anne's laughter bounced off the glowing mountainside. "Ah, the subtle poetry of the Land of the Rising Sun." She clapped her hands. "That's it, you've seduced me. Let's go to my tent."

CHAPTER THIRTEEN

Ripe Blood

Daisuke knelt before Anne, his muscles and bones protesting. It had been a long night.

This would have counted among the top ten hardest mornings of Daisuke's life, except that there were these beautiful soft arms and legs curling around him.

Daisuke explored the body pressed against him. Marveled at the way Anne gave when he sank his fingers into her skin. Generously yielding. Her mouth, parting in promise. Her soft moan in his ear. Her hair wrapping his fingers. Her scent.

"Would you stop sniffing at me?" she said. "You made your point. I know I'm totally gross, but hey, so are you."

I want to swim in a pool of your intimate scent. But he couldn't think of a way to say that in English without sounding disgusting, so he said, "It's okay. I like it."

Her throat vibrated under his mouth. "Enjoy it while you can."

"I will." His lips rose and fell across her like footsteps, laying a trail from one treasure to another. She moaned again, a signal in the wilderness. *Yes, go there!* And her hands pressed against his back, rubbing up his rib cage, down his waist. Searching for something.

Daisuke grinned against her navel. "You found me," he said.

But when he grabbed Anne's hips and tried to push her onto her back, the muscles on Daisuke's chest gave a sour *twang*.

"Tta!" he said, heart fluttering as if in memory of nearly being impaled on a crossbow bolt.

"Are you all right?" said Anne, and damn, the boiling honey was gone from her voice. She wasn't a tender goddess of love, but a concerned colleague on a disaster-stricken interplanetary expedition. "Daisuke, what's wrong?"

"Nothing," Daisuke said. "I'm all right. I'm actually surprised at how I am all right."

"Well then. Good." She snuggled up under his armpit.

He kissed her, rather more careful and clearheaded now, and tried to formulate a polite way to say, 'I still want to have sex, but I don't want to get you pregnant. Also, I should probably be on the bottom.'

He didn't get further than "I—" before Anne stuck her hand down the front of his pants.

"Very good," she said, and squeezed.

Daisuke pushed against her hand, his eyes filled with a vision of her face. The sweat beaded over her eyebrows. The pulsing emerald flecks in her irises. The freckles like stars. Daisuke's own eyes, he realized, were closed. Anne slid her hand up and those stars went nova.

Daisuke's muscles all went loose and he sank into the floor of the tent like gelatin into a mold. "Wow." Eyes still closed, he let the room spin around him, gentle currents lapping at his skin.

He drifted until, with a shock of cold air, Anne separated herself from him.

"No," Daisuke said. He squinted his eyes open and saw sunlight shining through the fabric of the tent just as it did through tents back on Earth.

"It's morning," said Anne.

"Good morning. Very good morning."

"We should get up."

She was on her knees over him, the light lining her wild hair with a corona of liquid gold, turning her eyes into deep pools the color of a Yucatan cenote. Her hands went to do up the lowest button on her shirt, drawing his attention to the tiny hairs on her skin, glimmering like diamond filaments in a line from between her breasts to her navel.

Daisuke was seized by the sudden imperative to give this woman an orgasm. Right now.

"But I want to…." *Make you do attention* would be gibberish in English, and he was pretty sure *make you come* would be crude. "It's my turn now."

That stopped her. "Your turn? What do you—"

Daisuke made a grab for her crotch.

"Whoa, now!" She put her hands to her mouth and stifled the yell, which became a giggle as Daisuke hooked her belt buckle with his finger and tried to pull her toward him.

"Stop that," she said again, smiling. "Later, Dai suki."

She was mispronouncing his name again, telling him she loved him. Anne kept one hand over her mouth, while the other worked to disentangle his fingers from the waistband of her pants.

"Promise me," Daisuke said, not surrendering a centimeter. "Promise me that I will get the opportunity to…" he flipped through several possible verbs, "…to return the favor."

"Yes," she said, tugging on his hand. "All right. It's a date. But not now. Everyone will be awake now and we don't have time."

Daisuke had been about to relent and let go. Now, however, he smiled and yanked Anne toward him, groin first. "Everybody?" he said. "What did I tell you about *everybody*?"

"Fuck 'em?" Anne needed both hands to stifle her burst of laughter, which left Daisuke's hands entirely free. He made good use of his opportunity.

Anne gasped and squeezed her eyes shut as Daisuke's fingers oriented themselves. She sank down as he rolled over, propping himself up on an elbow. He watched her churn against the floor of the tent. The thermal blanket stretched between her fists, breasts rolling out of her unbuttoned shirt, eyes shut tight, lips pursing.

*I've never had so much passion for Eriko. I was never…*the word came to him in English: *wild.* What would the preposition be? *I wasn't wild for her.* Daisuke leaned over and kissed her as his fingers continued their work. She breathed into his mouth and he smelled Earth. Human animals, wrapping their home ecosystem around them like a comforting blanket. Spreading themselves.

Anne screamed into the wadded-up thermal blanket.

Daisuke, whose mind had begun to wander, watched her press the blanket against her mouth and nose and thought, *I can't hear a thing. I bet you could smother someone under a blanket like that.*

It was a very weird thought to have during sex play. But it was true, Daisuke was sure. Daisuke knew how Pearson had died.

Anne clamped down around his hand as her head whipped back. Sweat beaded her upper lip. She gave a very small squeak and a long, draining sigh.

"Hey," she said. "Try not to look so smug."

"The word you are looking for is 'proud'," said Daisuke.

"Let's settle on 'satisfied'."

Daisuke tried to keep his expression blank as they left the tent and walked toward the people squatting around their pile of supplies.

"There you are," Hariyadi said. "At last."

"What is this glow I see in the air?" asked Misha. "Should I maybe applaud and throw roses?"

Anne responded in her usual manner. "If you needed us, you could have come to our tent."

"Next time, I will," said Hariyadi sourly, but Daisuke wasn't paying attention to the colonel. He squinted at Misha. And at Sing, who was sticking out from under the big Russian's arm, chin up, eyes focused on the distance as if she couldn't wait to be over the horizon. And, come to think of it, Rahman and Nurul had a particular glow about them too. The couple was sitting modestly apart, not even holding hands, but Rahman kept looking at his wife and grinning.

Well, it made sense. Yesterday had been a howling typhoon of death and exhaustion. They might or might not have made first contact. They might or might not have sacrificed one of their number to the spirits of the forest. They certainly didn't have enough food or water to get them to civilization. Why shouldn't they take the opportunity to enjoy life when it came?

"Because we all have duties," Hariyadi said.

Daisuke started, then realized that the colonel couldn't actually read minds. He was just responding to something Anne had said.

"Duties?" Anne said. "We're past duty, Hariyadi, and we're into necessity territory. We need water. We need wood to make a fire that can boil that water. Then meat. Then clean clothes and hair. Then, and only then, do we start to think about how we're going to get out of this valley."

"We saw campfires over there," said Daisuke. "Down the river on the eastern edge of the mountain opposite."

"Really?" Anne said. "Humans?"

"Unless you think there's some alien in the next biome over that can light fires," Nurul said.

If that was sarcastic, Anne didn't seem to notice. "It must be the Nun. Unless it's the rescue party. But why would they camp out at the edge of the Deep Sky Country? It would be one weird way to mount a rescue party."

"People," said Nurul. "How soon can we get to them?"

Misha made musing noises. "Maybe very soon. If we copy Sing and ride balloons across valley…."

"Don't be ridiculous," Hariyadi snapped. "I told you whether we arrive at Imsame later or sooner, it makes no difference."

Nurul made a shocked noise, looking at her commander as if he'd uttered an unthinkable blasphemy.

"Never mind," Hariyadi sighed, suddenly sounding very tired. The Indonesian had come to resemble a rotting strawberry, his face slowly sagging into red-brown wrinkles. The white stubble on his cheeks looked more like mold than beard. "There is…no need for hurrying. We shall rest here."

"It makes a difference whether we starve to death or not," Anne said.

"Sing says we can eat the animals here and burn the plants," Daisuke pointed out. "I think we can relax. Maybe."

"But will something explode or devour us?" Misha cocked an eyebrow at Daisuke. "Maybe."

Anne squinted at him. "So if you're done being sarcastic, do you want to go or stay?"

Misha shrugged. "Does it matter?"

"No," said Hariyadi. "I am in command and I say that we stay."

Now was not the time to challenge Hariyadi's command. "Sir," Daisuke said, nodding to the exhausted-looking soldier. "The water and firewood we need for a bath we will need anyway to drink and cook our food."

Hariyadi's pouched, bloodshot eyes focused on him. "All right, Matsumori," he said, "you and Houlihan are in charge of our survival initiative. Find water, find meat. Find something that will burn. Take Sing, take Misha to translate. Take Rahman with his camera and record the whole fascinating process in HD. Nurul and I shall remain here and guard the camp. Don't forget to take buckets as well."

It seemed Daisuke's deferential strategy had worked. "Thank you, sir," Daisuke said, and bowed low.

Anne giggled the whole way to the supply cart. "What?" Daisuke asked.

"Men is what," she said. "Sir, permission to wash my underpants! Underpants-washing permission granted! Sir, thank you, sir! My laundry will be both pretty and fresh-scented, sir! It's cute." She ruffled the hair on the back of his head as if scratching behind a dog's ears. Daisuke liked it.

They had planted their tents on the strip of muddy rock that girdled the mountain from the palisade. Clearly, that wall marked a defensive boundary, not a biological one, for toymaker biome plants still grew downslope of it. There were no kelp-trees here, but noodle-like brown tendrils waved in the slightly stinking south-easterly breeze. These grew small and thin as they descended, and the stink grew worse.

"Ugh!" Misha made a face. "This is even worse than on other side of mountain."

"Waste products building up," Anne said. "There are pathways in the climax ecosystem to recycle everything, but down here, we'll get a buildup of poisons."

"I don't understand," said Rahman. "Should I film this?"

"No," Anne said, picking her way down the muddy, stinking slope. "Save your film for when we get out of this wasteland." And as if to herself, "It *is* a waste too. On the other side, the toymakers made some effort to extract resources from glassland plants....Over here either the plants in the Ripe Blood Country have nothing in them the toymakers want, or— Aha! Look there."

Daisuke tried to figure out what had excited the biologist. All he could see was the curly brown tendrils of Toymaker Country grass. And even the grass was patchy and balding, like an old rug.

"Look at that dead place," she said. "What's that mound of stuff in the center?" She answered her own question, prodding the black dry material with the toe of a boot. "Dead material. And not from a kelp-tree. It looks more like...packing peanuts. Or little sponges. Washed up from the next biome, and clearly toxic as hell to this one."

Daisuke squinted. Now he could see other mounds of packing peanuts, some downhill, taller and surrounded by larger dead patches, others smaller, uphill, and grown over with curly brown weeds. He was reminded of the terraforming pools north of Imsame. Except....

"Washed up?" Daisuke said. "We are not in a marsh by the sea. We are on a mountain, and there are no waves here." He pointed at the clump closest to Anne. "So something carried those little sponges up here. Maybe to use as fertilizer?"

"Toymakers," Misha growled.

Sing's head came up. "Yes," she said.

Daisuke blinked. "Was that English?" She hadn't quite gotten the word right – it was more like 'yays' – but who was he to critique her pronunciation? Daisuke still sometimes slipped and pronounced 'yes' with two syllables.

"Yes," said Misha. "English. I teach her."

"Oh, I bet you do," Anne said. "So what, she's spending the nights in your tent now that her husband is dead?"

Misha drew himself up. "None of your business."

Rahman sniggered. "Before that. Back on glasslands, Misha and Sing walk out together...like dating?"

Which would explain why Tyaney was in such a foul mood climbing up the mountain. Some detective Daisuke was, for missing this affair going on under his nose.

He found himself looking at Sing, who gave him a hostile glare and took a step toward Misha.

"And she's what, ten years younger than you?" said Anne. "Sing, *dan Misha*, for Christ's sake?"

Sing turned her glare on Anne. "Misha good."

"*Tochno tak. Malysh.*" Misha squeezed her against his side. "Say again Misha is good guy."

Sing pointed east. "Down green, *an* wait. Here food *mekaletya.*"

Daisuke didn't understand that, but Misha evidently did. He let go of Sing, who squatted by the nearest pile of fertilizer. She had slung Misha's utility belt around her shoulder like a bandolier, and now she rifled through its pockets until she found a thick curling sheet that Daisuke realized must be a section of kelp-tree, cut lengthwise and unrolled. Sing used this sheet to scoop up and wrap the fertilizer, producing a large, stinking roll. This, she tied neatly with a twist of brown weed and secreted back in her utility belt.

"She needs to collect food for her pet toymakers," Misha explained.

"I see," said Anne, arms crossed, still scowling. "So, you're going to replace Tyaney now?"

"Replace that fucking bastard?" Misha turned to look at Anne. Daisuke found himself widening his stance, clenching his fists, preparing to defend her, but all the Russian said was, "If you were a man, I would beat you for saying that, but since I must be gentleman, I say only that you know nothing, so please shut up."

"Go?" Sing said. "Down green. Food go."

"I agree, my dear," said Misha. "Let us depart." The couple turned and strutted down the hill.

"Damn it, Misha," Anne called after them, "can't we go a day without interpersonal drama on top of the alien animal attacks and starvation?"

Misha looked over his shoulder. "What drama? I have Sing, you have Daisuke. Rahman has Nurul. Hariyadi has duty to Mother Indonesia. We go get water. Everyone is A-OK, okay?"

Daisuke suspected that everything was not A-OK, but Sing and Misha were already several meters down the mountainside, with Anne stomping after them.

"Come on, Rahman," Daisuke said. "Let's go before they leave us behind."

No answer from the Indonesian.

"Rahman?" Daisuke's shoulders tensed. What if this hillside was home to some kind of predator? What if the toymakers had followed them? His chest stung as if in memory of a flying crossbow bolt. Hand going for his knife, Daisuke ground the balls of his feet into the rocky mud. "Please answer me, if you can."

Daisuke spun, and found himself staring into the cold, unsympathetic eye of a video camera.

"Don't talk to me, please," Rahman said from behind the thing. "I am filming."

Daisuke closed his eyes and rubbed the place where his wedding ring had been. When he opened them again, he found he could smile. "Oh! I am sorry," he told his audience. "You surprised me. Yes! Well. Here we are on the other side of the…what we are calling the Outer Toymaker Mountains. We had quite an adventure…no…. One of us is dead…." He shook his head. *Bad idea.* "Cut that, please." He cranked the smile up a notch. "Now look at the place we have come to!"

The camera panned mercifully away from Daisuke, up then across the gray mist of the Death Wind Country, the lush yellow of the Lighthouse Country with its tiny trails of campfire smoke.

They would want Daisuke's voice over this. "Beautiful, isn't it?" he said, letting whatever words that wanted come. "That yellow color on the other side of the valley? What is that? We don't know, and honestly I hope we don't have to find out." He chuckled. "On this side of the valley, the plants are green, which means they might be something like the plants we find at home on Earth."

Rahman caught Daisuke's gesture. He panned down to focus on Anne, Misha, and Sing, then past them to where the mud became green weeds, which in turn became a pulpy sort of scrubland.

"What interesting forms the local plants take!" Daisuke enthused. "From here I can see no animals, but our native guide assures us that they are delicious." He laughed. "Well, let's go!"

With the camera's regard heating the space between his shoulder blades, Daisuke picked his way down the mountain toward a small stream that emerged from a cleft in the rock. Toymaker grass and curly soba-weed grew around its edges, inhabited by the snaillike creatures Anne called linguipods. The water itself was striped brown and green, perhaps from colonies of algae from two biomes? Daisuke would have to ask Anne, if he could make her stop shouting.

"It doesn't matter whether he was useful to us. It doesn't matter if none of us liked him. Tyaney was still a person and he's still dead." She turned to scowl past Daisuke. "Rahman, what the hell are you doing? Are you *filming*? Put the camera down!"

She stomped in the mud and Rahman retreated. He didn't stop filming, though.

"So?" said Misha. "Why so upset? Tyaney is dead. And?"

Anne whirled on him. "*And* we haven't talked about his death at all. We haven't done or said anything. We just...kept going. Hell, *you* didn't wait a day before—"

Misha went red. "I told you I'd hit you—"

Daisuke kept smiling, just in case the camera ever chanced to pass across his face. What if someone had thrown that toymaker at Tyaney back in the kelp-tree forest? With its blood or nutritive fluid on him, the other toymakers had swarmed the unfortunate Nun and given the rest of the party a chance to escape.

So. Sing had killed her abusive husband. Or Misha had killed him for her. Or Hariyadi, or Anne, or Nurul, or Rahman had killed Tyaney because it was that or lose their only guide.

Misha and Anne were talking to Sing, who of course couldn't understand them, or if she could, could not make her answers understood.

"Now you upset her!" Misha said when the Nun woman's yelling and flailing got too loud. "Quiet, little Sing. It's all right."

"I agree with Anne, though," said Daisuke.

"Of course you do," Misha said.

"I mean that we should say something about Tyaney."

"What you want?" Misha asked. "Death ritual for man chopped into little pieces by clockwork robots? You want to go back and collect pieces of him to bury?"

"No, but we need a ritual. A..." Daisuke found the word, "...memorial service even if there can be no funeral."

The camera focused on him. Of course, the audience would expect the memorial service right now. Daisuke had no choice but to close his eyes and bow deeply. "Of course, I will be honored to give that service." He straightened, wishing he could just lapse into Japanese. "Ah...Tyaney was...a difficult man. A difficult to understand man. He spoke with us, but did we listen? Or did we put the words in his mouth we wished were there? We wanted a native guide we could talk to, a person who would help us survive and understand this strange new world. But Tyaney was not a native. He was as much a stranger to Junction as we are. And he did not help us out of some sense of honor or nobility. He helped us because we had something he wanted."

Daisuke turned east, toward Imsame and the Death Wind Pass and the wormhole home.

"He wanted what we all want. Safety. Security in the future. Power so he could make his vision of the future true. A piece of this world."

"Well obviously!" Anne said, ruining the moment. "And remember none of this" – she spread her hands at the landscape around them – "would have happened without him. Tyaney told the world about Junction. Would you go back in time and stop him from doing that? 'Cause I wouldn't."

Daisuke cleared his throat. The camera turned back to him. "We should sympathize with Tyaney. Tyaney was selfish. He was ruthless. He was willing to hurt, or enslave, or kill to grab a piece of Junction for his people. He was just like us, and we did not understand that. We did not understand him, and he died."

"Amen, I suppose," Anne mumbled.

Daisuke nodded. "Now. Let us see what we have here. Good water to drink?" He squatted to dip his hand into the pool.

"No!" shouted Sing.

Daisuke jerked back. "Why can't we drink this water?"

"Water. Water no *nun*."

"Us," translated Anne.

"Us," Sing said. "Water no us. Water toymaker."

Daisuke looked at Misha, who shrugged helplessly.

"Water toymaker. No us." She pointed to the edge of the pool. "Water us."

What did she mean? Daisuke stood and walked to where she was pointing. The pool's uphill rim was flush with the soil, but the mountain sloped down while the spongy tube that contained the water maintained its height. It was as if someone had half buried a bathtub in the side of the mountain. Except this bathtub wasn't watertight. Droplets seeped out of the wall of the pool, creating a second, very different pool.

"Take a closer look at that, would you?" Anne asked.

Rahman knelt, dragging his camera from the stinking brown water of the upper pool, across the weeping wall to the lower pool. Green threads undulated in the water there, indistinguishable from algae on Earth. Fishlike creatures, all paddling legs and undulating tails, swam against the current, waiting for scraps of organic detritus to fall off the filter-wall. Tiny three-legged creatures skated across the surface tension of the water.

"It's clean," said Anne. "Do you get what we're looking at? This is like the settling pools at Imsame, except nobody designed it. That spongy wall is alive; a biological filtration system evolved all by itself!"

"What could we do with these things if we took them to Earth and used them in sewage treatment plants?" Daisuke said.

Misha laughed. "I was hoping for cure for cancer, but am willing to settle for cure for shit."

Fortunately, Daisuke didn't have to think of a segue for that.

"Look at this," Anne said. She was leaning over a bush by the river. The bush's branches were chains of puffy, thumb-sized segments, shading from ivory-colored near the ground to green at the branch tips. She gently squeezed one of the segments.

"They remind me of those ecofriendly starch packing peanuts. The ones you can lick and smoosh against each other so they stick together?"

"So is that what these...peanut bushes are?" asked Daisuke. "Structures assembled by someone else? Some*thing* else?"

Anne didn't appear to have heard his question. "You can build a pretty good model of a polypeptide that way. Or for that matter an anatomically correct mannequin of my biochem tutor."

"Would you two please take this seriously?" Daisuke said. "I don't want all of our footage cut."

"Daisuke, my sweet, I am operating mostly on endorphins at this point. You want to get more than impulses from my brain stem, you put some meat in me— Oh my Lord, that sounded filthy." She broke into a fit of giggling.

"All right," said Misha. "So enough with nature documentary. We must focus on two things. Making fire and cooking animal."

"No, keep filming," Daisuke said. "This is exactly what our audience wants to see. Anne, maybe we can burn some of those peanuts?"

She wiped her eyes. "Oh, hell, I don't have the faintest. Sing? Can we burn this plant? Okay? Fire?" She turned her hands palm up and wiggled her fingers. "Whoosh? Okay? Fire?"

Sing didn't appear to have any idea what Anne was talking about.

"Let's call that a 'yes'," said Anne. "Misha, hand over your knife. Daisuke, you gorgeous fillet of man-steak, catch me a fish to barbecue and I'll reward you with sexual favors."

Daisuke swallowed, and reached for his belt.

"Why my knife?" Misha said. "You have knife."

"I don't want to ruin my knife when this thing explodes or turns into acid or something." Anne held out her hand. "Lively now."

Misha handed his knife to her. "You want lighter also?"

"If you would be so kind, comrade. Here we go!" She sliced the branch off, revealing its hollow interior.

Faster than Daisuke could blink, that hollow space filled with paste. Pale foam bubbled out of the plant, hissing.

"Would you look at that?" said Anne. "It has its own insulation foam. Presumably the green photosynthetic cells will colonize the foam in due course. And look, the branch I cut off has its own blob of foam." She prodded it with the knife-tip. "As hard as a sponge already! I bet it'll burn up a treat too. Misha, hand me your lighter."

"Only if you give me back knife."

"Okay, serious science time. Let's say these things are sort of land-sponges. They grow by releasing a burst of paste from this thing here." She prodded the green tip of the branch she had severed. "The paste forms foam, which is then colonized by algae. Where's that lighter, Misha?"

The Russian reluctantly gave Anne his lighter, and she shuffled back, holding out the lighter to the severed branch on the ground. "Here we g—"

The flame raced over the branch. When it touched the tip, the branch burst, spraying foam that smothered the fire. The entire process took less than a second.

"Huh," Anne said.

Daisuke reached for an appropriate summary. "The firewood here comes with flame-retardant?"

Sing said something in Nun. She extracted herself from under Misha's arm and plucked another branch off the peanut-bush. She removed the bud at the end of the branch, unconcerned about the blob of foam that formed over her fingers, and handed the denuded branch to Anne. "Yes. Fire."

"Thank you." Anne applied the lighter to the branch, which, without the flame-retardant foam, burned to ash in five seconds. "Well, there's another problem. How are we going to build a stable fire if everything here goes up like tissue paper?"

"We catch fish in stream and eat raw," Misha said.

"First of all," said Anne, "they're more armored leeches than fishes...."

"And I don't want to eat them raw," Daisuke said.

"What kind of Japanese man are you?" Misha said. "You grab fish!"

Daisuke looked into the stream, where the crab-like creature walked slowly across the mud.

"Sing," Anne asked, "can Daisuke eat the fish? Daisuke fish *deb* fish okay? *Gum* fire? I mean, *ukwey gum*? She doesn't understand. Can you demonstrate, Daisuke?"

Daisuke snatched up the little crab. Its four legs wriggled. Eating this thing would look *excellent* on camera. "Fish!" he said.

"Daisuke eat fish okay?" Anne tried again. "Daisuke *deb* fish? Fish *dena* okay?"

"Yes, yes," said Sing impatiently. "Daisuke *adya hadya ara deb-lem-la-a* okay *ub-la*. Daisuke fish eat okay."

"Well, it doesn't get clearer than that," Misha said. "Rahman, you are filming, yes? Happy you're on that side of camera, yes?"

"Ya!"

"Tell them I died doing my job, and I loved every second of it." Daisuke put the crab into his mouth and crunched down. His eyes went wide, then crinkled up to match his utter confusion. *This is the face that's going to appear on the cover of my biography, I'm sure of it.*

"Ah. Mm! It's good," Daisuke said, the same as he did whenever he ate anything on camera. "Crunchy. Salty, with a very light sweetness and," he breathed in through his nose, "bananas?" The crab tasted like salty bananas.

"Ah," Misha said. "The fish made him crazy."

Daisuke swallowed. "It tastes like bananas. Sweet." He wiped his mouth, raised his hand to examine his fingers. "With red blood. Just like ours."

Anne turned to Sing. "What did you call this place? The Ripe Blood Country? Thank you!"

"Welcome," said Sing.

"Okay," Rahman said, lowering his camera. "Now we catch another meat for everyone. Take back to camp."

"Or," said Misha. "You go bring them here. This is better camping site than muddy rocky mountain side."

"No." Anne got up. "We all have to go back up the hill. They'll need help moving our stuff. But I agree, we should move camp."

"Camp?" Sing said. "Camp!" She pointed.

"What?" said Misha. "How do you know that word? What are you pointing at?"

They all looked east, where a fluted hill rose up above the pulpy foliage.

"Is that," said Anne, "smoke?"

Daisuke shook his head, searching in his utility belt for his spotting scope. "No, it's steam. Smoke moves differently."

"So what?" Misha asked. "We look at volcano?"

Daisuke fitted the scope to his eyes and the mound sprang into focus. The mound and the dark green-and-black globe that hovered at its apex.

"No," he said. "We're looking at another wormhole."

CHAPTER FOURTEEN

Death Wind

Dusk had fallen by the time Daisuke and the others got to the wormhole.

The green-and-black globe hung at the peak of a fluted mound of earth, steaming gently against the cool purple sky. It was very similar to the High Ground Hole, the one that led to Earth, except here the plants were like frozen splashes of muskmelon liquor. And this wormhole steamed.

"Look at that vapor plume," said Anne. "That wormhole must open somewhere warm and wet."

"That sounds nice," Daisuke said into her hair.

She swatted him on the nose. "Stop that. I'm theorizing. And it has lower gravity than Junction. Lower than Earth too, I reckon. The Ripe Blood Planet? Planet Oasis? Inhabited by packing-peanut-trees and lizard-bugs…."

He snaked his arm around Anne's waist and gave her a squeeze. "Can I do this while you theorize?"

"Easy there, Dice. I plan to clean at least some of the filth off me, warm up by the fire, eat some native wildlife, and then we can get down to the business of enjoying each other."

"How much can I help with bathing?"

"No."

Daisuke enjoyed the simple sensations of love and food. Too soon he would have to resume thinking about the deaths of Pearson and Tyaney, not to mention the task of hiking the rest of the way home. Daisuke sighed, looking uphill toward camp.

Where something moved. *Scuttled.*

"Anne?" he said.

"Dice?"

"Don't move."

Of course, Anne immediately spun, looking up at the hill of the Ripe Blood wormhole. Two creatures trundled down that slope like crab-walking acrobats.

"Hey!" came Misha's voice. "Lovey dovies! Do not let dinner escape!"

This order Anne obeyed, stepping into the path of the animals and waving her arms.

"Yah!" she said, and the creatures skidded to a stop, peering at her with bulbous eyes set at the tips of long, tube-shaped heads.

They looked either like spiky tortoises or giant shelled hedgehogs, with four sturdy legs under broad backs. A third pair of limbs ended in crab-like pincers, currently clasped below where the heads met the bodies. As Anne stared, unsure what to do, the farther animal lost interest and lowered its long head to the stream. Its eyes swiveled over the surface of the water while its broad, spiny tail curled up over its back, pulsing. The nearer of the pair kept its eyes on Anne. Mouthparts unfolded from its head like the implements in a Swiss army knife, and a pair of hairy antennae flicked out to taste the air like the tongue of a snake.

"Aha," whispered Anne. "Evolved your mandibles from limbs, did you, you clever little bastards."

"Don't worry, I'll kill them," whispered Daisuke.

Anne laughed. "Could you be any manlier? I'm not sure how you plan to…."

"Like this." Daisuke shuffled past her. He didn't get any closer to the two tortoise-hogs, but his path took him, as if by coincidence, to a point just behind them.

The first tortoise-hog stopped drinking and lifted its periscope head to focus its eyes on Daisuke. Its pincers snipped nervously at the air.

But Daisuke kept still, and those claws descended to clip pieces off the ground cover and pass them to the complicated mouth.

"Herbivores," Anne whispered. "And heavily armored. See the spikes on the tail, the legs. Those claws. These things won't be easy to hunt."

"Even so, if I drive it into the water…." Daisuke took another step forward, and the nearest creature's head and claws came up. Its legs swung out as if on hinges until the knees pointed sideways. The animal sidled away from Daisuke up the bank of the stream.

Daisuke darted forward to head the tortoise-hog off. It curled its spiked tail toward him and rotated its legs again, trying to get them into position to run forward into the stream. Daisuke got to it first and kicked it under the belly, flipping it neatly onto its back.

The second tortoise-hog scuttled away as Anne rushed to join Daisuke, but he seemed to have the creature well in hand. Its pincers waved at him, but Daisuke grabbed them at the base where they connected to the animal's body and twisted them off. He did the same with the head, leaving a body the size of a car tire, attached to four columnar legs and the spined, beaver-like tail. The legs churned ineffectually at the air while Daisuke yanked them off.

"Shades of Galapagos, isn't it?" Anne said. "I'm not so sure I like this."

But hunger evidently trumped conservationism. Anne helped drag the thing back to the firepit.

Hariyadi, who had been scowling over Rahman's attempts to keep the fire alive, turned at their approach. "Do you plan to butcher that thing here?"

"Let's call it a field dissection?" Anne said. "You can tell Rahman to bring his camera over."

"No time for butchery," said Misha, carrying the still-kicking body of the tortoise-hog. "Oasis plant life burns too fast. Just drop meat on fire."

He followed his own advice, and the big turtle-like body cracked and hissed amid the spurting yellow flames. It smelled delicious, if disconcertingly fruity.

"Like caramel corn," Daisuke said.

"Caramel what?" said Misha.

"Would you be quiet?" Hariyadi snapped. The Indonesian soldier had been in a foul mood since morning. He gritted his teeth and stared east, where the valley of the Deep Sky Country was visible, but still at least two days' hike away.

"Where's the other one?" Nurul asked, dropping an armload of foamy vegetation on top of the boiling carcass.

"Why do that?" demanded Misha. "Firewood goes *under* food. Put next armful to side."

"Why?" Nurul said. "I don't need to get more."

"We will need more firewood for more animals. I will go hunting."

Hariyadi harrumphed. "It is a bad idea to go off alone. Daisuke. Go with him."

Anne grumbled something about not hearing a 'please', but Daisuke could hardly refuse. "I will rest first, please," Daisuke said, sinking to his knees. It felt good to fold his tired legs, and the blazing fire felt even better.

"Aha," Anne said, in a different kind of pleasure. She was holding up one of the claws Daisuke had yanked off the tortoise-hog. "It's not exactly like a crab claw. True, the upper and lower parts of the limb are covered in hard armor, but see how it's fused together out of smaller elements? More like the carapace of a turtle than the shell of a crab."

"Oh good," said Misha, standing. "Lecture. I go see how Sing is doing. Daisuke, do not go hunting without me."

"I thought I was supposed to vocalize when I theorize," Anne said. "Right, Daisuke?"

Daisuke gave her a thumbs-up.

"Right. See how the little elements get smaller toward the joints and come uncoupled from each other? They turn into little scales." She flexed the arm, watching as the hide under the scales stretched and compressed in accordion folds.

"Are you going to cook that?" Nurul asked. "Or do you plan to just bite into it?"

"I don't think I could," said Anne, then seemed to register the sarcasm. "Hey, I'm just trying to get a feel for the anatomy."

She handed the limb to Nurul, who peered down at its length in surprise. "Oh," said the journalist. "There's no bone. It's meat all the way through."

"Of course," Anne said. "No internal skeleton. Since these banana-flavored beasties have broken their exoskeletons up into scales, they don't have to worry about molting and losing all their muscle attachments. They must shed bit by bit, like birds shed their feathers. And grow *much* bigger than Terran arthropods ever managed. The question is, what do their muscles anchor to? And we see…."

Anne recovered the limb and took a handful of meat. She pulled and claws clacked together. Nurul jerked back, eyes wide.

"There we go," Anne said. "What we have here is an armored tentacle. The limb of something very much like an insect trying to be a reptile."

"I see," said Nurul. "So this biome's life forms are originally from Earth."

"What?" Anne blinked at her. "No. At least, I don't think so. I said 'insect', but this thing isn't related to real insects from Earth any more than toymakers or shmoos. Insects have copper-based hemolymph for one thing, but this tortoise-hog has red blood like a vertebrate. Hemoglobin or something similar…."

"This is all irrelevant," Hariyadi grumbled. "The only matter of importance is if we can eat it for the long term."

Anne flexed her fists open and closed. "I don't know. I'm telling you everything I do know."

"Long term, sir?" asked Nurul.

Hariyadi's eyes shifted. Some species of confusion fluttered behind his blank expression.

Nurul inquired something in the tones of 'sir, what's wrong?' and Hariyadi waved her concern away. "We must stay here," he said in English. "I have decided we must rest and resupply."

Nurul threw the claw into the flames, where it clenched like a dying snake. She said something to Hariyadi, who responded sharply. Rahman asked Nurul something, which she shrugged off. Uncharacteristically angry, Rahman shouted at Hariyadi and stood, only to be coaxed back to his seat by Nurul. He and his wife glared at Hariyadi, who glared at the fire like it had betrayed his homeland.

"What's wrong?" Daisuke asked.

"Do you think we should only speak English for your benefit?" snapped Nurul.

Hariyadi spoke slowly, as if exhausted. "I said that we shall remain here."

"But, sir," she said something in Indonesian, to which Hariyadi replied in English.

"No, I will not go scouting down the valley. I will not let you or Rahman go, either. It isn't safe. It is pointless."

"Pointless?" Daisuke repeated. "We can be in the Deep Sky Country the day after tomorrow. Then maybe only a day back to the wormhole. We can tell the world—"

"What?" Hariyadi barked. "What can we tell them? That we have discovered a useless plain of glass and a forest of tiny monsters?" He bared his teeth at the fire. "And let us not forget the lizard-bugs. No, there will be no welcome for us back in civilization. Better we stay here."

"For how long?" Nurul asked the question in English, but Hariyadi's response was in Indonesian. He sounded as if he had lost all hope.

Why is it you are suddenly so eager to slow down, Hariyadi? Afraid of being held accountable?

Hariyadi glared at Daisuke as if the old soldier could read his thoughts. "Do not imagine you will escape the blame." He snorted with bitter humor. "And even if they do not find us all guilty of murder, they will imprison us for the secrets we know."

"Sir?" Nurul looked terrified.

"It's all right," Hariyadi said. "We can stop here now. Enjoy this day. We are alive. Isn't it enough just to be grateful for that? We survive."

"Learn more about what?" asked Anne.

Hariyadi looked at her like she was a tick on his sleeve, and cold fear bubbled up inside Daisuke's skull. "Anne," he said carefully, still smiling. "Let's eat. No more questions now."

"Oh, so the spirit of inquiry is all well and good when I'm exploring a telegenic alien environment or the front of your jocks, but when I'm trying to determine where we should go and how fast we should get there—"

"Not now please." Daisuke held up a hand.

"Don't you dare silence me, Daisuke."

"I'm going to bed." Nurul stood up and stomped off. Hariyadi watched her go, eyes narrowed. The sun was sinking, flushing the south-western sky the color of an angry shmoo.

Anne didn't seem to notice the deadly subtext flowing around them. "All right. And Daisuke, weren't you going to go away for a while? Chase down a critter for your dinner?"

Daisuke quashed his impulse to argue. Or to invite Anne to come with him. That might alert Hariyadi. What could the colonel be up to? And did his plans endanger Anne?

"I will go find Misha." Daisuke stood. "Then I will bring more meat."

He would ponder these questions away from the fire, where the air was clearer.

★ ★ ★

The tortoise-hog tripped and rolled to a stop.

"Wait!" Misha gasped. "Daisuke!"

Daisuke was gasping too, kneeling over the animal. His head was swimming, and his skin prickled. It had gotten cold awfully fast. There must have been a sudden change of pressure as they'd run down the mountain. That would explain his sudden headache.

Misha's silhouette moved in the rising mist. "Stay now, Daisuke. I coming to you!"

Daisuke was content to sit here and breathe until Misha closed on him. "I got the tortoise-hog," he said.

"You foolish Japanese," said Misha. "I tell you is not worth to chase one animal all way here. More live up by wormhole. Now we have to carry this one all way back up— Who is that?"

"Who?" Daisuke straightened and aimed his pounding head in the direction Misha was pointing. Yes, there did seem to be someone standing there in the mist downslope. Someone tall and thin.

"Rahman?" shouted Daisuke, and the figure moved. Leaned forward. Extended a pair of slender crab pincers to support itself.

"Oh," Misha said.

"Misha," Daisuke said, "please be calm...."

"We run away now," said Misha, backing up the hill. The animal loped forward to close the distance, as graceful as a crane, as grim as an undertaker.

Daisuke wobbled on his feet, trying to catch his breath. His heart raced. The creature was close enough now that nobody could mistake it for human. Its head was long and tubular like those of the tortoise-hogs, but bulged out at the top into a bulbous-eyed shape like a cartoon heart. Four pointed legs supported a round, spiny body. A third pair of limbs stretched up past the head, not pincers or praying mantis claws, but something more like baby fern fronds – tightly coiled tentacles, armored, articulated, and wickedly barbed. It stopped less than two meters away from him.

"Calm," Daisuke panted at Misha. "Don't look at its eyes. No sudden movements. Just back slowly away."

Its turreted chameleon eyes scanned back and forth, up and down, sometimes in synchrony, sometimes separately. Twin tongues flicked from its complicated mouth, tasted the air. The animal's fern-frond limbs curled tighter, rose, cocked with an audible click.

"Run!" Daisuke stumbled back, his legs nightmarishly numb and useless. He couldn't seem to find his balance. The creature darted toward him.

Horned ropes lashed the mist over Daisuke's head, flailed, coiled again for another strike. The animal reared onto its hind legs while its middle pincers stabbed at Daisuke. Bone-armored claws closed on his thigh, yanked, twisted. It hurt hardly at all. Like the work of a dentist after the anesthesia has kicked in. Daisuke was very cold.

"Help me," he whispered. It was getting hard to see. The creature wheezed and clacked above him, spittle flying from its insectile mouth. It was shivering. Its long, tubular head drooped. It sank onto its armored knees as if overcome with weariness, abdomen pulsing in grating, labored... breaths?

Daisuke was having trouble breathing too. His heart was beating even faster now, banging against his rib cage as if struggling to escape. His hands and toes had gone numb. *We are being poisoned.*

"Misha," he said. "Poison. My head hurts."

"What?" someone grumbled from upslope of him. "Speak English. Come on. Get up." A hand took hold of Daisuke's shoulder. "What happened to that monster? What's wrong? Ow! My head hurts."

Daisuke looked up at Misha's face, which was pale, though with hectic red staining his cheeks and lips.

"Shit!" Misha said. "You're *poisoned*."

The predator let go of Daisuke's leg. It fell heavily, wheezing in the dirt beside Daisuke.

"Something's wrong," he said, and realized he was speaking Japanese again. "Help me."

"Shit," Misha said again. "Come on." He dropped Daisuke. Grabbed him again. The Russian was wheezing too now. "Come *on*, I said. Damn it!"

Daisuke was dragged upright, stumbled on numb feet, fell. He hardly felt the impact with Junction.

How could he have been so stupid? So weak? Daisuke crawled. It was just a little farther. The peak of the mountain was there above him. He just had to keep pulling. He dragged himself another meter, vision a gray blur. Was he even going uphill anymore? He could no longer feel anything past his knees and elbows.

He was only very tired. Pleasantly warm. If he just stopped, stopped and breathed, Daisuke would not feel anything.

But Anne would go on feeling. She would never let herself stop surviving, and neither would Daisuke. *I must try harder.* He clenched his tingling teeth and forced himself up another centimeter.

* * *

Anne heard the cry from under the blanket of fog.

"It's Misha," she told Sing. "Come on!" But the other woman grabbed Anne's arm and tugged her back uphill.

"What?" Anne ripped her arm free. "He's in trouble, he's your bloody boyfriend, and Daisuke's down there!"

"No!" Sing snatched at her sleeve again. "Death wind." She pointed at the ground, where, Anne realized, a line of little corpses lay. Dead lizard-bugs like sea wrack on a beach. A high-tide line.

"A boundary between biotic zones?" Anne asked.

Of course Sing didn't know those words. "Ah!" she said, and darted to a clump of squat, tubular plants. "Death wind no. Plant, yes. Anne, plant yes!"

She wrestled a barrel-like growth from the ground and fumbled in her utility belt for Misha's knife.

"We don't have time for this," Anne said. "He could be being eaten by a – I mean poisoned by – and Daisuke isn't making any sound at all. Sing!"

"Sh sh sh," their guide hissed through her teeth as she sliced through the plant, making a wide hollow tube. This she forced over her head until it covered her nose and mouth.

"Mmmph!" she said, and thrust the remainder of the plant at Anne.

Anne shoved her panic aside, focusing on details. *Plant over mouth. Plant makes breathable air. Plant evolved to store up oxygen. Evolved on the edge of boundary. Boundary where a temperature inversion traps a bubble of gas that's light, colorless, odorless, toxic to anything with red blood. Carbon monoxide.*

The last thought slotted into place as the spongy plant material scratched down Anne's face. She breathed, gave the thumbs-up to Sing….

Who dove into the deadly swirling fog.

Anne had the presence of mind to yank out her flashlight as she followed, turning the oppressive gloom under the fog into something navigable.

Even the plants down here looked unhealthy, their foam bleached like dying coral. The fungoid ground cover had rotted to gray slime, and strange new plants sprouted from the soil like clumps of lead-colored cotton candy. Skeins of steel wool gleamed dully in the beam of Anne's flashlight, piles of metallic material the size of bushes. Some kind of plant?

Dead animals littered the ground as well as fuzzy rust-colored pellets. The breathing plant dug into Anne's nose and cheeks like a damp loofa. She took in a gulp of moist air, wondering how much of it was carbon monoxide. Commandeering her hemoglobin, turning her blood cherry-red as her tissues starved for oxygen. Was that movement in the corner of her eye? Something slick and black uncoiling from the steel-wool bushes? Or just her vision tunneling?

A muffled cry from Sing. Anne turned to look, and there, collapsed a heartbreakingly short distance downhill, were Daisuke and Misha.

Anne made a beeline for Daisuke. Grabbed his hands. Tugged, pulled him up the hill like pulling a corpse through treacle. He was too heavy. She needed help. Where was Sing? Tugging on her own lover, of course, and making even less headway.

They had to co-operate. Sing couldn't speak English. She wanted to save Misha.

The dismal calculus unspooled through Anne's brain. She couldn't pull

Daisuke to safety by herself. She couldn't ask Sing to help her without first taking care of Misha. But even working with Sing, it would take her time to pull the big Russian to safety. Time Daisuke might not have. And yet the only alternative was Daisuke's certain asphyxiation. What was that Hariyadi had said about leadership and making tough decisions?

Anne let go of Daisuke, grabbed hold of Misha's free hand, and pulled.

"I will kick you up this mountain myself," she told him. "Get up, you dipshit!"

Misha's eyes opened. He rolled over, making vague motions with his arms and legs that bore little relation to walking. Still, he was awake enough that when Anne and Sing got their shoulders under his armpits, he could stand. Together they hobbled up the hill.

Still agonizingly slow, though. By the time they'd gotten the huge Russian out of the Death Wind biome, Nurul and Rahman were there waiting for them. Not Hariyadi, though. Never fucking Hariyadi.

But Anne didn't have time to be angry. Sing was already shucking off the breathing plant. The Nun woman dashed off, not to comfort Misha, but to find fresh plants. Anne ripped her own mask off and took several deep breaths of fresh air.

"Carbon," she gasped, "monoxide. Daisuke's still. Down there. Come on. Put plants over. Mouth and nose."

She wanted nothing more than to just take a deep breath and run back down there. Carbon monoxide poisoning was slow enough that she might just be able to get out again. Or else she'd collapse and turn herself into another victim to be rescued. More tough decisions.

After some dizzying, agonizing span of time, Sing rushed up with four pineapple-sized breathing plants. These she sliced into shape and forced over the heads of Nurul and Rahman before they all plunged back into the Death Wind biome.

Dark, chill mist. Her breath against the inside of the plant and her tainted blood pounding in her ears. Was that headache from stress or oxygen deprivation? Spiked black fractals spun in her peripheral vision. But she remembered where Daisuke was, and there was his face, swimming up from the murk. His arm, warm and firm in her hands as she lifted. The corpse-strewn ground flew under her, as if Anne tumbled uphill. As if she dove.

The mist parted, and she could see the stars.

Anne, Rahman, Nurul, and Sing heaved Daisuke up onto the ground cover of the Oasis biome. He thumped to the ground between them, his face copper-colored in the light of the Lighthouse biome across the valley.

Entirely unaware of what she was doing, Anne put her lips against his.

Felt his breath.

Broke down crying.

★ ★ ★

Hariyadi was pacing around the fire when they trudged back into camp.

"What now?" he said, glaring at the barely conscious Daisuke. "How did he nearly kill himself this time?"

"A poisonous cloud, sir," Nurul said while Anne choked on her rage. "It fills the whole valley."

"Damn," said Hariyadi. "How are we going to get through it?"

"There are plants—"

"No," Anne said. Although she should just leave the dipshit to die alone in the mist like he had wanted to leave Daisuke. "The plants will keep you alive for five minutes in there, tops."

"So we'll walk around the valley to the mouth of the river," Nurul said.

"No." Hariyadi shifted into Indonesian, arguing over their route as if Daisuke wasn't lying there unconscious.

"Shut up," Anne said. Daisuke needed to get to their tent. She did too. Had either of them actually eaten anything? She would have to catch something. And get another fire going, since the shithead had let theirs go out. Shit, how much oxygen was Daisuke's brain getting? He was half-awake now, a stumbling zombie. Would he ever wake up the rest of the way? Anne was going mad and Hariyadi was still *talking* at her!

"Shut up, I said!" Anne bore up the sagging Daisuke, tugged him toward her tent. "We aren't going anywhere. Daisuke needs rest and I will *fucking murder* anyone who says otherwise."

"I am *not* saying otherwise, Ms. Houlihan," said Hariyadi, possibly not for the first time. "I agree with you. We must stay here. We cannot risk getting any closer to that poisonous gas."

"But sir," Nurul said in English. "We're already too close to it. What if the wind shifts?"

"Why, we have the wormhole," Hariyadi said. "We can simply cross over to the Ripe Blood planet and wait there until the air here is fresh again. In the meantime, we are within sight of the mouth of the valley. If we light a bonfire—"

"No one is coming for us!"

Had Nurul just raised her voice? At any other time, Anne would applaud. Now, though, she had more pressing concerns. She pulled Daisuke another step closer to their tent.

"We must arrive back in Imsame as fast as possible," said Nurul. "Nothing has changed."

"Everything has changed!" Hariyadi bit the words off as if tearing them raw off the bone. "We have two wounded men, men we *need*, Mrs. Astarina, and an impassable barrier in front of us. We shall stay here at least until Alekseyev and Matsumori recover."

Nurul's response was bitter. "Or until one of them dies."

CHAPTER FIFTEEN

Inversion

As he rose from the healing depths toward the chill surface of consciousness, Daisuke's muscles and bones began to protest. His head and joints ached. His diaphragm creaked with the effort of breathing. His finger- and toe-tips tingled. It was very much like the case of the bends he'd gotten coming out of the Caribbean Sea. Not to mention the fact that his chest still hurt as if he'd been kicked by a zebra.

It would have counted among the top ten hardest awakenings of Daisuke's life, except Anne was here, more solid and marvelous than anything he could have imagined. Still not entirely aware of what had happened to him or what planet he was on, Daisuke only knew that once again he had awoken in Anne's arms, and this time he wouldn't let the opportunity slip away.

"You're all right!" Anne squeezed him. "Are you all right? Stop that! How's your brain?"

Daisuke lifted his lips from her skin and considered the question. "Still dizzy," he said. "Trouble focusing. Nausea. What happened? I remember… mist. Dark mist."

"The Death Wind Country," intoned Anne. "It got you and Misha, but you were worse. He woke up after they dragged him out, but you've been unconscious almost all day."

Daisuke was glad to hear the darkness in the tent wasn't a sign of some scary neurological disorder, just the sun going down.

"What happened?" he said again. "Poison gas?"

"Carbon monoxide," said Anne. "And maybe anoxia. You fell unconscious suspiciously fast. Which is good, actually, because you didn't breathe in as much poison as you might have. So I'm hoping that means less brain damage."

Daisuke hoped so too. "But I can remember everything from before we ran into the Death Wind biome," he said. "And I can still speak English. Uh. Can't I?" He switched to Japanese. "So that you can take care of the drooling me, you have to learn Japanese, I suppose."

Anne slapped him on the shoulder. "Shut *up,* you awful man." She squeezed him again. "Just shut up and let me hold you." She bumped his forehead with hers. "And yell at you. We're on a different fucking *planet,* Daisuke. Every new biome we *come* to is a new planet. You can't just go prancing off into the bush like an eager little puppy and trust there to be stuff like air to breathe."

"I'm sorry," Daisuke finally said. "I will be more careful."

Anne sniffed wetly in his ear. "Damn right you will. Keep yourself safe, Daisuke."

They held each other until something jabbed him in the thigh.

"Ow!" Daisuke slapped at himself, battling with another wave of nausea as his eyes struggled to focus. There were – what? Chunky black and red beads? – scattered across his lower body. "Why...." he said, and one of the beads extended a proboscis.

"Linguipods," said Anne in disgust and brushed the parasites off Daisuke. "How did they get in here?"

Fear gripped Daisuke's heart. He remembered overturning one of his boots on a shoot in Thailand, and the pit viper that had plopped out. The ticks he'd found tangled in his socks after a hiking trip in Montana.

Daisuke tried to leap out of his infested sleeping bag, but all he managed was a sideways roll, eyes clenched shut against the dizziness.

"Why are you writhing around?" asked Anne. "However venomous those things might be to toymaker biochemistry, they're no match for your mighty Earthling body."

Right. Right. But who knew about allergic reactions? Daisuke passed his shaking hands down his body, searching himself for itching, sweating, tingling, and of course now that he was looking, he found them. He could be about to die or merely about to go mad.

"Relax," Anne said. "They bit Misha and nothing happened. So, buck up. We've got bigger problems right now and you can't fall apart."

"Anne," he tried to tell her. "I'm scared."

Anne screwed up her face. "What's there to be scared of? You just have to be more careful."

That hurt. As if Daisuke hadn't spent his whole professional life being *careful* as well as *bucking up* and all the other useless things you said to people when their painful death would inconvenience you. *If Anne really cared about me, she would see how worried I am.*

And there was something worse. The linguipods were from Toymaker

Country. Toymaker Country was a hundred meters up the slope. Those little aliens couldn't have gotten into Daisuke's tent without human help.

"Dice," she said, "we got to get up and out of this tent. There's no time for whatever it is you're thinking about."

Daisuke looked at Anne, then away. No, it was too melodramatic. The Iron Man of Survival should do what Anne said and get out of the tent. Throw himself at the next source of danger. Reveal the plot only after the murderer had been apprehended. But what if Anne was in danger too?

So what if a confession of fear would look silly and weak? So what if it wouldn't fit in this scene? Anne had saved his life. She had seen him at his weakest and most foolish. If he could not tell her how he really felt, what was the point of even being alive?

"Anne." He licked his lips, fear thrilling his heart. "I think one of us is a murderer."

She jerked back. "You *what*?" Her face twisted. "Fuck, Dice, I have to take paranoid bullshit from Hariyadi and Misha, don't you give it to me too!"

Daisuke slammed down his mask like a storm shutter. "Yes," he said. "I understand. I'm sorry."

He felt like screaming, but Anne didn't appear to notice. "'Impending doom,' indeed. I said it before, and it's just as true now. We have to work together or we'll die, right?"

"Yes," said Daisuke again, "I understand." His headache was back, his limbs as heavy as sacks of sour mash. He might as well be back under the Death Wind.

"We should leave the tent," he said. It was what was expected of him.

Standing was very difficult. Folds of dizziness and nausea draped across his vision and Daisuke swayed on his feet. What if this *was* brain damage? Would he be able to tell if his mind suddenly slipped into a lower gear? What if he started babbling and soiling his underwear?

Why, the same thing that would have happened to Pearson if he had not so conveniently 'died of his injuries', Daisuke answered himself. *I would myself have abandoned him in the kelp-tree forest along with Tyaney*. Daisuke knew he could look forward to the same sorry treatment if he outlived his usefulness.

"I'm sorry, Dice," Anne said, crawling out of the tent behind him. "You can't be feeling great right now, but we've got to get a move on. An ill wind blows and all that."

Daisuke barely registered her words. He knew why Tyaney had died.

Pearson too. The American had tried to keep them in one place, the Nun had almost driven away their guide. They had slowed down the expedition, and someone had killed them.

Anne didn't believe him, but that didn't matter. Daisuke was alone, as he had always been alone. Not just Man against Nature, but Man against everything. The venomous reptiles not only out in the bush, but sharing a bed with him.

Daisuke blinked, and his vision cleared. He was standing on the green slopes of the Oasis biome. Anne was behind him and Misha was in front of him.

"Ah," said the Russian. "You awake."

"In a manner of speaking," Anne said. "Come on, Dice."

Daisuke shrugged off her hands and wobbled into the chilly alpine dusk. The tops of the mountains across the valley still shone yellow, but the shadow of the Outer Toymakers crept ever upward. The Lighthouse wormhole had become visible against the darkness and, through some quirk of interplanetary orbital dynamics, so had the Oasis wormhole. Oasis daylight lent an eerie green vividness to the scene. The landscape was simultaneously darker and brighter than it should have been, as if the sun had been eclipsed. Creatures in the peanut-bushes fluted and rasped in panic.

"Yes," Misha answered some question Anne had asked. "We put almost all equipment now in wormhole. Hariyadi and Nurul there now, on Oasis Planet."

"Why?" asked Daisuke. Had the murderer been driving their expedition to this goal the whole time? Some insane colonization effort? "We can't live on the Oasis Planet forever."

Misha stared at Daisuke, then his beard parted in a smile. "You hurt head, my friend. I joke about brain damage, but please try to not thinking so hard, eh?"

So he could trust no one. But Daisuke would survive. It was the only thing he was good at.

Misha lifted his head as if scenting the air. "Now come on to wormhole. Here not safe. The wind is changing."

It was true. The wind had blown steadily from the north-west since they'd crossed the Outer Toymakers, but now a breeze from the east tugged at Daisuke's clothes, carrying the smell of smoke.

"That's bad," he said.

"Correct," said Anne. "You know what will happen when the new wind tears the lid off the temperature inversion over the Death Wind biome."

"It will vomit poison all over us," Daisuke said, understanding finally dawning. "We have to hide on Planet Ripe Blood until the Death Wind passes."

"Ya." That was Rahman's voice. "But Nurul and Hariyadi know what we will do, *insha Allah*."

Daisuke turned, very slowly and carefully, a hand pressed against the side of his head, to see the lanky cameraman walking up to them.

"Good, good. I happy to see friend okay!" Rahman patted Daisuke on the shoulder. "You okay?" He looked at Misha and Anne. "Damage brain?"

"Ehh," Misha held apart his index finger and thumb. "Maybe a little. Okay. Nurul and Hariyadi are on other side of wormhole. Now we help Daisuke through wormhole, yes? Then I go get Sing."

"I'm fine," said Daisuke. The wind ruffled his hair. Invisible, scentless poison billowing up the hill. Daisuke stopped himself from shivering.

Rahman pointed up the wormhole mound. "Nurul already go. She go in wormhole with Colonel Hariyadi. Make camp…um, emergency camp? Hariyadi says we wait there until, uh, weather stabilize. Nurul say weather never stabilize. The longer we wait…." He held out his hands, as if asking to be rescued. "They argue with each other! Always! I worry."

Daisuke remembered his odd conversation with the colonel the previous day. Hariyadi had certainly seemed angry at Nurul, but it was unclear why. The memory of Sing and Tyaney surfaced. The cameraman couldn't believe his wife was cheating on him?

I will solve this mystery, even if nobody else believes there is a mystery to solve.

"Good," said Misha. "You take Sing's stuff yet?"

Rahman shook his head.

"We should still be able to get at her through the wormhole," Anne said. "I was helping her consolidate her kit into a form we can transport and it's absolutely fascinating, Daisuke. She's halfway domesticated that colony of toymakers already."

Daisuke arranged his face in a way he hoped signified interest and respect.

"Toymaker?" Rahman said. "Toymaker stay here. I no like…I no…." He said something in Indonesian.

Anne said something back to him, scowling.

"What is it? This is no time to argue," said Misha.

Anne jerked her chin at Rahman. "Paragon of modernity here has decided Sing is a witch after all, and he doesn't trust her and her toymaker devil-box. As if you don't spend half your time pointing a camera at her."

Rahman shook his head. "Camera? What? I don't understand."

Anne said something sarcastic-sounding in Indonesian, to which Rahman angrily responded. The wind pawed at them.

"No time," Misha said again.

Daisuke just tried to stay upright, looking up at the wormhole. A shadow stretched down the mound from the silhouette at the top, outlined in dappled green light.

The animals in the bushes stopped singing.

Daisuke squinted. "Who's up there?"

The figure screamed.

"Nurul?" said Rahman, looking around, and shouted something in Indonesian.

"Monsters!" Nurul waved at them from the top of the wormhole mound, bloody shirt streaming out behind her. "They've killed Hariyadi!"

Daisuke's teeth clenched with the memory of bulbous, twitching eyes, limbs like coiled baby ferns.

"What?" Misha thundered. "*Dead?* God *fucking* damn it! You sure?"

"Killed? How?" Anne demanded.

Rahman said nothing. He only jerked like a startled deer and bounded up the hill toward his wife, camera thumping on his back.

"We aren't safe on the Oasis Planet," yelled Nurul, stumbling down the hill. "We have no choice but to pack up everything and move on. Oh, Rahman!" She broke into Indonesian as her husband embraced her.

"Move on where, Nurul?" Anne asked, while Daisuke's head pounded.

"No," said Misha. "Hariyadi can't be dead. Are you sure, Nurul?"

"Of course I'm sure," Nurul said. "Come. We must go up to the edge of the Toymaker biome."

"No. We need that body," Misha said, stomping up the mound toward her.

"Body?" said Anne. "There's a Death Wind coming. Would you please focus?"

Misha closed on her. "Even if he's dead, we need that body."

"Whatever for?" Anne asked.

Misha didn't answer. "Rahman," he shouted, "Daisuke, help me! Scare away those monsters!"

Rahman let go of Nurul. She clawed at him, trying to hold him back, but the cameraman was infected by the panic in Misha's voice. He churned up the hill, silhouetting himself against the wormhole that Nurul had just exited. It pulsed with green and white light.

Daisuke followed them, since it would look bad if he didn't. But why would they need Hariyadi's body? They hadn't even bothered to bury Tyaney. Not that there'd been much of him left to bury. And there was something strange about Misha's voice, but Daisuke could barely think. His head ached. His vision throbbed with the strobing of the wormhole's light.

"We need to go through anyway," Anne said. "Our supplies are in there and the Death Wind is coming."

"No," said Nurul. "No, not the wormhole. Up the hill. Rahman!"

The wormhole shimmered, throwing rainbows against the puffy bushes, the fluted mound, and the stricken faces of the people running toward it. Daisuke gaped. Blinked. Rubbed his eyes. Was he hallucinating?

"Wait a second," Anne said.

Nurul ran after Rahman, who had put his head in the wormhole. Weird lights played over the lower part of his body as the upper smeared like a reflection in a carnival mirror.

"Go!" Misha had reached the wormhole as well. He put his hands on Rahman's back, as if to shove him through.

Nurul screamed in frustration. "Listen to me!" she said. "That place will kill us! Our only hope is to go uphill. Get out of the wormhole!"

"Huh," said Anne. "I think she's right. Everyone?"

So maybe Daisuke wasn't hallucinating that multi-hued aurora around the wormhole. Should he stop and ask Anne what was wrong? No, she didn't want that from him. She wanted the Iron Man of Survival, who would climb any hill, leap into any danger. A spatter of raindrops ran down Daisuke's face. A breeze blew from the east.

"Go!" said Misha, and shoved. Rahman seemed to turn inside out, his image warped and wavering in a shower of rainbow light. The light pulsed faster, or maybe that was just Daisuke's racing heart playing tricks with his vision.

He and Anne were level with Nurul now. She beat ineffectually at Misha's shoulder, her snarling face awash with the garish light of the wormhole. Small animals plopped out of the bushes downslope, asphyxiated.

"Carbon monoxide! Go through the wormhole!" Daisuke reached toward its scintillating safety.

And went down in a cloud of dirt as Anne tackled him from behind.

"What?" Daisuke rolled over. "Let me—"

"Stay down!" Anne shouted at him.

The wormhole's light flickered like the light bar of an ambulance. The wind howled and Nurul reached toward the distorted image of her husband. His voice echoed through the wobbling hole in space and time.

The wormhole closed.

Rahman's form shrank as if he'd fallen down a well. The kaleidoscopic torrent of color peaked and vanished, leaving nothing where the wormhole had been but purple afterimages and poisoned air. Weight, the full gravity of Junction, crashed down on them.

Their doorway to Rahman, Hariyadi's body, and all their supplies was gone.

★ ★ ★

Sing stumbled as the ground lurched under her. It was as if she had just severed the stalk of a kelp-tree and was accelerating upward. The normal weight of things had returned, and the wormhole had fled. The Death Wind was upon them.

Sing looked down at the toymaker-food-maker she had spent so much frantic time disassembling for travel. Now she just dropped the useless thing. Her pitifully half-tamed toymaker tugged at the tether she'd tied around her wrist, and she gave it a petulant jerk. She shouldn't have wasted all this time tending it, but the thought of arriving home after all these years as a real toymaker-wielder as well as a real wife, of redeeming some part of her lost life, had seemed so ripe. But that dream, however ripe, had been too high up the tree.

And what were Misha and the Them doing up there on the wormhole's mound, anyway? Didn't they know it would be hours before the Death Wind dissipated and the wormhole felt safe enough to return?

"All right, everyone," she yelled up at the Them. "Let's get to higher ground before we all suffocate and die." Of course none of them understood her. They seemed to be arguing. Only Misha even bothered to look at her.

Sing waved. "Come on, love," she called to him. "The Death Wind is coming! Death Wind! Higher ground!" She pointed uphill and spoke in the Them language. "Run. Run! Up! Go!"

Misha jerked as if someone had speared him. He looked around wildly, beard flying. Then he barreled down the mound. "Go!" he shouted. "Go go go!"

"It's not that dangerous," said Sing. "It was only bad for you yesterday because you went too far down—"

Her man barely slowed as he scooped her up in his arms. Suddenly, Sing found herself being carried up the mountain, her toymaker bobbing behind them like an eager dog.

"What are you doing?" Sing demanded. "I can walk by myself."

Even if he had been able to understand her, Misha wasn't listening. He was babbling to himself in the Them language, of which Sing only understood the words 'Hariyadi' and 'dead'.

Sing looked back over Misha's jouncing shoulder. Yes, Hariyadi seemed to be missing from the group of Them. They were only now walking down the mound, waving and yelling questions at Misha.

Small animals fell from their perches. Larger ones ran uphill alongside the Them. A tortoise-hog stumbled and fell.

"Faster!" Sing called to the Them.

"Hariyadi," snarled Misha, as if to himself, "...dead."

"What happened to him?" Sing asked. "Did someone kill him with an animal, like Pearson and Tyaney? What happened to Rahman?"

Misha's feet slid over muddy rocks. They were at the edge of the Toymaker Country now, the balloon crowns of the kelp-trees swaying over their heads. Ripe Blood animals swarmed over the toymaker palisade wall, prompting a clicking, tapping chorus of alarm from its builders.

"Stop," said Sing. "We've come far enough. The Death Winds never come up this high. We're safe." She wasn't so sure about the Them, though. Daisuke, Nurul, and Anne were climbing much too slowly, swaying on their feet as if drunk.

Sing tugged on Misha's arm. "We have to go help them."

He only grunted and shook his head. Sing's man set her down before contorting himself to fumble with something on his belt.

"Misha!" Sing said. "Anne, Daisuke, Nurul! Death!" Why wasn't he helping his tribesmen? This was so unlike him.

Misha extracted something from his belt. Another Them artifact, all black and rectilinear. Sing flinched back, wondering if this was another *gun*, but Misha didn't hold it like a weapon. Facing east, toward the Deep Sky Country and home, he brought the contraption to his ear. Squeezing it, he spoke, although not to Sing.

The words were in Them, and Sing didn't understand anything. Who was Misha talking to? Was he praying?

If so, the only answer to his prayers was a Death Wind monster, breaching the fog layer that capped its murky home. Misha didn't seem to notice this terrible omen. He squeezed his artifact again and spoke, but it only hissed at him like a waterfall. Misha held up the device like he wanted to smash it on the ground, but seemed to think better of it. He clasped it to his belt and looked downhill at the other Them.

Daisuke and Anne had put their arms around Nurul, hustling her away from the Death Wind. They seemed to be all right. In any case, they had enough breath in their lungs to scream abuse at Misha for not helping them.

"I agree with the Them," Sing told her husband. "That was a selfish, cowardly thing you did, running away like that. Do you want your tribesmen to die? Do you want me to divorce you?"

But Misha wasn't looking at the Them anymore. He was staring at her, eyes bulging from his wildly hairy face.

"Sing," he said. "I go up. I fly. You help."

Sing took a step back. Her husband looked ready to smash someone's skull open. "You help," he insisted. "Help fly."

"What are you talking about?"

He spun around and pointed at the bobbling balloons of the kelp-trees.

"You want to balloon away," said Sing. "No, it's too dangerous. I was crazy to try it, even when I was an unmarried woman."

"I fly," he insisted. "Go up." He patted the blocky artifact on his hip. "Talk."

"You want to talk to who?" Sing slashed her hands through the air, her toymaker tugging at her wrist. "It doesn't matter. Your real tribesmen are down there and they need you. There's no one to talk to up in the sky but the Yeli and the Death Wind monsters."

Growling in frustration, Misha ripped his utility knife from its sheath and ran past Sing.

"What the hell do you think you're doing?" Sing shouted, but her husband smashed his way through the wild toymakers' barricade and just about launched himself at a large kelp-tree stalk.

"Curses!" Sing sprinted after him, but she was too late. Misha's wickedly sharp Them knife had already sawed through half the stalk that tethered the balloon, as well as his body, to the ground.

Sing scrambled up the stalk, adding her meager weight to his. "All right," she said. "I'll help you. We need to cut loops for your feet and hands. And we need two stalks. You understand? Two. One for each of us." With a tongue-clicked command, she made her toymaker harpoon the largest nearby stalk and winch it within arm's reach.

Soon, they were airborne.

★ ★ ★

Daisuke's vision was dark. His ears roared with blood. His heart swelled. His lungs spasmed and screamed for breath.

He did not breathe. He was the Iron Man of Survival, and he would pass out from oxygen deprivation before he let himself give in to the poisoned air around him. This was like when he'd fallen through the ice of that lake in Russia. No, it was like when he'd gone cave diving in Mexico. No, it was worse. Holding his breath and climbing this mountain was the worst thing Daisuke had ever done. And given that he was surely about to die, this was the worst thing he was ever *going* to do as well.

Welcome, gentle viewers, to the pinnacle of my career.

He fell forward.

And was caught again by Anne.

Her warm, solid back bore up under him, her strong legs carried him another step. Daisuke was reminded of riding a porpoise, although he wouldn't tell her that.

"You can breathe now," Anne said. "The woodland creatures have stopped dropping out of the bushes."

Daisuke breathed. Stopped. Tumbled to the ground with Nurul and Anne in a heaving tangle. He opened his eyes.

Stars and wormholes shone between rushing clouds.

The winds were changing. He was alive. Misha and Sing had abandoned them. Anne carried him around like he was some useful but cumbersome piece of equipment. And Nurul, he realized, was weeping.

CHAPTER SIXTEEN

Airborne

"Why did this happen?" Anne panted.

"I couldn't stop him," wailed Nurul. "Misha just shoved me out of the way and ran into the forest."

"No, I don't mean *people*," Anne said. She looked down at Daisuke, who was lying on the ground, barely conscious. Hariyadi was dead or at very least gravely wounded, trapped with Rahman on the other side of a vanished wormhole. "Wormholes can close. It must be some kind of safety cutoff. That flashing light was a—"

"Rahman's in there!" Nurul nearly spat the words.

"Well…with our supplies?" Anne didn't know if that was much comfort, but it made Nurul let go of her.

The journalist turned away, face crumpling, "Oh, Rahman, I'm sorry. Oh, Colonel!" She burst into tears.

Anne felt as if she'd been smacked on the back of the head with a cord of firewood. She was never great at making people feel better, and that was without the added confusion of partial carbon monoxide poisoning.

At least it wasn't ongoing. She had Nurul, and the barely conscious Daisuke had managed to climb far enough away from the valley that they could breathe safely. The wind was dying down as the temperature inversion clamped back down on the poison-spewing biome in the valley. The stars were back out. The Lighthouse biome shone across the valley.

"Why did Misha and Sing run off?" she asked. "Do they want something from the toymakers?" *Something more important than helping me figure out how we're supposed to survive now?*

"No," Nurul said savagely. "Misha abandoned us!"

Something large swept over their heads.

Anne's tired eyes tried to focus on the bulbous, dangling object. A flying jellyfish? A toymaker man-o'-war, bigger than any they'd seen so far? No. It was Misha, hanging from the hydrogen-balloon tips of a cluster of kelp-trees.

Note the bulbous tips, she thought. *Extra hydrogen storage for some sort of specialized fruiting bodies?* In the half light of the wormhole across the valley, she could see Misha waving goodbye.

"That *dog*!" Nurul was on her feet, face nearly unrecognizable with rage, shaking her fist at the departing Russian and shouting words Anne had never heard before.

Anne's fingertips and nose tingled. She wanted to slump down next to Daisuke and sleep, but Nurul, still yelling like a lunatic, was stomping toward the forest.

"Come!" That was in English, presumably directed at Anne. "Grab a tree!"

Another ballooner occluded the stars over them. Sing rode higher in the air, her tame toymaker trailing her like a baby duck.

"We're going to lose them," Nurul called from between the stakes of the toymakers' fence.

"You're thinking of following them?" called Anne. "In balloons?"

"Yes. Right now. So move quickly or I will leave you here."

She hadn't gotten a great look at Misha or Nurul's rigs, but Anne could guess how they worked. You get together three or four medium-sized kelp-balloons, tie them together, cut hand- and footholds into the stalks, sever the holdfasts, and off you go.

It was a lot harder to do than to think about, especially after she'd dragged the unconscious Daisuke up the hill. Anne lost a couple of balloons to twitchy, slime-slick fingers before she got herself and Daisuke tied up securely. *Hopefully securely. I suppose we'll find out.*

"I'm ready when you are," Anne called to Nurul, whom she couldn't bring herself to abandon.

"Finally!" Nurul cut away the stalks anchoring her to the ground. Anne did likewise and the dark forest floor dropped out from under her. The stalks of the other kelp-trees, still holding firmly to the boulders of this mountaintop, slid past her, along with their commensal communities of climbing log-worms and billowing windsock-eels. Then Anne and Daisuke cleared the canopy and the wind caught them.

The valley spread out under them, blobby peanut-bushes in the darkness below and ahead the bright, intricate filigrees that spread out from the Lighthouse wormhole. Anne worked her fingers into the strips of tough, gummy material she'd cut from the kelp-trees' stalks and swung her boots in the stirrups. Daisuke slept, trussed up like a roped steer. Everything seemed to be holding. Over the stink of the drying nutrient fluid from inside the trees, the wind carried hints of alien spices. Scents from other biomes swirled around Anne and Daisuke. They were airborne again.

★ ★ ★

Daisuke felt no wind. It was the strangest part of ballooning, feeling nothing, even as you looked down at the whipping trees. Or in this case, the currents in the mist of the Death Wind biome, where it bulged and folded like a blanket thrown over a sleeping ogre.

Water droplets hung in the cold air of the temperature inversion that protected oxygen-breathing life in this valley. Occasional eddies cleared the air enough for Daisuke to see pyramids of steel wool, twisted leaden columns, and lacy tripods that could be animals, plants, or sculptures. All these growths coursed with streams of black liquid.

Or maybe not liquid. Daisuke didn't like the way the stuff sometimes flowed uphill, or the spiny globs that swelled on the upper surfaces of the plant-things. He also didn't like thinking about how it would only take a gust of wind blowing in the wrong direction for the alien biome to belch up a suffocating wad of carbon monoxide.

Instead, Daisuke turned his attention upward. Anne was wound into loops in their kelp-tree stalk, her big boots just a few centimeters above his head. He examined those worn gray treads, crusted with layers of the mud of five different worlds, and wished he hadn't shown Anne his true face. Now she thought he was paranoid. An untrusting and untrustworthy manipulator. To win back her good opinion of him, Daisuke would have to put on the show of his career.

Daisuke attempted a smile. Anne couldn't see it, but she would be able to hear it in his voice. His face muscles stretched. Unnatural, he decided, but no more unnatural than usual.

Now, what would the Iron Man of Survival say to her?

"Is everything all right?"

"I wish we could make this thing go faster," Anne replied. "Can we, I don't know, spread sails or something?"

"No," Daisuke said. "The wind is moving at the same speed we are. If we had a propeller, we could make our own wind but…."

"So we have no way to catch them up. Or even stop ourselves from being blown way the hell off course," said Anne. "This was a stupid idea, wasn't it? Since when does Nurul give the orders in our party, anyway?"

Daisuke prodded his persona for something encouraging. "We will use the resources of Junction to survive and to explore!"

"Not really?" Anne said. "I'm beginning to think we should have stayed in the Oasis biome."

You're right, Daisuke thought, but said, "You wanted us to stay together."

"I guess I did," said Anne. "Now I wonder if we aren't all just marching into the lion's mouth together. Can you see Misha anymore?"

Daisuke looked out across the mist toward the suspended figure of Nurul and, much farther away, the hazy blot that was Misha and Sing. "Yes," he said. "I will reach the binoculars in my utility belt."

"Careful," said Anne, feeling the vibrations of his work. "Jesus, Dice."

"I am very careful." Daisuke managed to extract the binoculars. "Yes. I see Misha and Sing. The little man-o'-war is between them. I think I can see a string or cord? It connects Sing to the toymaker, and the toymaker to Misha."

"Of course *she'd* know how to get around up here," Anne said. "Or do you think Sing was kidnapped by Misha?"

"Maybe she is the leader here, and Misha is following *her.* We will find out when we land."

"If we survive the landing," said Anne.

Daisuke buried his true emotions under a mound of fake enthusiasm. "Of course we will!"

"Daisuke, I.... Huh."

The skin on his neck prickled. He had learned to dread that little expulsion of breath. Floating above a cloud of invisible, poisonous gas in an improvised balloon, Anne had just seen something interesting.

"What is it?" he said.

"Look at Nurul. Train your binoculars on her."

Daisuke did so. "She's looking downward."

"Yeah, yeah. Look at the mist under her."

Where a black bulk swam like a killer whale under a kayak.

The binoculars slipped from between Daisuke's numb fingers. Swinging on their loop, they tugged on his wrist until he recovered and fumbled them back against his eyes. The monster was still tracking Nurul.

"Another one of those things we saw from the plane, isn't it?" Anne asked.

"Another two." Daisuke had found Misha's and Sing's balloons, as well as the companion shadowing them. "Misha and Sing have one too."

"We don't, though?"

Daisuke dropped the binoculars again. Then he remembered Anne's habit of making statements with the intonation of questions. He peeked downward and saw nothing in the mist under his trembling feet.

"It doesn't make sense," Anne muttered to herself. "You don't just evolve flight for no reason. Is it some predator adapted to taking down these balloons? But in that case, why isn't anything hunting you and me?" She sounded almost disappointed. "We're hanging lower in the air column than anyone. I suppose it wouldn't be a predator per se if it ate floating plants. Maybe just a very aggressive herbivore? Sky hippos? Mist buffalo?"

Daisuke ground his teeth, reaching for control. He ought to be thinking about other people's danger, not his own fear. "How can we help them?"

"The buffalo?"

He sighed. "How can we help the people? Nurul and Sing."

"I don't know, Dice. I don't even know if they're in danger." An angry little jerk came vibrating down the kelp-tree stalk. "I'm never going to learn what's down there, am I? What sort of metabolic pathway throws off *carbon monoxide*, for God's sake? Are the structures down there made of ferrofluids or what? Who knows? I don't, and I can't find out because I have to chase after some stupid, cowardly bloody Russian! What the hell is he even running away from all of a sudden?"

It wasn't the first time Anne had asked the question, but it was the first time Daisuke had had the luxury of time to think about an answer. The machinations of fellow humans were infinitely more pleasant to consider than the impenetrable dangers that might even now be cruising the turbid air below.

"He could have run away from three things," Daisuke said. "The Death Wind, whatever force closed that wormhole, or us."

"Us? Why would he suddenly be scared of us? Oh, this is your stupid murder scenario again, isn't it? 'And Then There Were Nun'?"

Daisuke bit his tongue. Once again, he stuck his head up and she hammered it back down. He should just keep his mouth shut. On the other hand, what sort of Iron Man of Survival would Daisuke be if he remained silent just because he was afraid of being yelled at by his girlfriend?

"What if Misha is trying to escape justice?" he said. "What if he is the murderer?"

An irritating groan from above. "Why would *Misha* want to kill any of us?"

Daisuke remembered the linguipods. "He was killing everyone who slowed us down. Me, after I was poisoned. Hariyadi, who wanted to stay in the Oasis biome. Tyaney, who abused our native guide. Pearson, who wanted to stay on the glasslands."

"Christ Almighty, Daisuke, that's…." The stalks of the kelp-trees trembled as she shook her head. "Stop being so damn paranoid."

Why won't you listen? Why do you punish me for speaking the truth? Daisuke closed his eyes and bared his teeth, strangling the questions in his throat. The cool surface of the kelp-tree stalk pressed into the place on his left hand where his wedding ring had once lain.

"I mean, Misha the Russian hippie? He's in a hurry *now*, but he was dragging his feet from the plane crash until we lost Hariyadi and Rahman. I guess I could believe he offed Tyaney in a fit of passion, but that's not how that happened, either."

She went on like that for some time, but Daisuke was too exhausted to listen. He could never reveal his real face. Not to Anne, not to anyone. Because nobody was interested in Daisuke Matsumori – only the Iron Man of Survival was worth their attention. Daisuke would put aside his plans and emotions and focus on survival. It was what he did best.

He let his gaze fall to the toxic clouds below him, where a shadow bloomed.

"Oh my," said Anne. "That's certainly a big bloody thing."

The Death Wind organism looked less like an animal than a machine built by some far-flung and sinister future. Some deranged art student's idea of a lily, or maybe a spiderweb, all tangled wire and swirling black liquid, as large as a radio telescope.

"Can we, uh, fly away?" Anne asked.

"I'm sorry," said Daisuke. His teeth chattered audibly as the organism extended silently below them. "That there is nothing we can do to avoid that… death flower."

The death flower changed shape as he watched. Wires curved or protruded or coiled out of its central mass, which spread itself up their scaffolding like iron filings flying to meet a magnet.

Somewhere in the distance, Sing was screaming.

Daisuke could do nothing. No feat of derring-do would save them from the thing that uncoiled below them. Survival lay entirely outside of Daisuke's hands, which was some comfort. Nobody could blame him for dying.

A new mechanism took shape under the Death Wind flower. A coil of wire had attracted black skin, which turned it into a tube. A collar spun around the base of that tube, spiked and crackling, while the tube itself swung around like the barrel of a cannon…

"Anne," said Daisuke, "I have something to say to you."

...and aimed past them at Misha's and Sing's balloons.

"Huh?" Anne said.

A thunderclap passed through Daisuke's head, a wave of violated air. Something hurtled through the night, sleek and massive as a porpoise.

Sing screamed again. Her and Misha's balloons jerked down and to the side, suddenly weighted down by a wad of wire and black tar.

"Daisuke," said Anne, "your binocs."

"Binoculars?" They were still dangling from the strap he always kept fastened around his right wrist. Now all he had to do was convince the fingers of that hand to loosen their death grip on the tree.

Just imagine there's a camera on you.

Daisuke composed his face and brought the binoculars up to his eyes. He focused on the creature dangling from Misha and Sing's pair of balloons, glimmering gold and royal blue as it threw off whips of wire. No, not whips. Tracks. The creature flowed up the wires like a giant amoeba, bristling toward Misha.

"What are they doing, Dice?"

"Fighting each other," he said. Sing was wrestling with Misha for possession of...what? A gun? A knife? No. "Anne, Misha is holding a little radio."

"A bloody *what*?"

"A...a...." What was the damn word? "A walkie-talkie."

"Misha had a radio all this time? Why didn't he tell us? Why didn't he call for help?"

"Line of sight," said Daisuke, who remembered the days of wilderness exploration before communications satellites. "We cannot call someone we cannot see." Daisuke tried to stabilize his trembling arm against his body. "He is shouting into the radio. Listening. He is talking to someone."

"He's generating radio signals is what he's bloody doing," Anne said. "Doesn't he realize he's flying over an ecosystem based off the interactions of magnetic fields with ferrofluids in an anoxic atmosphere?"

"I...don't think he realizes that, no," Daisuke said.

The monster had developed a brownish crust, which cracked as it extruded a sheaf of wires like questing fingers, reaching up toward the radio Misha held against his ear.

"His modulated electromagnetic signals summoned a big bloody iron-eating monster," said Anne. "Do you think he's figured *that* out?"

"Sing has, yes," Daisuke said. "She is tugging on his sleeve, screaming. She wants him to—"

"To drop the radio. Obviously!"

Misha did not seem to hear her. Still shouting into his walkie-talkie, he tried to climb away from the monster, but there was nowhere for him to go. The monster flowed up its tracks with the speed of a locomotive.

There was no way Daisuke could have heard Sing's tongue-click from this distance. He must have only imagined it. That and Sing's toymaker's *sproing*!

Misha howled with pain – a noise Daisuke really *could* hear – and clutched at his shoulder, where, yes, a miniature ballista bolt protruded. His arm went limp, and the radio finally fell.

The amoeba monster twitched and dissolved. It dripped off the kelp-tree as skeins and loops of wire spread, acquired bristling black flesh, and became wings. The amoeba, now shaped like a manta ray, flapped clumsily after the plummeting radio.

Daisuke caught a glimpse of the rusty monster settling over the lower slopes of the mountains like a funeral shroud, stabbing its wires into the broken metal tool.

Daisuke gasped for breath, held the tree, tried to think. "Misha had a radio," he said. "All this time he had a radio. He was talking to someone. Why?"

Anne did not answer him. Daisuke was relieved. He should never have revealed himself to her.

CHAPTER SEVENTEEN

Coming Down

The wind did not conveniently blow Daisuke and Anne to where Misha and Sing had landed. It didn't even take them to Nurul. Instead, it threatened to bounce them back into the Death Wind biome. The wind pushing them south-east met another coming off the mountains, and the vectors seemed to be adding up to a course through the thickest part of the valley.

"We should cut the stalks," Daisuke told Anne. "Now, while we are over the Lighthouse biome and we know the air below us is breathable. Release the balloons one at a time."

"Maybe if we wait, we can catch up with Misha or Nurul," said Anne. "We can go faster by balloon than he can on foot."

"I think that's not true," Daisuke said, looking out over the sluggishly moving landscape. Morning sunlight lit the peaks of the Inner Toymaker Mountains and slanted out of the mouth of the Death Wind Pass. If Daisuke used his binoculars, he could see the green of Earth vegetation there. But below them spread the bare yellow branches of trees.

In daylight, the Lighthouse biome looked less like a glowing fairy garden than a blighted wasteland. That amber color, his instincts insisted, had to be a sign of pollution or disease. The fact that the animals didn't seem to be moving added to the impression of desolation. At least, Daisuke thought those things dangling from the skeletal branches were animals. Here was yet another new ecosystem, entirely unknown, potentially deadly.

"Cut the stalks now," said Daisuke. "If later, we won't be alive to regret it."

"You make a persuasive point." Anne fumbled for her knife. "Okay, I'm going to cut this one first." She gave one of the stalks a tug, sending vibrations down to where Daisuke dangled.

Daisuke started untying himself. He was no longer unconscious ballast on this flight, but he hadn't trusted his strength enough to loosen his trusses before now. His hands shook. His head pounded in pace with his pulse.

He kept feeling like he wasn't getting enough air, but that was probably psychosomatic. And his chest still twinged alarmingly when he spread his arms.

Has the Iron Man of Survival ever been in such a dire situation? thought Daisuke, glancing up at Anne's boots.

"Okay," he shouted, "cut them!"

One of their balloons floated away and they sank. Very slowly.

The yellow canopy reached up toward them, smaller saplings surrounding larger trees surrounding forest giants in overlapping fractal circles like ripples in a pond in the rain. Farther south, some other kind of plant (or giant animal?) had carved a clearing out of the forest, with reeds or fence posts growing in a spiraling pattern like the shell of a nautilus. It would be a better place to land than the forest, but Daisuke didn't see how they'd get there. As low as they were flying, their balloons would get hung up in the crown of one of the big cypress-looking trees, tens of meters above the ground. "Another one! Cut another balloon."

Anne didn't need convincing. She selected the smaller of their remaining balloons and set to work on its stalk while Daisuke carved grips for himself into the other.

They jerked as the second balloon tore away, and the trees swept up under them. Losing one balloon had had almost no effect on their buoyancy, but losing the second made them drop like a stone. *Typical. Well, this is no different from that time paragliding in Brazil.*

Teeth gritted in pain, Daisuke swung himself at the end of their last balloon stalk, turning himself into a pendulum, yanking them away from the sharp branches of one particularly tall tree. Those branches appeared to be tipped with little crystal spikes. He managed to pull his knees up to his chest, bringing his legs into position to kick out at the next tree that got too close. Crystals sliced his shins, but the sole of one boot connected with a solid branch, and he could give them a firm shove back the other way. Then it was time to spin and kick at the next tree and so on until their balloon finally got caught and wedged immovably into place.

Daisuke looked past his feet at the ground, maybe three meters away. In this higher gravity, in his battered condition, he would be a fool to let himself drop. His only other option, though, was to swing himself into the nearest tree trunk and climb down it.

"Get ready, Anne," he said. "I'm going to swing us into that tree."

"Oh," came Anne's voice from above. "Now you think to warn me. What about all that swinging you were doing before— Whoa!"

Daisuke let go of the kelp-tree stalk and struck the yellow tree trunk with three limbs and his knife. It was like stabbing a tube of PVC pipe. The knife blade jerked in his hand, sending agonizing shocks up his arms as his legs wrapped around the ivory-slick bark. But the tip of the knife had sunk in far enough to give him some leverage, and Daisuke managed to stop himself from plummeting to the ground.

He hugged the tree for a while, breathing.

"Okay," said Anne eventually. "So what now? We slide down this thing like a fireman's pole?"

"I think," Daisuke said, his forehead pressed into the bark, "we rest!"

"Normally I'd let you have all the rest you wanted, mate, but right now we have a traitorous Russian to catch."

Daisuke breathed deeply, searching for the reserves of strength he needed to play the survivor for Anne.

"Plus," she said, "I don't think you want that alien to catch you."

"Oh, *what*? What alien?" With a stab of pain from his much-abused head, Daisuke opened his eyes and focused on the growth dangling from the branch just above him and to his right. What he had thought was some kind of large fruit or flower was now moving toward him with slow purpose.

The animal was the same yellow color as the tree, and probably more massive than Daisuke. What he had thought were the petals of a flower now revealed themselves to be fleshy, flexible tubes capped with hard shell, ranging in size from pencil-tip feelers along the forward end to the six foot-long hooks that gripped the branch overhead. A seventh hook, even larger and more wickedly pointed, protruded from a cluster of horn-tipped tentacles at the front.

All of the tentacles, small and large, were in constant motion, swelling, shrinking, questing about as if in search of something to impale. And that complicated contraption hanging from the center of the body…was a mouth? A sense organ? A sex organ? Either way, Daisuke didn't like the way it was pointed at him.

"Would you stop looking at it and get out of that tree?" yelled Anne.

The body of the marigold-colored creature rippled and three of its legs shifted, pistons of tissue swelling, shell-tips scratching across each other and the plastic surface of the tree. How long before it would be in striking distance? What *was* its striking distance?

Daisuke tried to focus, but all he could think about was how hurt and tired he was. Well, at least a quick death smashed against the ground would be better than being slowly eviscerated by a carnivorous sloth-flower.

And if I break a leg but stay alive? Anne will just leave me. All right, enough thinking. Time for action! Daisuke squeezed his knees together and yanked the knife out of the tree.

He shot toward the ground, his knees hot against the slick plant, his knife vibrating and bouncing in his hands as he pressed it against the tree, trying to brake. He tore through branches and what felt like a man-sized spiderweb made of snot. Almost by accident, he found a grip on the knife that worked. Holding it perpendicular to the tree, he slowed his descent, peeling off a long curl of bark as he fell.

His ass hit the ground hard enough to compress his spine, but Daisuke barely noticed. He just rolled out of the way and gasped like a landed carp while Anne made her own rather more athletic landing.

"Okay," she said, hands on hips. "Let's go."

Now, what would be a more macho way to say, 'please let me rest, I'm tired'? "If you offered me the choice between getting up and another toymaker attack, I would let them chop me to pieces with their little hammers," said Daisuke.

Anne either didn't understand his message or ignored it. "Now's not the time, Dice. Up we go!" Anne grabbed him under the armpits and slid his body up a nearby tree trunk.

"No," he said flapping his hands. "No. I'm all right."

"Don't be stupid," she said, pulling him onto her shoulder. "You're weak and injured and poisoned. You can barely stand. Now put your bloody weight on me and let's get a move on, all right?"

Daisuke wondered why Anne bothered. Maybe she thought he'd be useful later on, or maybe she cared about his health, if not his feelings for her. Together, they hobbled eastward.

The understory of the Lighthouse biome was brighter than could be accounted for by the mere leaflessness of the trees. Those crystals redirected sunlight around obstacles, bathing Daisuke and Anne in a constant shower of light. Yellow plastic grass rippled around their feet – ribbons of tough material undulating in the steady south-easterly wind. Translucent bluish globs floated through the air or rolled across the ground like tumbleweeds.

"How are we going to find Misha and Nurul and Sing?" Anne asked.

"We can only hope that the others will want to go the same direction we do," said Daisuke. "East, toward home. If we go that way too, we will catch up to them."

"Or we won't catch up," Anne said. "Or they'll get lost and go off in different directions."

Where the hell did she get off being so pessimistic? Didn't she know they were still on camera? Daisuke glanced at Anne's bodycam and he smiled. "I think we will find them. Let's try."

"Ha," said Anne. "Thanks, Dice. Always walk on the sunny side of the shadowless forest." They slogged forward a few more three-legged steps. "I don't think we're going to make it to the mouth of the valley before nightfall, though."

Please don't leave me here, Daisuke thought, but he said, "We can survive that long without food or even water."

"Hoo, I wish you hadn't mentioned water, mate."

Daisuke thought of other ways to reassure her. "And we can stay warm when night comes."

"Were you thinking of sex? Or more along the lines of setting fire to the trees?"

Daisuke suppressed a flash of anger, then another, strong burst of self-disgust. Anne clearly had no idea how much she'd hurt him, but how could he tell her? How could he express his true feelings to someone who didn't want to see his true feelings? The only way to fix their relationship would be if Anne figured this all out and apologized without prompting.

Which is less likely than convincing these plastic trees to burn.

Anne stopped. "Can you stand by yourself for a moment?" she said. "I want to try something."

Daisuke found that he could stand, and even walk by himself, which was some comfort to his wounded pride if not his legs and back. While he tried some tentative stretches, Anne knelt in the undulating grass, pulling a lighter out of her utility belt. She reached for one of the stiff yellow grass blades, saying, "We have enough kindling— Ow!"

Daisuke jumped and Anne jerked upright, waving her hand as if the plant had burned her.

"What happened?" asked Daisuke, heart racing.

"The grass just shocked me. A nice little jolt of electricity." Anne sucked on her fingers. "Well, that puts the kibosh on collecting this stuff as firewood. I wonder if we could hack open the local fauna and sleep inside it? Unless the critters are electric as well."

"Critters?" Daisuke tried to remember if he'd seen any animals since the flower-sloth, but his mind was blank. Either he hadn't been paying attention to his surroundings or he had failed to form memories of his impressions. *It is possible, gentle viewers, that my career as a professional survivor is over. I can only hope that I can continue to survive as a hobby.*

Anne pointed at something off the path. "Animals like foot-wide sunflowers. Or I should say like sunflower sea stars. Land stars?" She snapped her fingers. "Land-asters."

Daisuke smiled and nodded, glad he wasn't expected to do more.

"I was wondering when we were going to finally see some good old-fashioned radial symmetry," Anne continued. "Except these things are more like mollusks than echinoderms, with those shell-tipped tentacles. And even there the analogy isn't great because mollusks have contractile muscles just like us, and *these* things – seems they've only got a sort of pneumatic muscular system of erectile tissue." She looked at him. "Does that make sense?"

"I didn't understand much of that, except for the part about erections."

Anne's laughter echoed weirdly between the yellow trees. "And in the end, what else do we really need to understand? Ah, there's a nice big turgid one."

She was right. At least about the 'big' part. Daisuke didn't know what 'turgid' meant, and didn't want to ask.

The animal sat on the edge of the path like a rococo boulder, its feeding apparatus dangling from the center of its body, a stalk of waving 'grass' caught within its jaws. As they walked past the creature, the grass broke with a *pop* and a flash of light.

"And I'm not sure what ecological role these fast little ones play. Look, you can even see them moving."

Clumps of blue aerogel wobbled on the backs of the ten-centimeter creatures as they made a comparatively speedy dash toward the big grazer. Erectile muscles swelled and contracted, pushing the little creatures up so that their spike-shaped feeding tubes could jab at the big land-aster.

"Little predators?" Daisuke asked, thinking about piranhas.

"I don't think so. Every now and then they'll stop treading about and this complicated apparatus unfolds from their underside and plugs into a hole in the ground." She pointed at one of the purple-filigreed cups that Daisuke had assumed were flowers. "I don't think the little animals are parasites, so are they like hummingbirds pollinating underground flowers? Hummingbirds sometimes mob bigger birds, try and drive them away. Or are they doing something else? Something more alien? Watch the grass."

Daisuke did. The paddle-shaped plants rose to a height of twenty to twenty-five centimeters, stiff at their squared-off tips but flexible at the base, where the stalk narrowed and met the bulbous root.

"A plant that makes energy through movement." Anne passed her foot through the grass, which *clack*ed. "But where do the purple ground-flowers come in? This grasslike stuff rewards animals that walk through it with some kind of nectar. Hummingbird-sea-stars, walking on treadmills for a sip of nectar."

Daisuke looked at the purple ground-flowers, remembering the bitterroot plants he'd filmed in college. How much he had enjoyed himself back then, in front of a camera. Now, he just felt like lying down. *I have been on this treadmill for too long, and for too little nectar.*

"What's up, Daisuke?"

He looked up. "Nothing." He could hear how flat his voice sounded, but it took all his effort to speak at all. Injecting emotion into his words was as impossible at this point as flying.

She looked him up and down, intense as an MRI. "You feeling dizzy? Headachy? Tired?"

Daisuke shrugged. "Yes, but none of that will stop me from walking." He faked a smile. "I will survive."

Anne looked at him dubiously. What would the Iron Man of Survival be expected to say at this point?

"The grass," Daisuke said. "Can we burn it?"

Anne shook her head. "I don't think so. Not without a furnace, anyway."

"What about those blue globs floating in the air? Maybe we could burn them."

"Blue globs?" Anne straightened and followed Daisuke's pointing finger to an irregular clump of translucent-blue gel around a meter across. She ran up to it and kicked it.

"Anne!" said Daisuke, but the clump just deformed around her boot and bounced off.

"It was like kicking jelly," Anne said, "except made with air instead of water."

"An aerogel?" Daisuke had seen a program on NHK about them. "What creature could excrete aerogel?"

Anne considered. "Maybe it's a tangle of some kind of ultrafine, ultra-hydrophobic fibers. Dense enough to trap air, light enough to be carried by the wind. But those little dark blots in the gel— Ha!" She laughed with real delight. "Animals!"

She trapped an aerogel with her fingers and held it out so Daisuke could see the creatures inside it. They were spherical and up to one centimeter in diameter. Ridges of iridescent cilia pulsed as the little animals slowly tunneled through their home.

"It's like a ctenophore," said Anne. "A comb jelly. Aerogelly?"

"I wish we could examine this creature," Daisuke said. "Stop and learn about it like in the old days." He peered into the depths of the aerogelly. The creatures moved within it, eating the detritus trapped by their sticky home.

"So?" said Anne.

"So what?"

"So are you going to try and light that thing on fire? 'Cause if not, we'd better get a move on before we freeze to death."

"Oh, right." But Daisuke didn't move. An idea had occurred to him. "Maybe there is something better I can do." He pressed the aerogelly over his left arm. It spread and stuck to itself, forming a tube from Daisuke's wrist to his elbow.

Daisuke waved his arms experimentally. "The one with the aerogel feels much warmer," he confirmed.

"Good," said Anne. "Now watch those things excrete acid and eat your arm off."

Daisuke watched the little animals within the aerogelly, which were indeed clustered around the fabric of his sleeve. "Easily fixed...." he said, and reached into the gel with forefinger and thumb. He plucked out one of the creatures and he tossed it away. It flew a few tens of centimeters before ballooning out a new cushion of aerogel and floating off, light as a soap bubble.

Daisuke repeated the procedure until he had made a small cloud of drifting baby aerogellies and an uninhabited bracer of gel over his left forearm. He and Anne spent the next few minutes tracking down aerogellies and converting them into insulating clothing.

"Brilliant, Daisuke," said Anne, now blue with gel. "I think we might just live. Come here and let me do your back. You'll have to do mine too."

She looked up at him, and Daisuke felt a little better. So what if he couldn't tell Anne how he felt? They were both alive, weren't they? And now, no longer cold.

CHAPTER EIGHTEEN

Plots

"*Tek-lum! Keb tek-lum!*"

Misha opened his eyes. His eyes hurt. So did his left little toe and his scalp and everything in between. What *especially* hurt was his right scapula, where Sing's little toymaker had shot him. And the place on the back of the head where she'd hit him with a tree branch. That, and the knowledge that he'd been betrayed.

The natives had put him in some kind of cage. It was made of alien plants – flat yellow paddles as wide as his body and about twice as tall. They had been planted around him at angles to each other, forming a spiral. And between the gaps in the spiral....

"*Keb-lum!*" A man stood beyond the wall of paddles. He looked just like Sing, minus the breasts and plus a bizarre yard-long codpiece of twisted yellow plastic. Some kind of translucent blue jelly glinted on his narrow, wiry shoulders. A white thong had been tied over his brows, with feathers, bones, and thorny alien mandibles woven into his hair. He held another paddle, this one only the size of a cricket bat, which he used to reach into Misha's cage and prod him in the chest.

"You're going to have to do more than that to impress me," Misha told the man he assumed was Sing's brother, watching the bat. It was the same yellow plastic as the codpiece. Someone had scorched its edges, then pressed pointed teeth into the softened plastic to create saw edges. Those teeth looked very much like human canines.

"Okay," said Misha. "That is pretty impressive."

"Sing," he said. "Where is she?" No, that wasn't what he should say. He had a mission that was more important than any native women he might have taken a fancy to. "Listen, I go. I go to my persons."

"Misha," said the Nun war chief, followed by an incomprehensible spate of words. He turned, addressing someone behind him, putting his back to Misha.

Who grinned and smashed him into the paddles.

The pain was so intense it felt like nothing at all. A pop like an old-fashioned fuse blowing, and Misha was on his back, his teeth chattering, his heart smashing against his ribs, his hands throbbing, the smell of burning hair in his nose.

"Misha. Okay. Okay, Misha."

That was Sing's voice. Misha managed to loll his head sideways and saw Sing between the electric paddles of this alien torture chamber. "Okay is," she said. "No go. Hurt more."

Misha cursed in Russian.

"Misha, this is Yunubey," Sing said. "He is...." She pointed to herself, then to the native, then mimed giving birth.

He couldn't be her son, and he was too young to be her father. "Sing," said Misha. "Help me. I have to go."

"No," said Sing. "Here is people of you." She gestured around her then pointed to Misha. "*Nu....*" – she pointed to herself and Misha – "*Nun-ak ang...*" another gesture around her – "*...ulu-na.* We are...with the Us."

Misha blinked, and human figures melted out from between the electric paddles. 'The Us' surrounded Misha, Sing, and Yunubey, mostly male, mostly short and skinny, all armed, literally, to the teeth. Sing's people, but not Misha's. Not while he had his mission to fulfill.

"Okay, Misha?" Sing asked again.

"Yes." Misha licked his numb lips. He would be all right. He had gotten through to base before that monster ate his radio. The Indonesians' little coup had failed, Misha's people had control of the wormhole, and someone was coming to pick him up.

Misha would survive, although he'd have to disappear for a while. Anne, Daisuke, and Nurul might make it out of here if they had the sense to stay away from him. Misha looked at Sing, the woman he loved even though she'd put him in a cage. Hell, he would have done the same thing in her place.

He took a deep breath and hauled himself to his feet. "You got to go," Misha told the war chief. "Go from here. Death comes. Death flies." He pointed toward the sky, wondering how the hell he was going to convey 'helicopter'.

Sing said something to Yunubey that might be her attempt at a translation. Yunubey frowned and asked her a question. She launched into a story that Misha recognized from her gestures as their encounter with the flying monster, not the helicopter.

"No," Misha said. "Wrong. New death comes. New *deibukna.* Death *will* come. Not from Death Wind Country. From *my* country. My…." Sing wouldn't know the word 'comrades'. "My people. My Us. My Nun. They're coming to kill you."

How long did Misha have to make himself clear? He didn't even know how long he'd been unconscious. He checked the sky above the paddles. It was dark, but the air was full of a weird yellow radiance. Straight, smooth branches stretched above them, shedding enough light to read by.

Sing squinted at him. "People of you…come kill? Me kill? Yunubey kill? They Misha not kill?"

"Yes," said Misha. "My people are coming here. I called them. They'll kill everyone but me."

Yunubey bared his teeth and shook his cricket bat at Misha. "*Dan? Danya yak-nam-ak do?*"

"Who come?" Sing asked. "People of you are who?"

"Who are my people?" Misha could only shrug. Unlikely as it was that any journalist would ever interview these poor, doomed people, the chance was still there. And he was still wearing the bodycam, if his brush with the paddle-cage hadn't fried it. So he couldn't very well say 'Americans', could he?

★ ★ ★

When they found her, Nurul looked like a corpse reanimated by vengeance. Her hair hung in tattered curtains across her waxy skin. She clutched at herself, shuddering, her lips pulled back from chattering teeth.

"Shit, what happened to you?" Anne rushed to fold her arms around the shivering journalist. "We thought a magnetovore got you."

"What? No. I only got…turned around," Nurul said. "Cold. I need… help."

"Christ, you need gel," said Anne. "Daisuke, get her some gel."

Daisuke, who had hoped that Nurul was just a hallucination, groaned as his brain creaked over this new information. He was hurt, hungry, exhausted, angry at Anne, and despairing of his future. And now a journalist had joined their party.

"Why were you walking west?" he asked.

Nurul's eyes widened. "I was going the wrong direction?"

"It's a good thing you found us," said Anne. "Let's get some insulation on you before you freeze."

Nurul watched with distaste as he and Anne caught some aerogellies and spread the excretions over her body, but her shivering slowly subsided.

"Where did you become lost?" Daisuke asked.

Nurul pointed behind her, in the direction they were supposed to be going. "There's a river. I tried to go around it."

Daisuke shivered in sympathy. Nurul would very likely have died of hypothermia if she had gotten wet. "Is it deep?" he asked.

Nurul shook her head. "Waist-high."

Daisuke looked at Anne. It was clear she felt no better about wading through icy mountain water than he did.

"Any ideas how we're going to cross that river, Dice?" she asked.

Daisuke thought. It was a very great effort. "We might chop down a tree to make a bridge if we had an axe."

"We've also got no grappling hook or shovels," said Anne.

Daisuke looked around, and his gaze snagged on one of those big starfish-looking grazers. Land-asters moved so slowly. It should be easy to capture enough of them. "I have an idea, but I don't know how to explain it," he said. "How does the saying go? We will cross that river when we get there." Yes, that sounded properly telegenic, although now they had no cameraman. "For now, we should walk."

They set off, just as slowly as before. Nurul stumbled alongside them, hugging herself and shivering. Her color seemed better, though, at least what Daisuke could see of it under the blue tinge of the gel.

The poor woman. She had lost so much. Had Daisuke even expressed his condolences? "I'm sorry about Rahman," he said.

Nurul closed her eyes and nodded silently. Anne only shot Daisuke a puzzled glance.

"What are you sorry about?" she said. "He's probably safer than we are."

Nurul stopped walking. "What?"

"What what?" asked Anne. "The Oasis biome is warm, and you can eat the animals there."

Nurul looked like she was going to cry.

The part Daisuke was playing couldn't confront Anne about the callous way she treated his feelings, but he could certainly defend Nurul. "Why did you say that? It's cruel."

"Cruel? You guys are the ones talking about Rahman as if he's dead," Anne said. "And he isn't. He's just on the Oasis Planet."

As if it made any difference whether Rahman was still alive, trapped as he was uncountable millions of miles away. Daisuke massaged the base of his thumb. "Don't be so pedantic."

"Wait," said Nurul.

Anne stared at Daisuke. "Are you angry with me? What did I do?"

"You are talking about my husband as if he *isn't* trapped forever on an alien planet," Nurul said.

"Well, yeah," Anne said.

"'Yeah'?" repeated Daisuke. "He *is* trapped forever?"

"Don't shout at me," Anne said. "Yeah, he *isn't* trapped. Unless something eats him before the wormhole reopens."

Nurul put her hands to her face and sank to her knees in the electric yellow grass.

"You think we should have waited for him?" Anne asked. "I'm really mystified here. I thought you wanted to follow Misha to Imsame and organize a rescue party. That's what it makes sense to do, anyway, so we can be some help to him when he comes out."

"Why didn't you say any of this before?"

Anne threw up her hands. "I thought that was obvious. The wormhole shuts off when the air gets toxic, then turns back on again when things are safe. Remember Misha's question about supernovas?"

Daisuke tried to think back to their conversation on the other side of the Toymaker Mountains, when he had been worried about things other than simply surviving.

"The wormholes were designed with an automatic shutoff," said Anne. "That's why there are no supernovas or volcanoes spewing fire over Junction. That's why the flooding of the Mekimsam doesn't spread to New Guinea. And I bet that's why—"

"So Rahman might come back?"

They both looked down at Nurul.

"What am I doing here?" She rose in a smooth, athletic motion. "We must go back for him."

Anne put her hands on her hips "How? Don't be stupid."

Daisuke winced, but had to agree. "We can't survive a trip back to the Sweet Blood Country by ourselves."

"And can Rahman survive on the Oasis Planet by himself?" Nurul asked. "We must turn back! If you don't have the courage, I do."

Daisuke didn't know what to say. How much courage did he have? He couldn't even tell Anne how he felt.

"We can get help for him in Imsame," said Anne. "He just has to hang on until then."

Nurul looked down. "I suppose…we still have a mission. This is all the more reason for us to hurry."

She was right. They hurried, and the wind whistled, the animals around them clicked, the grass rippled. None of it would pause if the three of them died. Only humans cared about other humans.

They found the river, which ran clear, fast, and icy-cold through a gully overgrown with more of those grasslike plants. These blades were as tall as Daisuke's shoulders, undulating in the water.

"Turning the current into energy," Anne said, as if to herself. "Probably via the flexion of piezo-electric crystals at the base of their blades. Maybe sucrose?"

"This is where I got turned around," said Nurul. "How can we cross it?"

"I suppose we could try and make a bridge," Anne said, but for once, Daisuke had a better idea of how to use the local environment.

Daisuke looked around for land-asters. "I have a plan. We can make…." Hell. What was the word in English? "Flying rocks? Jumping rocks?"

"Jumping…rocks?" said Anne. Stupid English. Why would the default meaning of that phrase be something entirely impossible like 'rocks that jump' rather than 'rocks that are for jumping on'?

"I understand," Nurul said. "Walking rocks. Rocks for footing."

"What the hell are you two—" Anne blinked. "Oh. Stepping-stones. You see any rocks around here, Dice?"

"No," he said. "But…." He walked to the nearest place where the paddle-reeds parted and found a grazing land-aster the size of a *kotatsu* foot-warmer table. He flipped it over with a boot and pushed it down the embankment.

The reeds hummed as the creature crashed through them, coming to rest at the edge of the water. It stayed there, its back broad and dry in the middle of a writhing nest of horn-tipped tentacles.

"That's one," said Daisuke. "Quickly, we must get others. They move slowly, but they do move."

The land-asters were unused to attack from above, and incapable of moving faster than real starfish. Daisuke sent them rolling while Nurul pressed the hinged, reedlike plants into a sort of ramp. Anne placed each creature in the water, apologizing under her breath as she did so.

Their immersion didn't seem to bother the aliens. They kept moving in any case, inching their way closer to the nearest bank, slow and silent as snails.

The sun was still high when Daisuke hurled the last land-aster into the shallows on the opposite bank. Aerogellies sparkled in air cold and sweet as shaved ice, tumbling through spotlights cast by the crystalline branches above. More blue gel stretched between the gently clacking reed-blades – something like spiderwebs, perhaps?

Daisuke stood there, surveying his 'stepping-stones'. No envenomed tentacle jabbed his foot. The nodding kinetotroph weeds did not zap him with electricity. No poisonous cloud fell on him. No monsters dropped from the trees or leaped out of the water to devour him. The many worlds of Junction were finally giving him a break. *Knock on wood and pretend to be a mulberry tree....*

Something exploded above them with a sound like a thunderclap funneled through a foghorn.

Daisuke jumped up the embankment in a single terrified bound and stood there, hair bristling, heart and head pounding. He caught a glimpse of a little brown ball as it flew up from the forest to the east and exploded in another noisy burst of red powder.

"Is that a signal?" he asked once the echoes had subsided.

Anne nodded. "That looked like a kelp-tree balloon. More of Sing's so-called witchery, I guess."

"Who is she signaling?" Nurul asked. "Us? Or someone else?"

"You think she's signaling her people?" asked Anne. "Or the people Misha was trying to radio?"

Nurul whipped around, staring at her. "Radio? What radio?"

"The one that attracted the ferrofluid monster?"

Nurul closed her eyes. "Anne, remember how we talked about externalizing your thought processes?"

A petty part of Daisuke was glad to see that Anne's social obliviousness hurt more than just him. But his more gallant persona demanded he say, "We are all tired and we have a long way to walk."

"Toward Misha's signal?" Anne asked.

Nurul shrugged. "There's no better way to reach Far Side Base. And if Misha succeeded in calling someone there, I think we had better find him before they arrive."

The trees were sparser on the other side of the stream, the ground cover taller and more dense. Oar-shaped plastic blades came up to Daisuke's waist. The blades resisted him as he pushed through them, as if the hinges at their bases were rusty. They hummed softly as they righted themselves behind him.

"That radio must be why he pulled that stunt with the balloons," said Nurul as they walked. "He was trying to get line of sight with Far Side Base."

The paddles had grown to shoulder height now, and he could see the tips of still taller blades rising to the east and north. South, the reeds grew shorter, and Daisuke could see a subtle pattern in their growth. Triangles pointed their apexes east, then north-east, then north, leading uphill in a contracting spiral like a nautilus shell.

"No," Anne said. "That doesn't make sense. Misha couldn't have just been in a hurry to phone home. He could have gone balloon riding days ago when we first crossed over the Toymaker Mountains. But Misha only abandoned us when…when what? When the Death Wind came up? When the wormhole closed? When Hariyadi died?" She smiled at Daisuke. "Ha, look at me, getting as paranoid as you were when you woke up with linguipods in your bed."

When I woke from near death and confessed my real fears to you and you ridiculed me? When you showed me that you preferred my actor's persona to the real man I am? Daisuke swallowed the words, nearly choking as he struggled to keep his face blank.

Nurul looked at him. "What's wrong, Daisuke?"

"Nothing," said Anne. "He just had this cockamamie theory that someone was trying to murder us one by one."

Daisuke couldn't think of what the Iron Man of Survival would say now. He could only stop himself from screaming at Anne.

"Oh," Nurul said. "I understand. Anne, you don't realize that Daisuke is angry at you, do you?"

"Angry? Why would he be angry?"

Daisuke pushed aside another, taller paddle, and it bent at an angle, leading them uphill of their original path. "We have to be careful," he said. "Try to go downhill at the next opportunity. We don't want to turn around in a circle."

"Don't avoid the subject," Nurul said. "Daisuke, what's going on?"

He felt like a mussel being attacked by a starfish. Nurul was trying to pry him open.

"Listen," she said. "The man we are following may well be a spy. What if Misha is lying in wait for us? What if we catch up with him? Clearly he is trying to beat us back to Far Side Base. What does the Russian plan to do when he gets there? I suspect it's nothing good."

"You're not suggesting we kill Misha?" said Anne, and Daisuke swallowed. Next to this tale of betrayal and international espionage, his personal problems sounded ridiculously small. He couldn't bear to speak them.

Nurul came up behind him and put a hand on his shoulder. "The longer you lie, the harder it becomes to tell the truth."

What, was she telepathic?

"It doesn't matter," Daisuke said. "It is a personal problem, and right now it is more important just to survive."

Nurul's hand was on his shoulder. "No. We have a higher mission."

"Maybe you do." Daisuke shook her off. "I only want to live until we can return home."

"Oh, for Christ's sake, Daisuke!" Anne whacked a paddle downhill of them. "Ow! Fuck, that hurt." She rubbed her hand, glaring at him. "Why are you doing this to me? Trying to make me guess your bloody fucking mental state? I don't know why people do things, I *told* you that."

"And what did I tell you?" Daisuke snapped back.

"I don't know! Lots of things!" Anne flexed the paddle back and forth. It was taller than she was. "You know I'm the kind of person who can tell that these paddles only bend in one direction in order to guide animals walking in them into a spiral so they can trap the animals' kinetic energy. What I can't figure out is what's wrong with you."

Daisuke raged at her unfairness. "So I have to spend all my life with you explaining why I'm feeling what I'm feeling like I'm some kind of alien?"

Anne's eyes went wide. "You want to spend your life with me?"

The English sentence arrived on Daisuke's tongue, and without hesitating or considering how it would sound, he spoke. "Only if you don't make me play a part. Let me show sometimes that I'm afraid."

Anne looked from the paddle to Daisuke. "I have no idea what you're talking about."

"Why can't you understand?" Daisuke yelled. "I told you I was afraid someone was trying to murder me. Someone killed Pearson and Tyaney and Colonel Hariyadi."

"Oh no!" Nurul said. "You mean it was Misha all the time?"

"Yes," said Daisuke. "You wouldn't believe me when I said he tried to kill me."

"Of course. With the linguipods," Nurul said.

"Maybe you don't trust me or you think I'm stupid?" shouted Daisuke. "But I will not be the Iron Man of Survival for you. I need only one person with whom I can be myself."

All the color had gone out of Anne's face. "Oh," she said. "Oh *shit*."

Nurul steepled her hands. "This is good. I think you can both be happy together. But if Daisuke is right and Misha is the murderer, we are in great danger." She pushed aside the paddle in front of them, angling farther uphill. "We must go."

"Shit," said Anne. "Toxic linguipods, Dice."

"What are you talking about?" Daisuke had thought he was exhausted before, but now he felt like lying down in this energy-stealing trap of a grove and dying. He had shown Anne the small-minded, selfish, cowardly person under his professional mask, and she didn't seem to care. Daisuke might as well have unloaded his terrible secrets to a land-aster.

"Daisuke!"

His head snapped around. Anne's expression wasn't angry or confused. She was terrified. Her eyes darted between Daisuke and Nurul.

"Toxic," she hissed. "Not venomous, and Misha knew that!"

And Daisuke understood. "Anne," he said, voice tight. "Stay back."

Anne stopped. She listened to him. She knew what he meant. "Yeah," she said. "Yes, Daisuke."

The two of them were downhill of Nurul. Nurul, who had been with Pearson when the shmoo attacked, who had known how to attract the wrath of the toymakers, and had been alone with Hariyadi on the Oasis Planet. Who didn't know that linguipods were harmless and tried to use them to kill Daisuke.

"What's wrong?" asked the murderer. Her voice sounded normal, but Daisuke could see how her hand strayed toward her pocket. He remembered the dark bulk that had tracked her through the mist of the Death Wind biome, attracted, Daisuke was suddenly sure, by the metal in the gun Nurul had looted from Hariyadi's corpse.

"You should be happy," Nurul said, her body tensing. "You have your whole lives ahead of you." And now her hand was in her pocket. How could she lie so well? Daisuke had to admit he was impressed.

"Fucking now, Dice!" shouted Anne and Daisuke lunged. There was no thought, no choreography, no awareness of the camera on the murderer's chest. No fear, only the actions he needed to perform in order to survive.

Nurul's shoulder jabbed into Daisuke's chest. She was half turned away from him, shielding her weapon with her body. If he just had another moment to reach around her body and grab her right wrist....

Nurul didn't give Daisuke the chance. She stepped back and pivoted, turning inside the circle of his arms. The barrel of her gun jabbed into his belly, sending a wave of nauseating pain up his body.

Nurul bared her teeth in a feral snarl of fear and anger and hopelessness. The gun nosed deeper into his intestines and Daisuke knew he would die out here in the wilderness, his guts turned into hamburger. Die of shock or cold or blood loss or sepsis even before the slow predators of this country could descend on him. *But at least I know I am a real hero. I even got the girl.* He wondered if he had time to give his dying speech.

"Anne," he said, and she barreled into him.

Anne's tackle sent Daisuke and Nurul reeling backward through the fence of yellow paddles. Electricity tingled over Daisuke's skin. From much too close, the noise of the gun rang his skull like a bell. He stumbled backward, Anne pulling on his wrist.

She was pulling him back through the gap his body had made in the yellow fence. Nurul fell away from him, mouth open in a silent scream, smoke trailing from the barrel of her gun as it swung to follow him.

It was like pulling a trout from a stream in Kamchatka. With his free hand, Daisuke snatched the gun.

Daisuke and Anne tumbled onto the ground and the broad plastic plants snapped back into position.

The paddle had about the heft of a baseball bat, moving too slowly to do any real damage. The electric shock it administered to Nurul's face, however, was more than enough to send the murderer reeling back. Daisuke could even hear the pop of the spark. Nurul screamed in pain.

Daisuke put his hand to his chest. Tried to breathe. Tried to think. They had imprisoned the murderer.

"Bonza!" Anne pumped her fist in the air. "Biology! To finally be able to predict something bad *before* it actually happened! Thank God she never listened to me when I talked about the local wildlife, or she might have exposed you to something actually dangerous." Anne rolled against Daisuke. "Oh my God, Dice. You almost died. *Again*! Stop doing that!"

Daisuke put his arms around her. "We won," he said, and from a dozen hidden places around the trap-grove, people cheered.

CHAPTER NINETEEN

Confessions

Daisuke had never been in such prolonged pain. *Nor have I felt so grateful to still be alive to feel it.*

"We did it." He rolled off Anne and tried to sit up. "We found people."

"The Nun." Anne got to her hands and knees, but very slowly. "The signal from Sing's pet toymaker must have brought them here. They must have known we would come this way so they hid. Let us stumble into this… 'trap-grove', would you call it?"

Daisuke closed his eyes. "I don't care," he said. "Just tell me I can rest."

"Yeah," Anne said. "Good show. Now the question is if Nurul was killing all of us, why? And why did Misha run away? And how did he get the Nun to co-operate with him?"

"I didn't!" came a voice from farther inside the spiral of the trap-grove. "They held a stone knife to my throat and told me not to make a sound."

"Hello, Misha. So, the Nun were seeing whether they could trust us, maybe?" said Anne. "But now I'm curious about how they—"

"Ask them if they plan to kill us," Daisuke said, eyes still closed. He would prefer they didn't. He had a lot of things to do once his body started working again.

"Oh, right. Um, *Nun*, uh, *nu deibuk do?*"

"No. You safe."

That was Sing's voice. Daisuke opened his eyes and saw their guide emerge through the paddles of the trap-grove. Behind her, other Nun bent and tied the paddles to each other, creating a path back to freedom without triggering the plant's electrical defenses.

The men were short and wiry, with heavy features and well-defined muscles under beaded smocks and strands of yellow plastic. The same stuff formed their axes, bows, and arrows, melted around knapped stone or sharpened wood. All of the Nun were coated in aerogel, and many had floating toymakers tethered to their shoulders. The domesticated aliens tracked him and Anne with underslung crossbow bolts like the stingers of giant, clockwork wasps.

These were people who had mastered the art of surviving in alien biotas. People who had figured out how to turn the strange lifeforms they found into tools. These Nun weren't starving and smeared with half-understood exobiology like Daisuke, and they weren't reluctant wormhole guardians like Tyaney's tribe. They were Junction natives. Sing's people.

"Hello," said Sing, walking toward them. "Peace."

"Take us to your leader," Anne muttered.

"Too late," came Misha's voice. "He's already here."

"Yunubey is leader," said Sing, nodding toward a man with a distressingly long codpiece. "He is brother me."

"Good day," Anne said. "Now, I have some questions. Um. *Heib? Heibna? Heina?*"

"Yes yes," said Sing, treating Anne to one of her own impatient hand-flutters. "Long time we will talk. After we not die."

That sounded ominous. "Does that mean that we won't die after we talk, or we will talk after we don't die?" Daisuke asked, sitting up.

"I don't suppose I could convince you all to run away," Misha called to them. "The Nun might take it badly and attack, but you'd stand a better chance of survival than if you wait around here."

I suppose that answers my question. There was something strange about Misha's voice, and the things he was hinting, but Daisuke didn't have the capacity to untangle more than one mystery at a time. "What will happen if we stay here?" he asked.

"I'm afraid my friends are coming to pick me up," said Misha.

Anne stomped in frustration. "What the hell is going on? I thought we'd caught the bad guy."

A bitter chuckle from behind the fence of trap-grove paddles. "Bad guy?" Nurul said. "Don't you know what Misha is?"

"Not a *mur*-der-er," Misha sang from his own prison.

"I am a *patriot*!" Nurul's scream wiped away the smile growing on Daisuke's face. *Hell. I'm going to have to sit up, aren't I?*

"I love my country," Nurul said, her voice compressed. "My country, which finally has the chance to achieve the greatness it deserves."

"Huh?" Anne said.

"*Dan?*" said Yunubey the Nun.

"Say again," Sing commanded.

"She means that she and Rahman were spies the whole time," said Daisuke.

"No! Rahman was just—" A muffled sob from behind the paddles. When Nurul spoke again, it was through her teeth. "He *is* just my husband."

"But Nurul took orders from that idiot Hariyadi," Misha said.

"Of course," said Nurul. "And of course I knew Hariyadi was a narrow-minded, power-hungry fool, but I also knew too that when our people had control of both sides of the wormhole, we could start letting through *colonists*."

"Colonists!" Anne spat. "Of all the insane fucking megalomaniacal ideas...."

"We could settle this new world. *All* these new worlds." Nurul did not sound insane. She sounded like a TV weather reporter announcing the beginning of swimsuit season. "Junction could be the beginning of a great new experiment. A society that's faith-based, civilized, unified, democratic, just."

A brief lull while Sing translated that for Yunubey. Then a longer pause while Yunubey looked expectantly at Sing, she looked at Anne, and Anne looked at Daisuke.

So I am still the host of this bizarre little drama. With a sigh, Daisuke stood up.

"But?" he prompted.

"But!" Nurul growled. "Of course you Westerners weren't going to let us have it. No, empire building is only something *you're* allowed to do. At first I thought that stupid pretend plane crash was just to prevent Hariyadi from being present for our coup, as if that would stop us."

"Pretend crash?" said Sing, "Coup?"

"Yes," Nurul said as if Sing had asked for clarification rather than vocabulary. "A coup. Our government was just rolling over for America. Again! But certain components of the Indonesian army thought they had a chance to seize Junction."

Yunubey said something and Sing raised her hands. "I don't understand."

"I think I do," said Anne. "Hariyadi was supposed to lead the coup from this side. He was waiting for somebody back on Earth to launch their attack, but it seems the Americans found out about that."

"'Course we did," said Misha. "But we couldn't prove anything. We couldn't arrest the commander of an allied armed force. We couldn't even stop the movement of troops on the Indonesian side of the wormhole."

"Wait, '*we*'?" Daisuke had realized what had changed about Misha's voice. "Your accent...you're an American!"

"Well, obviously," Anne said.

Misha sniffed. "I most certainly am not an American."

"Your accent sure as hell is," Anne said.

"I am Russian," said Misha. "I was born in Russia and lived there until my parents emigrated in '91. I tried to go back, but there was some…" he cleared his throat, "…disagreement about my military service. I ended up in the American embassy, where, you know, work was found for me."

"So you're a dog for the Americans," Nurul sneered. "That's even worse than I thought. At least the Russians have pride."

"You don't know what you're talking about," Misha said, voice tired.

Anne blinked, eyes focused inward, brow wrinkled. "So this whole thing: the plane ride, the crash, the hike through the wilderness, was all a ruse to get Hariyadi out of the way."

"We weren't going to kill him," said Misha, "just remove him from play so that the Indonesian coup would fail."

"Well, why *didn't* you kill him?"

"World War Three, remember? We're still wearing bodycams for exactly that reason."

Daisuke rubbed the tender spot on his chest, thinking of all the great footage Anne and Sing were surely failing to capture in this scene. "But then why did they drag *me* into this?" It wasn't something the Iron Man of Survival would say, but Daisuke found that role easy to ignore now.

"You gave our plot a veneer of verisimilitude," Misha said. "Plus, somebody in Washington owed somebody in Tokyo a favor."

Yunubey grumbled something and Sing translated. "Say again. Misha is American Them, Nurul is Indonesian Them. Them two for country Nun fighting, right?"

"Yes," said Anne. "Stupid geopolitics killed three people and made us march across five different alien biomes."

"We were supposed to stay by the plane and wait for the helicopter to pick us up," said Misha, his tone disgusted. "But you idiots couldn't just sit down and take orders. Then *this* bitch kills Pearson…."

"I had no choice." Nurul paced behind the electrified paddles like a caged tiger. "At first I was glad I only crippled him. But then Pearson got drunk and started talking about my country's plans. He knew about the coup! So I waited until his next dose of morphine, then I smothered him with a thermal blanket while he was unconscious."

"And Hariyadi?" Daisuke asked.

"And Hariyadi! The traitor!" Nurul's voice dropped from pride to scorn. "The *coward*. Just because the day of the coup had come and gone, he was ready to give up. Give up! I sacrificed everything for our mission and Hariyadi just let it slip away." Her voice went dull. "Now my country has nothing. I have nothing."

"I understand," said Sing. "Anne and Daisuke are good. Misha is a little bad. Nurul is a little bad."

"A *little*?" Anne said. "She would have killed us!"

"That is bad." Sing looked at her. "But Nurul killed Tyaney. That is good."

Swarms of aerogellies swirled and twinkled through shafts of light. The kinetotroph grass hummed and ratcheted around their ankles. Slow predators oozed along the branches on pneumatic claws. The paddles of the trap-grove hummed with stored power.

"That ass threatened to drive off our native guide," Nurul said into the high-tension silence. "And just when we were entering territory she knew. It was infuriating." And a moment later, "Anne, and Daisuke, to you I am sorry. I couldn't find my way through the yellow jungle, but if I let you come with me into Far Side Base, you would have said too much."

"What the hell is that supposed to mean?" said Anne.

Misha cleared his throat. "It's the same reason my buddies will kill you when they land here. You're evidence of a stupid blunder on the part of my bosses and Nurul's. What is the Pentagon supposed to say when this story comes out? 'Well, what we were *trying* to do was keep Hariyadi alive, but, whoops, we let one of his subordinates kill him'? Nobody will believe that."

"But it's the truth," Anne said.

"It *looks* like an open declaration of war," said Nurul. "One that the Americans didn't even bother to cover up. It would be better if nobody from our expedition ever came back."

Daisuke swallowed.

"She's right," Misha said. "When my people get here, they'll only have two options: put you in jail forever, or shoot you out here where nobody will see it."

"Fucking *what*?" Anne stomped her foot and everyone but Yunubey winced. "I can't bloody believe this. You were so committed to your role as Misha the Russian stoner that you couldn't step in and stop the murder of the people you were supposed to protect. That was the whole point of this stupid farce, wasn't it?" She waved her free hand at the glowing trees, the scowling Nun. "Now you're willing to let us die again to save the story of your incompetence from getting out."

"I tried to leave you behind," Misha said. "Why did you have to follow me? I was going to tell them that I was the only survivor."

"Oh right," said Anne. "A great ending for your bullshit story. What were you going to tell them about me and Daisuke, that we heroically sacrificed ourselves to get you home?"

Yes. It would have been a good story. Daisuke could see it playing well.

"I would have told them you stayed in the Oasis biome," said Misha. "If you had just stayed there, you could have waited a few months or a year until the political situation calmed down—"

"Or we died from lack of some critical amino acid," Anne said.

"Since you're all here now, I can leave you with the Nun," said Misha. "They can take care of you until you can present yourselves to the international authorities. Will you explain that to them, Anne?"

"And what do you think Rahman's chances are of surviving until then?" Nurul said. "And what about Sing's people popping all of us into cookpots?"

"No!" said Sing.

Anne sighed. "The Nun aren't going to eat us."

"No, just kill us and impale our bodies on spikes to scare off their enemies."

Sing shrugged. Hopefully only because she didn't understand.

"What do you expect me to do?" Misha asked.

It sounded like a real question. Daisuke surprised himself by coming up with a real answer. "Stay," he said. "You should stay with Sing."

Anne made a questioning noise while Nurul snorted. Sing smiled at Daisuke in approval.

"I can't stay here," said Misha.

"That is what you want to do," Daisuke pointed out. "You allowed Sing to go with you when you left the rest of us on the other side of the valley. But you knew she could never go back to America with you."

"She wanted to be back with her people," Misha said.

"I think she also wants to be with you."

Daisuke raised an eyebrow at Sing, who said, "Yes. Misha Nun live with. Nun protect him."

"I wish I could," said Misha.

Daisuke tried to compose his thoughts in English. A bright sort of night was falling. Even as the sky shifted to red and purple-black, the ground and trees around them did not darken. Light reflected off the mirrored crystals at the tips of the branches of the spangle-trees, spotlighting their trunks. In contrast to the darkening sky, the forest around them gained a hallucinatory radiance.

The setting was wrong for a discussion about political intrigue. *This should be the backdrop for confessions of love, not murder.*

"The only real thing is love," Daisuke said. "What Misha feels for Sing. What Nurul feels for Rahman." He looked at Anne and found the courage to say, "Me and you. That is real. Not politics. Not ideals. Not missions."

"Psh," said Anne. "Allergens are pretty damn real. So are digestive enzymes. Extended phenotypes. Poisonous gasses. Electromagnetism." She looked at the spangle-tree branches and the corners of her mouth turned up. "Light." She turned to face Daisuke. "And I guess hormones too. The hormones I'm feeling now are pretty real."

Daisuke's heart clenched. All those wasted hours of feeling betrayed. He had clung so desperately to his persona, his pride, protecting himself against the one person who might actually help him.

"I love you too, Anne." He was crying. His nose was running, and he wiped at it. The gesture would look absolutely awful on camera.

"What the hell are you talking about?" said Misha.

"Anne and I will go home together," Daisuke said. "We will tell the Americans our story, and our story will be the truth, as Anne believed until a few minutes ago. We were on a very dangerous journey. One by one, our companions died. We lost Nurul in the Oasis biome. We lost Misha here. We know nothing about politics." He held out his arms to Anne. "We only survived with each other."

"What," said Anne. "You mean we have to lie?"

"Think of it as maintaining a persona," Daisuke suggested.

"Hoo boy," Anne said. "I'll try."

"It can't work," Misha said. "The bodycams have recorded this whole conversation."

"I know," Daisuke said, walking to Anne. A week ago, this would have been unthinkable.

Daisuke bent down as if to kiss her. Instead, he slipped his fingers under the strap of her bodycam and lifted it from around her neck. "You can't have this." The black rectangle swung on its strap, heavy with the sum of the best work of Daisuke's career. "Nurul must sacrifice her bodycam as well."

"Done," said Nurul. "I agree. I'll stay in the wilderness forever. I'll die there when my amino acids run out or whatever. Just let me try to reach Rahman."

"We owe you nothing," Misha said.

"But should we kill her?" Daisuke considered the next sentence. Conditionals were tricky. "In another world, we would have been friends. Let her find her husband. Let us go home." He nodded at Sing. "Let yourself stay home."

"Plus, you know," said Anne, "I still have Nurul's gun, so I'll shoot you if you don't play along."

"You don't need to threaten me." Misha snorted as if at a private joke. "Just give the bodycams to Sing. There's no reason to destroy them."

"Ha," said Nurul. "You just want blackmail material for when they finally track you down."

Daisuke took a breath to prevent yet another digression. What they needed to do now was ask the Nun chief if he had understood any of their conversation. But Yunubey wasn't looking at Daisuke. His head was raised, his eyes half-shut as if in concentration. As if he was listening to something.

The noise came from the east, like the wingbeats of a glasslands bumblefly or the mating buzz of an Oasis biome lizard-bug.

"The helicopter," said Sing.

Daisuke nodded at their guide. "Thank you," he said.

Sing nodded back to him, tears in her eyes, and turned to explain the situation to her brother.

★ ★ ★

"Yunubey, release my husband."

"Ugh, Sing, really?" Yunubey said. "Husband? He looks like a huge, half-cooked tree-kangaroo."

"Misha is my husband," said Sing firmly. "He killed the evil Tyaney, brought me to you, and the secrets he knows will be of great use as we explore Junction."

Yunubey screwed up his eyes. "Explore what?"

"It's their name for all the countries on this side of the High Earth Hole."

"Why would you need a word for that?" Yunubey shook his head. "I still don't like this. It is proper for the woman to go live with the man's people, not the other way around." He waved his spear at the trap-grove. "This Misha creature can't even speak. He isn't one of the Us."

Sing let some spines show in her voice. "Tyaney was one of the Us."

Yunubey grunted as if punched. "I already apologized for doing such a poor job of protecting you. You don't need to make me feel any worse by coupling with a...a...."

"Scorched tree-kangaroo?"

"I'm trying to think of a less flattering comparison. What was that monster you described from beyond the Outer Toymaker range? Some kind of giant spiny bag full of caustic poison?"

"You, brother, need to broaden your mind." Sing looked back to where Misha lay caged, softening her voice. "These people may be Them, but they are people. They laugh. They look with wonder at the Nightbow. They weep over their dead. They fall in love with each other."

"I'll just bet they do," Yunubey grumbled. "Well, at least they're done gabbling. Ugh. Here come the ones who won't shut up."

"Sing." It was Daisuke, leaning on Anne, holding up one of the black amulets the Them carried on their chests. "*Douzo*," he said, and passed the amulet to her with both hands, lowering his head as he did so. "*Onegai shimasu.*"

Sing took the amulet, looking to Anne for explanation. "What do they want now? Is this a gift?"

"A gift," said Anne. "Daisuke want you gift. Uh. Gift you!"

Yunubey chuckled. "Either she wants us to take that amulet as a gift, or she's offering to sell you to the Them in exchange for it."

"What are you doing standing around making sarcastic comments?" Sing said through her smile. "They're giving us their most valuable possessions. Go get something nice to give them."

"Eh?" said Yunubey. "But they're Them. They don't know about proper gift exchange."

"Just give them something, Yunubey. They're my in-laws now."

Her brother sighed, casting about for suitable bride prices. "Well, I'm not giving them a pig. They wouldn't know what to do with a pig if…by the Rainbow Worm, Sing, you're not back a day and you're already putting me in impossible social situations!"

"Give them an interesting animal," suggested Sing. "Anne likes them. The weirder the better. Something from a country far away."

Yunubey brightened. "Oh! We did buy a specimen from a toymaker caravan out of Howling Mountain Country. We can't eat it or make anything useful out of it, but it sure *looks* bizarre. Do you think we could unload it on these rubes?"

"If you mean 'would they like the Howling Mountain specimen in exchange for their amulets?', I think yes," said Sing. "Go fetch the specimen. And somebody let Nurul out of the trap-grove. She has her own husband to find. And get Misha hidden. Hurry. We don't have much time before the helicopter lands."

"Helicopter?"

"It's what's making that noise," Sing said. "A toymaker big enough for many men to ride inside. My new husband knows how to fly them."

When she looked around at Yunubey, his face had gone stiff. "I think," he said slowly, "that we will need to teach him to talk soon."

Sing smiled. "He will be a very great asset to the Us."

CHAPTER TWENTY

The Next World

"Hey." Anne rubbed Daisuke's face. "No crying."

"I don't care," he said. "There are no cameras."

"But what about the soldiers?" She had to shout to be heard above the rotors of the helicopters, which were still making that annoying screaming noise, even though they weren't turning that fast. Also, the soldiers were shouting at her.

Daisuke sniffed and coughed and brought his hand up to rub his eyes. Then he turned to yell back at the soldiers. "We're Daisuke Matsumori and Anne Houlihan. Blah blah blah. No, everyone else is dead. Blah blah. Bodycams blah. Would you please not shoot us or detain us indefinitely?"

Anne let him yell while she examined the heavy box in her hands.

"Ms. Houlihan? What are you holding? Show us what you're holding!"

The soldiers were nervous. The two Americans who had stepped out of the helicopter had not shot Anne or Daisuke yet, but they clutched their weapons and peered fearfully around the bright and deserted clearing.

The spangle-trees shone with the reflected light of a dwarf star. The paddles of the trap-grove rippled and sparked in the backwash from the rotors. Aerogellies whirled through the air like agitated snowballs. And the Nun's gift moved in Anne's hands. It *sloshed*.

The soldiers took the gun that Daisuke had taken from Nurul. Nurul had probably stolen it from Hariyadi while she was alone with him on the other side of the Oasis wormhole. Or something. Anne didn't care about the gun anymore. She could barely bring herself to care about these lads who were shouting at her.

"Where is Colonel Pearson? Colonel Hariyadi? The pilot? The journalists?"

Daisuke shook his head, face grave. "We are the survivors."

The soldiers decided to be civilized, which was a nice change. "If you'll come with us, ma'am," one of them said, reaching past his machine gun toward her. "We'll have you home in no time."

Dice was crying again. "Survival," he said. "It is very beautiful."

"Come on now," Anne shouted at him. "There, there. Now stop blubbing and ask me what's in this package."

"What?" He couldn't hear her, which was just as well. Anne supposed she wasn't being very supportive of her boyfriend's emotional breakthrough. But that was the nice thing about biology. You didn't need to talk to appreciate nature's marvels.

The box was Lighthouse biome plastic, finely cut and melted together. It could have come from Ikea, except for the gauche yellow color. It was open at the top, and Anne could see that within a nest of very expensive-looking gray satin padding, there nestled a rock. What appeared to be a rock, anyway.

"Let's get out of here," shouted one of the soldiers. He turned to the other one and Anne caught "…light enough to take off?"

The other one, the pilot, gave the light-scattering spangle-trees a look of deep suspicion, but eventually gave the okay sign.

"Just make sure you don't fly low over the Death Wind biome," Anne said.

"What? What does she mean?" asked the pilot, but Daisuke had the matter well in hand. Flying monsters in the mist. Blah blah blah.

The specimen in the box was shaped like an old pomegranate, gray and pitted and roughly round, its surface composed of tiny triangular scales. Anne was reminded of the sclerites of the Oasis zone's animals, or the tiles of the shell of a glasslands land urchin. Or for that matter, the plates in the test of an Earth sea urchin. The plates of a human skull too. Not a rock, then. No, this was something that had once been alive.

The soldiers sat them next to each other in the helicopter, and wasted more time shouting into Anne's face about whether the thing in her hands was dangerous.

How the hell should I know? That's what makes it exciting! But Anne didn't say so out loud. She let Daisuke do the talking, that manipulative, adorable son of a bitch. Niche partitioning, that's what built a good relationship. Let the actors act and the scientists science.

Anne picked up the specimen. It was much heavier than she had expected. Those little scales ground against each other, allowing the thing to shift slightly in her grip, sloshing and rattling in her hands as if filled with mercury and rock salt.

Daisuke pressed against her, put his warm lips to her ear. "*Is* that thing safe?"

Anne shrugged. Something tugged on her hand and she almost dropped the specimen before she saw that its resistance was only because part of its packing material had snagged on…no.

The aperture at the end, what would have been the flower on the bottom of the pomegranate, had spilled forth a shimmering flood of…spun glass? The stuff covered the folds of packing material inside of the box. No, Anne realized, there was no packing material, only this shimmering stuff, as fine as wild silk. Depending on how she tugged and pressed on the material, it turned as stiff as metal, stuck like Velcro, or flowed like water over Teflon. The stuff's color changed as well, gray in certain angles of the helicopter's lights, transparent in others, black as charcoal or white as a wedding veil.

"Solar sails," said Anne, as Daisuke kissed her ear. "This is a space animal."

Anne turned its dense little body in his hands. Star-silk spooled in glittering skeins. "A 'star-wisp'," she named it. "Or maybe a 'full metal jacket'. Want to bet it's magnetic?"

She imagined it alive and in its natural habitat. Heavy and spherical, its outer surface terrifically hard, flinging out and reeling in this net of a material fine enough to harvest starlight. Funneling matter and energy into its mouth, spinning order from entropy. *Just like the rest of us.*

"If it came from space, how did the Nun get their hands on it?" Daisuke had to shout now, even though he was sitting next to her. The rotors were spinning up, the illuminated forest dropping out from under them.

"That's the million-dollar question," said Anne, although she doubted he could hear her. "The several-billion-dollar question, actually. Where is the wormhole that leads from the surface of Junction to the Nightbow? And can we go through it?"

"Yes," he said.

Daisuke was thinner now, his eyes sunken and his chin overgrown with uneven black hairs. He should have looked ten years older than when he'd first come through the wormhole onto Junction, but really he looked younger. Maybe it was his expression. Like grand vistas were opening before his eyes.

The Earth wormhole and its mound swung past the windshield as the helicopter pointed its nose toward home. But Anne knew she'd be coming back soon. They wouldn't be able to keep her away. She'd discovered bloody space-aliens.

Daisuke must have had a similar idea. Careful not to make her drop the star-wisp, he put his hand over Anne's and pressed his face up against her ear. "Do you want to go to space with me?"

Anne laughed, and now there were tears in her eyes too. "I do, Dice," she said. "I do."

ACKNOWLEDGMENTS

What I really wanted to do was write a field guide to alien animals. The fact that this is, you know, a story, is mostly thanks to my alpha-readers, who read each chapter as I wrote it and pretended there was some sort of coherent plot there. Melissa Walshe bonded with Anne and told me how to make her more… Anneish? Tex Thompson upped the Daisuke-osity, and reminded me to add some emotional resonance to the explosions and slime. Pavlina Borisova told me when I'd gotten things wrong (mostly by not including enough kissing). On Tumblr, Spugpow, Exxon-von-Steamboldt, and Turbofanatic helped me make creatures. Timothy Morris corrected my typos and Australian dialect. The Codex Writers' Forum answered my stupid questions (How do you wrestle a cassowary? You don't, idiot).

Like a viscid monstrosity clawing its way up from the abyss, the resulting manuscript-shaped blob then devoured countless souls in its determination to achieve the light. I think we were up to 'epsilon-readers' by the end? Benjamin Poulsen told me when I needed more sensory details and which parts were 'clunky.' Kim Moravec wanted more wonder (and to know where the hell the action was taking place). Kalin Nenov suggested anime references. Kacy Nielsen gasped in all the right places and said "Huh?" when the places weren't right. Daniel Newman dug the aliens and what people could do with them. Brent A. Harris lined up character emotions with scene tone. Carrie Patel informed me, gently, that I hadn't actually mentioned any wormhole in the first chapter. Jesse Sutanto and Franz Anthony told me where I'd messed up with Indonesian language, politics, and culture (as well as good old-fashioned typos). Eric Fischl told me that methane doesn't have a smell and 'commander' isn't a real rank in the army. Anne Tibbets depth-charged the mediocre first couple of chapters and in general hoisted the story up out of the abyss. Rachel Westfall saw how I could clarify the characters' goals and personalities. Richard Campbell Powel asked pointed questions about the evolutionary biology of kelp-trees and ferrofluid monsters. Nicholas Hansen told me what parts I shouldn't cut. Maiko Shigemori helped me with the translation of Daisuke's conversation with his bosses in Chapter One. My agent, Jennie Goloboy of Red Sofa, made me go back and put in the mystery and romance elements I promised her at the beginning. My copy editor at Flame Tree, Imogen Howson, fixed the quotation marks and defused several potentially disastrous continuity errors. Finally, thanks to Don D'Auria, my editor at Flame Tree, who dragged this beast out of the murk and hammered it into a shape you'd be glad to mount over your mantel.

Thanks to you all. I cannot express how terrible this book would have been without you.

And there actually was some real research too! For examples of the real New Guinean Mek languages, see transnewguinea.org/language/eipomek, diva-portal.org/smash/get/diva2:631006/FULLTEXT02.pdf, and www.transnewguinea.org/language/ketengban. For anthropology, see *Scripture in an Oral Culture: The Yali of Irian Jaya* by John D. Wilson and (in a more general way) *The World Before Yesterday: What Can We Learn from Traditional Societies?* by Jared Diamond.

For biology and some of the wonders evolution can produce, see Richard Dawkins's *The Ancestor's Tale.* For some of my more specific questions, I turned to the *Cassowary Husbandry Manual First Edition December 1997* edited by Liz Romer, "The Influence of Carbon Monoxide and Other Gases upon Plants" by H.M. Richards and D.T. MacDougal, and 'Outcome of children with carbon monoxide poisoning treated with normobaric oxygen' by K.L. Meert, S.M. Heidemann, and A.P. Sarnaik.

Undaunted Courage: Meriwether Lewis, Thomas Jefferson, and the Opening of the American West by Stephen Ambrose was my inspiration in more ways than one, as was *Bird Woman (Sacajawea) the Guide of Lewis and Clark: Her Own Story Now* by James Willard Schultz.

FLAME TREE PRESS

FICTION WITHOUT FRONTIERS

Award-Winning Authors & Original Voices

Flame Tree Press is the trade fiction imprint of Flame Tree Publishing, focusing on excellent writing in horror and the supernatural, crime and mystery, science fiction and fantasy. Our aim is to explore beyond the boundaries of the everyday, with tales from both award-winning authors and original voices.

•

Other titles available include:

Thirteen Days by Sunset Beach by Ramsey Campbell
Think Yourself Lucky by Ramsey Campbell
The Haunting of Henderson Close by Catherine Cavendish
The House by the Cemetery by John Everson
The Toy Thief by D.W. Gillespie
The Siren and the Specter by Jonathan Janz
The Sorrows by Jonathan Janz
Savage Species by Jonathan Janz
Kosmos by Adrian Laing
The Sky Woman by J.D. Moyer
Creature by Hunter Shea
The Bad Neighbor by David Tallerman
Ten Thousand Thunders by Brian Trent
Night Shift by Robin Triggs
The Mouth of the Dark by Tim Waggoner

•